Break in Two

Break in Two

MJ SUMMERS

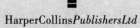

HarperCollins*Publishers**Ltd**

Break in Two
Copyright © 2013 by Gretz Corp.
All rights reserved.

Published by HarperCollins Publishers Ltd

Originally self-published by the author in 2013.
First published by HarperCollins Publishers Ltd in ebook and
trade paperback editions in 2014.
This mass market paperback edition: 2017.

HarperCollins books may be purchased for educational, business,
or sales promotional use through our Special Markets Department.

HarperCollins Publishers Ltd
2 Bloor Street East, 20th Floor
Toronto, Ontario, Canada
M4W 1A8

www.harpercollins.ca

Library and Archives Canada Cataloguing in Publication
information is available upon request

ISBN 978-1-44343-907-7

Printed and bound in the United States of America
QUAD 9 8 7 6 5 4 3 2 1

For J, who is my Cole,
only hotter and without the horse

Dear Reader,

Thank you so much for choosing this book! I hope you love the characters as much as I loved creating them. *Break in Two* is a work of fantasy, therefore Cole and Claire do not have to practise safe sex. In real life, please always be safe while you are with an intimate partner.

On the next page is a list of songs that inspired me as I wrote. I hope you have time in your life to make a playlist and listen to it as you read (it may enhance your experience, as it did mine), or even just to put the book down for a while and let your mind (and other parts of your body) wander. So, pour yourself a glass of wine and enjoy.

I wish you love, great sex and happiness always.

MJ

Break in Two Playlist

"Just a Fool" by Christina Aguilera and Blake Shelton
"Do Right Woman, Do Right Man" by Aretha Franklin
"(Everything I Do) I Do It for You" by Bryan Adams
"Hero" by Enrique Iglesias
"Have a Little Faith in Me" by Jewel
"Fix You" by Coldplay (X & Y)
"Sadeness" by Enigma
"Almost Full Moon" by Enigma
"Return to Innocence" by Enigma
"Have You Ever Really Loved a Woman?" by Bryan Adams
"My Hero" (acoustic live version) by Foo Fighters (Skin and Bones)
"Let's Get It On" by Marvin Gaye

PART ONE
They Meet

ONE

Seattle

Rain streamed down the windows of Claire Hatley's car as she sat parked in front of the house that would never again be her home. She had just finished cramming the last of her things into her car and leaving the key on the kitchen table before walking out forever. Beside the key was a note that read: *Antonio, I hope she's worth it. Fuck yourself. Claire.* He hadn't been home since their big fight two days earlier. It was clear to both of them she would be leaving, and he had stayed away, probably at Stacey's apartment.

Claire leaned her head on the steering wheel, willing herself not to tear up again, exhausted from packing and crying since she had found out Antonio had moved on without bothering to tell her. She started up the engine and took a deep breath as she pulled out onto the road. Without so much as a glance back, she headed onward to a new chapter in her life.

Claire needed to get out of Seattle, even though it was June, her favourite month there, and it was a city she loved. She needed to be away from the rain, the memories and the people she had thought were her friends, friends who had betrayed her by not bothering to mention Tony's affairs. She didn't know what hurt more—his cheating or her so-called friends hiding it from her.

As she pulled onto the freeway, her cellphone rang. Hitting the hands-free button, she saw it was her sister, Janet, calling from her home in London.

"Hey, sis, just calling to check on you. You okay?"

Claire stifled a sob. "Been better."

"Where are you, hon?"

"I'm on my way to Colorado," Claire replied with a sigh she could not contain.

There was a noticeable pause and then Janet used her softest voice, the one she used only when Claire was doing something she might regret later. "Sweetie, why don't you just come here? You can stay with Ted and me for as long as you need. Right now, you should be with people who love you."

"I can't. I appreciate the offer more than you know. But I just can't. I need to be on my own for a while. If I can't handle this, I promise, I'll come running to you. Besides, I don't want to go from one rainy city to another. I need some sun." Claire suddenly realized she was shivering and turned on the heat.

"Well, maybe if you need some sun, you and I could meet, say in Spain, or Florida, even, and have a holiday together. I promise it would be fun! We can make little voodoo dolls of Tony the fuckwit, drink too much, eat too much . . ." Her voice trailed off as she waited for a response.

"Thanks, Jan, but I really have to do this. I need to be in Colorado by Friday for the job interview. I told the owner of the ranch I'd make it there by then. He needs a chef right away."

"You really think you'll be happy living on a dude ranch, cooking for a bunch of rough cowboys and middle-aged yuppies having mid-life crises?" Janet took one last shot at talking her out of it.

Claire dug in her heels, not wanting to be pushed. "That's kind of a snotty way of thinking, Janet. The guy is trying to change the image of his ranch; he wants to have the upscale cuisine these wealthy clients expect. He wants to turn the cookhouse into a proper restaurant. It'll be a chance for me to run my own show, choose the menu and help redesign the kitchen. It's what I've always wanted to do, and it gets me the hell out of Seattle, where I have to see Fuckwit's face on billboards everywhere I go. Okay? So, can you just be excited for me, please?" She didn't have patience for anyone who doubted her right now, even her big sister. She was too busy doubting herself.

"You're right. I'm sorry. I am excited for you. Promise me one thing—you'll sleep with the first sexy cowboy you see and fill me in on all the glorious details."

Claire managed a laugh. "Okay, deal. For now I better pay attention to where I'm going. I'll text when I can to let you know where I'm at."

"You'd better, or I'll have the state troopers out looking for you. Bye, sweetie! Love you! Be safe!"

"Love you. Bye."

Claire drove for thirteen hours, well into the night, stopping twice for gas and to stretch her legs. She grabbed some coffee and fast food, which she barely picked at. She went from crying to being terrified to feeling excited at least twice an hour.

When she really thought about it, her relationship with Antonio had been bad for much longer than it had been good. He *had* been excellent at courting her and making her feel beautiful and special. They had a whirlwind romance, and after only four months, he took her to the Mayan Riviera and asked her to move in with him. She didn't hesitate for a second with her answer. Looking back now, she could see *that* was the moment when he had lost interest in her. The chase was over, and for Tony, that was the best part. He quickly downgraded her from sexy girlfriend to more of a mother figure. He beamed at her when she cooked for him or did his laundry, but he stopped wanting to be romantic or

{4}

go out together, and then even making love had become rare. He was always too tired from his work as a realtor or from going to the gym. When they did go out, he was flirty with the waitress and gazed lustfully at other women. At first, she would argue with him about it, but eventually she gave up. He would say things like "Who cares where I get my appetite, as long as I eat at home?" or "I'm with you, but that doesn't make me blind. I can't help but look. I'm a man; we're very visual."

For the thousandth time in two days, her mind drifted to their last fight. They were standing in the kitchen and Tony was leaning against the counter, his keys in hand, ready to run. Claire was screaming at him and crying. When she had finally exhausted herself, she stopped and stared at him for a long minute and asked, "Why?" in a quiet voice.

"I don't know. She was there, she's young and she really gets me, and I thought, 'Tony, this may be your last chance to get a girl so young.' And I went for it. YOLO, right?"

"YOLO? YOLO. That's your reason? You only live once," she said incredulously. "Wow, all this time I thought you were one of the good ones, and it turns out you're not only a cheater but a complete idiot as well."

"Screw you, Claire. You asked, so I told you the truth." With that, he stomped over to the door and out of her life forever.

If he's a complete idiot, what does that make me for not seeing it? She thought as she drove on.

"Okay, Claire, make a list of all the things you hate about Tony," she said out loud to herself as she popped some trail mix into her mouth. "Then forget he ever existed."

She drew a deep breath then started her list.

"Number one: The way he primps before going anywhere. He spends more time plucking, shaving and fixing his hair than I do. NOT sexy.

"Number two: His wandering eye. Asshole.

"Number three: His wandering dick. He's more than an asshole. He's the devil.

"Number four: How he belittles my appearance with suggestions that I spend more time at the gym and less time tasting my own cooking. Yeah, that one alone should have tipped me off that he was the devil.

"Number five: His little comments about my clothing choices. 'Are you really going to wear that? We are supposed to be dressed up.' Prick.

"Number six: His wandering dick. That deserves to make the list twice.

"Number seven: How he replaced me with a twenty-two-year-old moron with the body of a fifteen-year-old boy. Have fun with that, dickhead.

"Number eight: How he always makes irritating and horrible suggestions when I'm working on a new recipe. He's a realtor for God's sake, not a chef. He doesn't even know saffron from cilantro, but he acts like he's the world's authority on the subject.

"Number nine: How he never helps out around the house. He leaves his shit all over the place, never once in four years picking up his clothes off the floor. He waits me out, knowing it'll get to me and that I'll end up doing it for him. When I complain, he makes the same joke every time, about the maid coming on Friday. Good one.

"Number ten: How he never agrees to go visit my sister and her husband in London. He always has some lame-ass excuse but is certainly ready and available to go on golf trips with his buddies. Son of a bitch.

"Number eleven: How I feel around him. I always feel a bit nervous, as though I am constantly seeking his approval. I can never be myself and never dare to show my sense of humour because to Tony, 'funny girls are not sexy.' Yup, I'm *glad* to be rid of that shithead."

The more she thought about it, the more she realized she was a fool not to have seen years ago that he was bad for her. For four years she had tried so hard to make it work, thinking if she gave it enough time and effort, things would get back to how they felt at the beginning. She hadn't realized it was an impossible task since she was the only one engaged in that fantasy.

Her thoughts wandered to her own parents' marriage when they were still alive. It was a world apart from her relationship with Fuckwit. They had been true partners. As a teenager, Claire was always embarrassed by how in love they were. Her sister and her husband, Ted, were happy, too. They had met in high school and had been together ever since. They frequently went out on dates and took romantic trips together. They laughed easily and finished each other's sentences. They just seemed to *get* each other.

Why can't I find that? What is wrong with me? she wondered.

She stopped at a Super 8 along the interstate, so tired she wasn't sure if she was in Idaho or Utah. By the time she checked in and sluggishly dragged herself to the room, it was after midnight. She had a long hot shower, ate a few handfuls of trail mix and collapsed into bed.

* * *

Claire woke eight hours later, having had a solid night's sleep for the first time since discovering Antonio was cheating.

"Shit! Shit! Shit!" She should have been on the road two hours ago. She hastily brushed her teeth, threw her things into her bag, ran down to the lobby to check out and grabbed a complimentary coffee before getting back on the road.

An hour into the drive, she was shocked to realize she hadn't thought about Antonio once since waking. Of course, it helped knowing there was no way she would run into him, or any reminders of him, for that matter. She could leave him behind, but would she ever shed the feelings of humiliation and self-doubt that came with being cheated on? Those nagging questions—*Am I not sexy enough? Am I not smart enough, pretty enough, interesting enough to keep a man?*—occupied her thoughts. Her sister had tried, unsuccessfully, to reassure her that it was not Claire at all but purely selfishness on Fuckwit's part that had caused him to cheat. But Janet had to say that. She was her big sister.

At thirty-one, Claire felt old and used up. She had been traded in for a twenty-two-year-old hostess whom she herself had hired to work at the restaurant a year earlier. The owner had tasked Claire with finding a sexy hostess to attract high-paying clientele. As it turned out, the hostess had also managed to attract Antonio. Claire's mind wandered back to the moment she had found out. She had called the restaurant from home to make a schedule change, and Stacey, the perky little hostess, picked up, thinking it was Antonio. "Hey, Tony, did Fatty leave already? You calling to talk dirty to me?"

There was a pause on the line and then Claire spoke up. "No, Stacey, it's me, Fatty. Why the hell would Tony be calling to talk dirty to you?" Stacey, the cowardly bimbo, hung up.

TWO

Colorado

As Claire drove through Denver, there wasn't a cloud in the sky. The sun shone brightly, bringing her a sense of renewal. Each mile took her further from her hurtful past and toward an unknown future. Her heart pounded as she admired the scenery of the rugged Rocky Mountains to her right and the expansive plains to her left. This was a place like nowhere she had ever been, and the beautiful, unfamiliar scenery brought her a sense of exhilaration and also created a nervous knot in her stomach. She could hardly believe she was really doing this. Up until now, she had lived a safe, mundane existence, and here she was, about to completely change her life. Colorado Springs seemed like just the place to do it. When she had seen the job posting, something about it just felt right to her. A ranch close to the mountains seemed like a wonderful place to breathe again and get back on her feet after what had happened. No reminders. No connections. No humiliation. Just sunshine and fresh air to soothe her bruised ego and help her find her worth again.

When Claire finally pulled up to Black Canyon Ranch at 4:30 p.m., her eyes were burning and her body was sore and sweaty from the long drive. She turned off the car and took a moment to check herself in the mirror. She knew she didn't look exactly put-together. Although it probably didn't matter as much out here in Colorado as it would in Seattle, she hated the thought of making a bad first impression. She pulled out a tube of her favourite lip gloss and tried to make a few minor improvements. She managed to find a comb and a hair elastic in her purse and quickly pulled her hair up in a ponytail. She took a deep breath and stepped out of the car with her heart in her throat, trying to convince herself she was ready to make a fresh start.

Cole Mitchell stood near the barn door watching as the woman pulled in and parked her car. He figured she must be the new chef he was expecting that afternoon. He was caught off guard by the realization that he found something sensual about watching her in a private moment as she applied her lipstick and tied up her hair. He had yet to see her face up close, but he was somehow drawn to her already. As she got out of the car and stretched, he strode over to her and welcomed her with a warm smile.

Claire watched a man who looked to be about her age, early thirties maybe, wearing jeans, a fitted white

T-shirt and a straw cowboy hat walk toward her. His gait was confident and self-assured, not in a hurry but not slow either. *Fuck me. There really* are *hot cowboys here*, she thought.

When he reached her, their eyes locked. Claire couldn't look away even though she knew she should. He was tall, so she had to tilt her head up to look at his face. It was all she could do to keep her jaw from dropping as she took in the sight of his gorgeous hazel eyes, his kissable mouth, his chiselled features and his short, sandy-blond hair poking out from under his hat.

"You must be Claire. I'm Cole Mitchell. We spoke on the phone." His voice was just as sexy in person as it had been when they had spoken a few days earlier.

"I am. Nice to meet you," she said, extending her hand. His handshake was firm, and he held on maybe a second too long. She could feel that he had strong hands from working hard and was slightly shocked at herself when she realized she was imagining that the rest of his body would match. As she glanced down at the veins bulging in his forearm, she could feel her face heating up with thoughts she had no business thinking.

A large grey and white sheep dog came running up beside Cole, wagging his tail to greet her. He looked up at Claire and gave her a single bark as if to say hello.

"This is Otis. He loves everyone as long as I like them." Otis sat down beside Cole, panting.

Claire looked down at the dog. "Hi, Otis."

As if on cue, the dog walked over and nudged her hand in hopes of being petted. She grinned as she crouched down to comply with his request. "Aren't you a sweetheart?"

Cole watched her with an appreciative smile. "How was the drive?"

"It was long but good. It was a nice chance to see the country," Claire answered as she stood up again.

"You must be beat. I was thinking we could do the interview tomorrow if that's okay with you. I had something come up at the last minute that I can't get out of, and I need to leave for a few hours," Cole replied, looking apologetic.

"That would actually be a relief to me. I could use a good night's rest to be at my best for the interview."

"Great. I'll show you to your cabin, then. I can help you carry some of your things before I go. It's a bit of a hike to the staff quarters from here."

Claire opened the hatch of her car and a garbage bag full of clothes tumbled out. Cole caught it before it hit the ground, but not before a pair of lacy pink panties fell out. He caught those with his other hand and gingerly handed them back to her with an amused grin. "You sure know how to make a first impression."

Claire's face instantly burned with embarrassment. She quickly took the panties from him and shoved them into the pocket of her jeans. "Those aren't mine. I have no idea how they got in there," she said in mock denial.

Cole laughed at her reaction. He had a warm, deep laugh that made her heart skip a beat.

Taking the bag of clothes along with a large suitcase, Cole waited while Claire grabbed her overnight bag, her purse and another small suitcase. As they walked down the paved path by the restaurant and lodge, she got her first chance to really take in her new surroundings, and she looked around in awe. Cole watched her as she gasped a little at the sight of the large lake. It was surrounded by tall grass that led up to the mountains on the other side of the water. "It's beautiful here," she said with quiet reverence.

Down the path they passed by a handful of two-storey guest cabins. They continued walking along until they reached the staff lodgings—much smaller one-storey versions of the guest cabins. They stopped at the last in the row, and Cole put her bags down on the front porch and fished a key out of his pocket.

"This one's you," he said, unlocking the door. "It's pretty small, but I think it has everything you need if you decide to stay. Let me know if there's anything missing."

"I'm sure it'll be just fine. The view alone is more than enough."

He carried her bags inside and set them down on the floor in the small open-space living room and kitchen before handing her the key. They walked out together back down the path to the parking area.

"My brother, Ben, and his wife, Alicia, are making supper for everyone tonight in the restaurant. Nothing fancy, but I hope you'll join them. Dinner will be ready in about an hour."

Just then, two young ranch hands appeared at the door to the barn. Both were tanned and lean, wearing well-worn cowboy hats. Cole called to them, "Trey, Dustin, this is Miss Claire. She'll be our new chef."

As the two walked over, Cole watched them, saying, "Trey and Dustin are my little cousins. They're working here until they decide to get off their butts and go to college."

"Not gonna happen, Cole. We were born to be cowboys," called Trey, the taller of the two. Both men tipped their hats to Claire and said hello.

"I have to run over to O'Reilly's. I'd like you two to help Miss Claire bring the rest of her things to her cabin, and then you're done for the day, alright?" Even though he asked if it was alright, there was no doubt in anyone's mind that it was an order, not a request.

Both young men headed toward her car. "Sure

thing, boss," Dustin replied, giving Claire a little wink.

Cole turned back to Claire. "Ben and Alicia are in the restaurant if you need anything. Make sure you go get something to eat in a little while. Sorry again that I have to go."

"Please don't worry about me. I'll find my way around. Thank you, though," she said, realizing she had forgotten how good it felt to have someone show concern for her.

Cole climbed into a big white Chevy pickup truck, and Otis jumped in beside him. He gave her a little nod before driving off with a horse trailer in tow. Claire just stood there and watched the truck pull out of the yard, forgetting completely that Dustin and Trey were waiting to unload her things.

"Sorry," she said as she tried to shake the feeling of attraction she had for her new boss. "I'm a bit tired from the drive." She quickly unlocked the doors of her car and started unloading the rest of her things from the back seat.

"No worries," Trey said, taking a couple more large garbage bags stuffed full of clothes from her.

She handed two more bags, full of shoes and boots, to Dustin. He looked at the bags with a surprised expression. "How many feet do you have anyway?" he joked.

Claire gave a little laugh. "Just the two, but they are very spoiled."

She picked up a backpack and another couple of bags, and the trio headed in the direction of her cabin. Claire thought it couldn't hurt to get a little background info in preparation for her interview the next day, even though the way Cole had introduced her made it sound like she had the job already. "So, what's it like to work here?"

Dustin replied first. "Well, if you work here, you work hard, but Cole and Ben are really good to their people, too. They are very fair. The only things they won't tolerate are laziness and being rude to the guests."

Claire felt relief sweep over her. "Well, I don't think I'll have a problem with those rules."

After the bags had been dropped at her cabin, Claire thanked the guys and followed them out onto the small porch. Trey glanced back at her as they started down the path. "Now, don't get all caught up organizing your shoes and miss supper! Alicia's making her famous lasagna."

Claire laughed. "I'll try not to!" Claire grinned a little to herself as she watched them stroll away, relieved to have received such a warm welcome.

* * *

As Cole drove toward the O'Reilly ranch, he should have been thinking of the horse he was about to pick up. He should have been trying to figure out how they were going to load her up, given the fact that no one at the O'Reillys' had even managed to get within ten feet of her since they had brought her home from the auction. Once he had figured that out, he should have been thinking about how he was going to train the horse. Instead his mind kept bringing him back to the pretty new chef that had just arrived. Claire Hatley. Somehow he had found himself riveted by her, even just watching her from the barn door as she tied her hair back before stepping out of her car. There had been something so intimate about seeing her in that moment that he couldn't shake the feeling as he pulled onto the narrow dirt road.

He thought of her voice—sultry, even though that wasn't at all what she had been trying to project—and her embarrassed laugh when her panties had spilled out of her bag. It was a pleasing sound. He thought about her panties. They were lacy and tiny. His mind wandered to what those might look like on that curvy body of hers. *No way, Cole, you better shut that down. No matter how pretty she is or how good she'd look in those panties, she'd still be your chef in the morning. And that would be a problem you don't need right now.*

* * *

Claire dropped onto the couch, staring at all her bags. The sum total of all her belongings sat in front of her in disarray. Too overwhelmed to face the pile right then, she walked over to the fridge to see if there was anything in it. She was surprised to find it stocked with milk, a dozen eggs, cheese, some fruit, spinach, a loaf of bread and a six pack of beer. Claire grabbed a beer, cracked it open and stood at the kitchen window staring at the view of the lake in the late-day sun. It shimmered a deep blue, with the Rockies acting as a majestic backdrop.

A feeling of excitement passed over her when she thought about all the possibilities of this place. And if she was honest with herself, when she thought about her new boss as well. He was sexy as hell and seemed so thoughtful, too. Her mind went over every detail of what she knew about him so far. On the phone, Cole had told her that he and his brother had taken over the family ranch a couple of years earlier. From their conversation, she had gotten the sense that he was ambitious but also kind. Seeing him with his cousins, she could tell he had an air of calm authority in addition to that warm smile.

Soon, Claire's mind couldn't help but wander to how clean he smelled, as though he had just stepped out of the shower in an Old Spice ad. His freshly shaved face, the touch of his hand as he shook hers, his sculpted body carrying her heavy luggage with ease. Her cheeks suddenly flushed as she remembered the panties she had stuffed into her pocket. She pulled them out with a little laugh of embarrassment and tossed them onto her suitcase. Digging around in her purse, Claire grabbed her cellphone and texted Janet to let her know she had arrived safely. When she hit send, she realized her stomach was growling. She hadn't eaten more than a few bites in days. She freshened up quickly, then, slipping into her flip-flops, she walked over to the restaurant.

As soon as Claire opened the door, she instantly fell in love with the place; it was both rustic and luxurious at the same time. The windows on the back wall reached up to a peak in the centre, interrupted only by a large stone fireplace in the middle. The tables were cherrywood, and each one had a candle in a glass jar as a simple yet elegant centrepiece. Wrought-iron chandeliers lit the seating area with a lovely warm glow. Near the fireplace, groups of brown leather couches and armchairs were arranged in cozy sitting areas, perfect for relaxing after a long day on the ranch. The walls were lined with black and white framed photos of the ranch over the years. Claire slowly walked along the room studying each photo. She stopped at a picture of two boys in swim trunks sitting on a dock and wondered if it was Cole and his brother.

A voice broke her concentration. "You must be Claire." A tall, willowy woman stood in the doorway to the kitchen, smiling in her direction. "I'm Alicia, Ben's wife. I imagine you're starving."

"You're right on both counts. Nice to meet you, Alicia."

"Have a seat. What can I get you to drink?"

"I could use some water, thank you," Claire said as she chose a table near the window.

A minute later, Alicia came back with a Caesar salad and a glass of water. "I thought you might like a salad to start with. I made lasagna, but I wasn't sure if you were a vegetarian, so I thought I'd better ask before I brought it out."

"That sounds lovely, thank you. I'm not a vegetarian. I can serve myself, though. I feel silly sitting here." Claire gave Alicia an uncomfortable look.

"No, tonight you are our guest. You must be exhausted after your long drive. I just feel funny serving a real chef my poor attempt at a meal."

"Oh no, please don't be nervous. I'm sure I'll love it," Claire replied, giving her a reassuring smile. "Trey told me it's your famous lasagna."

Alicia turned back toward the kitchen as she called out, "Yeah, but famous for what?"

She came back carrying two plates piled high with lasagna, followed by a tall man in jeans and a ball cap. He bore a striking resemblance to Cole, except for his nose, which was slightly crooked, as though it had been broken more than once. He greeted Claire as he set down his own plate of dinner, introducing himself as Ben, Cole's big brother.

"Do you mind if we join you?" Alicia asked.

"I'd love it. I've had only my thoughts for company the last few days, and I can tell you, the conversations aren't always worth having." Claire gestured for them to sit down.

Claire felt immediately comfortable with the couple. They were very friendly and asked her a few questions about herself, but not so many that she felt as though she was being interrogated. They talked about the ranch and how it had been in the family for over a hundred years. Ben explained that their parents had decided to hand the ranch over last year, choosing to travel around the world while they still could.

It was obvious from watching them that Ben and Alicia were very much in love. Claire felt a little stab of envy. She had never felt as in tune with Antonio as these two seemed to be. They laughed easily and seemed enthralled when the other talked. At one point, Alicia reached up with her napkin and wiped a tiny bit of food off Ben's cheek. Claire wondered if she would ever feel this at ease with a man. She had always felt a bit nervous around Antonio, as though she couldn't really be herself. They didn't share a sense of humour, and when he was around, most of her jokes landed with a thud. She knew she never quite measured up to his expectations of what his girlfriend should be. She wasn't skinny enough for him and didn't have the breeding he was looking for in a wife, which was why he had never made her one.

As they finished eating, Claire stood up to clear the table. Ben gently took her plate from her hand. "We've got it, Claire. You're our guest tonight."

"Thank you. I feel bad not helping, though," Claire said.

"Don't even think about it," Alicia said. "Now, you must have some unpacking to do, or if you like, we have a swimming pool and a hot tub behind the lodge. I know I always want to soak after a long drive."

"Really? I would love that!" Claire exclaimed with delight. "I think I'll take a few minutes to get settled in and then go for a dip. Thanks again."

They said their good nights, and then Claire sauntered lazily back to her cabin, breathing in the fresh mountain air and listening to the evening sounds of the frogs croaking. She was surprised to realize how peaceful she felt, even though she was in a completely new place, surrounded by strangers.

She unpacked her toiletries and searched her suitcases for her swimsuit. It was a royal-blue two-piece that brought out the colour of her eyes. She had worn it on a trip to Mexico with Antonio four years earlier and had felt so beautiful in it then. That was at a time when he was still interested in taking her on trips and in making love to her. She tried to shake that thought as she undressed and put the suit on, pulling on a black skirt and a grey T-shirt for the walk down to the pool.

* * *

The sun was just beginning to set as Claire climbed into the hot tub, immediately feeling her body relax in the warmth of the water. She sat with her back to the jets while she took in the view of the mountains with the sky growing pink and purple behind them. She gave an appreciative sigh at her new surroundings.

It didn't take long for her mind to wander back to Cole. She had been hoping to find out more about him at dinner. What he was like to work with, if he was with anyone. He didn't have a wedding band on, but that didn't mean anything. *Okay, Claire, you just left a four-year disaster of a relationship, and he is your boss. You need to get your head out of the clouds right now*, she thought to herself. *There is no way he is going to want you, Claire. He's probably got a girlfriend who was just crowned Miss Colorado or something.*

She climbed out of the hot tub and walked over to the pool, plunging into the deep end with a graceful dive. As she lifted her head out of the cool water, she was surprised to see Cole standing at the other end of the pool, dressed only in black swim trunks, looking at her. The sight of him nearly undressed was a lot to take in. His tall frame was entirely covered with lean muscle, and he had a light tan. Unlike Antonio, Cole's muscles came from hard work, and his tan from being outdoors. Antonio's muscles, such as they were, came from hours at the gym, his tan from a tanning bed.

"Oh, hi, sorry . . ." she stammered, brushing drops of water from her face. She suddenly worried that she was out of line using the swimming pool before she even had the job. "Alicia told me about the pool, and it was just too tempting. I hope that's okay."

Cole smiled. "Of course it's okay. I'm glad you're making yourself at home." Tossing his towel on a lounge chair, he kicked off his flip-flops. "Ben said they had dinner with you. I'm sorry I missed it."

"Oh, yes, it was delicious. Alicia is a great cook, and they were both so welcoming."

"Good. I'm glad you had a chance to meet them."

He walked across the pool deck to the shower and turned on the water, soaking himself. Claire couldn't help but stare at him, biting her bottom lip, as the water washed down his sculpted body. When he put his arms up to run his hands through his hair, she could see all the muscles in his arms and back flex, causing them to ripple.

"Wow," she whispered in spite of herself.

He dove into the pool, coming up a long way

from his entry point. He swam a few laps, displaying considerable skill. She treaded water in the deep end while trying not to gawk at him as he moved gracefully and powerfully through the water. He propelled his body forward with purpose and confidence. After a few minutes, Claire realized she had to stop drooling. She could feel his eyes following her as she climbed the steps out of the water and walked over to the hot tub. She hoped she looked as good in the bikini as she had the last time she wore it. She suddenly regretted that second piece of lasagna, knowing that her tummy was sticking out a little more than usual. She stepped down the stairs into the hot tub and settled in.

A minute later, Claire allowed her head to turn toward the pool. She was just in time to see Cole get out, using his muscular arms to pull himself onto the deck in one long move. He strode over to the hot tub and sat down on the edge with his feet dangling in the water. "I'll never get sick of that view," he softly exclaimed as he slid his body into the water. Claire looked up, startled.

"I meant the Rockies," he said, looking a bit panicked.

Claire's face flushed. "Of course you did. It's amazing." *Shit. First the panties and now I seem totally vain.* "I feel like that about the ocean, especially the sunsets."

Cole gave her a pensive look. "You're pretty far

'from the sea." He searched her navy-blue eyes for any hint of whether she might suddenly disappear back to Seattle to whatever—or whomever—she was running from.

She gazed out at the lake for a moment and then turned her focus back to Cole. "To be honest, the sunsets in Seattle have nothing on the one I'm seeing right now."

A spark flew between them as their eyes met, the sexual tension building. Claire took a deep breath and ran her hands through her hair, causing her bikini-clad breasts to lift out of the water. She fought the urge to lick her lips as she gazed at him. Suddenly aware of how inappropriate it was for her to be in a hot tub eyeing her new boss the night before their interview, she decided she'd better go straight back to her cabin. "I should go get settled in. What time would you like to meet tomorrow?" she asked. They still focused on each other, unable to look away.

Cole cleared his throat and glanced at the lodge. "I'm up early. Alicia said she'll keep cooking over the weekend, if you like. Why don't you head to the restaurant for breakfast around eight, and we'll get the interview out of the way right after. I'll come find you when I'm done getting the guys started on their morning chores at the stables."

Claire climbed out of the hot tub, sucking in her tummy as she rose out of the water. Feeling more than a little self-conscious at being so exposed in front of a man with a body that should grace a Calvin Klein underwear ad, she quickly put on her T-shirt and skirt before sliding into her flip-flops. "Sounds good. See you tomorrow."

* * *

Cole sat in the hot tub waiting for his erection to go down. It didn't help that thoughts of Claire sitting across from him in that bikini kept creeping back into his head. She was short, with a sexy little curvy body, like Salma Hayek. His brain flashed to an image of her staring into his eyes while she untied her bikini strings. He let out a low groan. *Nope, nope, nope. I need to nip that thought in the bud.* He climbed out of the hot tub and dove into the pool, hoping the cold water would help. He swam twenty laps while going over the sports highlights he had watched the night before, to get his mind off her. It almost worked.

* * *

Claire went back to her cabin and climbed into bed, feeling dizzy from the hot water and from being so close to a nearly naked, hot-as-hell cowboy. She hadn't felt so sensual in years. Even though she was exhausted, she tossed and turned in bed for an hour with thoughts of Cole filling her head. She fantasized about him crossing the hot tub and untying her bikini strings, his mouth lowering to hers, the feel of his large hands all over her body . . .

She got up and splashed some cold water on her face. "Stop that!" she scolded her reflection in the mirror. He might be married or have a girlfriend, and even if he didn't, a man that hot would never be interested in boring old Claire. She couldn't even keep Antonio's attention, and he was nowhere near the man Cole was.

Her mind wandered back to the last time she had tried to seduce Antonio, six months earlier. It had been weeks since he had showed any interest, and he was watching a football game he had recorded. Claire had the night off, which was rare for her, so she decided to make the most of it. She stopped at a lingerie shop on her way home and picked up a small, frilly black negligee. She showered and put her hair up in a messy, tousled bun on top of her head. She took her time applying her makeup, then sprayed herself with perfume and dressed in her new purchase, along with some black heels. Feeling sexy, she walked into the living room and found Antonio on the couch, absorbed by the game. She sauntered in front of the screen and bent down seductively to pick up a throw pillow that had fallen onto the floor. Without looking at her, he moved his head so he could see the TV around her.

She stood straight up, tossed the pillow at him and put her hands on her hips.

He glanced over for a second, looking her up and down before speaking. "Babe, not tonight, this is an important game. Nice outfit, though."

The humiliation of that moment still stung when she thought of it. She had gone to her bedroom, taken off the nightie and heels and thrown them into the garbage. Then she had put on fleece pyjamas and gone to sleep in the spare room. She had been carelessly rejected by the man she loved. In hindsight, it made a little more sense. He'd probably had sex with Stacey or some other woman earlier that day.

THREE

The next morning, Claire woke to the sun shining brightly into her room and the sound of birds singing. It was 6:30 a.m. She was surprised to find that she could feel so energetic within days of her break-up. Deciding to go for a run to calm her nerves, she quickly hopped out of bed. She rummaged around to find her running shoes, some shorts and a sports bra, then she changed and headed out the door. She walked at a fast pace for a couple of minutes, making her way over to the dirt trail along the lakeshore. When she reached it, Claire broke into a run, feeling freer and more alive than she had in a long time, maybe years, even. The feeling of the sun's warmth on her skin renewed her enthusiasm for life. She had shed the weight of a lousy relationship and was getting a chance to start over.

Thirty minutes later, she was back at her cabin showering and getting dressed for her interview. Claire took extra care getting ready. She told herself that she was doing it to look professional, but a part of her that she wouldn't acknowledge was doing it for Cole. She dried her hair and put it up in a loose bun, leaving a few pieces to hang and frame her face. After applying her makeup with an expert hand, she selected a black pencil skirt, a white blouse that was just a tiny bit sheer and a pair of nude high heels to make her legs look longer. When she saw her reflection in the mirror, there was no trace of the broken woman who had left Seattle earlier that week. She looked radiant, with a slight flush to her cheeks left over from her run. Feeling confident, she walked out of the cabin and headed over to have some breakfast.

Arriving at the restaurant just before 8 a.m., she opened the door to the delicious smells of bacon and eggs frying and fresh coffee brewing. She was surprised by how busy it was, with at least ten men dressed in jeans and work shirts helping themselves to food at the buffet table or sitting and eating. Trey and Dustin were among them. Trey called out to her, "Well, there she is! Miss Claire, our new chef extraordinaire!"

Claire blushed as all the men looked up at her. She suddenly felt overdressed and out of place.

"Hello," she managed to say, shyly waving to everyone.

Dustin walked up. "Oh, I like your shoes! You might want to stay out of the stables with those, though. You'll never get the manure off them." The men laughed.

Claire, not one to allow herself to be intimidated, gave him a sassy grin. "Thanks for the tip. Is that how you wrecked your heels?" The room exploded with laughter.

One of the men called out from his chair, "This new cookie has a little sass in her. We're going to have some fun with . . ."

His voice trailed off as he spotted Cole standing at the door staring at him. Claire blushed with embarrassment and walked over to the buffet table and picked up a plate. She hoped Cole wouldn't think she was flirting with the men or that she was the type to cause trouble.

Everyone went back to eating as Cole walked over. He smiled warmly at Claire, putting her mind at ease. "Morning. How did you sleep?"

Claire looked up from the fruit tray she was picking from and nodded. "Really well, thank you. I feel much more refreshed today."

"I'm glad. I'm heading over to my office. It's on the main floor of the lodge. Come over when you're done eating so we can get the interview out of the way, okay?"

"Will do."

With that, he was gone as quickly as he had arrived.

*　*　*

Claire found her way over to Cole's office twenty minutes later. He was sitting at his desk talking on the phone and waved her in. Otis, who had been lying on a dog bed beside the desk, lazily got up to greet her as she took a seat opposite Cole. She patted Otis warmly as she sat, looking around, hoping to find evidence of a wife or girlfriend (or rather, hoping not to). His office was not messy but was obviously a place where a lot was happening. Neat stacks of papers sat on his desk. On the shelf under the window were rolls of what looked like blueprints. Next to the rolls sat a picture of an older couple on a beach—she assumed they were his parents. No other photos were in sight, so no sign of a significant other yet. On the wall behind the desk was Cole's bachelor of business degree from Colorado State, framed in silver with a dark green mat.

Whomever Cole was talking to was irritating him. He spoke in a quiet, even tone, and although he sounded calm, there was an edge to his voice that was undoubtedly making the person on the other end squirm. Otis wandered back over to his bed, made a circle and lay down again as the call ended. Claire watched as Cole took a moment to write something before looking up at her. "Sorry about that."

"Oh, please don't be," she responded, trying not to notice how sexy his eyes were with their long, curved eyelashes. He wore a light-blue button-down shirt, open at the top to reveal a white T-shirt underneath. She knew he had jeans and light brown cowboy boots on from his brief appearance at the restaurant. It was impossible for her not to think about that hard body hidden beneath all those clothes.

The interview seemed more like a getting-to-know-you conversation. Cole spent some time talking about the new image he was trying to create for the ranch. With the recent downturn in the economy, they needed to attract clients with money. Those clients had higher expectations of luxury, fine wines and cuisine, and excellent service along with a somewhat authentic ranch experience. He and Ben had realized all of this a couple of years earlier and managed to put together some cash to have the swimming pool and hot tub installed in addition to renovating the rooms at the lodge. They had plans to add some luxury cabins along the lakeshore over the next few years but wanted to create a world-class dining experience first. They wanted to attract more local people to the restaurant as well. He told Claire they would welcome any marketing ideas she had, although he didn't want her to feel pressure, as he understood she wasn't being hired for that purpose.

As Claire listened, she couldn't help feeling excited. Cole's eyes lit up and he was passionate about his plans as he talked. She loved the idea of running a kitchen that provided a world-class dining experience. It was what she had always dreamed of.

"For now, I know we aren't anywhere near that level. We don't have enough regular customers to have much of a staff in the kitchen. It'll be you and Alicia to start. This means everything from prep work to menu design to cleaning up the kitchen. I know these aren't considered the typical responsibilities of a chef, and I hope that won't be a problem for you." Cole paused, waiting for her reaction.

"It won't be a problem at all. I love the idea of helping to build something to its full potential, and I want to be a part of it in every way possible, even if it means scrubbing the sinks and counters. I think the plans you have and the timeline sound realistic. It seems like you have a perfect location here—close to Colorado Springs but still with that out-in-the-wilderness feel to it. I have a lot of ideas for the menu, traditional favourites as well as trendier fare that some of the wealthier clients will be expecting. It'll take me about a week to finish and present it to you, if that's okay."

Cole nodded at Claire, looking relieved that she hadn't turned her nose up at the less-than-glamorous duties. "That all sounds excellent, Claire. We have a couple of weeks until the busy tourist season starts, so you can take your time and fine-tune the menu as you go. Tomorrow is Sunday, so why don't you take the rest of the weekend to finish getting settled in and unpacked? You can work with Alicia in the kitchen if you feel like it, and if you don't, that's alright, too."

"I'm eager to get started. I won't need more than a few hours today to get unpacked and set up. I'd like to help out with supper tonight, if Alicia won't mind."

"That should be just fine. I'm sure she'll appreciate the help," Cole said, looking down for a moment at the list of interview questions.

"So, Claire, what made you want to become a chef?"

"Well, it's all I've ever wanted to do, actually, since I was a little girl," she answered. "I love creating something new. I love the smells, the textures, the tastes. I love the feeling of washing fruits and vegetables under a rush of water, the sounds of raw veggies being chopped and bubbling liquids and sizzling pans. Most of all, I love making something carefully, paying attention to every little detail, and then seeing other people derive pleasure from experiencing the flavours and textures I wanted them to enjoy . . ." She trailed off, suddenly feeling as exposed as she had in her bikini the night before. She felt like she had said too much and sounded strange. She glanced at Cole, trying to see if he was put off by her. Instead, he seemed riveted, unable to look away.

"Wow," he said quietly, "that was some answer. I almost feel like I've just watched you make an entire meal." His voice was low and sounded thick with desire.

"Sorry, I think I went on a bit. I sound like an artsy nutball."

"Not at all, Claire. You sound like someone who loves what you do. It's rare to find people with such passion about their work. That's how I feel about the ranch. I could talk about it for hours if anyone wanted to listen."

I would listen, she thought. *I would listen to you read the phone book with that low, sexy voice coming out of those gorgeous lips of yours.* "I would love to hear about it sometime. I need to learn more about what you do here if I'm going to be a part of it all."

"I'd like that very much," he replied with his eyes still locked on hers. He couldn't help but notice how her shirt was just a bit see-through, showing the outline of her bra, and how her hair was done up, with a few pieces falling around her face. An image of her taking her hair down and ripping her shirt open flashed in his brain. In his peripheral vision, he took in the sight of her legs as she crossed them. An image of him sliding his hands up under that skirt overtook his brain for a moment. *Get it together*, he reprimanded himself, looking down at his paper again. As he scanned his other questions, he realized they all sounded lame. "You know, I think that just about covers it, unless you have any questions for me."

Claire paused for a moment, her face falling a little, as though disappointed, before she regained her smile. "Nothing I can think of. If I think of something later, I know where to find you." She licked her lips.

"Right," he said, watching her mouth. "Okay, then. Good. I'll let you get settled in," he said, looking down again.

As Claire made to leave, Cole discovered he had one last question. "Oh, Claire, there's something else. I'm wondering if you're planning to stay long."

Claire's head shot back in confusion. "I wouldn't have come all this way if I intended to leave." Her tone had a slight edge.

"I've offended you. I'm sorry. I only meant that for me, it's important to find a chef who will be here for the long haul while we get things up and running. It'll take a couple of years for that to happen, and although I know I can't ask you to commit right now for that length of time, I need to know if there might be something or someone waiting for you back in Seattle that you might have to go home for suddenly."

Claire paused a beat before responding. "Seattle isn't actually my home. I've lived there for the past eight years, but there's nothing there for me to go back to. I grew up in upstate New York and went to college there. My parents have both passed away, and I have a sister who lives in England, but that's it."

Cole felt a stab of regret for making her answer such a personal question. For a moment he didn't know what to say. He could see she was upset by this conversation and knew there was something more to it when she said there was nothing for her in Seattle. The way she had obviously packed and left town in such a hurry, throwing her clothes and shoes into garbage bags, managing to get to the ranch in only a few days, spoke volumes. He knew better than to push it, though. He still wasn't 100% sure that she wouldn't leave to go back to whomever she was running from, but he had to try to trust her. For him, that was a tough thing to do.

"I'm sorry about your parents, and I'm sorry I've upset you by asking you to explain your situation. I just really want this to work out, and the thought of having to start over to find a new chef is simply too much for my brain these days." He wished he could offer a more eloquent apology.

"That's alright. I understand why you need to know. It's all just a little raw for me right now. But I am really excited to get started here and to move on with a new chapter of my life." Claire managed a tight smile.

"Thanks, Claire. I'm really pleased to have you here, and I want you to feel comfortable coming to me with any concerns or questions you have, especially as you're getting used to things."

Cole stood and came around his desk, offering her his hand. Claire rose from her chair and shook his hand, feeling electricity pulse through her as their skin connected again. She wondered if he felt it too, or if it was just wishful thinking on her part. She had been lonely for a long time without really realizing it.

As he walked her to the door, Cole cleared his throat. "Oh, and Claire, I don't want you to feel like you have to dress up, unless you feel more comfortable that way. Not that you don't look good—you look great—but you can just dress however you like."

Claire looked up into his eyes and gave him a flirty smile, knowing he was the one feeling nervous now. "Thanks, boss. I'll keep that in mind."

"Great. Welcome aboard, Claire."

* * *

Back in her cabin, Claire changed into jeans and a light pink V-neck tee. She began unpacking and putting her clothes into the closet and dresser drawers. It would be a tight fit to get all of her things in, especially her shoes. In the end, she decided to store most of them in her suitcases, under the bed, knowing she would have use for only a handful of pairs here.

She laid out her makeup and other toiletries on the counter in the bathroom and put framed pictures of her sister and Ted as well as her parents on the bookshelf in the living room. She took a cream-coloured plush blanket and some coral throw pillows out of a bag and arranged them on the couch. It felt nice to have her own space. Everything at the house in Seattle had been Antonio's, and he hadn't wanted her to "make the place too girlie." She decided she would find some fresh-cut flowers as often as she could to keep in a vase in the living room. There were several books already on the shelf, and she quickly looked them over—mostly romance novels and mysteries, as well as couple of travel guides.

Feeling satisfied with her work, she decided to go for a walk before lunch. She wandered over toward the stables. She could see a man in a cowboy hat working with a horse. As she got nearer, she realized it was Cole. He was training a rather beautiful and very skittish horse. Cole was trying to lead her around the arena with a rope, but the horse was having none of it. She reared up and whinnied loudly at him, trying to intimidate him. Cole stood his ground and spoke quietly to her. He continued to stand holding the rope with his body turned to the side, instead of facing her directly. His demeanour was calm and reassuring and he spoke softly and gently, keeping his moves slow and deliberate. The horse eventually began to give in and move in step with him as he guided her around in large circles. He soon managed to reach up and touch the side of her face. The horse stopped resisting, turning her head to him calmly. Claire watched as Cole reached into his pocket for apple slices, which he held up to her. The large animal nuzzled his face a bit, fully surrendering to him. *Lucky horse*, she thought. *I'd eat apple slices out of his hand, too, if he offered them.*

Cole knew just what to say and how to move his body to calm the horse. Claire could tell he would know just how to make her relax into his arms. He looked up from his work with the horse and saw her watching him. He touched his hat to her and continued to lead the horse around for another minute before returning her to the stables.

Claire didn't notice Trey walking up behind her. He startled her when he spoke up. "Cole's one of the best horse trainers around. Some folks up the road asked him to pick up that horse yesterday because none of them could get near her. They've been trying for weeks. He got this far in one morning."

"Wow. That's pretty impressive," Claire replied.

"Yup." Trey nodded. "You like horses, Claire?"

"Love 'em. My grandparents had horses when I was growing up."

Just as Cole walked up, Trey asked, "Well, maybe you can come for a ride with us later? A few of us are heading down to the river after lunch to see if it's shallow enough to cross with the cattle. You could join us if you aren't too busy."

"That sounds wonderful, but I should really

help with supper. I haven't lifted a finger since I got here."

Cole smiled. "Well, that's just because you didn't work here until a couple of hours ago. You should come along. Alicia's got supper all planned out already—it's just steak and potatoes, so I doubt she'll mind if you come along. It'll give you a feel for the area, which is actually important when you're talking to guests."

"Okay, thanks!" Claire beamed. "I'll mention it to Alicia first, though. I hate the idea of skipping out on her."

"Sure thing. Let's head down and have some lunch."

* * *

"No problem! Of course you should go," Alicia replied, giving Claire a wide smile. "I have the steaks marinating, the baked potatoes are wrapped already and I just need to cut up the mushrooms and make a salad. I'm actually going to go for a swim this afternoon to relax for a while."

"Thanks so much, Alicia. I haven't been on a horse in years—I am *so* excited." Claire's face shone with happiness.

Cole watched her as she ate her tuna sandwich and fries with gusto. He loved how enthusiastic she was about going riding. He thought of how different she was from Gabriela, the woman he had at one time hoped to marry. Gabriela hated riding and certainly would not dig into a plate of fries.

Cole's eyes followed Claire as she got up to clear her dishes and take them into the kitchen.

"Hey, little bro, you seem lost in thought over there," Ben said, sharing a smirk with Alicia.

She lifted a knowing eyebrow at Cole. "Uh-oh, I've seen that look before!"

Cole broke from his trance with more than a little embarrassment. "What? Come on. I'm just thinking about that new filly I was training this morning. She's coming along nicely."

Ben broke into laughter. "I think there might be another nice filly you want to work with even more."

"Shut up," Cole said, trying to hide his grin as he got up and took his dishes to the kitchen.

* * *

It was a perfect afternoon for a ride. There was not a cloud in the sky, and though it was warm, there was a slight breeze to keep them cool. Cole saddled up a chestnut-brown horse for Claire.

"This is Nellie. She's pretty calm, so she's a good choice if you haven't been on a horse in a while."

He led Nellie out to the yard, along with his horse, Dudley, a large horse with a sleek black coat. The two obediently followed him out into the sun.

The others joining them on the ride were already heading out of the yard, leaving Cole and Claire last.

Claire felt butterflies in her stomach as she walked over to Nellie. She stopped in front of the large beast and stroked her face, speaking quietly. "I'm Claire; is it okay if I get a ride? It's been a long time since I've done this, but I'll do my best to remember how."

Nellie nuzzled her nose up to Claire's cheek. Claire gave a little laugh and patted her on her long neck. Cole stood behind her as she prepared to get on. Putting one foot into the stirrup, she tried to swing her leg over. She had underestimated how tall Nellie was and didn't lift herself high enough, slipping back toward the ground. Cole caught her by the waist and gently helped her down.

She smiled sheepishly. "These are my skinny jeans. I should have worn yoga pants so I could stretch."

Cole gave a little chuckle. "You'll be just fine. Nellie's tall. I'll help you on."

She lifted her foot back into the stirrup again, and this time, as she tried to hoist herself up, Cole gave her a little boost using both hands on her bottom. "Oh my!" she exclaimed as she swung her leg over. Her heart jumped a little at the feeling of those strong hands touching her.

Cole mounted Dudley with ease and turned to Claire. "You ready?"

"Yeah, now that I'm up here, I should be okay."

"Giddy-up," Cole told Dudley, and they began moving forward at a slow pace. Once they were out of the gates of the yard, the horses started trotting quickly.

Claire relaxed into the saddle, feeling happier than she had in a long time. The sun on her face and the beautiful beast carrying her out toward the mountains were pure bliss.

Cole rode beside Claire, matching her pace to keep an eye on how she was doing. "You're a natural!" he said.

"This is one of my favourite things to do in the whole world!" she answered, giving Cole a huge smile.

They rode along for over an hour, a few minutes behind the rest of the group. Cole told Claire about the area they were riding through and what the cattle drives were like. She asked a lot of questions and seemed genuinely interested in learning about ranch life. He had always wanted a woman who would like to ride with him just like this. He was struck by how beautiful she was moving up and down in the saddle. A piece of her hair blew forward onto her face, and he watched as she carefully tucked it behind her ear as she spoke to him. He felt a longing to kiss her stirring inside him.

When they reached the river, the other guys were standing by the bank, skipping stones as their horses drank from the water's edge. The river looked shallow near the shoreline, but it was wide and moved quickly. The clear water rushed over the rocks, making a calming sound. Cole climbed off Dudley and walked over to help Claire slide down off Nellie. He held her waist with both hands and looked right into her eyes as he lowered her down.

"Thanks." Claire's voice came out almost as a whisper. He leaned his face down to hers, bringing his lips close to hers.

The moment was interrupted as Trey called back to them. "Cole! What did you pack us to drink? We're all thirsty as hell over here!"

"Water!" Cole called back without taking his eyes off Claire.

Claire cleared her throat. "Here, let me help you before there's a mutiny."

Once everyone had their drinks, Claire walked along the riverbank, taking in the view and the smell of the fresh mountain air. She sat on a fallen log and took her boots and socks off. Rolling up her jeans, she slowly walked over the rocks to the river's shallow edge and dipped her toes in. The icy water felt refreshing after the hot ride. She waded in up to her ankles and allowed the water to rush over her feet, feeling invigorated. Something shiny under a rock caught Claire's eye and she bent down to try to reach it. The object was just a touch too far, and as she stretched forward, her feet slipped on the wet rocks and she lost her balance, landing in the river with a loud splash. She let out a muffled shriek as the cold water hit her chest and face, soaking her front. She quickly popped up back onto her feet, hoping no one had noticed.

"Shit, that's cold!" she exclaimed under her breath.

When she turned around, all the men were staring at her. Dustin started a slow clap, and pretty soon they all joined in, some of them whooping. Claire tried to pull her T-shirt away from her breasts, realizing all of a sudden how see-through it had become now that it was wet. Her lacy, lavender-coloured bra was very visible now.

"Well, of course this would happen," she muttered to herself.

Cole strode over quickly, trying to hide the grin on his face. "Alright, you idiots, calm down. Haven't you ever seen a lady fall into the water before?"

He walked up to her and reached out his hand to pull her out of the river. Her feet slipped again, and he grabbed her just as she was about to land on her ass in the water.

"Whoa! I got you," he said as he picked her up and lifted her back over to the log to sit down.

"Those rocks are more slippery than they look," she managed to say, her face flushed with embarrassment.

"That they are," he answered, glancing down

at her shirt as he sat next to her. "You know, if you want me to see your underwear, you could just have me over and lay them all out on the table for me to have a look."

She laughed out loud, surprised by his joke. "I'll keep that in mind," she replied, then paused to look down at her soaking clothes. "Thanks for rescuing me there. You have quick reflexes. You could join Cirque du Soleil and be the Amazing Reflex Man or something."

"Well now, that's a great idea if this whole ranch thing doesn't work out," he replied as he started unbuttoning his shirt. Taking it off, he revealed his white T-shirt and those powerful arms he had been hiding. "Here. You can throw this on to keep you from flashing the whole team on the way home. It would take forever if all the guys start riding backwards so they can stare at you."

"I don't think this view would be that distracting for anyone, but I will take you up on that offer, if you don't mind."

Cole gave her a confused look. "Claire, there isn't a man on the planet who wouldn't be riveted by the sight of you in a wet T-shirt."

Claire blushed. "You're too kind. Wrong, but kind. Maybe you should make an appointment with your optometrist soon."

Cole put his hand up to her chin and gently turned her face to his. "That guy really did a number on you if you don't know how completely stunning you are."

Claire's head jerked back. She was surprised he would allude to Antonio. "Thank you for the shirt. I'm going to go change behind that shrub over there."

She hid behind the shrub and took off her wet shirt. *What the hell does he know about it anyway?* she thought, feeling more exposed by his comment than by her state of undress.

When Claire walked back to find her socks and boots, Cole was riding his horse across the river to test its depth. She watched as he eased Dudley across the current, fearless and confident in the saddle. Her anger melted away as she breathed in the scent from his shirt and remembered the feeling of his hand on her chin. She realized she was just scared to fall for another man, to believe sweet words only to be hurt again. She couldn't handle it right now, and it wasn't going to do her any good to get involved with her boss only to end up out of a job and a home again. She sighed, resolving to keep things professional from here on out.

There was a distance between Cole and Claire on the ride back that was obvious to both of them. They barely spoke two words to each other, keeping closer to the group. Claire listened quietly, suddenly feeling out of place again, as they all chatted about sports and the upcoming cattle drive. When they reached the stables, Claire managed to slide off Nellie on her own, feeling both pride and regret at not having Cole's hands on her waist again. Dustin took the reins from her to lead Nellie back to the stables. "Thanks for the ride, Nellie. Sorry about being so wet."

Claire hurried off to her cabin to get changed before dinner. At least she could help Alicia clean up.

After supper, Alicia and Claire worked together washing down the tables and scrubbing the pots and pans. "You seem quiet tonight, Claire. Was the ride alright this afternoon?"

"Oh, yeah, sorry, Alicia. I think I'm just tired. The ride was very nice, even with the dip in the river. I had forgotten how much I love being on a horse."

Alicia smiled at her. "Yeah, I love it, too. Such a sense of freedom."

"Exactly!" Claire smiled back, happy to connect with someone about that feeling.

"Everything else okay, Claire? How do you think you'll like it here, so far?"

"So far I love everything about it. I just hope I don't mess things up and end up having to leave."

Alicia gave her a confused look. "I can't see that happening. You seem to fit right in around here."

"Well, I hope you're right. I just really want this to work out."

Alicia smiled. "I do, too. You are the nicest person to work here that I can remember. It's also really great to have a woman my own age to talk to."

"Thanks, Alicia, you've made me feel so at home here." Claire gave Alicia's hand a little squeeze.

FOUR

The next week flew by as Claire and Alicia worked on the new menu together in between preparing meals. Claire had plans to add some healthy smoothies to the breakfast menu, as well as some vegan options to each meal. One day at lunch she tested out a sandwich with baked brie, grilled chicken, fig jelly and roasted apples on ciabatta buns. For a side she prepared a spinach and strawberry salad with caramelized pecans. The meal was a big hit. One of the casual ranch hands called into the kitchen, "Claire, marry me and make this sandwich for me every day!"

Claire appeared in the kitchen doorway and called back, "Yeah, Bill, but what's in it for me?"

She caught Cole smiling at her and shaking his head as she disappeared back into the kitchen. It was the only sincerely warm moment they had shared that week. They both seemed to have come to a silent agreement to keep things professional, having realized they had been treading on dangerous ground. Their working relationship couldn't be sacrificed by their attraction to each other, which caused an air of sexual tension that frustrated them both equally.

Cole was also busy getting ready for the next week's cattle drive and the arrival of the season's first guests. He needed to make sure the horses and cattle were all healthy enough to make the trip, in addition to overseeing the packing of supplies and preparation of the guest rooms. Claire had caught glimpses of him as he moved quickly around the ranch, calling out orders and working hard himself.

On Saturday when the new guests arrived, things got worse. The guests included a group of seven guys in a stag party. The groom's fiancée had decided she would rather have them out in the wilderness with some cowboys and horses for a week than in the wild streets of Vegas for three days. The men were rowdy and looking for a good time, forcing Cole to put on an air of fierceness in order to keep them under control during their stay. Claire was surprised to see this side of him. He became short with everyone when the guests were around, rarely smiling or talking. She grew uncomfortable with both the guests and the way Cole was acting.

When she and Alicia were cleaning up after supper, Cole turned to her as he passed through the kitchen and growled, "You'd best stay away from the pool with that little bikini of yours while these morons are here."

Claire felt like she had been slapped in the face. He had such a harsh tone and seemed to be accusing her of acting inappropriately with the guests, even though she had been nothing but professional and friendly, if detached. She was so shocked that she was speechless as he stormed out the back door.

"What was that about?" Alicia asked, looking stunned.

Claire's eyes filled with tears. "I don't know."

The next morning, things felt frenzied as the group was preparing to head out on the cattle drive. Cole came into the kitchen to find out where the food supplies for the trip were. Claire and Alicia were still putting everything together, not expecting the men to leave for another hour. Ben was in the kitchen helping himself to coffee.

Cole was visibly irritated when he saw they weren't finished. "What's the holdup? We need to get these guys on the trail!"

After two days of him being a prick, Claire snapped. "You know what? I've had just about enough of your crap. You said you were leaving at 10 a.m., so we'll be ready for 10 a.m. If you've changed your mind, then wash your hands and start helping. Otherwise, go bark at someone else."

"Oh, really? You've had enough of my crap? Well, you've got some nerve, coming onto my ranch—"

Ben interrupted him, his voice calm. "Say, Cole, why don't you and I go saddle up the horses and leave Claire and Alicia to finish up here? Or you and Claire could go out back and have sex and just get it over with."

Claire and Cole both turned to Ben, clearly pissed right off.

"Shut the hell up, Ben," Cole said, slamming the door behind him as he left.

Alicia and Claire glared at Ben.

"Sorry, it's what everyone was thinking. I just thought I'd say it," Ben said in a sheepish voice as he walked out to help with the horses.

An hour later, Claire and Alicia had all the food and supplies packed onto the back of a wagon Bill was sitting on. A large horse was harnessed to it, ready to go. Trey smiled at Claire and with mock affection called out, "Beautiful Claire, promise you'll wait for me."

Out of the corner of her eye, Claire noticed Cole staring at them. "Oh, Trey, I promise!" she said in a dramatic voice. She could see Cole's body stiffen as he watched the pair flirt, and a part of her was pleased to see him upset after how he had been acting.

Cole got up on his horse and gave Claire a long, serious look. She couldn't read his expression, but she knew he wasn't happy. She lifted her chin and glared back, her eyes daring him to say something. He turned his horse away without accepting her challenge.

Ben opened the gate to the corral, freeing the herd of cattle it held. The stag-party guests let out big whoops as they got started. One of them almost fell off his horse. Ben, Alicia and Claire watched silently as the group rode off. Things felt a bit awkward after what Ben had said in the kitchen. Claire felt foolish for her part in it all.

Alicia knew just what to say to ease the tension. "Claire, honey, we've earned a swim. You go grab that bikini of yours, and let's hit the pool! Ben, I'm sure there's some sporting event on TV," she cooed as she kissed him on the cheek. "Go relax for a while."

* * *

The next five days were a complete roller coaster for Claire. When she and Alicia were working on the new menu together and cooking, she felt relaxed and happy. As soon as she was alone, she felt angry and confused and anxious all at the same time. She had been too familiar with her boss—a huge mistake that might cost her both her job and her new home. He had no right to talk to her the way he had, but she certainly could have handled the whole thing with more tact. She also couldn't deny her feelings of longing for him. He was the sexiest man she had ever met, and she had never felt more feminine than when he looked at her. Thinking about those brief moments when she had felt his touch made her ache for him.

Each morning she would start out with a long run to try to ease some of her tension. It worked for a while, but by evening, she was a mess again. On the fourth day, the old fridge in the restaurant kitchen called it quits. Ben had a look at it and said they probably shouldn't bother spending the money to fix it again. They would have to make do until Cole got back so he could take a look at it. Ben and Alicia decided to put the food into their own fridge as well as Cole's.

The three started over to Cole's cabin, Ben taking most of the food Alicia was carrying from her. "I don't want you trying to carry such heavy things anymore."

Claire's eyebrows went up, but she decided not to ask.

Alicia turned to Claire, seeing the expression on her face. "Well, Ben, I think you let the cat out of the bag."

Ben gave a wide, proud smile. "Yup, Claire, we're going to have a baby!"

Claire smiled back. "Really? Oh, wow! I'm so happy for you! You two will make wonderful parents. And what a perfect place for a child to grow up. When is the baby due?"

Alicia gave an excited smile. "It's early still. I'm only eight weeks along, so the baby should be here in mid-January if everything goes well."

Claire grinned. "That is just terrific! I would hug you if we weren't carrying all this food."

When they got to Cole's cabin, Alicia put down the bag she was carrying and unlocked the door. Claire had yet to set foot into Cole's cabin and was curious to see what it was like. It was much larger than hers, with two stories and a wraparound porch. She walked in to find a cozy, homey place with a lot of framed family photos as well as many books lining the shelves. She was surprised to find that he had a wall of CDs and vinyl records, everything ranging from classical to rock to blues, with only a little bit of country. She tried not to gawk as she and Ben brought in two big boxes of food.

"He's quite the music fan," Claire called to Alicia.

"Yeah, he sure is. He loves to read, too."

I really don't know this man at all, she thought. *How can I even begin to think I'm falling for him?*

* * *

Cole, meanwhile, was in a private battle all his own. Try as he might, he couldn't stop himself from thinking about Claire and how badly he had messed things up with someone who he needed to turn the ranch into a sustainable business. He was glad his dad hadn't been there to see him make such a fool of himself. On more than one occasion, his dad had told his boys, "You never get your bed where you get your bread," meaning don't mess around at work. Cole wished he could take back the first weeks of Claire's time at the ranch and start over. Feeling stupid about how forward he had been with a woman he barely knew and who also worked for him, he cringed, remembering how he had snapped at her before setting off on the trail ride.

He was doing his best to forget any attraction he had for Claire as he prepared himself for her inevitable departure from his life. He had screwed up and knew it was only a matter of time before she would go. The thought of it left him in a bad mood with very little patience for the rowdy stag-party guests. He was getting sick of hearing them talk about all the women they wanted to bang, and he wished they had gone to Vegas after all.

On Friday afternoon, the first sight of the ranch brought Cole both relief and tension. He would be glad to see the guests leave the next day but was half expecting Claire to be gone by the time he got back. And if she was there, he wasn't entirely sure how to handle what he knew would be an awkward situation.

* * *

Claire and Alicia had spent the afternoon in the kitchen, preparing a big steak dinner for the returning group. They had beer in large, ice-filled tubs on the restaurant patio as well as a table of appetizers waiting. Ben poked his head into the room around four to say he could see the party on the other side of the lake already. When the men returned, the guests made their way up to the restaurant first, while Cole, Ben and the other ranch hands got the horses fed, watered and settled in for the night. The beer was flowing quickly, and by the time Cole and the others arrived at the restaurant, the guests were well into their third round.

The groom, Woody, had tried hitting on Claire each time she came out with more food. She smiled politely and said little things like "Oh, you!" or "What would your fiancée say?" or even, "That's flattering, but no thank you. My heart belongs elsewhere." She was trying to not offend him but at the same time make sure he knew he wouldn't get anywhere.

When Cole arrived, he could see Woody trying to grab Claire around the waist as she cleared empty bottles off the table. She slipped away with great agility and a tense smile. Cole's body coursed with rage as he watched. He decided to sit at Woody's table and keep an eye on him. Each time Claire came out, he stared at Woody with a territorial look that was impossible to miss. Woody, already drunk, seemed to take it as a challenge.

Cole got up and went into the kitchen. "Why don't you stay in the kitchen, Claire, and let Ben and me finish serving dessert. I don't like the way Woody is carrying on right now."

Claire, still angry with Cole, did not want him marking her as his territory. "Thanks, but I can take care of myself. I'm a big girl and I have lots of experience dealing with drunken idiots. In a little while, he'll go sleep it off and tomorrow he'll have a nice hangover on the plane home." Her words came out with more venom than she intended.

"Suit yourself," he said with a shrug as he walked out of the kitchen.

"Ben, keep an eye on our esteemed guests, will you? I need to go have a shower," Cole said as he walked out.

The party went on for another two hours. It was after dark when Claire finished up the last of the dishes and started heading back to her cabin. Alicia had left earlier to get some much needed rest. As Claire walked along the quiet path, she picked up her pace, sensing someone behind her. As she reached into her pocket for her keys, she hoped it was her imagination. Suddenly, she felt two hands on her waist, grabbing her roughly from behind and yanking her off the path. She was turned and pinned up against the outside wall of a guest cabin, staring into the wild eyes of Woody. Pressing one hand over her mouth, he used his other hand to grip both of her wrists, forcing her hands over her head.

"Shh," he slurred. The reek of beer mixed with sweat was overwhelming to Claire's senses. She stood rigid and terrified.

"I am looking to have one last night of fun before I strap on the old ball and chain, and you're the lucky lady who gets to have me last," he snarled as he pressed his lips into her neck.

Claire struggled, but he overpowered her with his heavy body. She tried to bite his fingers.

"Oh, you like it rough, hey? Me too," he hissed in her face as he slammed her head back into the wall. Pain seared through Claire's head, causing her to see stars as tears of fear rolled down her cheeks.

Suddenly, out of the darkness, she saw a figure approach. In one swift movement, Woody's feet were kicked out from under him, knocking him onto his back. Before Claire even realized it was Cole, he had jumped on Woody, delivering three quick punches to his face. Woody was out cold on the ground, but Cole continued to punch him with brutal force. Suddenly terrified that Cole might kill him, Claire yelled, "Stop, Cole! Stop! He's out."

Cole's arm pulled back and then halted in mid-air as he got a hold of himself. Otis was next to him, growling and barking in Woody's face. Ben came running up from the direction of the lodge, followed by two of Woody's friends.

Cole glared at the guests. "Get him to his room and make sure he stays there. Tomorrow morning, I'm putting you all in a cab before breakfast. You are not welcome here anymore." He spoke with such levelled rage the two men had no choice but to pick up their friend and drag him away. Ben followed them to make sure they went back to their rooms.

Claire stood against the wall, breathing heavily and shaking, her knees starting to give out as the reality of what had just happened sank in. Cole caught her as she slid down the wall, pulling her up and holding her arms to keep her steady.

"You okay, Claire?"

She nodded bravely as her eyes filled with tears again. "I really think he would have . . ." She couldn't even bring herself to say the words.

Pulling her to him, Cole pressed his lips to the top of her head as he wrapped his arms around her. His voice was hoarse as he spoke. "Don't let your mind go there." She heard him let out a long exhale as he held her.

"I'll call the police. You should press charges," Cole advised.

"No. You stopped him, and I think you might get charged with assault," Claire responded quietly.

"I don't care about that. He should be charged after what he did to you."

"Cole, I don't want to go down that road. I would just have to relive the whole thing in detail over and over. And think of the bad publicity for the ranch. Let's just leave it alone."

"I couldn't care less about the publicity, but I'll handle this any way you want, Claire. The only thing that matters is keeping you safe." He looked down at her. "Are you hurt? Should I take you to the hospital?"

"I think I'm okay, but he slammed my head into the wall. It really hurts," Claire said, her voice breaking.

"Come on, I'll take you back to your cabin and have a look."

Cole kept one arm around her while they walked farther along the path, and he tried to get a sense of how steady she was on her feet. Otis followed along and then sat on the porch as Cole unlocked the door and the pair went inside.

Claire dropped down onto the couch with a despondent look on her face. Picking up her throw, Cole wrapped it around her shoulders. "Here, you rest for a minute. I'll make you some tea."

He quietly walked over to the kettle and lit the burner under it. Claire watched him as he washed his hands and opened the cupboard, finding a box of camomile tea. It was hard to imagine that this gentle person had only moments before viciously pummelled a man. When the tea was ready, he walked over and handed her a mug, being careful not to spill any.

He knelt down in front of her. "I'd like to take a look at your eyes and your head, just in case you have a concussion. I've seen my share of them around here, so I'm pretty sure of what to look for."

Staring into her eyes for a moment, he lifted his hands to her cheeks. "I'm checking your pupils to make sure they're the same size and aren't dilated. They look good." He moved around behind her before gently combing through her hair. "You're not bleeding, but you've got a pretty decent-sized bump here. I'll get you some ice for your head, okay?"

Claire nodded, too upset to talk. He grabbed a small bag of frozen peas from the freezer and wrapped it in a dishtowel.

Claire sipped her tea and then, after a long moment, looked up at Cole. "Well, I guess we can't expect a good review from *those* guys on TripAdvisor."

She tried to laugh and then started to cry instead. Cole carefully took the tea out of her hands and placed it on the coffee table before wrapping her in his arms and holding her tight to his chest. She could smell his aftershave and feel his warmth as he held her. His heartbeat provided a hypnotic sound against her ear, and she realized she had never felt this safe with any man, not even with Antonio when they were still happy. She knew without a doubt that Cole would do anything to protect her. The anger she had felt at him in the past few days completely dissolved as she began to understand why he had acted that way.

"You knew what those men were capable of," she said quietly.

"I had an idea. Something about that guy just didn't sit right with me from the start."

"So that's why you've been . . ." her voice trailed off.

"Such a prick this week?"

"I wasn't going to put it that way. I was going to say you've been in a bad mood."

"I was both. I'm sorry for how I acted before we left. I could have handled things a lot better."

"Me too."

Cole held her close, soon feeling her body relax as she fell asleep. The sight of her under that blanket, so shaken and fragile, stirred something deep inside him. Even though they hadn't so much as kissed, the thought of another man touching her made him feel physically sick. Cole sat reflecting on the intense rage he had felt when he saw what was happening—it was something he had never experienced before. He knew that in that moment he would have killed Woody with his bare hands if that was what it took to get him away from Claire.

As he listened to her breathing grow steadier, he admired her efforts at bravery in the face of such a horrifying situation, how she had tried to stand up to the guy and then tried to make a joke about it. Holding her as she slept, he drank in the smell of her hair and took in the feeling of her body's perfection against his. He had an undeniable feeling of yearning he had never felt before. Gently sliding her onto his lap, he stood up with her in his arms and carried her to her bed. Carefully taking off her shoes, he tucked her under the covers. Cole stood and watched her for a minute and then couldn't help reaching out and touching her soft cheek with the back of his fingers. Her skin felt like silk, just as he had imagined it would.

FIVE

When she woke in the morning, Claire was in her bed fully dressed, with the blanket still wrapped around her shoulders. Looking out the bedroom door, she saw Otis lying on the floor. She stood up and called him over so she could pet him. As she did, she saw a note on the kitchen table.

Claire,

I left Otis so you wouldn't have to wake up alone. I hope you didn't mind sharing your cabin with a dog for the night. Rest up and come to the restaurant when you're ready. It's Alicia's day off, so I'll get breakfast for the guests.

Cole

She sighed gratefully as she read the note. Looking over to the couch, she saw a pillow and blanket neatly folded. *He must have slept here in case I needed him.* The thought of it almost brought tears to her eyes. Otis walked over and nudged her hand for more pats. As she made herself coffee, she mentally replayed the events of the last evening in her mind. She shuddered to think of what would have happened if Cole hadn't been there. As she looked over at the couch, she was flooded with the memory of him holding her in his arms and how completely safe she had felt. Claire sipped her coffee, realizing he must have carried her to bed when she was asleep and tucked her in. The thought brought a mixture of emotion—embarrassment, gratitude and, underneath, a longing to be back in his arms, safe and warm.

"If only I could fall asleep like that every night, Otis." As she heard the words come out of her mouth, she knew it was a ridiculous thought. "I'm not going down that road. I am not ready for anyone in my life right now."

Otis looked up at her and wagged his tail in response.

After having her coffee, Claire took a long hot shower and got dressed in jeans, a black, long-sleeved T-shirt and black ballet flats. She did her hair up in a ponytail and put some mascara on. Her heart pounded as she hurried past the spot where she had been attacked. As she walked up the back steps to the restaurant, she sighed with relief when she saw Cole through the kitchen window. She opened the door and gave Otis a quick pat before going in.

"Thanks, buddy," she said.

Cole looked up from making scrambled eggs and pancakes. There was a strainer full of strawberries in the sink, waiting to be cut up and arranged.

"Good morning. How are you feeling?"

"My head is a little sore, but otherwise I'm okay. I'm so embarrassed that I fell asleep on you last night. Sorry about that. Thank you for putting me to bed and leaving Otis for me." She smiled gratefully at him.

"It's the least I could do. I only hope that idiot didn't make you rethink being here. I sent him and his buddies off in a cab at seven this morning. I didn't want you to have to run into him again." Cole didn't look up as he stirred the eggs.

Claire crossed the kitchen and touched his arm gently as she stood beside him. "Thank you, Cole. You managed to make me feel so safe, even after what happened. I have no intention of leaving. Besides, there are assholes everywhere you go, really."

As she touched his arm, her shirt sleeve rode up, exposing bruises on her wrist from the night before. Cole's shoulders dropped as he saw the purple marks. He put down the spatula he was holding and gently ran his fingers over her wrist. "Aw, fuck. That shouldn't have happened. I should have kept a better eye on that dick."

"I'm alright, really. You know what cheers me up? Cooking," she replied as she picked up the spatula and flipped the pancakes on the griddle. Handing it back to Cole, she walked over to the sink to cut up the strawberries. The two worked well together, making breakfast for the remaining guests and the ranch hands. They seemed to find an easy rhythm as they filled the plates and served up the food.

When the meal service was over, Cole smiled at her. "I have to run over to my office for a bit. You going to be okay here alone?"

"I'll be just fine now that numbnuts is gone." She smiled bravely.

Cole started to walk toward the door and then stopped. "Alicia told me about the fridge. I took a look at it and I can't fix it. It's pretty old, so I think it's time for a new one. Would you be up for going into town with me to buy a new one this afternoon? I think you should pick it out yourself."

"I sure am. Come and get me when you're ready."

Cole nodded as he put his hat on and headed out the door. "Will do."

* * *

Cole walked out to the barn to get his tools. The latch on the arena gate needed repairing and he wanted to see to it himself. There was a little trick to it that no one else knew. There were so many things like that around the ranch, little bits of information that only he knew, that made it his home. He wondered if that was why what had happened last night had affected him so deeply. Because it had happened at his home—a place that was supposed to be safe and secure.

As he walked out into the sun, he took in a deep breath of fresh air, trying to force out the sick feeling that had settled itself in his chest since he had come upon Woody and Claire. The thought of her so shaken twisted at his heart as he opened his tool kit and selected a screwdriver. She was so fragile underneath that tough act she had going. He hadn't even wanted to leave her alone in the kitchen this morning, a foolish thought now that Woody was long gone. Was it just because it had happened at his home or was it because it had happened to her? There was something about that woman that made a mockery out of his belief in keeping things professional as her boss. He had done a decent job of drawing that line since they had been down at the river, but if he were really honest with himself, that line was in sand and nothing more. He wanted her, and not just her body—he wanted all of her. Something had shifted the night before, making it feel as though giving in to his desire for her was right. He wouldn't act on it, though, unless she made it very clear that it was what she wanted too. And after what she had been through, he doubted she would have any thoughts of romance on her mind for a very long time.

* * *

Just after lunch was cleaned up, Cole walked into the kitchen. "Hi, you still feeling up for some appliance shopping?"

Claire smiled. "You bet, I just need to go grab my purse from my cabin."

"I'll walk you."

"Thanks." Claire felt better having Cole walk with her. Even in the sunlight, the memory of the night before was still too fresh for her to feel at ease along the path.

They walked into her cabin and Claire headed for her bedroom and shut the door. "I'll just be a minute."

She quickly washed her hands and face, put some BB cream on her face, touched up her mascara and threw on some tinted lip gloss. She changed into a royal-blue yoga shirt with extra-long sleeves to hide her wrists before coming back out of her room. She found Cole studying a picture of her with her sister, taken in London a few years earlier.

"That's my sister, Janet."

"I figured she was your sister. You two look alike. Do you miss her?"

"Yeah, I do. But she's so happy in London, and we talk and text all the time so she doesn't feel quite so far away."

They left her cabin, headed over to his truck and climbed in. The interior was clean, and when Cole started the engine up, the Foo Fighters came on, an acoustic version of "My Hero."

Claire looked over at him. "This is hands-down one of the best songs ever recorded."

"I think so, too. Have you ever seen them live?"

"No, but I'd love to."

"I saw them in Denver once. They were unreal. Maybe if they come back, a few of us could go," Cole replied.

On the way to Colorado Springs, the pair chatted and laughed as Claire took in the scenery on the beautiful drive from the base of the mountains to the city. The big pines gave way to low shrubs, tall grasses and red earth under the blue sky. Claire looked from the window to Cole, noticing that things felt as comfortable between them as they had on their ride out to the river. She told some funny stories about the more memorable patrons at her restaurant back in Seattle, loving the sound of Cole's laughter as she talked. It was deep and genuine. When they reached the appliance store, Claire was having so much fun she was sorry the ride was over.

* * *

As soon as Cole and Claire entered the appliance store, a saleslady with a name tag that read TANYA AT YOUR SERVICE zeroed in on them. She strode over with a too-wide smile. "Good afternoon, you two! What can I help you with today?"

"We need to get a new refrigerator," Cole said.

The saleslady turned to Claire and asked, "So, do you know what type you're looking for?"

Claire smiled. "Something with a large capacity. A Sub-Zero would be best."

"Oh!" Tanya practically jumped with glee. "Now, does your husband here know what that's going to run him?"

Cole gave Claire a playful grin. "It doesn't matter. Nothing's too good for my little lady." He grabbed her around the waist with one arm and drew her to him. Claire breathed in his aftershave, feeling suddenly giddy with delight.

It took about forty-five minutes for them to pick out a Viking Sub-Zero, which would be delivered in two days. As they were about to leave, Tanya beamed at Claire and said, "This one's a keeper. It's a rare man who will spend that much on an appliance to make his wife happy and still have a smile on his face! You hang on to him!"

"Will do, Tanya!"

When they got back to the truck, Cole opened the passenger door for Claire and offered her his hand. "Your carriage awaits, Mrs. Mitchell."

She took his hand and climbed in, putting on a regal air. "Thank you, darling."

Cole started the truck and looked over at Claire. "It's just you and me for supper. I gave everyone the afternoon off as soon as the last of the guests cleared out. Alicia and Ben went into town to have dinner at her mom's place. Would you mind coming with me to run a few errands and then grabbing a bite somewhere before we go back home?"

"I'd love to."

"Excellent. I know the best burger place in the state."

* * *

The sun was about to go down when they got back to the ranch. Cole parked beside the barn.

"It looks deserted here," Claire said. A feeling of disappointment crossed over her as he took the keys out of the ignition, signalling the end of their wonderful afternoon together. She watched as he glanced over at her, his eyes asking what he couldn't. If she had been reading him properly, he seemed every bit as into her as she was into him. After she had flirted for hours, her instincts told her that if she wanted to cross that line, he would come with her.

Cole got out of the truck first and came around to open Claire's door. She jumped down, using the hand he held out to help her. She stood with her back against the truck for a minute as he locked it up. She looked up at him, willing him to touch her.

He gave her a sexy grin and a peck on the cheek. "Good night, Mrs. Mitchell."

No longer able to stop herself, Claire reached out and tugged on Cole's shirt with one hand. "You can do better than that."

She locked eyes with him, her stare daring him to kiss her. It was suddenly too much for either of them. All common sense was tossed aside as their lips met urgently. Cole grabbed her ass with both hands and squeezed hard, pulling her to him and pressing his body against hers. Claire parted her lips, inviting his tongue into her mouth. His kiss was even better than she had imagined—it was like nothing she had experienced before, and it made her instantly desperate to have him.

After a few deliciously frenzied moments, Cole stopped abruptly and pulled away, holding her face in his hands. "Is this okay for you?" he breathed heavily.

"Only if you don't stop," she answered.

Claire slid her hand off his collar and rubbed

his chest, thrilled to find that it felt every bit as muscular as it looked. She ripped his shirt open, grateful that it had snaps instead of buttons. As she ran her hands over his smooth skin, she felt herself becoming immediately wet. He pulled her shirt up over her head, revealing her in her bra. Their desire for each other had them completely oblivious to the fact that they were outside and could get caught at any moment.

Cole's hands slid over her breasts, squeezing them gently as he groaned with pleasure at having his first chance to feel their ample size and firmness. His large hands were more than filled. He moved one hand up to hold her face while the other explored her breasts. His touch moved from her jaw to her hair and, wrapping it around his hand, he pulled her head back so he could kiss her full on the mouth. He heard her breathing become heavy, and she gave a little gasp when he gently pulled her hair again. Letting go, he slid both hands back down to her ass, and in one quick move picked her up so that her legs were straddling him. He gave a low moan as he felt her pressed up against his hard length through their jeans.

Claire wrapped her legs around his waist and pressed herself against him, feeling his erection for the first time. She wanted nothing more than to have him inside her right then. She felt as if she might burst from frustration if he didn't take her.

She had never known this much need for any man, certainly not for Antonio. Her head was spinning as Cole carried her to the back of the pickup, holding her up with one hand under her ass as he opened the tailgate and carefully set her down on the back of the truck. She urgently reached for his belt and struggled to unbuckle it, their mouths never parting. Helping her with the buckle, Cole then moved his hands to pop open the button on her jeans while she quickly tugged his pants down to reveal him standing in front of her, shirt open, in boxer briefs, hard as a rock.

"I wish you were wearing a skirt," he murmured into her ear.

"Me too," she breathed.

She put her hands down on the tailgate to prop up her body as he pulled her jeans off in one quick move and then paused to look into her deep blue eyes, his stare full of lust. He urgently slid one hand inside her panties, finding her wet and ready. Claire rocked her hips forward to push his fingers inside her. She grabbed at his boxer briefs and yanked them down, unleashing him so his cock was now pointing straight at her. A small gasp escaped her mouth as she got her first look at him this way. He was magnificent.

Cole's mind was reeling now, and that little gasp caused his cock to twitch with excitement. He had never wanted anything as badly as he wanted to feel Claire around him. He picked her up with both hands again and moved her panties aside as his thick length found his way inside her. She wriggled her hips from side to side to help him work his way in deeper. He lifted her up and down, rubbing her along his length as she squeezed him with every muscle in her core. He was so large and so hard that it was almost too much for her, but as she looked at him, she wanted everything he had.

"You're so fucking beautiful," he said to her as his eyes locked onto hers again. She had never felt so feminine, so sexy, so turned on in all her life. The smell of him, the feel of his chin, slightly rough with stubble as he kissed her, the touch of his skin on hers all made her wild with desire.

His strength amazed her as he continued lifting her up and down, with his powerful hands cupping her ass. Their breathing joined up in the same rhythm as he thrust himself into her, and she pushed down on him with her entire body. He was in so far and was so big, it was almost painful at moments, but it was such an exquisite pain she didn't ever want it to stop. She leaned back in his arms and pulled her bra down under her breasts, exposing her hard nipples. He exhaled as he took in his first view of her ripe, pink nipples and lowered his head down to her full breasts, sucking on her, gently at first and then with increasing intensity. He moved his mouth over to her right breast and flicked her nipple with his tongue, then plunged his mouth over it, sucking hard, as he moved in and out of her. This sent Claire over the edge, an explosive orgasm erupting from inside her, drenching him as she came. She had to bite down on her lip to keep from crying out so they wouldn't be discovered.

Cole felt her coming on his rock-hard length. She was so unbelievably tight and wet. As he looked up to see her face as she came, her desire was more than he could take. He surrendered to his own orgasm, his entire body shuddering with its strength.

"Fuck! Oh fuck, fuck, fuck!" was all he managed to say as he came inside her. He held her up around his waist, kissing her and firmly pressing her body to his until long after he was finished.

He didn't ever want to put her down; he didn't ever want to let her go. "You're amazing, Claire."

Claire was, for the first time in her life, completely satisfied. She pulled back and gave him a flirty little smile as she gazed into his perfect hazel eyes. "I knew you could do better."

He grinned back and leaned against the tailgate of his truck, holding her for a moment longer before placing her down gently to stand in front of him.

"I've been wanting to do that since I first laid eyes on you," Cole said as he lowered his head to kiss her again.

"Really? I thought it was just me," Claire answered in a sultry voice.

"You don't know what you do to me. I've never been this irresponsible in my life. Anyone could have pulled up here," Cole said, trying to catch his breath. "Next time, we should probably try to make it at least as far as my cabin."

"Hmm, that's a little presumptuous, don't you think? Maybe I'm a love 'em and leave 'em kind of girl. Have my way with you and then move on to the next cowboy? Or maybe it just wasn't that good for me?" Claire wrinkled her nose uninterestedly.

Cole's eyes widened with surprise. "Not possible. That was amazing for you," he said as he tapped her on the bottom with his hand.

Claire giggled. "You can do better than that, Mr. Mitchell."

She watched Cole pick up her panties and jeans. He dusted them off and slid her panties onto her legs and into place, then did the same with her jeans. A little tremor went through her body as his hands slid up her legs. The combination of his thoughtfulness and his touch had her desire for him building again.

"Mmm, you keep doing things like that and I might give you another chance to impress me." Claire buttoned up her jeans as he reached for his own clothes and started to dress. She reached over and grabbed him by the shirt again except this time she started snapping it shut for him.

"Why am I putting your shirt back on for you?

There should be a law against you wearing anything that covers up my view of your chest."

Cole laughed. "I was thinking the same thing about you, except your whole body." He pulled her in close and started kissing her again. First her lips, then her neck, then he nibbled on her earlobe, causing a little moan to escape her throat. She could feel him getting hard again and was shocked at how quickly he had recovered.

"Already, Cole? You're a machine." Her eyes were wide with surprise.

"Only you can do that to me. These last few weeks have been torture for me. Having you around but not being able to touch you. I have never wanted anyone so bad."

Claire bit her lip. "Okay, I just decided. I'll give you a chance for a round two, but that's probably going to be it."

"Well, I better make the most of it, then, if it's going to be the last time." Cole picked her up in a fireman's carry over his shoulder, causing Claire to squeal with laughter.

* * *

Cole carried Claire all the way back to his cabin and unlocked the door. When they crossed the threshold, he gently lifted her off his shoulder and slid her body down his until she was standing. Their eyes locked, and their mouths came together in hungry, passionate kisses. Claire unbuttoned Cole's jeans and ripped open his shirt again, as he undid her jeans and roughly pulled them down. She kicked them off and pulled her shirt over her head, so she was standing in front of him in her lacy pink bra and panties.

He pulled back from her to take off his shirt, unable to stop his eyes from admiring the view of her looking so sexy. She pulled her ponytail holder out of her hair, causing soft waves to fall around her face. She could see that under his boxer briefs he was hard again.

"Let's take this to the shower," he said as he picked her up over his shoulder again and carried her up the stairs.

Claire started laughing. "You know, I can walk."

Cole caressed the inside of her thigh with his free hand. "I know, but you're going to need to save your strength. If I only get one more chance to impress you, I'm going to make it count."

He set her down in his bathroom and flicked on the light. This was Claire's first time seeing the second level of his cabin, and she was surprised by how spacious it was. A skylight interrupted the sloped, cedar-panelled ceiling, giving the bathroom an airy feeling. White walls and an oversized shower with a long bench added a modern flair. The sun had just set outside, and Claire could see the moon peeking in through the skylight. She looked over at Cole in his underwear, admiring his rippling body, suddenly feeling shy about her own curves in contrast to his chiselled perfection. She bit her lip with a nervous expression on her face.

Cole, who was watching her, immediately noticed the change in her demeanour. His face softened. "What's the matter, Claire?" he asked as he cupped the side of her cheek with one hand.

Claire looked away, suddenly embarrassed to say how she was feeling. "It's just that you're so insanely hot, and I'm feeling really unsure of what someone like you could possibly see in someone with this body."

She put her arms up to hide her chest and rested her chin on her fists. With that same calm and gentle manner she had seen Cole use with the skittish horse, he kissed her on the forehead and then on the tip of her nose, folding her into his arms. "Oh, Claire, you are unbelievably gorgeous. How do you not know that? Your eyes are an incredible shade of blue, your beautiful long hair, your sexy smile . . ." he said gently as he kissed her neck. "The smooth curve of your neck . . ." He slid his body behind her and turned her to face the mirror above the sink.

"Look at yourself. You are perfect," he said, gliding his hands up to hers and carefully pulling her hands down to her stomach.

"Look at these." He ran his hands over her bra, cupping and gently squeezing her breasts. "They are just the right size for my hands—and I have big hands." He reached behind her and unfastened her bra, slid it off her shoulders and let it drop to the floor. She immediately put her hands up to hide herself. He covered her arm with his, wrapping her tight in his warm embrace.

"Look at your hips, how they curve out from your small waist. Everything about you is delicate, feminine, beautiful," he said as he gazed into her eyes in the mirror and ran his hands down her sides to her hips.

She could feel his erection pressed against her back. "Can you feel how hard you're making me just by standing here in your panties?" He reached up, taking one of her hands and bringing it behind her to prove the effect she was having on him.

"Can you see what I see?" he asked, bringing her hand back up to his lips and kissing each finger slowly. "Can you see how completely gorgeous you are? Any man would be lucky to have you. I would kill to be with you."

A shudder of desire coursed through Claire as she brought her hand up onto the back of Cole's neck, exposing herself completely now. Suddenly, she could see her own beauty like never before, and she became wet and ready at the sight of herself standing with this sexy man holding her.

Cole slid his hands to her breasts, rubbing his thumbs over her nipples. Claire moaned with desire as she took in the reflection of her pink buds responding to his touch.

She reached behind her back and placed her thumbs into the waistband of his boxer briefs, pulling the band out and down, freeing him from the confines of the fabric. His underwear fell to the floor as Claire slid off her own panties, wriggling her hips until there were no barriers between them. Cole let out a low moan from his throat as his eyes hungrily devoured the view.

Leaving one hand on her breasts, Cole brought his other down her body, sliding it between her legs. He rubbed her wet, smooth sex as he carefully let one finger slide inside her. Rubbing her clit gently at first, he increased his force as he felt her becoming wetter. Claire turned her head and their mouths joined, greedily exploring each other. Claire moved one hand behind her back and stroked his cock in long motions. He now had two fingers inside her, moving them in and out with a delicious rhythm, causing a sound to escape her mouth that was pure animal. His fingers swirled inside her as he kissed her hard on the mouth. The sight and the sensations rippled through every fibre of her body as she came undone before him.

"Mmm, God, yes," he said as she came on his fingers. "Look at you. You are perfection." Claire looked in the mirror at Cole's face, his expression full of a passion she had never seen before. When he eased his fingers out of her, she made a little unhappy pouty sound, causing him to chuckle softly. Turning her body to face him he crushed her lips with one long kiss.

"You distracted me," he said. "Weren't we going to have a shower?"

He strode over and opened the door to the shower, turning on the water. His body moved with such confidence and ease, Claire couldn't help but sigh with pleasure at the sight of his strong back and his perfectly sculpted ass. He tested the water, then turned to her and reached back with his arm outstretched and his huge erection unashamedly aimed right at her. This time as his eyes looked her up and down, she felt beautiful. She took his hand and he pulled her into the shower and closed the door.

The warm water rained down on their naked bodies as Cole tilted Claire's head up with his hand under her chin. He kissed her, his tongue expertly exploring her mouth. He reached for the soap and began washing her, starting with her arms, then her back and her bottom; he brought the soap around to her chest, kissing her as he ran the soap over her breasts, now full with desire. He washed her tummy next and then knelt down in front of her as he rubbed the bar over her legs and lifted her feet, one at a time, to wash them. He ran his fingers between her toes, massaging them. As he looked up from his position below her, he stared into her eyes and glided the soap up the inside of her legs and over her sex. Lifting himself to standing, he replaced the soap in its holder, then plucked the shower head down with his other hand. Spraying her body, he stopped when he reached her core, using one hand to massage her. The sensation of his skilled fingers along with the vibration of the water was an intoxicating combination that had Claire ready again. Replacing the shower head, Cole ran his hands over her wet skin, taking in the feeling of the warm silk of her body.

He moved his lips over her neck again, then rained slow, sweet kisses down each arm, stopping at her wrists to kiss away the bruises. Kneeling down again in front of her with his hands on her lower back, he slid them around then in between her legs as he looked up with a little smirk. "How am I doing so far?"

Claire's answer of "Good," was almost inaudible as he planted a delicate kiss on her sex. He parted her legs with his fingers as he leaned in to lick her slowly. Carefully sucking on the edges of her hot, ripe core, he entered her with his tongue, this time with small, flicking motions.

"Ahh . . ." She let out a soft cry that seemed to come from deep inside her chest. Thrusting his tongue in further, he pressed his palm to her sex, spreading her lips open with his fingers to allow him more access. Claire grabbed his hair in both hands and pulled his head back and forth as he worked his magic on her.

He stopped long enough to say, "God, you taste good," in a deep growl and then pushed his tongue back inside her. Claire rocked her body over his mouth as she let go with a long shudder that curled her toes. "YES! Oh yes!" she cried as she came on his warm mouth, tightly weaving her fingers through his hair.

He waited until her body released all of its tension on him before standing and caressing her all the way up with his hands. The water rushed over them as they kissed with wild abandon. Claire put her hands on his chest and pushed him down firmly onto the bench in the corner. He kissed her breasts and sucked on her nipples hungrily as she lifted one leg at a time and straddled him. She reached her face down to meet his, and their tongues twisted together in perfect unison. With one hand wrapped behind his back, she pulled him closer to her, pushing her breasts against him. He could feel her erect nipples against his chest. Claire reached down with her other hand and stroked his rock-hard length. Positioning her body until they were perfectly aligned, she moved in slow circles over him, teasing him until Cole groaned with desire. He wanted to thrust deep inside her, but she was holding her body too high for him to reach.

Her eyes locked onto his as she continued her exquisite torture until he couldn't hold back any longer. He grabbed her hips and pulled her down onto him forcefully, rocking her back and forth as he did. She gasped as the full length of him was buried in her. It was almost too much for her, and yet she couldn't get enough. She lowered her body as she spread her knees along the wet bench and then lifted up, squeezing him as hard as she could. Cole's head snapped back and he bit her lip gently, then thrust his tongue into her mouth, mirroring the moves he was making deep inside her core. Their breathing became heavy as he pulled her back and forth and then in long, slow circles over him.

His eyes met hers with a look of pure and all-consuming desire. "Oh God, Claire, I'm going to come."

"Yes, Cole. Give it to me!"

His breath became ragged as his body jolted with the waves of his orgasm. Claire reached around behind herself and pressed his balls against her firm ass as they both came. Cole erupted with a force he had never felt before. He came in long waves as she squeezed his length with her tight warmth. Moaning, Cole realized this pleasure was one he had never experienced with another woman. As Claire nuzzled her face into his neck and he caressed her curves with both hands, he didn't want her to ever get off his lap.

"How was that?" he asked, feigning concern.

Claire laughed. "Hmm, you can do better."

"What?" he said incredulously. "You seemed to be satisfied more than once already, if I recall."

"Satisfied and impressed are two entirely different things, Cowboy."

"You might be a little high maintenance in the sex department."

"Every woman is. They just don't admit it." Claire gave him a sassy grin. Lifting herself off his lap, she stood to wash her hair.

Cole sat, recovering. He gazed at her as she shampooed, her breasts lifting with her arms. "I could watch you do that all day."

She smiled down at him and then took the soap over to him and began running it over his body, as he had done for her. In one night, she had experienced more intimacy with Cole than she had ever known with any man, including Antonio. Sex with him had been rather dull in comparison. He liked missionary or spooning in bed with the lights out. More often than not, he would try to push her head under the covers for a blow job, although he was never one to reciprocate. He certainly wasn't what Claire would call a generous lover. The more time she spent with Cole, the more grateful she was that Stacey had come along, getting her out of that mundane existence and into a world of ecstasy. This one night alone was worth the humiliation she had suffered weeks earlier. She felt drunk with bliss as Cole shut off the water and they stepped out of the shower.

He grabbed two large towels off a shelf and wrapped one around his waist. He fanned out the other one and wrapped Claire in it before rubbing his hands over it to warm her and dry her off. Pressing the towel into her long hair, he kissed her on the nose, then on the forehead. "You hungry?" he asked.

"I could eat. We worked those burgers off a long time ago," Claire answered as she dried off her legs.

Cole handed her his bathrobe and quickly patted himself off before throwing on a pair of grey pyjama pants that hung low at his waist. "Come on, let's grab something to eat."

"Sure," Claire answered. "I'm just going to comb out my hair, and I'll meet you down there."

Claire evaluated herself in the mirror as she combed her hair. For the first time in years—maybe ever—she loved what she saw.

* * *

As she descended the staircase, Claire was completely at ease. Cole looked up at her in his bathrobe; it almost dragged on the ground, she was so small. "How about some strawberries and beer?"

"Mmm, sounds great. Although, I feel as though I'm drunk right now," Claire replied as Cole opened a bottle of beer and handed it to her.

He opened his and they clinked their bottles together. "To appliance shopping," he stated with a sexy grin. "Who knew it could get a woman so hot?"

Claire laughed. "I thought that was common knowledge. You men need to pay more attention."

Cole picked up a strawberry and popped it into her mouth before taking one for himself. "Stay with me tonight."

Claire looked deep into his hazel eyes, knowing there was nowhere on earth she would rather be. "Alright."

He gave her a lingering kiss and then carried the bowl of strawberries and his beer over to the dining table. He turned on the stereo, allowing John Mayer's voice to ring out as they settled themselves at the table to share their snack. Claire could hardly believe that this incredible man was sitting across from her, bare chested, feeding her strawberries. It felt like she was living someone else's life.

When the bowl was empty, Cole stood, taking her hand and pulling her to her feet. He closed the small distance between them. As Christina Aguilera and Blake Shelton sang about being fools, Cole started swaying with the music, looking at Claire with such tenderness it melted her heart. He pressed his lips to her forehead and laid his cheek on her hair; he wrapped both arms around her waist to hold her. Claire hugged him tightly, swaying to the beat along with him.

When the song faded out, Cole put one arm under Claire's knees and lifted her up. He carried her up to his bed. After weeks of yearning for her, he finally felt satisfied, but he knew this one night wouldn't be enough for him. He was filled with a need he had never felt before, as if his very breath depended on her being with him. He laid her down on the bed and took off his pyjama pants, revealing his already hard cock. The sight of her on his bed in his bathrobe, with her hair falling over his pillow, stirred a deep sense of possessiveness that was entirely new to him.

He lifted himself onto her body and nuzzled into her neck, kissing her lightly and sucking gently on her ear. Claire moaned in anticipation, shocked to find that she could become wet again at his slightest touch. The weight of him was perfection. He leaned on one elbow and used his other hand to open the sash of the bathrobe, moving it aside. He pressed his skin onto her body and lowered his mouth to hers. Her lips were slightly swollen from what they had done before, making them appear plump and unbelievably sexy. He wanted to feel those lips all over his body. Almost as if she understood his thoughts, Claire started to kiss Cole's neck and chest. She pushed him onto his back and moved her way down his body, kissing him until she reached his midsection. She licked up the length of his cock in slow, firm strokes before placing her full lips over his head. He let out a low groan as she plunged her mouth over him. The sound was enough to excite Claire as she lifted her mouth up and back down, over and over. She moved her hand to work his thick length, and her mouth down to his balls, licking and sucking on them with increasing intensity. Cole reached down to pull her up and rolled on top of her again, kissing her hard on the mouth. Their tongues found each other as he started grinding his hips into her, parting her legs and pushing himself against her sex. She opened her legs into wide splits as he entered her, slowly moving his hips in circles as he brought himself carefully all the way inside her. She wrapped her legs around his mid-back and locked her feet together.

"Hmm, bendy," he said, thoroughly impressed.

"That's nothing," she said with a coy smile.

"It's a good thing we're already fucking, because that is the kind of information that would make me hard as a rock."

Claire laughed out loud before tilting her hips up, bringing Cole in deeper. He grabbed onto the wrought-iron headboard with one hand and used the strength of his arm to pull himself forward in a slow, hard motion. His other hand held her arm above her head, their fingers interlaced. She squeezed him with her entire core as he pulled forward into her. Thrusting himself inside her with long, hard movements, the intensity built for both of them as he moved faster and faster. Cole looked into Claire's navy eyes as he moved over her, until, overcome, her entire body tensed.

"Oh yes, Cole, fuck me! Fuck me so hard!" she cried out.

Those words brought on an orgasm so powerful it caused Cole to see stars. He plunged his tongue into Claire's mouth as he came, every muscle in his body flexing with the force of it. She could feel him pulse inside her in the most perfect spot, causing her own orgasm to erupt wildly and for what seemed like minutes.

They were both left glistening with sweat as they tried to recover their breath. Cole lifted himself off Claire and lay down on his side, the length of his body touching hers, with one arm holding her around her waist.

"That was . . . just . . . wow."

He reached down and tugged the covers up to tuck them in. Claire gave him a sleepy smile. "I would tell you that you can do better, but I frankly don't have the energy left to experience round four."

Cole kissed her neck softly. "Rest up. What I have planned for tomorrow will make tonight seem boring."

"Really? Are we going shopping for a new

dishwasher?" She planted a firm kiss on his lips and then turned away from him onto her side, snuggling into him with the back of her naked body.

He wrapped his arm around her top arm and held onto her hand, lacing his fingers through hers. Claire fell asleep immediately with a sense of peaceful bliss she had never felt before. Cole lay awake for a while, feeling slightly panicked at how strong his feelings were for someone he hardly knew.

SIX

The next few days were heavenly. Claire and Cole decided not to tell anyone about their new-found relationship; they attempted to act professionally while managing to steal a few moments together to drive each other crazy. After the supper cleanup each evening, Claire would sneak over to Cole's cabin, and they would make love until late into the night. Claire felt like she was in a constant haze brought on by a combination of exhaustion and lust. When Cole wasn't around, she had a reminder of him in her somewhat sore muscles and her slightly raw sex. She was completely caught up in him, thinking only of the next time she could touch him, kiss him, feel him inside her. She had no desire to sleep, and she barely thought about eating, even though she was around food all day.

Cole's feeling of panic on their first night together had subsided. He could see how well they worked together and loved hearing Claire's ideas for the restaurant. Everything about her seemed to scream out that she would stay, which was all he really wanted. Sex with her was the most intense and amazing experience of his life. She was always ready for him, sometimes waking him up in the middle of the night to make love. He had never been so tired or so happy before.

One day while Alicia and Claire were cleaning up after breakfast, Alicia asked, "So, how are things with Cole?"

"Oh, great," Claire said, avoiding eye contact with her new friend. "He's a great boss. Really open to new ideas and very positive all the time."

"No, I meant how's the sex," Alicia replied with a wry smile.

Claire's face flushed to a bright pink hue. "Oh God, is it that obvious?"

"Let me put it this way, honey. Ben figured it out, and he doesn't notice anything."

Claire covered her mouth with her hand and laughed with embarrassment. "Okay, I don't want to kiss and tell, but let's just say I can hardly walk some mornings when I wake up, and I don't even care."

"Wow, really? Sounds like he takes after his big brother."

The two friends giggled naughtily just as Cole walked into the kitchen.

He picked a grape from the fruit tray and

popped it into his mouth as he looked from one woman to the other. "What's so funny?"

Claire gave him a sheepish look. "Apparently you and I aren't fooling anyone."

Cole closed his eyes for a moment, waiting to cringe at the thought of being found out. She was the new chef, and he definitely shouldn't be involved with her romantically. Opening his eyes, he walked over to Claire and said, "Fuck it. I'm glad if people know you're mine."

He put his arm around her back and kissed her hard on the mouth, bending her body back into a dip. When he let go, he gave her a slap on the ass and walked out the back door. Claire's face was flushed again—this time with excitement

Later that morning, Claire snuck into Cole's office while he was on the phone. She quietly shut the door and locked it, then crossed the room to stand in front of his desk. Giving him a naughty grin, she started swaying her hips from side to side as if moving to a sexy beat. Then she lifted her pink sweater over her head, revealing a lacy light-blue tank top underneath. Her blue bra was clearly visible through the shirt. She tossed the sweater to Cole and watched as his jaw dropped and he had to adjust himself on his seat.

Claire kept swaying and licked her lips slowly as she pulled her tank over her head and tossed it at him next. He caught it with one hand and a big grin.

His expression changed suddenly as he became aware of the person on the other end of the phone. "Sorry, can you repeat that? Someone came into my office and distracted me for a minute. Uh-huh . . . okay . . . okay, can I get back to you on Monday? I'll just have to check on that."

Claire turned her back to him and ran her hands up and down her sides and danced in a little circle. She unbuttoned the top button on her jeans and wriggled them down her hips a little, revealing a lacy blue thong.

"Okay . . . right . . . right. Yeah . . . no, I meant no, of course not. Okay. Talk to you Monday." Cole hung up the phone and exhaled with a moan. "You are trouble, you know that?"

Claire bent forward, pressing her head down to her knees with her legs perfectly straight. He watched as loose curls of her long hair touched the floor. She arched her back and lifted herself to stand up.

"Yoga," she said simply as she stopped dancing. She leaned over onto Cole's desk and snatched her tank top back. With a nonchalant look, she slipped it back on as if to say, "That's all you get. No big deal."

She grabbed her sweater and slid it over her head, then buttoned her jeans. Cole groaned. "Oh, come on!" he said in exasperation.

"I need to get lunch prepared," she said with a

shrug. And with that, she blew him a kiss, turned and walked out the door, leaving him with an erection and very little clue as to what he had agreed to on the phone.

Claire laughed as she exited the lodge, thinking of the expression on his face. She had never felt this sexy before. She felt wild and powerful around Cole, like she could do anything.

* * *

That afternoon the next group of guests arrived. They were to stay one night at the lodge and then camp for two nights, followed by one more night back at the ranch. Claire was clearing tables on the restaurant patio, which gave her an excellent vantage point to see the guests exiting the airport shuttle. A feeling of dread passed over her as she watched them. It was a group of tall, thin women in their early twenties, each one hotter than the last.

"Shit," she muttered. It was her worst nightmare. The thought of Cole watching over them as they rode and camped made her feel nauseous. She was suddenly deflated. In an instant, there was no trace of that sexy woman who had done a striptease in Cole's office that morning.

Trey, Dustin and the other guys seemed to appear out of nowhere to welcome the girls, looking like kids on Christmas morning. Alicia, who had seen Claire standing motionless, came out onto the patio and stood beside her.

"It's a group of volleyball players from Colorado State. They were the national champs last year, and they're here for a celebratory trip. Yuck, right?"

Claire never took her eyes off them. "Yeah, this is going to be a challenge for me. My ex tossed me aside for a tall, twenty-two-year-old stick bug without bothering to mention to me that we were over."

Alicia put her arm around Claire's shoulder and gave her a gentle squeeze. "Well, Cole is hot, and they may try to get his attention, but it won't work. I've known him all my life, and I have never seen him come close to cheating. I've also never seen him this crazy about anyone before." Alicia paused. "Still sucks balls, though, doesn't it?"

"Yeah." Claire sighed as she rested her head against Alicia's shoulder for a second. "I have a bad feeling that I'm not going to handle this gracefully."

"Just keep reminding yourself that he's one of the good ones, and if he did mess around—which he won't—he wouldn't be worth your tears anyway."

Claire nodded as she saw Cole exit the lodge to greet the girls. "I'll try." She took a deep breath and turned back to Alicia. "Let's cook."

* * *

When supper rolled around, the guests and ranch hands all piled into the restaurant and onto the patio. There was an excited energy making the place feel more like a nightclub than a ranch cookhouse. The dozen volleyball girls were done up in casual, sexy clothes, some in their own spin on western wear. They had spent the last couple of hours with the guys, testing their horse-riding skills.

Before dinner, Claire had rushed back to her cabin to freshen up her makeup and change into a sexy black top in a clingy fabric with a low V-neck. She winced at her reflection in the mirror and tried to convince herself that she looked every bit as good as those girls out there. It was a stretch, though. At five four and thirty-one years old, she knew they were in a whole different league.

Cole arrived a few minutes later than the rest of the group, along with a tall blond girl, Brittany. From the kitchen window, Claire observed their entrance. Brittany, it seemed, was a novice rider and needed some "extra attention." She was gushing over Cole, who was smiling and trying to reassure her that she would be just fine tomorrow.

One of the other girls, who was sitting next to Trey, called out to her, "Brittany! You and Cole should come sit with us!"

Brittany waved back. "Okay!" She reached for Cole's arm in a far too familiar way. "Come on!"

He excused himself to head back to the kitchen

and told her he hoped she enjoyed her dinner. Brittany gave a pouty look, walking over to her friend and dropping onto the chair.

Cole stepped into the kitchen, happy to find Claire on her own. "There's my bendy girl," he said, giving her a peck on the cheek. "I've been missing you since your little dance earlier—I can't wait to see the rest of it."

Claire gave him a brief, fake smile and turned back to the oven to take some chicken out. "Oh, hey," she said with very little enthusiasm. She was suddenly humiliated by her brazen attempt to seduce him in light of the new arrivals.

"What's wrong, Claire?" Cole asked, his tone full of concern.

Claire didn't look up. "I'm just having a crappy afternoon, that's all," she said in a tight voice.

Cole walked up behind her and put his big hands on her shoulders to massage her. "How can I help make it better?"

Her body stiffened in response to his touch.

"Okay, what's going on, seriously?" he asked as his hands dropped to his sides.

"Can we talk about this later? I am really busy right now trying to feed a bunch of starving volley-ball goddesses."

"Oh. So that's what this is about," he said with a hint of amusement. "You're jealous?"

"I'm not sure what's so funny about that to

you. You're about to leave with those girls for two nights, and it's pretty obvious that at least one of them would like to ride something other than a horse during her trip." Claire's words cut through the air like a knife.

"Hey, relax, okay? It doesn't really matter what they want. It matters what we want. And I want you. Going away for two nights won't change that."

"Well, I hope you'll still feel that way when you're out in a tent surrounded by a bunch of horny college girls who look like supermodels!" Claire retorted, her voice rising.

"Shh! Calm down." Cole spoke in a low tone and made a downward motion with his hands while giving her an urgent look that told her to be quiet.

Being shushed was not high on Claire's list of likes. Seeing red, she pointed her finger at him and yelled, "Calm down? Calm *down*? You calm down!"

Cole walked to the back door. "You're right; we should talk about this later," he said as he let the door slam shut behind him.

Claire reached into the oven for a pan, forgetting her oven mitt and burning her fingers. She dropped the pan, spilling the chicken onto the floor with a loud crash.

"Fuck!" she cried.

Just then, Alicia rushed back into the kitchen. "Oh, Claire, you okay?" she asked. "Here, run your hand under some water. I'll get this cleaned up."

Claire's eyes filled with tears. "I knew I wasn't going to be graceful about this. Shit." She paused for a moment. "Could everyone hear me out there?"

Alicia winced. "Well, maybe not everyone. I don't think Bill had his hearing aid in."

"Ugh, I have fucked this up fast, haven't I?" Claire said, now moving into the ugly cry.

"Well, it's not anything you can't come back from, I'm sure. Cole will understand once he knows what happened with your last relationship. For now, let's figure out what to feed these people."

Claire nodded with resolve and blew her nose into a tissue. "Okay, you're right. There's salmon in the fridge. I can spice it and throw it on the barbecue fast. In the meantime, maybe see if anyone would like a bowl of wild mushroom soup while they're waiting."

"I'm on it!" Alicia said, moving quickly.

* * *

After the dinner service was over and the guests had left the restaurant, Claire turned to Alicia. "You go home and spend time with Ben. I'll clean up."

"You sure? I was thinking you might want to go talk to Cole."

"I will. I just need to figure out what I'm going to say first, so I could use some time to think," Claire replied.

"Okay. You hang in there. I'll see you in the morning."

"You bet. And Alicia?" Claire turned from the sink to look at her. "Thank you so much—for everything. I don't know what I would do without you here."

* * *

After finishing the dishes, Claire turned out the lights and locked up for the night. She looked warily in the direction of Cole's cabin. It was completely dark. Sighing heavily, she headed in the direction of the stables instead, hoping to catch him getting ready for the trip the next day. When she got there, she found him alone, brushing Dudley, his back turned to her. She watched him for a long moment. He seemed so calm in comparison to the bundle of nerves that she was.

She finally got up enough courage to speak. "Hi," she said quietly.

Cole stood frozen for a minute and then continued to brush Dudley without turning around. "What's up?" he replied impassively.

"I'm sorry, Cole. I was being completely unfair and irrational earlier," she croaked as her voice broke. "I embarrassed both of us, and I would give anything to take it all back."

Cole turned to her and tossed the brush down

onto a table nearby, then leaned against the gate of the nearest stall and folded his arms. The sight of him closing off from her like this made her ache with longing.

Cole's eyes were cold. "Yeah, you really lost it tonight—in front of the staff and guests, no less. It would be one thing to have a big freak-out when we're alone, but to do it in the restaurant? The reputation of this ranch needs to come first, Claire. When we're working, we are *at work*, regardless of what you and I've got going on. We need to act like professionals. I just can't believe that I have to tell you that. And, honestly, I can't for the life of me figure out what the hell happened there."

Claire leaned her body against the door, tearing up. "Everything you're saying is true, and I know I really screwed up. And I'm just so sorry, Cole. I am. I have never done anything like this at work before in my life. I totally lost it today. Those girls are my worst nightmare. Antonio, my ex, was cheating on me with a very young, tall, skinny girl from my restaurant. It had been going on for months before I found out. Turned out everyone else there knew but me." She sighed. "That is why I left Seattle. He made a fool out of me, and now I've been a fool again, by lashing out at you in front of everyone. It's no excuse, though. I know I'm responsible for what comes out of my mouth. It's just an explanation, I guess," she said, shaking her head. "I felt so threatened when I saw them get off the shuttle this afternoon. It's just that you're so hot, you could have any woman on earth, and I don't measure up to any of those girls. They all have legs that go on for miles, and they are so athletic. They probably look so graceful riding, and I doubt any of them will fall into the river. And then when I saw you walk into the restaurant with that girl, I thought, 'Well, she looks more like who he should be with.' I'm not fit like them and—"

Cole interrupted. "Stop it. That's enough."

Claire gasped at the harsh sound in his voice. Her heart jumped to her throat. She had messed up this relationship before it could get started.

Cole looked her dead in the eyes. "I'm not going to stand here and listen to this."

Claire's stomach twisted into knots as she turned to hurry out. "I understand," she whispered.

Cole caught her by the elbow and spun her around. "I'm not going to listen to anyone talk shit about you, not even if the words are coming out of your own mouth. I can stand up for you against any-one—and I intend to—but I can't protect you from yourself. If you want to tear yourself apart, I can't stop you. You can see where that's gotten you, so you are going to have to figure out a way to trust that I am right when I tell you that you are beautiful, smart, fun and sexy as hell. You are also going to have to find a way to learn to trust *me*, or this will never work. I'm not your ex. I have never cheated on anyone, and I would never do that to you. You are the only woman I want to be with, but if you push me away, I will go."

Claire stood in front of him, tears streaming down her face. "Okay." She nodded. "I'm a bit screwed up right now, but I'm not broken beyond repair. Do you think you can be patient with me while I work this out?"

Cole reached out, taking her hands in his. "That depends, Claire." He paused for a moment and looked at her with a little gleam in his eyes. "Are you going to finish your striptease for me or not? I couldn't get it off my mind all afternoon."

Claire gave a little laugh through her tears. "You've got yourself a deal, Cowboy. Can I give you a rain check on it, though? I'm still feeling really embarrassed, which would come through, making the whole thing awkward rather than sexy."

Cole nodded his head. "Good point. What if we just go back to my place to grab something to eat? I'm starving."

"Sounds perfect. I forgot you didn't have supper. I actually didn't eat either. There's leftover salmon in the fridge at the restaurant. Do you want to stop in and pick it up?"

"Mmm, yes." Cole took her hand and the two walked over to the restaurant.

* * *

Claire unlocked the door to the kitchen and flipped on the light. "Okay, let's get some food into you." She reheated the salmon and some rice and put together a salad. Cole opened a bottle of white wine from the cooler and poured two glasses. He took them into the seating area and lit some candles to brighten the nearly black room before connecting his phone to the stereo and selecting a Coldplay album for background music.

When Claire walked through with their plates, she stopped and smiled at him. How could he be so romantic after she had been such a shit earlier?

They ate quietly, both needing nourishment after such an emotionally draining evening. Cole spoke up first. "This might be the best salmon I've ever eaten. Even if you weren't the sexiest woman on the planet, I would want you for the food alone."

Claire smiled at his compliment. "Well, thank you, sir. I'd keep you around just to watch you eat."

When the meal was over, Claire got up to clear the table. Cole stood and took her hand.

"Come here," he said, taking her in his arms. He danced with her slowly to "Fix You," holding his head low so his cheek was touching her temple.

"I'm sorry," she whispered, tearing up again at his tenderness.

"It's over. Let's move on. It was a learning

{116}

experience for both of us. It will be a long time before I try to shush you again," Cole said, looking down at her with wide, teasing eyes.

A loud laugh escaped Claire's mouth. "You learn fast."

Feeling a wave of relief, Claire reached up on her tiptoes and planted a solid kiss on his lips. Cole returned her embrace, at first tentatively, opening his mouth slightly over her bottom lip. She opened her mouth, and he accepted the invitation to let his tongue slide in between her lips, tilting his head to the side.

Claire's hands moved down to Cole's muscular bottom. She cupped his ass with her hands, feeling it flex at her touch. Cole mirrored her actions with his own hands and then slowly slid one hand up and into her shirt. The touch of his fingers against her skin sent a ripple of arousal through her, and she became hungry to have him inside her.

Cole moved both hands to the bottom of Claire's shirt and pulled it up over her head. He undid her jeans, pulling them down roughly to her ankles. He kissed her chest over her bra then moved slowly to her mouth again.

"Hmm, I believe I've seen this bra and these panties somewhere before. From what I recall, they made quite an impression on me." He kissed her full on the mouth while using one foot to hold her jeans down so she could step out of them, her shoes coming off with her pants.

He took her hand and moved it down over the front of his jeans. "Oh yes, same reaction as before."

"Why, Mr. Mitchell, are we going to have make-up sex?" Claire was breathless as Cole ran his hands over her bra.

"Yes, and I believe we are about to violate all kinds of health codes as well," Cole answered, giving her that sexy half grin again.

Claire pulled his T-shirt over his head and tossed it aside, then grabbed him by the waistband of his jeans and pulled him toward her, kissing him again, their tongues colliding as she struggled to undo his buckle. Cole helped her with his belt and pulled his button fly open in one quick motion. He hooked his thumbs into her panties and pushed them down to her feet. Claire yanked his jeans and boxer briefs down to his knees in a frenzy of movement.

Cole sat down on the chair behind him. "I should take my boots off," he said.

Claire climbed on top of him with her knees resting on the sides of the chair. "I'm not interested in your feet," she said, pressing her lips to his earlobe and sucking gently.

Cole closed his eyes for a moment and moaned. He reached behind her and unhooked her bra, then slid his fingers over her shoulders to slide it off, gazing at her breasts. He took her breasts in his hands, leaving her nipples exposed so he could suck each one slowly until they were both rigid. He pulled her closer to him so their chests were melded together, skin on skin. He breathed in her seductive perfume, caressing her back and her hips with his fingers.

"Mmm, my sexy Claire is back," he murmured, sending a thrill through her entire body with his words.

Claire climbed off the chair, putting her feet on the floor one at a time, keeping her lips on his. Cole groaned as she pulled away, but when she dropped to her knees in front of him, his enthusiasm came back full force.

Claire looked up at him seductively as she settled her body between his knees, her breasts pressed against the inside of his thighs. She took him in both hands and slowly lowered her mouth over his length. Cole let out a moan, thrilled at the sight of her mouth over his cock, her delicate hands stroking him as she sucked. Moving her head up and down in a slow rhythm, she moved one hand in unison with her mouth and used her other hand to massage his inner thighs.

She lifted her mouth off his shaft and licked him from the base to the tip in long, slow movements. She then pressed her hands to the sides of her breasts and lifted them around his cock, enclosing his thick length in the silk of her skin. She arched her back to rub her full breasts up and down his smooth, wet skin, her peaked nipples rubbing against his lower abs as she moved. The sight and the feeling of it was too exquisite for Cole; he needed to stop her before he came.

"Wait, wait, wait. Come here." He took her hand and pulled her up to him. "I want to be inside you."

He drew her close to him, kissing her breasts and sucking on her nipples again. With one hand he rubbed her sex, now wet and plump with desire. She turned her back to him and lowered herself onto his lap, using her hand to guide him inside her. His lips caressed her back and neck as she lifted herself up and down and swirled her hips in slow circles, filling herself completely with him. Just a couple of hours ago, she had thought she would never have him inside her again, and the incredible relief that she could touch him now made the moment all the more erotic.

Cole reached in front of Claire with his hands, using one to explore her breasts while the other pressed firmly against her sex, tightening her around his length. Claire gasped with pleasure. "Oh, Cole, yes, just like that," she said breathlessly.

Cole took his hand off her breasts and reached up for her chin, turning her to face him. Their mouths met as they kissed urgently. Claire reached around and grabbed the back of Cole's hair with her right hand. She took his left hand in hers and held it to her breasts, pushing it firmly against her skin as she moved faster over him.

The moment overtook them both and they

came in unison, with Claire crying out, "Yes, Cole! Oh yes!"

Their bodies shuddered as waves of ecstasy swept through them. Claire could feel him coming inside her and squeezed him tight with each new burst. When it was over, Cole wrapped her naked body in his strong arms and held her against his chest for a long time, kissing her neck and cheek.

"I don't want anyone else, Claire. Only you."

Claire nodded. "Me too." She sat against him for a long while, basking in the tenderness of his embrace, before slowly leaning forward to lift off him.

As they got dressed, Claire said, "You know, back home there was a country bar that claimed to be 'the most fun you can have with your boots on.' I think we just proved them wrong."

Cole laughed. "Sexy and funny—double-threat girl." He pulled her toward him and kissed her again.

SEVEN

The next morning, Cole got up early as usual and made a pot of coffee. He took a quick shower while the coffee brewed and then wrapped a towel around his waist and took a mug upstairs to Claire.

"Good morning, sexy girl," he said, planting a kiss on her cheek.

Claire, who was sleeping on her tummy, turned over to face him. "Mmm, that's my second favourite look on you. Maybe just throw your hat on so I can decide for sure." She sat up and took a sip of her coffee. "Oh, on second thought, let's try hat, belt and boots, lose the towel."

"You are objectifying me in a way that is making me feel really uncomfortable." He gave her a mock serious look.

Claire laughed out loud. "You do realize I'm only with you for your body, right? So, if this is going to work out, you're just going to have to get used to being objectified." She got out of bed and walked casually across the room wearing Cole's T-shirt as a nightie.

Cole watched her walk over, pick up her jeans and slip them on. "You know what I could get used to? Seeing you in nothing but my T-shirt. On second thought, lose the shirt."

Claire laughed. "Like this?" She turned away from him, lifting it over her head, revealing her naked back. Cole watched her as she put her bra on and slipped her own shirt over her head. Claire walked over to the bathroom to brush her teeth and put her hair up in a ponytail. Cole threw on his jeans and a white T-shirt and followed her into the bathroom. He squirted toothpaste onto his toothbrush.

"What time are you heading out today?" Claire asked.

"After lunch. We're doing a three-hour ride today. The girls wanted to stay here and hang out at the pool for the morning instead of doing the hike once we get to the first campsite," Cole said.

"Alright. I should run back to my place to shower and get dressed. It's going to be a busy morning." Claire gave Cole a long kiss and smacked him on the ass. "See you later, Cowboy."

She took a few steps, then turned back to him. "Oh, Cole . . . I think I'm going to hide out in the kitchen and see if Alicia minds serving the guests today. I don't want to make anyone uncomfortable, including myself."

"Sounds fair. I'm really going to miss you, you know." Cole gave her a serious look.

"Me too."

Claire walked back to her cabin, feeling completely happy. She took a quick shower and put her hair up in a loose bun at the back of her head, with some hair spiking out to give it a funky look. She put on her makeup, and threw on a flirty A-line minidress in white with a delicate floral pattern, a skinny brown belt and mid-calf, slouchy, dark-red cowboy boots. As she looked at herself in the mirror, her courage was bolstered. "There. That ought to leave him with a good impression," she said to her reflection.

As Claire hurried down the path to the restaurant, she saw Brittany and her friend jogging down the path in short shorts and sports bras. Both were tanned, with not even the slightest hint of cellulite.

"Shit," she sighed, feeling as though they had trampled her confidence with their size-nine running shoes.

The morning was a blur, with Claire and Alicia serving breakfast and making lunch as well as preparing all the food for the three-day trip. The two worked at a furious pace, double- and triple-checking their lists as they went.

Cole popped in to eat a few minutes before noon. He gave Claire a long look up and down when he saw her. "I haven't eaten all day, but seeing you in that little outfit makes me want to forgo lunch and take you back to my place."

Claire glanced at him with a nonchalant expression. "Oh, this old thing? I only wear it when I don't care how I look." She had gotten that line from the movie *It's a Wonderful Life*, but he didn't need to know that.

Cole ate in the kitchen so he could spend some time with Claire before getting back to the stables to finish loading everything up.

"What can I take down with me now?" he asked.

"Oh, if you can grab the big cooler, I'll bring the others over to the stables with Ben and Alicia once lunch is served."

"Sounds good, gorgeous," he said, giving her a quick peck on the cheek.

* * *

When the guests finished eating, they went back to their rooms to get packed up for the trail ride. Claire, who had been hiding out in the kitchen, took that opportunity to write a quick note to Cole.

> *Hey, Cowboy. I'll see you in three days for a replay of last night. I think there are some health codes we haven't violated yet.*
>
> *XOXO, Bendy Girl*

She tucked into it her bra and grabbed a cooler to carry over to the stables.

When she got there the building was empty. *Perfect*, she thought. She found Cole's overnight bag on the back of the supply wagon and unzipped it to slip the note in. Sitting neatly on top of his clothes was an economy-sized box of condoms.

Claire's heart refused to believe her eyes. He must have something else in there. She opened the box to make sure. Indeed, there were several packages of condoms in the box. Claire ripped up the note and tossed it into the trash can on her way back to the restaurant, her eyes filled with tears. She managed to pull herself together when she got to the kitchen, dabbing her eyes with her fingertips as she walked in. Alicia was loading Ben's arms with the other coolers and picking up a couple of smaller bags.

"We're already packed up, Claire," Alicia said as the pair exited the kitchen.

"Great. Thanks, you two. I'll get started on the lunch cleanup." As soon as Ben and Alicia were gone, Claire wrote another note, this time for Alicia.

I ran back to my cabin for a bit. I have to make a phone call that can't wait. Please leave the cleanup for me, and I'll come back as soon as I can. You and Ben go relax for the rest of the day. Thanks for everything! Claire

Claire walked quickly back to her cabin, hoping not to run into anyone. A brief wave of relief washed over her as she shut the door, having made it back without being noticed. As she locked the door behind her, she burst into angry tears.

Twenty minutes later, Cole was knocking on her door. "Claire?" he called out.

When she didn't answer, she heard him move away from the door and head up the path. Her phone soon buzzed with a text.

> I can't find you. Wanted to say goodbye. I hope everything's okay. See you in two days.

* * *

Inside her cabin, Claire was on the phone with her sister, Janet, filling her in on her discovery.

"Well, better to find out now, when you're only a few weeks into the whole thing, than wasting years on him," Janet said.

"It's just so strange. He really didn't seem like the type. I honestly thought he was falling in love with me. If you had seen his face and heard all the things he said to me, it's so hard to believe it was all lies."

"I can't see any logical reason he would have condoms in his bag, other than he plans to have sex while he's away. I know how hard this must

{127}

be, coming fresh out of your relationship with Fuckwit, honey, but it seems like you found another asshole." Janet paused, hearing Claire sob at the other end of the line.

"I'm such a fucking idiot to fall for these men. What is wrong with me? Seriously?" Claire sobbed.

"Nothing's wrong with you, except maybe you're a bum magnet. Just come here and stay for a while. Now that you have two men to get over, you definitely need your big sister. I can hardly feed you ice cream and hug you while you're all the way over there. When you're ready, I'll hand-pick a decent guy for you."

Claire sobbed into her hand for a moment, considering her sister's offer. She quickly made up her mind. "I can't leave until they find a replacement for me. Alicia is really struggling with morning sickness right now. She can't go more than a few hours without puking. I couldn't do that to her after she's been so wonderful to me. I'll tell them to look for someone else and then stay clear of Cole until they either hire another chef or Alicia's feeling better. Then I'll come stay with you."

"You sure you can handle it? I really think you should worry about your own needs rather than someone else's right now."

"I'll be okay. He's away now and then next week there's another group coming in, so I'll only have to avoid him for a few days until he's gone again. I can hide out in my cabin in the evenings or go into town."

* * *

The next day, Claire woke up early with her eyes puffy from crying. She went for a long run along the lake without even noticing the sun lighting up the mountains as it rose. Her mind raced along with her body, wondering if Cole had slept with one of those girls last night or if he would tonight.

She showered and threw on a navy T-shirt, old jeans and some flip-flops. She walked down to the restaurant and started getting breakfast ready for the staff who'd be at the ranch that day.

Alicia came in a few minutes after her. The moment she saw her, she stopped. "What's wrong, Claire?"

Claire had decided not to tell Alicia about the condoms. She didn't see how it would help anything to sully Cole's reputation with his sister-in-law, and she wasn't ready to admit to anyone else that she had been such a fool twice in a row.

"Oh, my eyes? It's just allergies today. I might have to run into town to pick up some antihistamines later. How are *you* feeling this morning?" Claire kept cutting up fruit so she wouldn't have to look Alicia in the eye.

"Well, better this morning. I think it's because

I had such a good rest yesterday afternoon and evening. Thanks so much for that, by the way." Alicia got a bowl out of the cupboard and started cracking eggs into it.

"I was thinking maybe you should take a rest every afternoon for a while until you're feeling better. It's no problem, really. I could handle lunch cleanup and dinner prep."

"Thanks, Claire, you're a good friend. I'm so glad you're here. Ben and I were just talking last night about how much less worried we feel about the baby coming with you around to handle the restaurant. Before you got here, we weren't sure what we were going to do." Alicia beamed at Claire.

"Oh, Alicia, I'm glad I can be here for you." Claire gave her a quick smile and then looked away, feeling guilty that she wasn't going to be there much longer. She needed to change the subject. "Say, I need to get a haircut. Do you think I could get in to see your stylist within the next couple of days? I thought I'd try to go while we don't have any guests."

"Sure, my stylist is pretty good about squeezing me in. I can give you her number. She's great."

EIGHT

The next morning, Claire drove into the city to Sky Salon and Spa for a cut, colour, manicure and pedicure. Alicia's stylist, Sammi, had agreed to come in at 9 a.m. so she could have Claire back to work in time for lunch. Claire had spent the night moping again and decided she had wasted enough time letting cheating bastards get her down. Now her goal was to look as good as possible and make Cole sorry he had ever met her. He would be able to look but not touch, and she intended to make the sight of her hurt.

Sammi was a genius. She changed Claire's hair from a typical all-one-length cut to one with sexy layers that flowed beautifully and bounced up into flirty beach waves with the slightest help from a diffuser and some spray. She coloured Claire's hair a rich shade of chocolate brown that brought out her blue eyes much more than her lighter brown hair had done. Claire chose a very feminine light pink colour for her nails. When she was done, she hurried back to the ranch with her new look, feeling armed and ready to take on Cole.

When she arrived home, she quickly changed into strappy wedge sandals, her best push-up bra, a fitted navy tank top and a dark denim miniskirt. She put on pink lip gloss that stayed wet-looking and made up her eyes carefully to accentuate her best feature.

"There," she said feeling satisfied. "Eat your heart out, asshole."

She walked over to the restaurant to see how lunch was coming along. Alicia had told her she would cover the morning as there were just a handful of people to feed. The tour group wasn't due back until shortly before supper.

She checked her cellphone. There was a text from Cole.

What's up? I haven't heard from you. Everything okay? Missing my bendy girl.

She deleted the message.

* * *

At that exact moment, Antonio was boarding a direct flight to Colorado Springs. He settled into his chair, checking out the flight attendant's ass. He deserved a little diversion after spending weeks trying to track Claire down. No one seemed to know where she had gone. She had just disappeared into thin air. He had finally managed to sweet-talk the restaurant's assistant manager, Denise, into helping him. Claire had left her new address so the restaurant could send her last paycheque. Denise had been easily convinced of Antonio's undying devotion to Claire and how grateful she would be when she found out Denise had played a key role in their romantic reunion.

He put on his headphones and then checked the breast pocket of his jacket to make sure the little black velvet box was still there. Smiling to himself, he decided to take a nap. He would need to rest up for all the make-up sex he was going to have that night.

* * *

Cole was completely irritated as he checked the horses' hooves. They were running two hours late getting back to the ranch, and he was tired of managing the group of giggly girls and the younger ranch hands, all of them raging with hormones. Everyone had stayed up far too late flirting both nights, causing them to oversleep. Cole had been the last one to go to bed each night, hoping to prevent his guys from trying to sneak into the girls' tents or vice versa, and now the lack of sleep and constant delays had used up all of his patience.

Finding that one of the horses had somehow managed to lose a shoe, he swore under his breath as he reached into his saddlebag for some pliers. He eased out the nail that was still embedded in the hoof before dropping the pliers and slipping a boot onto the horse's foot to protect it for the long ride back. He stood and lifted his hat to wipe the sweat off his brow.

It was getting to the hottest part of the day, and he just wanted to be back home and find out what was wrong with Claire. He couldn't understand why he hadn't heard anything from her and why she hadn't come to say goodbye. Part of him was worried, and the other part was annoyed that she had seemed to go off the deep end again. He wasn't sure if he wanted to invite so much drama into his life, even if it did come with the best sex he'd ever had. When things were going well, he and Claire were amazing together; but when they were bad, it was like dealing with a thoroughbred— Claire was easily frightened and skittish, needing expert handling. Cole wasn't sure if he had it in him to try to keep her from getting spooked while trying to manage the ranch, the lodge and all of his plans for expansion.

Feeling worn out, he turned back to see how the others were coming along. "Let's get moving, everyone!" he called in a sharp tone.

When Claire reached the kitchen, Alicia was slicing up veggies. She looked up at Claire. "Wow, Claire! You look amazing! Cole is going to blow a fuse when he sees you."

"Aw, thanks, Alicia. You're so good for my ego. I love Sammi; she *is* the best! I feel like I look better than I have in a long time."

"I love the colour—it really brings out your eyes, and the cut really flows. Sammi knows what she's doing," Alicia agreed. "Oh, Cole texted Ben a while ago. They're going to be late getting back, probably close to six. Apparently it's been like more like a party than a trail ride. They've had hardly any sleep, and they got off to a late start this morning."

Claire quickly opened the fridge door so Alicia wouldn't see her wince. She tried to sound casual. "Okay, well, maybe we should have supper ready for seven. It would give them a bit of time to get cleaned up. We could just have the salads and a couple of appetizers ready earlier."

"Sounds like a plan," Alicia replied.

Claire looked over at her friend with concern. "Thanks for covering for me this morning, by the way. You must be exhausted. Why don't you go lie down for a while? Maybe come back close to supper if you're feeling up to it. I can take it from here."

"I was hoping you would say that. I feel like

death warmed over. Last night I told Ben if he wants more kids after this, *he* can have them." Alicia finished cutting up the veggies and arranging them on a tray and then washed her hands.

"I'll be back before six o'clock for sure." Alicia opened the door. "Thanks, hottie!"

Claire laughed. "See you later!"

Her afternoon was spent trying to concentrate on preparing supper, although her mind was racing with all the things she wanted to say to Cole when he got back. Her hands were a blur as she made five trays of lasagna—three with meat and two vegetarian—as well as garlic bread, shrimp skewers to grill, and two large salads. Dessert would be cinnamon apple crisp with vanilla ice cream. The closer the time got to supper, the more anxious she felt. She didn't want a big scene again, and it would take all of her willpower not to say anything to Cole until she had him alone. Her urge to scream in his face and call him a snake would have to be overridden by her desire to prove to herself that she could remain calm and handle this with dignity.

* * *

At 5:30 p.m., Antonio drove out of the car rental lot with the car's GPS guiding him to Black Canyon Ranch. He turned west toward the Rockies, casually popping some peanuts into his mouth. If he didn't hit any traffic, he would be there within an hour to start over with Claire. He couldn't wait to see the look on her face as she rushed into his arms. He'd have her at hello.

* * *

At a quarter to six, Alicia walked into the kitchen. "Sorry I'm so late! I fell asleep and was shocked to see the time when I woke up."

Claire gave her a warm smile. "Don't worry about it at all! Everything's under control here, and you obviously needed the rest. You're making an entire human being—that has *got* to be exhausting."

Alicia laughed. "I never thought of it that way. Thanks, Claire. Now, what can I do to help?"

Claire removed the trays from the oven and pulled off the covers to brown the cheese on the lasagna. "Well, I put out the metal tubs and filled them with ice and drinks so everyone can help themselves. I thought we'd go buffet style, so I moved a table over to the side wall, and I was going to put out silverware and plates. Do you mind finishing that for me?"

"No problem," Alicia replied as she got right to work. She saw the horses coming in as she set out the silverware. "They're back!" she called to Claire.

Claire's heart started to pound and she felt as though her stomach had moved up into her throat.

She found her purse, applied some lip gloss and sprayed her mouth with breath spray. *Why am I bothering?* she asked herself.

*　*　*

Forty-five minutes later, the volleyball team began trickling into the restaurant, having first gone back to their rooms to freshen up. They were a sight to behold in their short skirts, made up and full of energy even after a long day of riding. Claire could hear them talking excitedly about their experiences over the past few days and going on about the guys. She turned up the stereo system using a remote in the kitchen so she wouldn't have to hear any more.

It didn't take the guys long to shower and catch up, even though they needed to tend to the horses first. When they came in, there was a surge of life in the room. Cole wasn't with them. He had walked over to his cabin to have a shower and get cleaned up. He needed some time alone to try to get his patience back before he faced Claire. Returning to the restaurant with a cleanly shaved face and a little more energy than before, he opened the back door of the kitchen quietly and stood for a long moment watching Claire. She looked gorgeous. Her hair was different; the sexy waves that fell over her shoulders seemed to move with her. He wanted nothing more than to walk up behind her and lift up that skirt and get his hands inside her panties. She turned and jumped a little in surprise to see him standing there, gazing at her.

"Oh, Cole. Hi," she said with an icy stare. Her eyes looked like pools of deep blue sea water, but their expression was dead cold. She walked over to the oven to pull out what looked like dessert.

Cole watched as Claire bent over to take the trays out, her skirt moving up as she did. Feeling himself harden at the sight, he decided maybe she was worth all the hassle after all. He walked over to stand beside the stove, leaning against the counter so he could face her. "I missed you, Claire. I know something is wrong, and I want to know what."

"You're very perceptive. I really will have to talk to you later, though. I'm very busy right now, and I don't want a repeat of the other night."

"Fair enough. I'm going to go eat, and you can come to my place when you're ready. Don't leave it too late, okay? I'm really worn out," he said.

"I *bet* you are," Claire said sarcastically as she turned away and grabbed a bottle of wine off the rack.

"Oh, we're back here again, are we?" Cole said with an edge in his voice. "You know what? Why don't we forget the whole thing?"

Claire looked him dead in the eye. "My sentiments exactly."

Cole walked out the back door to his cabin, preferring to be alone.

Claire fought back tears as she brought out the dessert. She rounded up the dinner plates with Alicia without making eye contact with anyone.

Trey smiled up at her, and as she walked by he gave a low whistle. "Well, Miss Claire, I do believe you got a new hairdo! If you get sick of that old man you're dating, you should come find me."

"I'll keep that in mind," Claire said without looking up as she walked back to the kitchen.

She placed the plates on the counter and went back out with another tray of dessert. She almost dropped it when she heard Antonio's voice.

"Hi, Claire Bear," he called as he moved toward her from the doorway, wearing that smile he had practised in the mirror for hours before his first billboard shoot. "Guess who's come to get you!"

Claire stood completely still, her feet feeling like they had suddenly been cemented to the floor.

"You have *got* to be kidding me," she said, dropping the tray onto the table with a thud and turning back to the kitchen. The restaurant grew silent, everyone waiting for the show to start.

Antonio followed her through the kitchen door.

Claire kept moving. "Alicia, this is Antonio. He's just leaving. I'm going to help him find his car. I'll be back in a minute. Do you mind putting out the last dessert tray and the ice cream?"

"Sure thing, Claire," Alicia answered, keeping her eyes on Antonio. He tried the same smile on her but it faded when she glared at him.

Claire opened the back door to the kitchen and walked out quickly without breaking her stride. Tony hurried to keep up with her.

"Claire, I know you're angry with me. I came all this way because it's over between Stacey and me. I want you back. We are meant to be together."

Claire continued to walk in the direction of the parking lot. Antonio grabbed her by the elbow and turned her to face him. "Stop. I need to talk to you, Claire. Just give me a few minutes of your time. I flew here for you; it's the least you can do."

"Not really, Fuckwit. The least I can do is nothing, which is exactly what I'm going to do," Claire said, yanking her arm back.

"Come on, Claire. I wouldn't have flown out here if it wasn't important. I'm only asking for twenty minutes of your time. We have a lot to sort out," Antonio said, keeping pace with her.

"I have nothing to say to you, and I don't give a shit what you have to say to me," Claire replied, giving him a look of pure venom.

He touched her arm again, gently this time. "Claire, beautiful Claire, please just give me twenty minutes. I've come all this way, and I know you'll want to hear what I have to say."

She pulled her arm away and wiped it off.

The thought of him touching any part of her made her nauseous. As she took in his perfectly coiffed McDreamy hair and the two-day stubble that he meticulously kept the same length, she didn't know what she had ever seen in him.

He looked down at her. "I know you were hurt by what happened. But I need to talk to you. If you won't hear me out, I'll just keep coming back until you do. I'll march into that restaurant over and over until you listen to me."

Claire sighed and shook her head with disgust at what she was about to do. "Fine. I'll meet you in town at nine tonight. I'll come to the Starbucks on Centennial Boulevard. I won't wait for you. If you aren't there on time, forget it. I'll give you fifteen minutes, and then you leave me alone forever. Got it?"

Antonio smiled at her. "That's my girl. I knew you would come around. I'll see you at nine, Claire Bear."

Claire turned back to the restaurant and walked away, shuddering with disdain.

* * *

"So, that's your ex?" Alicia asked when Claire returned.

"Unfortunately." Claire sighed, feeling suddenly exhausted.

"I take it he wants you back?"

"Looks like it. I don't know. I agreed to meet him at Starbucks in town later to hear him out. He threatened to just keep coming back here otherwise. I have a few choice words for him, so it might be worth it."

Claire started loading the dishwasher with the stacked plates.

* * *

At eight-thirty, Claire was on her way to Starbucks. She had changed into dark boot-cut jeans and thrown a crocheted, off-the-shoulder taupe beach sweater over her tank top. She had also changed from her wedges to her navy ballet flats to give her aching feet some relief.

She wished she could talk to Janet right now, but it was the middle of the night in England. The second-best option would be to crawl into bed with a bucket of rocky-road ice cream and watch some romantic comedy, where the endings were always happy. Instead, here she was, driving to meet her scumbag ex-boyfriend, and then she would need to go back to the ranch and break it off with her current scumbag boyfriend. After that, she would have to find a way to start her life over again for the second time in two months. But that thought would have to wait. Right now, she had her anger to occupy her mind.

When she pulled up to the coffeehouse, she was five minutes late. She saw Antonio sitting at a table on the patio. She clenched her jaw as she got out of her car and tossed the keys into her purse. It was a hot summer evening, and even though the sun had been down for a long time, the air remained warm.

Tony waved to her and stood up as she approached the table. He tried to kiss her on the cheek, but she pulled away and sat down quickly.

"Thanks for meeting me, babe. You look just amazing. I don't know if you've ever looked this good. You are hot as hell." He paused, hoping for some response. Not getting one, he went on. "I ordered you a chai latte, your favourite."

"Thank you," Claire said, leaving it on the table. "So, what's so urgent that you had to come all this way?"

"Claire, I can't stop thinking about you. I hardly eat or sleep. Losing you was the biggest mistake of my life. I want you back. Things will be different this time. I'm done messing around. It will be just you and me forever. I promise."

"Stacey got bored when you stopped having to sneak around, right?" Claire looked down at her fingernails as she spoke.

"Well, she did leave me," he stammered, "but it was because I was so heartbroken over you. As soon as I came home and found that you were really gone, I couldn't take it. I went nuts. I need you back

{144}

for good." Antonio slid off his chair and bent down on one knee.

"What are you doing? Get up, you idiot," Claire said with a look of pure disgust.

"Claire Bear, I know it's what you've always wanted. I know I'm late, but please, Claire, will you marry me?" he asked, pulling out the ring box.

The people at the surrounding tables were staring now.

"Sit down, Antonio," she ordered quietly. "You're causing a scene."

He did as he was told.

"Do you honestly think I would consider marrying someone who cheated on me for months, maybe even years, for all I know? Are you insane?" she hissed.

"I do. I am. I'm crazy for you. I want to spend the rest of my life making it up to you. It will be a fresh start. I've left the real estate business. I want us to open up a restaurant together, wherever you want. Not here, but, you know, maybe San Francisco or New York or something. You can be with me all the time now, which I know was always an issue for you." Antonio searched her eyes, hoping to see her soften.

Claire sat perfectly still for a minute and then burst out laughing. She laughed for a couple of minutes straight until tears were streaming down her cheeks.

"Sorry, sorry," she said finally, "it's just that I can't believe I was so upset about you a few weeks ago. You're just such an idiot. And your time is up." Claire stood up to leave.

"Wait! Claire, don't go. I need your help. I . . . I lost some money. I got a great backdoor lead on a real estate deal and I got in early, but it fell through. I'm broke, Claire. I'm going to lose our house."

"What?" Claire spat out.

"I borrowed against the house to make the deal. Now I just need a little more cash to get back on my feet. You're the only one who can save me. I need you behind me so I can launch my comeback." Antonio's voice was pleading now.

"Stop it. You are embarrassing both of us," she replied, starting to walk to her car.

Antonio followed her like a little puppy. "Claire, please. I know we always kept things separate before, but if we get married and use your inheritance money, I know we could make a go of it. A restaurant, another real estate firm, whatever you like. We could have anything we want."

"Wow!" Claire stopped walking, rounding on him with an incredulous look on her face. "This is a new low even for you. You are actually telling me you want me back for my money. Well, *that's* an offer I can't refuse. Marriage to a cheating bastard who needs me for my inheritance from my dead parents. That's just what every girl dreams of!"

Claire opened the door to her car. "You're incredible. Get yourself over to the airport, and get the hell away from me. Don't think of contacting me again. Ever," she said in a quiet, even tone. She got into the driver's seat and slammed the door.

Antonio punched the top of her car, yelling, "Yeah, well, fuck you! You were always a cold fish, and now apparently you're a bitch, too!"

Claire unrolled her window a crack. "You know what, Fuckwit? Stacey didn't leave you because you were heartbroken. She left you because you're a horrible lover. You're a one-trick pony whose only trick is mediocre at best."

With that, Claire pulled away, shaking her head at the scene they had just caused. She sped off down the street, driving for a long time before realizing she was heading in the wrong direction.

"Son of a bitch," she muttered as she made a fast U-turn and started back to the ranch.

It was pitch dark as Claire left the city, now sobbing angry tears. She was furious at Antonio, at Cole, at her sister for moving so far away and at herself for ever falling for either of those two assholes. Speeding down the highway, she flipped stations on the radio, searching for a song that would suit her mood. Finally, she hit on "Blow Me (One Last Kiss)" by Pink and blasted it, belting out the words as loud as she could.

As she took a sharp curve, she saw something

black dart out into the road. She swerved and slammed on the brakes, causing her car to skid sideways. Suddenly, everything went black.

NINE

The next morning, Cole woke up with a terrible feeling. He had managed to get some rest, despite downing a couple of beers before he went to bed. He realized now that he had overreacted to Claire's silence and attitude when he got back the day before. He had been exhausted and out of patience yesterday and had taken it out on her to some degree. He regretted telling her to just forget their relationship. He doubted she would take that lightly.

After quickly getting dressed and brushing his teeth, he jogged out the door and down the path to Claire's cabin with Otis following along. When he got there, he knocked on the door. No answer. He knocked louder. *She should be up by now*, he thought. He tried calling her phone, but it went straight to voice mail. He hurried over to the restaurant to see if she was there already, but it was all locked up.

Taking one last shot at finding her, he jogged to the path by the lakeshore, thinking she might have gone for a run. Cole doubled back to her cabin to knock again. If she had been in the shower, she should be out by now. "Claire! Claire!" he called.

When no answer came, he walked back over to the restaurant. The door was unlocked now, and when he entered, his face fell a little when he saw Alicia there alone. "Hey, Alicia, have you seen Claire this morning?" he asked, feeling concerned now.

"No, I haven't," Alicia said. "Maybe she's still asleep?"

"I don't think so. I was just over at her place and then I went down the trail to see if she was out running. I can't find her anywhere."

"That's odd," Alicia said slowly. "Her ex showed up here last night during supper. She got him out of here fast and then agreed to meet him for coffee in town later. She said he insisted on having a conversation with her. Said he'd keep coming back if she refused."

Cole fought the urge to show any hint of the shock he was feeling. This was the last thing he had expected to hear. He felt like he had been punched in the gut. He stood quietly for a minute and then said, "If she doesn't show up for breakfast, do you need a hand?"

"No, I'll be fine, Cole, but what about Claire?

I'm worried about her. What if something happened to her? I can't see her just leaving like that and not showing up for work."

"I think the most likely thing is that she ended up staying with him, they spent too much time making up and she overslept." Cole looked sick as he thought of that possibility.

"What? No, Cole." Alicia shook her head. "That just doesn't sound right. She was really pissed at him."

"Well, all we can do for now is wait and see. I'm going to head over to the office. I need to make up the bills for the volleyball team. They're leaving right after breakfast, which is not soon enough for me. Let me know if you hear anything from Claire." Cole walked out the back door, letting it slam shut behind him.

He searched the parking lot and discovered that her car was missing. "Fuck," he muttered to himself, rubbing his hand over his jaw.

* * *

Claire woke up in a bright room. She was lying down and could hear a beeping sound. She tried to lift her head, but it hurt too much when she moved. She gasped at the pain, letting her head fall back. After a moment, she held up her arm and saw that it was attached to an IV line. She slowly started to put it all together in her mind, remembering driving and singing and then seeing something run out in front of her car. Then, nothing.

A few minutes later, a nurse came in to check on her. "Look who's awake. Welcome back, Claire. You gave us quite a scare last night. How do you feel?"

"My head hurts. What happened?" Claire croaked.

"You were in a collision last night; you hit a deer." The nurse paused. "You're going to be okay, but you'll have a headache for a few days, and you're going to be really sore for a while. Your body got pretty bruised and you have a bump on your forehead, but nothing is broken. You got really lucky. We've seen much worse injuries from this type of collision."

The nurse gently raised the head of the automatic bed and held out a cup of water for Claire to sip through a straw.

Claire blinked slowly at the nurse, trying to digest all this information. "What time is it?" was all she could think to ask.

"It's 6 a.m. I'm going to give you some more pain medication now so you can rest, okay? Do you want us to call anyone for you?" the nurse asked with a concerned look.

"Alicia. I have to let her know I can't come to work," Claire replied slowly.

"Okay, your cellphone was brought in with your

other personal belongings. I'll go get it and then you can call her. My name is Dawn, and I'll be here for you until the shift change in two hours."

"Thanks," Claire whispered. She shut her eyes for a minute, waiting for Dawn to come back.

Six hours later, she woke up again and saw her cellphone on the tray beside her bed. She turned it on in a haze, knowing she had to do something with it. It took her a few minutes to figure out she needed to call Alicia. She searched for her number, dialed and then heard Alicia's voice mail come on. Claire's voice was raspy as she started to leave a message.

"Alicia, it's me. I'm sorry. I'm here. I don't really know where this is," she said, pausing to look around the room. "It's definitely a hospital. I got hit by a deer last night. I'm sleepy now. Good night, sweetie . . . Oh, it's Claire."

* * *

Cole had spent the day in a simmering rage. After he finished up the bills for the volleyball girls and got them on their way, he went back to his office and slammed the door. He tried to concentrate on getting through some paperwork, but his mind kept wandering. He was shocked Claire would disappear like this, after everything they had said and done together. He had started to trust her and really believed she would stay in his life. He still had no idea why she was so angry at him when he got back, and he couldn't believe she would just up and leave with her ex.

As the day wore on, he became increasingly humiliated. Everyone had seen that guy show up at the restaurant, and then she had disappeared. It reminded him of how stupid he had felt when Gabriela had taken off back to Brazil. She'd moved all of her things out of his cabin while he'd been out on a trail ride. He hadn't even had the faintest clue Gabriela was planning to leave until she was already gone. Cole wondered if Claire had been in touch with Antonio while he was away. Maybe they had been in contact the whole time. Maybe she had been using him to make her ex feel jealous or as a way to boost her ego after having been jilted.

In the mid-afternoon, after still having heard nothing, he decided to clear his head by going for a ride. He saddled Dudley up and took off, encouraging his horse to run his fastest, wanting to get as far away from the ranch as possible. He dismounted at the river's edge and threw rocks into the water as hard as he could for a long time.

It was after 4 p.m. when Cole finally returned to the ranch, feeling slightly calmer. He had decided that he would start looking for a new chef first thing the next morning, and that it was better things ended now rather than after another year of being with Claire. Even though he had strong feelings for her, he hoped he could forget her quickly.

Cole took a long shower before feeling ready to face the paperwork he had been putting off. He decided to take a plate of dinner to his office so he could be alone. As he locked up his front door, he heard Dustin shouting to him from near the lodge. *Oh, for God's sake! Can't they handle anything themselves?* he thought.

"Cole! Come quick! Claire's in the hospital. She had some kind of accident!" Dustin yelled, running toward his cousin.

Moments later, Cole burst into the lodge with Dustin on his heels. "Alicia? What the hell happened?!" He had a look of pure panic on his face.

"I got a message from Claire; she sounded so confused. She hit a deer last night. That's why she didn't come home. I've been calling the hospitals to find her. She's at Memorial."

Alicia, Dustin and Cole rushed out of the lodge just as Ben hurried toward them from the barn. "I just heard. Is she gonna be okay?"

Alicia answered, "We don't know anything yet. We're on our way over now."

Ben said, "Give me a minute and I'll drive you."

"No," Cole answered. "I need you to sign off on that delivery of feed. It should be here by five. Come over after, okay? Dustin, can you stick around and help Ben unload it?"

Dustin nodded.

"Sure thing, Cole." Ben said. "Call if you need anything."

Cole barely registered the drive over to the hospital. He felt sick to his stomach at the thought that Claire had been lying in a hospital bed while he had thought she was off with her ex-boyfriend. His anger had melted into desperation. *Please let her be okay. Please.*

"Alicia, about what I said earlier, about Claire being with her ex—" Cole started.

"Forget it, Cole. I won't tell her. What were you supposed to think under the circumstances?"

"I should have trusted her more than that. I should have gone out looking for her," Cole said as he turned into the hospital parking lot.

Moments later, the two were hurrying through the front doors and up to the front desk.

"We're looking for a patient who came in last night, Claire Hatley. She was in a collision," Alicia said to the woman behind the desk.

She peered at Alicia over her glasses and said, "Well, let's see if we can find her. Are you family?"

Cole spoke up, his voice shaking a little. "We live together. Her family is in England."

The woman paused for a minute. "Okay, you can go see her. She's in room three-seventeen."

Alicia and Cole took off toward the elevators. When they got to the room, Cole pushed the door open and saw Claire lying in her bed, hooked up to an IV and monitors, sleeping. She had horrible bruises on her face and neck, along with a huge purple bump on her forehead. What they could see of her collarbone was dark purple and badly scraped from her seat belt. Cole's knees felt weak at the sight of her looking so beat-up and fragile. He held on to the door frame to steady himself. Alicia pulled two chairs up to the side of her bed and motioned for Cole to sit down. They sat for a few minutes quietly watching her sleep.

"I'm going to run to the ladies' room," Alicia said as she got up.

Cole nodded. When he was finally alone with Claire, he let out a stifled sob. Claire stirred and opened her eyes. Her mouth curved up into a tiny smile when she saw him. Her voice came out as little more than a whisper. "Hey, Cowboy, come here often?"

Cole's eyes shone with tears. He sniffled, rubbed his face with his hand and then said, "Oh, Claire, you had me so worried."

He took her hand in his and held it carefully, as if he never wanted to let go. He lowered his forehead to her hand and rested it there for a moment.

"Judging by your face, I guess I look pretty rough. I haven't seen myself yet."

"You look like you've been through something, yeah. There's a big bump on your forehead and lots of bruises. Can you remember what happened?" Cole asked.

"Sort of. I was driving back to the ranch. I came around a corner and saw something run across the road and then I woke up here. They told me I hit a deer," Claire said.

Just then, Alicia walked into the room. "Oh, Claire, honey, you're awake," she said, crossing the room and standing on the side of the bed opposite Cole. She gently brushed the hair off Claire's forehead. "Can I get you anything?"

"I'd love some water," Claire replied.

"Sure thing, sweetie." Alicia held the cup up to Claire for her to have a drink. "Listen, before the nurse comes in, we better mention that Cole had to tell them you two live together so we could get in. He told them your family is in England."

Sadness and confusion crossed over Claire's face before she sighed. "Okay. Thanks, Cole. I appreciate your saying that. It's nice to have company."

A nurse came in, along with a doctor, to check on Claire. "Can you two wait outside while I see how our patient is doing?"

Alicia and Cole nodded and walked out into the hallway.

"She looks pretty beat-up," Alicia said.

"Yeah, it's hard to see her like this," Cole said, his voice thick with emotion.

Ben met them in the hallway. "Hey, you two,"

he said, giving Alicia a quick kiss on the forehead. "How's Claire?"

"She'll be okay, I think," said Alicia. "We don't have much information yet, but she's awake. The nurse is in with her now."

A moment later, the nurse came out. "We're going to take her upstairs for some tests. It'll take about half an hour. We don't like more than two visitors at a time, so maybe just a quick hello, okay?"

* * *

An hour later, when Claire was wheeled back into the room, Cole was waiting for her. "Ben and Alicia went back to the ranch. They're going to handle things so I can stay with you. Do you need me to call anyone?"

"No, I'll call my sister after I get all the test results back. I don't want to worry her for nothing. Thanks, though."

"You look tired. Do you want me to go so you can get some sleep?" Cole asked quietly.

"Would it be strange if I need to sleep, and I want you to stay, too?" Claire replied. She couldn't bear the thought of being alone right now.

"Not at all."

Cole found the light switch and turned off the lights. He gently kissed her cheek and sat down beside her in the chair, holding her small hand in his.

Lying there with her eyes closed, drifting into a medication-induced sleep, Claire couldn't stop a horrible feeling in the pit of her stomach. She wanted nothing more than for this sweet man to be the one, but she already knew he was not. He had cheated on her, or at the very least, had strongly considered it. There was no way she could stay with him now. She could sense the loneliness that was about to hit her when she told him what she knew and ended the relationship. Why had she asked him to stay? She was just torturing herself, allowing him to take care of her like this.

* * *

Cole watched Claire for a long time, thinking about their relationship so far—the roller coaster of it all. He tried to figure out what had upset her so badly a few days earlier but came up blank. He knew that right now none of it mattered. The only thing that mattered was to be there for her until she could grow stronger and heal. Having almost lost her, he had a completely new perspective. He was certain now that he wanted to be with Claire and try to work through the things that spooked her. What he didn't know was whether she would want to be with him when this whole ordeal was over.

Claire had been asleep for a couple of hours when the doctor came back in and turned on the lights. Cole had been dozing in the chair beside her.

"Claire?" the doctor touched her arm. "Claire, it's Dr. Olsen. I have your test results."

Claire opened her eyes. She nodded, trying to look brave, but the fear in her eyes was unmistakable. Cole held her hand, giving it a gentle squeeze.

"Everything looks pretty good. No sign of a hematoma or nerve damage, no swelling so far, so those are all good signs. We'll need to keep you here for a couple more days, though, to monitor your brain and make sure it doesn't start swelling. So far, it doesn't look likely, so I'd say you got pretty lucky."

Claire squeezed Cole's hand. "Thanks, Dr. Olsen," she said, tears filling her eyes. "That's a relief."

The doctor smiled at her. "Hey, you remembered my name, so nothing wrong with your short-term memory either," he said with a wink. "Get some rest, and I'll be back to check on you tomorrow, unless anything changes."

Cole stood up and shook the doctor's hand. "Thanks, doc!"

"I didn't do anything, really. I just get to be the lucky guy giving good news for a change." With that, he walked out, leaving Cole and Claire alone.

Claire looked up at the ceiling, trying to blink

back her tears. Cole sat on the bed beside her and gave her a long, careful hug. "You have no idea how scared I was. I can't remember ever worrying that much about anyone."

Claire looked up at him. "Thanks, Cole, for being here. I know we haven't been on good terms the last few days."

"We can talk about that later, or not at all, Claire. It doesn't matter to me anymore. I just want to be here for you."

"Not at all? That would be convenient," Claire replied, glaring at him.

"What?" Cole responded, pulling away from her. "I just meant it doesn't matter to me that you got so insecure again. I'm over it."

"You may be, but I'm sure as hell not. Before you left with the volleyball girls, I went into your bag to leave you a note, and I found the box of condoms."

Cole sighed heavily, suddenly understanding why she had been so angry with him. "Well, now it makes sense. I'll admit that looks pretty bad . . ."

"It doesn't just *look* pretty bad, Cole. It is."

"I know it's going to sound hard to believe, but I didn't bring those for me. I brought them in case any of the girls and my guys seemed like they were going to hook up. At the time, I thought it would be better to hand out the condoms than have any accidents. Then I thought better of it and realized if I was handing out condoms to my guys, it would be like saying it was okay for them to have sex with the guests, and it isn't. In the end, I just stayed awake until after everyone was asleep to keep an eye on them. I also made sure I was awake first. Nothing did happen that I know of." Cole paused, waiting to hear what Claire had to say.

"You're right, Cole. That is hard to believe," Claire said with a sigh.

"I'm sure it is, but it's the truth, Claire. I never had any intention of sleeping with any of those girls. Not even for a second. I only want to be with you. I told you that before I left, and I'm a man of my word, Claire. I've never given you a reason not to trust me."

"Well, Cole, the condoms in your bag are a pretty big red flag, don't you think? What would you think if you were me?"

"I hope that I'd trust you and take you at your word, but I also know you've been cheated on before, which makes it a pretty tough thing for you to do."

Claire stared at him for a moment, trying to figure out if he was indeed telling the truth. "It's more than tough for me, Cole. It's damn near impossible. I just won't be a trusting fool ever again."

Seeing Claire's battered face, he had no desire to fight with her. "You know, Claire, I figure what that asshole did to your heart is just about as bad as what that deer did to your body. You've been hurt really badly, and now I've done something that has made you question me. But I promise you, I was *never* going to use those condoms. I would never do that to you. Ever."

Claire looked him in the eye as he spoke. He seemed so sincere, and everything in her wanted so badly to believe him. It was all so confusing to her. He *had* never given her any reason to doubt him, but how could he expect her to believe he didn't want to sleep with any of those girls? They were gorgeous and willing. She needed to keep her guard up and be smarter from now on.

Cole looked down at her. "I can understand why you got so angry. It looks really bad."

Claire started to tear up. "I'm just really confused right now, Cole. I don't know what to think."

"Claire, I would never cheat on you. I hope you realize I'm telling the truth, because there's nothing I want more than for what we have to work out. I've never met anyone like you. You are amazing, you know that?" Cole paused, giving her a little half smile. "Twice in the last two days I thought I was going to lose you, and to be honest, it just shook me to the core."

Claire nodded, tears streaming down her face.

Cole wiped her tears with his thumb. "Don't cry. We'll figure this out together, okay? For now, you need to rest and not worry about anything. Let me take care of you, and when you are stronger, you can kick me to the curb if you still think I'm a cheating bastard."

Claire laughed a little at his words. Nothing would have pleased her more than if he was the real deal. He seemed almost perfect. "Okay, Cole. I'm pretty sure I'm going to believe you when these drugs wear off. No promises, though."

"Smart girl. You shouldn't make important decisions when you're high as a kite. Have a sleep. I'll be here when you wake up."

TEN

The next morning, Claire had to go back for another brain scan. Cole left for a few hours to get showered and changed and have something to eat. Claire called Janet to update her on how she was doing. She shared with Janet what Cole had told her about the condoms.

Janet sounded skeptical. "I know you want to believe him, hon, but seriously? It doesn't sound right to me."

"I know," Claire sighed. "I'm just going to wait and see. Keep my guard up. I'm sure we'll talk about it some more, and then I'll just have to go with my gut. If I had listened to my instincts about Fuckwit, I would have left him years ago. I just kept ignoring that voice in my head screaming for me to leave him."

"What is your gut telling you about Cole?"

"As insane as it sounds, I think I believe him."

"Hmm, are you sure it isn't just your vajayjay wanting you to believe him?" Janet replied.

Claire laughed and then winced in pain. "Ouch. Shit. No more jokes."

"Sorry, Claire. You okay?"

"Yeah, I'll be fine. I should get some sleep."

"Okay, sweetie. I wish I was there right now. This sucks. I would totally kick his ass and then take care of you myself," Janet said, her voice full of regret.

"Good night, you."

"Have a good rest, Claire. I love you."

"Janet?"

"Yes?"

"I figured out the difference between Cole and Antonio. With Antonio, I wanted it to work even though everything inside me told me it was all wrong. With Cole, my gut is telling me he's the one, but my brain is looking for reasons for it to fail. I'm terrified of how I feel about him. I'm falling hard, and I have a horrible feeling that if I let this whole thing go on too long, I'll be crushed if it doesn't work out."

"In that case, go with your gut, Claire, but keep your eyes open for the truth."

"Will do, sensei. G'night."

* * *

At that moment, Cole was back at the ranch, trying to get through as much work as he could as quickly as possible. He called the towing company that had Claire's car and got them to deliver it to his mechanic. Ben came by the office to take over, bringing some cinnamon rolls Alicia had made for Claire. Cole went over some instructions with Ben and then hopped into his truck, his heart beating a little faster in anticipation of the reception he'd get when he arrived at the hospital.

When he got in Claire's room, it was empty. He stood by the window, waiting for her to return, a feeling of dread in the pit of his stomach. After their conversation the night before, he wasn't sure if he could regain her trust. Their relationship was so new, and it had certainly been tested a number of times in a matter of weeks.

After a few minutes, Claire was wheeled back in by a porter. Cole smiled at her, even though seeing her so beat-up made his knees go weak again. Claire gave him a little grin when she saw him. Cole walked over and helped her out of the wheelchair and into the bed.

"Thank you," Claire said, her eyes moving to the tray of cinnamon rolls on the night table. "Are those for me?"

Cole nodded. "From Alicia. Can I get you one?"

"Only if you'll have one with me," Claire said. "I hate to eat alone."

"I won't turn down that request," Cole said, grabbing two napkins and placing the rolls on them. "So, how did the tests go this morning?" he asked, searching her eyes for some sign of how she was feeling about him.

"Pretty good, I think. They said everything looked the same as yesterday, so that's good," Claire said, popping a piece of the roll into her mouth.

"I'm so glad to hear that, Claire. Nothing is more important than getting you well again."

Claire gave him a thoughtful look. "Cole, about our conversation last night, I really want to believe you. You have been nothing but wonderful to me since I've known you, and my gut is telling me to trust you, so I'm going to try really hard to do that. It may not be all that easy for me to do, I hope you understand that."

"I do, Claire. You've been hurt before, and when you've been hurt, it changes how you see the world."

"It really does."

Cole gave her a long look before he spoke up. "You know, the morning after your accident—before we knew what had happened—Alicia told me you had gone to meet your ex. I spent a good part of the day thinking you had gotten back together with him. When we found out where you were, I felt awful that I had been willing to believe the worst of you when here you were in the hospital."

"You thought that? Really?" Claire asked, sounding a little hurt.

"Yeah, well, we kind of broke up that evening, then he showed up and you disappeared. I didn't know what to think. This whole thing is still pretty new. Trust is something that takes time to build."

"It is. We might have to slow down a bit," Claire replied.

"Maybe. There's no rush, right?"

"No, there isn't."

They ate in silence for a moment before Cole looked back over at her. "You know what, Claire? Even if it is all pretty new, you really are the only woman I want to be with."

"I feel the same way about you, Cowboy."

That afternoon, things grew more comfortable between them. Claire listened as Cole described in excruciating detail what it was like to babysit a bunch of horny twenty-somethings. He managed to make her laugh a little as he painted a vivid picture of how panicked he had been, trying to make sure no one slept together.

After, as Claire filled him in on her dealings with Antonio, Cole was shocked and angry on her behalf. He held her hand as she fell asleep, then sat beside the bed reading while he waited for her to wake up.

Dr. Olsen came back to see Claire in the late part of the afternoon. He was pleased with the test results and told her she could go home the next day, but there was to be no work or other physical activity for the next two weeks. He gave her a pamphlet on brain injuries, with a list of things to look for in case she seemed to develop any new symptoms over the coming days.

Cole slept on the chair beside her again that night, even though Claire tried to persuade him to go home and get a good sleep. "Your back must be killing you. You seriously do *not* need to stay. Come back in the morning."

Cole gave her a serious look. "Three days ago, I thought we were breaking up. Two days ago, I thought you might not make it. If you think I'm going anywhere, we should send you for more brain scans. I'm staying right here with you." He kissed her softly and pressed his cheek to hers.

"Mmm, careful," Claire said. "Dr. Olsen said no physical activity for at least two weeks."

"Oh, I don't think he meant sex, do you?" Cole said, shaking his head and trying to sound serious. "We could ask him, but I'm pretty sure it's okay."

Claire smiled wistfully at the thought.

* * *

The next morning, Claire was released from the hospital. Cole carefully drove her back to the ranch and set her up in his cabin to finish recovering. He brought over a lot of her clothes and toiletries, her tablet and some books, made sure she got into bed and brought her a coffee and some lunch.

"I have to run down to the office for a bit. Your cellphone is right here if you need me. You're supposed to take your pain meds at 2 p.m. I'll be back in time just in case you fall asleep." Cole gave her a quick kiss. "Will you be okay while I'm gone?"

Claire nodded. "Yes, I will. I'm just so glad to be here instead of in the hospital."

Cole smiled and touched her cheek with the back of his hand. "I'm so happy you're here, too. See you in a bit."

Otis stood beside the bed, wagging his tail at Claire. Cole turned to him. "I know what that looks means. But you are not allowed on the bed." With that, he gave his dog a pat and headed downstairs.

* * *

Over the next few weeks, as Claire stayed in bed, she began to think of plans for the ranch. She had some new ideas to increase business during the slow seasons, including hosting weddings, reunions, girls' getaway weekends as well as romantic couples' weekends. Cole's face filled with excitement listening to her ideas when he popped in to see her during the day. In the evenings, he curled up with her in bed to watch movies and they talked late into the night. All the talking with no opportunity for sex somehow created a new level of intimacy between them. They were growing closer each day.

But the days began to drag, leaving Claire feeling lonely and bored. One morning, Cole brought Trey over to ask for Claire's help. He had decided to apply for college, having seen what he was missing when the volleyball team came to the ranch.

"I would *love* to help, Trey! I am bored to tears," Claire said with a smile, getting up from the couch and walking over to the kitchen table.

"Thanks, Claire. I've been finding all these forms pretty overwhelming, actually," Trey admitted.

The two got straight to work. After a few minutes, Cole left to get back to his desk, giving Claire a peck on the cheek before he left. He looked over at his younger cousin. "Now, don't stay too long and tire her out, Trey."

"You got it, boss," Trey replied. "Don't worry."

A couple of hours later, Trey received a text from Cole telling him to let Claire rest. As he packed up his things, he shook his head at Claire. "My cousin sure has it bad for you, Claire. I've never seen him like this before. He guards you like you're made of china or something."

"He certainly takes good care of me," Claire agreed.

"Yeah, he does. Sometimes he goes a little overboard with the whole protective thing, though. When we went on that trail ride with the volleyball team, he wouldn't let any of us guys anywhere near them. He spoiled what could have been an epic time."

"He did, did he?" Claire asked. She wanted him to say more but felt wrong asking him about Cole.

"Yeah, he pulled us all aside before we rode out and made it real clear that we'd be fired if we were caught messing around with them," Trey replied, putting his boots back on. "Then, the whole time, he acted like he was their dad."

"Well, he won't be at college with you, so I guess you can have some fun. Just make sure you get your butt to class. I didn't do all that paperwork just so you can get laid."

"Oh yes you did!" Trey said with a loud laugh as he walked out the door.

As Claire made her way back up the stairs to go lie down, she thought about what Trey had said. It put to rest the nagging questions that had plagued her mind about Cole's trustworthiness. Before she took a nap, she sent Cole a quick text.

> Just going to take a little nap. Can't wait to see you tonight! XOXO

* * *

The rest of the two weeks crawled by for Claire. She was improving quickly, her bruising now a faint yellow colour, and the bump on her forehead was finally gone. As she healed, she started to feel more energetic, which made it all the more difficult to lie around doing nothing.

When Cole got into bed at night, they cuddled and kissed, but he put the brakes on as soon as Claire tried to grope him or seemed to get a little too aggressive with her kisses. One evening, Claire took Cole's hand and placed it between her legs.

"No, Claire, we have to be patient," he groaned. "After your follow-up visit with Dr. Olsen, okay?"

"But this is killing me, to be so close to you and not be able to touch you and feel you inside me." Claire pouted.

"Believe me, it's killing me, too. But I just can't be with you that way until I know I won't hurt you somehow." Cole kissed her forehead. "How about we watch a movie?" he asked.

"Oh, alright. Let's see if we can find something dirty on Netflix."

* * *

The next morning Claire got up early with Cole. "I want to work today. I promise to sit down while I chop food, and I won't overdo it, okay? I just can't lie here anymore."

Cole gave her a concerned look. "Claire, the more you rest now, the quicker you'll be back to a hundred per cent. Alicia's fine and we have my aunt coming in to help out, remember?"

Claire growled at him in frustration. "Seriously, Cole, I'm a grown woman. I make decisions for myself. Now, I appreciate how you've cared for me—more than you can know—but I *really need* to get out of here for a few hours and be useful. I'm doing it." She slapped him on the ass as he bent over to pick up his jeans.

Cole flinched. "Alright, alright. There's no need to get violent about it. But hold that thought for after your appointment."

A little while later, Claire walked over to the restaurant with a skip in her step. She took pleasure in the feeling of the warm breeze blowing that morning, the sun shining down and the peacefulness of the lake framed by beautiful mountains. She took deep breaths, filling her lungs with fresh air and smiling as she went. She was happy to be out of bed, but most of all, she was grateful to be alive. Otis followed her, having spent most of his time over the past couple of weeks by her bed. Claire crouched down to pat him and touched her forehead to the top of his head. "Thanks, buddy, for keeping me company. You're the best." She was rewarded with a wet lick on the nose.

When Claire stepped into the kitchen, Alicia and Cole's Aunt Fern were already there, working.

"Good morning!" Claire called.

"Claire! You're up and around!" Alicia came over and gave her a big hug.

"I am, and I feel great. It's good to be alive," she said happily.

Fern wiped her hands on a dishtowel and walked over with a smile. "Claire, it's a pleasure to meet you. I've heard such great things from everyone." She shook Claire's hand warmly. Fern looked to be in her fifties. She was short and a little plump, with a big smile and short curly blond hair with little bits of grey mixed in.

"It's so nice to meet you, Fern. I am so grateful for your stepping in to help out while I've been off. I would have been really worried about Alicia if you hadn't been here."

"I'm happy to help," Fern said. "Besides, I've seen a whole lot more of Trey and Dustin than normal, which is every mother's wish. Those boys are almost never home other than to sleep."

Alicia gave Claire a concerned look. "I hope you're here to visit. I don't know if you're supposed to be working just yet."

Claire gave her a confident smile. "I'm here for both. I promised Cole I would sit as much as possible. I just had to get out of that bed and get back to being productive again. I swear I'll go back if I start feeling even a bit worn out. Now, what can I do?"

* * *

Three hours later Claire was back in bed, propped up against some pillows, reading. Cole came by to check on her. "How you doing?"

Claire grinned. "I feel great. I was a little tired, so I thought I better quit while I was still ahead. It was so nice to be with Alicia and your Aunt Fern. She's a sweetheart. I'm going to start helping out with breakfast for a few days, and then breakfast and supper."

Cole sat next to her on the bed. "Okay, as long as you don't overdo it."

"I won't, I promise." Claire gave him a long, lingering kiss. "I'm going to have to find a way to make all of this up to you. You've been amazing."

She kissed him again and ran her index finger down his shirt until she reached his belt buckle. Cole didn't stop her, so she reached down further and placed her hand over his groin. Cole slid his tongue into her mouth for the first time in weeks. Claire shuddered with pleasure at the feeling and opened her mouth a little wider, inviting more. When he stopped, she bit his bottom lip gently and gave a little frustrated moan. She could feel how hard he was through his jeans and felt herself becoming wet.

"I want you, Cole. I need to have you inside me," she whispered. "Please fuck me."

Cole moaned. "Oh, gorgeous, I want you so bad."

He slid his hand under the sheet and into her

panties, rubbing her with long, slow strokes. "You're so wet," he murmured.

"You do that to me. I just have to look at you and I'm ready." Claire sighed, kissing him on his neck.

Cole pressed his fingers exactly where he knew she wanted them, rubbing her in unhurried circles. Claire arched her back against the pillows and spread her legs open. Cole kissed her mouth with such tender passion that she was almost ready to come. He pulled his mouth away from her, and for one horrible moment, she thought he was about to stop. She let out a little cry of desperation. Cole lifted up her shirt with one hand and pressed his lips to her nipples, one at a time. He cupped her left breast with one hand, working her nipple with his teeth and fingers until it was rigid, then he slowly moved over to her right breast to give it the same attention. He could feel how slick she was becoming, and he now ached with desire.

He slowly made his way down to her waist, taking his hand out of her panties and using both hands to slide them off as she lifted her hips to help him. Cole kissed her navel and then spread her legs with his hands, kissing her inner thighs and her core gently. Claire made a fist around the sheet with one hand and caressed her breasts with the other hand. "Oh, Cole, yes, yes," she breathed.

Cole slid his tongue into her sex with a deliberately careful movement, sending a rush of passion through her entire body. He put his hands under her bottom and lifted her hips as he continued pressing his tongue into her. He reached around behind her, rubbing her ass with the tips of his fingers as he hungrily licked and urged her to come with his tongue.

His own excitement was becoming uncontainable. He felt trapped in the confines of his jeans. His need to feel her tight, wet skin around him, squeezing more than just his tongue, was almost more than he could take. Ignoring his own need, Cole continued working her with his mouth and fingers, increasing his pace and force until he could feel her coming on his mouth.

Claire cried out with the pleasure of it, her entire body shuddering. Grabbing his hair with her hands, she pulled him to her until every last pulse was over. When she stopped and released him, he kissed her inner thighs and made his way back to her face, stopping to pay homage to her tummy, breasts and neck on the way up. She kissed his lips and the taste of herself on him sent a flicker of excitement flowing through her. She could still feel his tongue inside her, thrusting and licking. He used one hand to prop himself up and the other to hold her cheek and jaw as he kissed her.

"Cole," she whispered, "take me now. Please, I need you inside me."

Cole rolled off her suddenly and stood up. "I can't, Claire. I want to so much that I'm physically in pain, but I just can't until I know you're okay. Please don't ask me again."

With that, he walked into the bathroom and shut the door. A moment later, Claire heard the shower go on. "Shit," she muttered under her breath.

Cole stood under the tepid water with his head against the shower wall. The thought of her pretty mouth begging him to take her was all he could think of. His body was raging with lust and he was as hard as stone. He wrapped his fingers around his thick length and started pulling with force. *Take me now, Cole. Please, I need you inside me.* He didn't hear the door to the bathroom open and was startled to feel her behind him, her body pressed up against his, her hands reaching around his waist.

"I'm sorry, Cole. Let me at least give you some of what you've given me." She put her hand over-top of his, lacing her fingers through his. Together they stroked slowly and firmly. Claire used her other hand to hold and massage his testicles as the water cascaded over their bodies. She kissed his back as she pleasured him. "Just think of all the things we are going to do to each other soon. I want to feel you come inside me. I want you to fuck me until I can hardly stand."

"Oh, Claire!" he moaned as he came, his orgasm coursing through his entire body. Claire held him tightly to her and felt his body shudder with pleasure.

When it was over, he turned around to face her, wrapping his arms around her and pulling her to his chest. "Only you can do that to me. You can bring me to the edge with one word, the slightest touch. Promise me you'll never leave. I need to be with you, only you."

"I promise, Cole. I promise I will stay," Claire whispered. He tilted her head back with his hand and they kissed again, this time with pure emotion instead of lust.

ELEVEN

A week later, Claire finally had her follow-up appointment. She and Cole had managed to keep their hands off each other until that day, although it had been excruciating. They had busied themselves with detailed plans for marketing the ranch and setting aside dates for the Girls' Getaway Weekend and the Couples' Romance Weekend. Cole decided it might be a good idea to build a gazebo on the lakeshore for weddings and other events. They shopped online for a do-it-yourself kit, settling on a large cedar package. The gazebo would be lined with benches on the inside, with room to accommodate a small wedding party or a table and chairs for romantic dinners for two. Claire's car came back from the shop, all repaired, and she had to spend some time dealing with the insurance company.

On the afternoon of Claire's appointment, Cole drove her to the hospital. On the ride over they were both feeling a bit nervous. Claire had had another

MRI the day before and she was going to get the results. They tried to make small talk but it was difficult while they were thinking about what the test might show.

"Maybe we could go for supper after to celebrate?" Cole said.

"I was hoping you'd ask," Claire said. "I realized you and I haven't really gone out on a proper date yet, unless you count fridge shopping."

"Wow, I can't believe that's true. I'm going to have to step up my game, pull out the romantic Cole."

"You've been extremely romantic. What do you call taking care of someone when they're sick?" Claire asked.

"I don't know. Not romance. Love, maybe?" His heart skipped a beat as he said it.

Claire's face flushed and she felt her stomach flip with excitement. "Would you call it love, Cole?"

He pulled into a parking space in front of the hospital and looked over at her. "I would," he said.

Claire unhooked her seat belt and lunged across the seat to him, wrapping her arms around his neck and kissing him hard on the mouth. They lingered there for a few beautiful moments before Cole stopped and said, "You're going to be late, and I don't know about you, but I don't think I can wait another minute to find out when we can finally do all those things you've been talking about."

"Good point, Cowboy. You know, you are more than just a handsome face," she said, giving him a playful look. "Let's go get this over with." Her anxiety had suddenly been replaced by a rush of exhilaration from being told for the first time that he loved her.

An hour later, they walked out of the hospital. They made it only a few steps before Cole spun Claire into him and kissed her with wild abandon. Without their mouths separating, he grabbed her bottom and hoisted her up around his waist.

A security guard watched them for a minute and then walked over with wide eyes. "Okay, you two, you're in front of a hospital. Can you take it home, please?"

Cole set Claire down on the ground, and the two apologized sheepishly before hurrying to the truck, red faced. They drove for a few blocks and then suddenly Cole turned off the road into the parking lot of a large hotel.

"Where are we going?" Claire asked.

"I don't want to wait till we're back at the ranch. Let's spend the night here," he said, pulling up to the front entrance. He looked over at her. "Okay?"

"I like how you think," she said, pulling him by the shirt to bring his lips to hers.

The two got out and practically ran to the front doors. Cole tossed his keys to a valet who wore a knowing look. Cole could hardly keep his hands off Claire at the front desk. When the clerk asked for their names, Cole told her, "Cole and Claire Mitchell."

"Right," the clerk said with one eyebrow raised. "It's none of my business, but you two clearly are not married," she said as she handed over the key card.

*   *   *

When the elevator doors closed, their bodies pressed together, hands moving everywhere as they started to undress each other. Claire unsnapped Cole's shirt in one quick move, leaving him bare chested. She stood back and gazed at his muscular chest, running her hands over his smooth skin. "Oh yes."

Cole tugged Claire's cardigan off her as he locked his mouth onto hers. They reached their floor and the doors opened, revealing an older couple dressed up to go out. All four looked startled. Cole closed his shirt and they walked past the couple, holding hands with their eyes down. Once the elevator doors had shut, with the onlookers safely behind them, Cole swept Claire up in his arms and practically ran down the hall to their suite. He had to put her down to try the key card. They frantically waited for the door to unlock.

"Come on, come on," he said as he jammed the card into the reader a third time. Finally, the green light came on and Cole shoved the door open, pulling Claire with him by the hand. The door shut behind them as they stood in the entrance to the bright suite, grabbing at each other's clothes. Claire pulled Cole's shirt the rest of the way off and threw it to the floor, yanking at the front of his jeans greedily. With no belt to contend with, she was able to just tug at the buttons, popping them open. Cole helped pull his pants down and then leaned against the wall to tear off his boots and socks. His jeans finally came all the way off as Claire tried unsuccessfully to unzip her dress at the back. Cole spun her around and unzipped it for her then slid it off her shoulders with his fingers, letting it drop to the floor at her feet. He hastily unfastened her bra and spun her back to face him. She grabbed at his boxer briefs, yanking them down unceremoniously before staring directly at his erection and breathing out, making a little *O* with her mouth. "I missed that."

Cole yanked at her lacy thong with such force that it ripped open.

"Oh shit, sorry," he said as he pulled her to him by her hips.

Their kisses became frantic, so full of need and desire that they both could have come if they had stayed there, groping each other long enough. Cole picked Claire up by her bottom and pressed her up against the wall with her legs wrapped around his waist. He started grinding his hips into her and she could feel him rubbing along the length of her sex. Claire clawed at his back, pulling him closer to her. "Oh, now, Cole, right now!"

Cole groaned with desire and carried her over to a low footstool positioned neatly in front of an armchair. He sat down on it with her still wrapped around him. "I want you on top, so I don't hurt you," he said, pausing between words to kiss her and suck on her bottom lip.

Claire grabbed the back of Cole's head and gave him a fierce look. "I'm fine. And I'm not waiting another minute."

She lowered her legs until her feet reached the floor and lifted her hips up off him, rubbing his lower abdomen with her wet heat. Cole held the base of his erection and guided it to her until she pushed herself down over it.

"Oh!" They both gasped as he entered her completely. Claire rocked her hips in circles as she pushed against him, tightening her pelvic muscles as she moved.

"Claire, slow down. I don't think I'm going to last for you," Cole whispered as she started grinding her hips faster.

"I'm so close, Cole, don't stop me. I need to come now, and I want to feel you come with me," she gasped. "Give it to me, Cole, please," she breathed.

Cole grabbed her ass with both hands and pushed her down onto his cock forcefully. The effect was immediate, causing the pair to climax simultaneously. Claire cried out, "Yes! Cole! Yes! Just like that! Yes!"

Cole lifted her up and down on his lap, both of their bodies pulsing with delirium. Claire could feel him jerk inside her with each release as she tightened herself around him to squeeze out every drop he had. She bit down on his collarbone to keep from crying out again. Wrapping her hair around his fist, Cole pulled her head back so he could kiss her mouth as he finished. Their tongues found each other again as they panted with exertion.

Claire sat on Cole with her core tight around him for a long time, trying to recover. They pressed their foreheads together, trying to catch their breath. She sucked on his earlobe and kissed the base of his neck and his collarbone, where she had bit down. Cole moved his hands up to her back, embracing her fully to keep her close. He could never get close enough— never get enough of her—even in this moment.

"Are you okay?" Cole asked, suddenly remembering her injuries.

Claire nodded, her eyes welling up with tears. "I've never felt this good, I promise."

"Are you crying?" he asked, bringing his hands up to hold her face.

Claire nodded. Cole looked at her with such tender concern. "What's wrong? Did I hurt you?"

Claire shook her head. She tried to look down,

but Cole tilted her face up to his and held her gaze with his eyes. "No, of course not. It's just that I've never felt so loved before. It's just *so* much, you know?"

Cole hugged her tighter. "You deserve to be worshipped. You're perfect, Claire. You're *my* perfect Claire. I thought I had lost you to Antonio, and then I thought I might lose you to your accident. I don't want to ever lose you. I won't ever let you go."

Claire's eyes shone with tears of pure bliss. This moment, with this magnificent, muscular, sexy and sweet man, was the most romantic moment of her life so far. They sat like that until Claire felt a little shudder go up her spine from growing chilly.

"You're getting cold. Let's go shower and then get some food," Cole said.

"You read my mind," Claire said, slowly getting up from his lap.

She looked around the room. "Wow! This is an amazing room. I didn't even notice until now. It's huge! And check out that bed!" She walked over to the French doors that led to the balcony. "We have a balcony, and look at that view of the city, with the mountains in the background! Mr. Mitchell, this is going to cost you a fortune!" She glanced over at him with wide eyes, looking concerned.

Cole shrugged, enjoying her enthusiasm. "Totally worth it. That view is only made better by you standing in front of it so wonderfully naked.

Wow." Cole paused, looking thoughtful. "Although, you could stand in front of a Dumpster nude, and I would enjoy the view."

Claire laughed. "Let's check out the bathroom." She wandered in. "Oh my God! It's enormous! Not as big as you of course, but still very nice." She poked her head out and winked at him. "Let's forget the shower and have a bath instead. It's a soaker tub with jets, and it looks like it would fit at least four people."

Cole cocked his head to the side. "Are you planning to invite guests? You are a kinky girl, aren't you?" he teased as he followed her into the bathroom. His thoughts wandered to the first time he had stayed in a hotel with Gabriela. She had been so unimpressed with their surroundings, having grown up rich. Her own childhood bedroom would probably have been twice the size of this suite. He remembered feeling disappointed at how cavalier she was about everything, as though nothing had much appeal to her, other than him for a little while.

He walked into the bathroom and found Claire bending over to turn on the taps and pour some bubble bath into the tub. Cole gave a low whistle, causing Claire to straighten up. "No, no, do that again."

The sun was starting to set outside, giving the bathroom a soft pinkish hue that made Claire look all the more lovely. She stepped into the tub and slid into the water, motioning for him to come join her. Cole got into the tub behind her, even though there was ample room on either side of her for him to sit down. He pulled her shoulders back to rest her upper body on his chest.

"Come here, sexy girl."

She rested against him, loving the feeling of his hands skimming over her tummy and chest in a slow, lazy motion.

"Tell me about one of your exes, Cole," she said suddenly.

His hands stopped. "That might kill the moment, don't you think?"

"No. I want to know all about you. I feel like I don't know anything about your past, or how you got to be who you are. I thought maybe if you told me a story about someone you dated, I would get a glimpse. It doesn't have to be anything tragic or major. Maybe you have a funny story you want to share with me? Something that makes you smile when you think of it?"

"Hmm, well, that's a tricky one. Let me think for a minute." He went back to caressing her with his fingers. "It's just so hard to think when you're completely naked in my arms. I am not getting enough oxygen to my brain."

"Quit stalling, Cowboy."

"Okay, I'll tell you about the first girl I ever slept with," he replied. "I was seventeen, and she was probably in her early twenties, I guess. She was the niece of a friend of our family, visiting here from New York for a summer. She had never been on a horse, and her family brought her over to go on a trail ride. She enjoyed it and asked if she could come back for riding lessons while she was here in Colorado. Her uncle dropped her off every Wednesday on the way to his golf lesson and picked her up after it was over. A few weeks into this, she decided she wanted to ride something other than a horse, and I was more than happy to oblige.

"The first time we had sex was in the stables. The whole thing took about two minutes but she handled it well. She must have been expecting it to go quickly, because she gave me another shot the next week. Well, the fourth week, her uncle drops her off as usual and then heads off himself. We go into the stables and get undressed, only she didn't realize she had forgotten her helmet in the car. Being the concerned uncle that he was, he drove straight back and came to the stables. He found me with his niece bent over in one of the stalls, going to town. She started screaming, he started yelling and I started running. He grabbed a rake and dashed after me. I must have run clear across the pasture, buck-naked, dick pointed straight in front of me, before he gave up. Needless to say, I never did get paid for those lessons. We also stopped getting invited to their family barbecues."

Claire laughed as he told the story. "I can almost

see you running. In fact . . . I would like to see you running naked with an erection. Is there any way we can replay that scene sometime?"

"Not likely—it's not as sexy as it sounds," Cole replied.

"What was her name?"

"Jessica."

"I say we order some food and some champagne and drink to Jessica," Claire said.

"You sure you don't want to go out for supper? We still haven't had a proper date yet."

"I don't think I'll ever want to leave this hotel room. Besides, someone who doesn't know his own strength tore my panties apart, and I don't have another pair with me."

"I actually prefer to go on dates with women who don't have panties on. But since you're so happy here, we should stay," Cole replied. "What do you feel like eating? And don't say 'just a salad,' 'cause I know you're not that kind of girl."

"You do know me. I would kill for a clubhouse sandwich and fries right now."

Cole ordered their meal using the phone next to the tub. "We've got fifteen minutes," he said as he placed the receiver back into its cradle and Claire reached forward to turn on the hot water.

"Ah, that's better," he said as she turned the water off and settled back in between his legs. "Now you tell me about your first time."

Claire leaned her head toward his chest and stroked his arms. "This story isn't funny like yours, but I suppose it's only fair that I tell you. As you know, my parents died in a car accident the summer I was nineteen. I felt exactly as lonely and empty as you might expect. That fall when I started college, I was completely numb. I went to a frat party the first week of school and met a guy, Todd, who seemed nice enough. He was a pledge. We got to talking, and I told him about my parents. He got me a couple of beers and stayed with me for the evening, showing me a nice time. He said he wanted me to feel better, even if just for the night. I wanted to feel something other than numb, so I agreed to go upstairs with him to make out. I thought since I was in college, I better hurry up and have sex, so I decided that would be the night. The whole thing was over in a few minutes. Todd said he would call, but of course he didn't. I found out later it was part of his pledge requirement. Pretty soon, it seemed like everyone on campus knew about it." Claire paused for a moment, and Cole hugged her tightly. "Oh well, at least it was before the days of camera phones. My humiliation was limited to rumours spread by some idiots. If it happened now, the whole thing would be uploaded to Facebook or something."

Cole pressed his lips to her temple. "That is a fucking awful story. I hope I run into Todd someday so I can kick his ass."

Claire laughed. "Better yet, you hold him, I'll kick his ass."

"I like your style, Ms. Hatley," Cole replied.

They were interrupted by a knock at the door. Cole climbed out of the tub and wrapped himself in a robe. "Meet me in the bedroom?" he asked.

"Be right there."

* * *

Claire raised her wine glass. "To Jessica!" she said.

Cole clinked his glass to hers. "To Jessica, wherever she may be," he said with a formal nod.

The two sat on the balcony in bathrobes, eating supper and enjoying the warm night air.

"Claire, how come you didn't have a boyfriend before you were in college?"

Claire looked a little embarrassed. "I was a chubby nerd. Teenage boys aren't exactly into fat girls or smart girls, and they certainly don't want to date a girl that is both of those things."

Cole nodded his head. "Boys are fucking idiots until they're almost thirty."

Claire laughed. "I've often wondered about that."

Cole's face suddenly turned serious. "Do you want to hear about the first time I made love that really mattered?"

Claire gave him an intrigued look. "Yeah. That I would like to hear."

"Well"—Cole gave her a little grin as he began—"I took this sexy-as-hell chef fridge shopping once. It turns out she had some type of appliance fetish, so lucky me that I didn't send someone else with her. I wanted to be with her from the moment I first laid eyes on her. She was in her car, putting her hair in a ponytail and putting on some lip gloss, and there was just something about her that got to me. Anyway, a few weeks later we went and bought a fridge. We got back to the ranch after she wolfed down a burger and fries, and she jumped right on me and we made love right outside in the daylight, then in the shower, then in my bed . . ."

"Sounds hot. Maybe I could get a replay of that night?"

"Sure, it was actually more amazing than it sounds. I just have to save up for another fridge," he said as he refilled their wine glasses.

Claire laughed. "I was thinking of testing out that bed. Wanna come?"

Cole grinned back at her. "I always want to come with you."

"That was too easy," she said. "Oh, just heard it myself. I said *easy*."

Cole stood up and took Claire's hands, pulling her up to him. He opened the French doors to the room and led her over to the bed and then turned her to face him. He lowered his mouth to hers, tasting the wine on her lips. Untying the sash of her bathrobe as he kissed her, Cole parted the robe and placed his hands on her hips and then ran them over her back and bottom. Claire shivered at the feel of his fingers barely touching her. She could tell that he was already hard, and the thought of him inside her, along with the feeling of his skin on hers, had her moaning with desire.

With one hand behind Cole's neck, Claire used her other to open his bathrobe. She touched his chest with her fingers, feeling his muscles flex. She could feel a shift in their connection to each other; it was somehow more intimate than before. In that moment, her heart was so full of emotion it felt like it might burst.

Cole took his time, exploring her with his hands. He slowly moved them up and down her back then slid them up her sides, feeling the curve of her breasts with his thumbs. He brought his hands up to her shoulders, causing her bathrobe to fall to the floor. Her shudder as the cool air touched her body brought out Cole's protective instinct. He opened his own robe, wrapping it around her. She was so tiny in his arms, and his heart stirred at the thought of always wanting to keep her warm and safe.

He picked her up and carried her to the bed, placing her head on the pillow. Standing up, he rolled his shoulders a bit, causing his robe to slide off as Claire got under the covers. She looked him up and down, watching his sculpted form as he climbed into bed, lying on his side, facing her. She lifted the covers over Cole so they were cozy and warm together.

Using one hand to prop his head up, Cole slowly traced the curves of her body with his other, as though painting a picture of her. His eyes followed his finger as he took in the view of her completely nude.

He was the first man Claire had allowed to see her like this without feeling at all self-conscious. The look in his eyes was just about the sexiest thing she had ever seen. His expression, along with the feeling of his finger brushing against her skin ever so lightly made her tingle with anticipation.

"You have perfect breasts," he said as he made slow circles around her nipples and then ran his tongue over each one. Claire arched her back, wanting him to take her breast in his mouth, but he moved on, brushing his finger, followed by his tongue, down her in a straight line from the space between her breasts to her belly button.

He moved over to one of her hips. "I love how your body curves right here," he whispered and then traced his finger across to the other hip. "And here."

Cole continued to move his finger over to her inner thigh and then his mouth followed. Claire lifted her ass a little, willing him to move over to her centre, but he proceeded down the inside of her thigh instead. Claire let out a little sigh of frustration, causing Cole to stop and look at her with a hint of amusement.

"Hmm, somebody is getting impatient . . ." he teased as he kept moving down toward her foot. "I intend to take my time."

Once at her ankle, he moved over to the other one and back up her other leg. When he reached the top of her inner thigh again, just inches from where she wanted him, he flipped her over so she was lying on her stomach. Claire let out a little gasp of surprise.

Cole groaned at the sight of her naked backside as he moved her hair to one side and kissed her neck. He let his fingers travel along her spine all the way to the top of her ass, causing her to shiver.

"I feel bad for you, Claire. You're never going to get to see this flawless ass." He continued using his finger and tongue to caress her bottom until he reached the top of her legs. She tilted herself toward his mouth to offer him full access to her. Instead of taking advantage of the opportunity, he hovered for a moment before starting down the inside of the back of her leg. Using his large, skilled hands, he massaged her ankles, feet and legs with such methodical movements that it seemed as though he were trying to touch every inch of her.

"You're perfect." He skimmed his hands over her ass and then started massaging her back, shoulders and neck, then her arms, one at a time. Claire sighed, this time with the bliss of being touched, adored and cared for.

"Oh, I forgot something," he said as he moved his hands back down to her ass. He rubbed her bottom, teasing her, with his thumbs getting closer to her core and then moving away. Claire tilted herself up again, this time rewarded by his thumbs gliding slowly along her sex. She moaned as he brought the tips of his thumbs in further. He kept them there, caressing her, feeling how hot and wet she was before moving his hands under her hips and lifting her up onto her knees. Claire turned her head and looked over her shoulder, her face flushed with excitement. Cole answered her look with his eyes full of lust as he lowered his mouth over her ass.

With deliberate strokes of his tongue along the length of her, he brought her breathing to a quickened, almost frantic pace. She tried to wriggle from side to side as his tongue reached her centre, but he refused to stop there or plunge his tongue into her as she ached for him to. Instead, he followed his tongue with his hand, rubbing her sex and slipping one finger in only as far as its tip, stroking just barely inside her.

Claire felt as though she would burst if he didn't bury himself inside her, either with his tongue or his erection. The moan that escaped her throat was one of complete desperation. Cole had been rock hard the entire time he was touching and massaging her, excited by what was going to happen, excited by his ability to give so much pleasure, knowing how badly she wanted him even though she had just had him such a short time earlier.

Claire splayed her knees apart, lowering her body closer to the mattress and opening her core to him, her breath and the small circles she made with her hips indicating that she was begging him to enter her.

"You are so fucking sexy," he growled as he moved his mouth along her spine up toward her neck. When his lips settled on the nape of her neck, he lowered his body to cover hers. Holding himself up with one hand, Cole wrapped the other hand under her and pressed his fingers against her sex.

Claire gasped, silently pleading for him to take her as she turned her head to bring her cheek close to his, her mouth searching for his. He slid his fingers inside her slowly as he plunged his tongue into her mouth. Her lips opened to hungrily accept it.

Cole took his fingers out and held his length in his hand, pressing it to her sex, teasing her with it and then spanking her with three hard slaps. Claire pushed her body back onto his length on the third motion, rocking her hips from side to side to bury him inside her. Cole let out a low moan and pulled himself out slowly almost all the way. Claire let out another shameless cry of pleading. She was far beyond the ability to refrain from begging now.

Cole thrust himself inside her to the hilt in one quick move, feeling her tighten around him with such force as to never let him go. The feeling was explosive for them both. There was no stopping it now. They were both overtaken by a need so primitive and overwhelming they had to obey it. Cole pulled himself back halfway and then plunged in again, feeling himself move in and out with his fingers over her sex. He rocked his hips in an upward motion when he reached the end of each thrust, lifting her off the bed a little each time. He held her firmly with his hand, pulling himself back and forth over and over. She could feel his entire body working to fuck her, his powerful legs against the backs of her thighs, his arm that kept him from collapsing on her, his core as he slammed himself into her, his hand that rubbed her and secured himself inside her. She was completely filled with him and had never felt such a strong need to come in her life.

"You're so wet, so tight. I want you to come all over me, Claire. I want to feel you coming."

"Yes, yes, Cole." She could hardly speak. "I'm ready," she said, urging him to increase his pace and his force.

She turned her head to reach his mouth again. Their tongues melded together frantically as their bodies reached the breaking point. He continued to ram himself into her until they both came with a violent pleasure. She pushed her ass into him with all the strength remaining in her arms to accept his orgasm and fuel her own. They remained fused together for a long time until they collapsed to the bed, exhausted. Cole lay on top of her, his legs entwined with hers, with his cheek pressed to hers, wet with sweat. Claire felt the full weight of him on her body, connecting her to the bed, keeping her warm. Slowly, they caught their breath, feeling completely satisfied for the first time in weeks.

"I love you," Cole whispered so quietly it was almost inaudible.

Tears welled up in Claire's eyes. "I love you too."

He pulled off her, bringing himself to lie beside her. Claire rolled onto her side to face him. Their lips met for lingering, sweet kisses until the need for sleep overtook Claire. She flipped over and pushed her naked body into him. Cole wrapped his top arm over her and laced his fingers into hers so their hands were nestled against her chest.

A few minutes later as they were drifting off to sleep, Cole said, "Claire? If I had known you when you were a teenager, I would have wanted to be with you. I know I would have seen you. You know? Really seen you."

"How do you do that?" Claire asked, turning her face to his.

"Do what?"

"How do you take something that hurt me and make it okay?" Claire asked.

"It's a gift," Cole said, lifting his eyebrows, trying to sound mysterious.

"I'm serious. You're incredible." Claire lifted her head and kissed him. "You'd better be careful, Cole. If you keep this up, you're never going to get rid of me."

"That's my plan," he said, scooping her into his arms and closing his eyes. "Now, let me get some sleep. I have a sexy girlfriend who's a bottomless lust pit. I need to rest up so I can try to keep her satisfied."

Claire giggled and closed her eyes, feeling completely peaceful.

* * *

Sometime in the middle of the night, the pair found themselves ready for each other again, making love slowly this time as the moon shone through the French doors. When it was over they lay together, bodies sweaty and entwined, in the silvery light that fell upon them.

Cole lay on his back and Claire on her tummy, resting her head on his chest. Claire lazily caressed Cole's chest with her hand. "Tell me about your parents, Claire," he said suddenly.

Claire lifted her head and looked at him for a moment. "You know, most people are uncomfortable talking about my parents once they know they're dead. It's too sad, and they don't know what to say. Not you, though. You just dive right in. I love that about you."

"They're your parents. I want to know about them."

Claire nodded. "Well, my mom, Vivian, was a beautiful woman. She had brilliant blue eyes and blond hair that shone in the sunlight. I can still hear her warm laugh in my mind, and she had a great sense of humour; she loved to tease my dad and us girls. She played the cello and gave lessons at our house in the evenings and on weekends. I still love the low sound of the cello. It makes me feel calm and peaceful. My parents were quite young when they had my sister—only twenty. They got married shortly before she was born and made a go of it.

"My dad, Conrad, was a family lawyer. He somehow managed to finish his law degree while working full time to support us. He had quite a successful practice. He's the reason my sister, Janet, is a lawyer now. He was tall with black hair and green eyes, and he loved to cook. I used to spend hours with him cooking and creating new recipes. When he was in the kitchen, I got to experiment with whatever ingredients I wanted. Sometimes my mom would get a little pissed if I ruined, say, the shrimp she had bought by putting them into some new sauce I'd created that tasted awful. She would say, 'Can't you let her practise with just one or two shrimp? Why *all* of them?' Dad would just smile and say, 'My Claire is creating art, and I will not stand in the way of that. Someday, she will be the world's greatest chef!'"

"They sound wonderful."

"They really were. They were one of those couples that just belonged together. They started dating in senior year, and even at the end, they couldn't get enough of each other. They were always laughing, talking or touching each other. On Friday nights, they would have an at-home date. They would make pizza for us, and my mom would put us to bed, while my dad would whip up some fabulous meal for the two of them. They would light candles and eat and talk. They set the standards of what love should be pretty high for us. My sister and her husband, Ted, are like them. They've been together since high school. I always wanted what they had, that connection— you know? I thought I'd meet my soulmate before I was twenty and that would be that. But here I am, at thirty-one, still searching."

Cole kissed her on the forehead. "Well, maybe you've had a longer search, but I'm here now."

Claire's eyes filled with tears. "You are, aren't you?" she whispered.

TWELVE

As they drove back to the ranch in the morning, Cole reached for Claire's hand, kissing her knuckles. "I'm wishing we had another week in that hotel room."

"It's kind of nice being the guest for once, isn't it?"

"It *is*. We're going to have to promise ourselves we'll do it again as soon as we get a chance. No guests till tomorrow, though, so we'll have two more nights before the next cattle drive anyway."

"I can think of a few ways to spend it. But for the moment, let's think about where we'll go when we get another chance to get away."

"Hmm, well, my parents spent a few weeks down in Mexico over the winter. They made it to a place called Tulum, which looked pretty perfect to me. I'd love to take you there, find some secluded beach to laze around on, do some swimming and some other fun things together . . ."

"Sounds wonderful," Claire said, reaching her hand up and rubbing the back of his neck. "Say, I must have been in such a sexual daze last night, I forgot to ask about your parents! I just realized I don't know the first thing about them."

"Oh, right, well, you'll meet them sometime soon, I expect. They usually show up every few months for a visit. They stay for a couple of weeks and then get back on the road. They bought an enormous RV, and after years of running the ranch, they're seeing the world. They've been travelling up in Canada since May. I think you'll like them, and I know they'll like you.

"My mom, Mary, is a great horsewoman and is tough as nails. She doesn't mince words, and you always know where you stand with her. She married my dad when she was nineteen. She kept all the books for the ranch. My dad, Jake, grew up on the ranch and is one of the most respected horse trainers in the state. He's really patient and pretty quiet most of the time, but he has a dry sense of humour, and he can tell a great story once he's had a beer or two."

"Well, I look forward to meeting them sometime," Claire said. "What are they like together?"

"I would say they aren't necessarily passionate like your parents were, at least not that we saw, but they're definitely great partners. They both work hard, and they work well together."

"That's important."

They drove for a while in silence before Cole spoke up again. "I'm almost sorry we have to go back home today. I would like it if we could just keep driving and go somewhere with no responsibilities for a while."

"Me too, but at least we'll be together for now. I love that we can sneak over and see each other whenever we get a chance."

"That is a great perk, isn't it?" Cole smiled. "I love how you always try to look at the positive side."

They pulled into the ranch a few minutes later and parked. Claire put her hand on the door handle.

"Wait! Allow me, my lady. We haven't had a proper date, but I can give you a preview of what it will be like." He got out and walked around to her side of the truck, opening the door and holding out his hand for her.

Claire took it and stepped down. "Thank you, Cowboy. It seems like you have some real potential."

Cole spun her over to him, grabbing her around the waist with both hands, pulling her close and kissing her long and deep.

"How's that for potential?" he asked.

"Not bad, I guess. What else you got?" she retorted with a sexy grin.

"This . . ." he said in a low tone as he kissed her hard on the mouth. He lowered his hands to her ass and gave her a squeeze, lifting her dress up as he did and exposing her to the sun and the mountain air.

Claire could feel him getting hard against her stomach as she moved her hands up his chest and around his neck, causing her dress to lift even higher.

"There you—oh! Oh my!" came a woman's voice from across the parking lot.

"Oh shit," Cole muttered.

They quickly straightened themselves out, Cole tugging her dress down and Claire standing in front of him to hide his erection. She turned, her face bright red.

"Hi, Mom, hi, Dad. You're back!" Cole said in a weak voice.

"Oh shit is right," Claire whispered, overcome by complete panic.

There stood Cole's parents; his dad had a wide grin under his black cowboy hat, and his mom was wearing a shocked expression.

"Well, you must be Claire," his dad said heartily, walking forward to meet them, pulling his wife with him.

Cole and Claire stood rooted to the spot, mortified.

When they reached them, Cole's dad hugged Cole and then reached his hand out to Claire. "I'm Jake, nice to see you," he said, still with that same amused look.

Claire took his hand and meekly said, "Nice to meet you, sir."

Cole's mom looked her square in the eye. "No need for such formalities now that we've seen your bottom. That's a surprising lack of underwear. I hope that's not how you dress when you're cooking. It's certainly against health codes."

Claire's face burned with humiliation. "No. No, of course not. I always wear underwear. Well, not always . . . I mean, not in the shower, but otherwise, I'm very big on panties. Today was a special case, no, um, more *unusual* than special. It's not like I don't wear them on special occasions, because I do. I definitely do . . ." Claire's voice trailed off.

Cole gave her hand a little squeeze. "Claire was just about to go get changed and head over to the restaurant," he said, then turned to her and added, "See you in a bit, Claire."

Claire excused herself and walked away, wishing a sinkhole would open at that very moment and swallow her up.

Cole turned back to his parents and gave his mom a hug. "Good to see you Mom, Dad. I've missed you. It's lonely without you here."

His dad shot him a wry look. "You didn't look that lonely a minute ago. In fact, you looked like you had your hands full."

His mom fixed him with a disapproving look. "Honestly, Cole. You're messing around with the new chef? Does that seem like a smart way to run the ranch?"

Cole exhaled sharply. "I know it looks bad, Mom. But I know what I'm doing. It's going to sound crazy to you because she's only been here a couple of months, but I'm pretty sure I want to marry her."

"Is that so, son?" Jake replied, slapping Cole on the back. "Well, she looks real nice to me. I can see why you'd want to hold onto that." He gave a big, hearty laugh and walked over to the barn, leaving his son alone to face his mother's scowl.

* * *

"It's not funny," Claire hissed into her cellphone. "Stop laughing, you witch! Seriously, help me the fuck out."

Janet had spent the last three minutes trying to think of some way her sister could handle this situation and was only able to come up with a series of puns like "You sure were em-bare-assed!"

"Okay, okay. Sorry. For real, this time. I'm done," Janet said, still laughing. "There really is only one way to play this. You need to get dressed—including panties this time, maybe two pairs, just to be safe—and then go to the restaurant and cook a fabulous meal. Act professional, be very polite and try to have a good sense of humour about it, but only if someone else brings it up. Don't make light of it yourself. You don't want them to know you're a total floozy. Just laugh along if someone else brings it up."

"Alright, thank you. That makes a lot of sense. I don't know if I can do it, but it makes sense." Claire paused. "I'm thinking dark boot-cut jeans and a plaid button-up shirt, nothing too fitted or low cut."

"At this point, honey, you might as well just show them your tits. At least then they'll have seen the whole package!" Janet exploded with laughter again.

"I have to go. You're an awful human being. I love you. Goodbye." Claire hung up and switched into high gear.

She looked in the mirror. "Okay, Claire, now you really have to wow them with your professionalism and your cooking. You can do this."

She put her hair up in a ponytail, put on just a little makeup, jeans, the button-up plaid shirt and tan Skechers. She took a look in the mirror and decided to swap her push-up bra for a T-shirt bra instead. Once she had changed, she decided to do up one more button than she normally would at the top. *Alright, casual and yet respectable enough.*

She got a text message and grabbed her cellphone to read it. It was from Janet.

Hey, baby girl, I feel bad about laughing. Listen, you are a talented, smart, fabulous woman. If they don't like you because of one little awkward moment, fuck 'em. Love you.

Claire texted back: Thx. Love U 2.
She grabbed her keys and walked out the door.

Okay, Claire—professional, polite, sense of humour, wow them with your cooking.

* * *

When Claire opened the door to the kitchen, Alicia was already there, cleaning up from lunch. As soon as she saw Claire, she dropped her dishtowel and rushed over with her arms open. "Oh, Claire, I'm so happy about the test results!" she exclaimed, giving her a big hug.

Claire smiled. "Thanks, Alicia. It's just such a relief that all of that is over. How are you feeling?"

"A bit better today, which is nice. I'm hoping I've turned a corner here," Alicia replied as she turned back to the sink.

"Let me finish up. You've been covering my butt for weeks now. You should go rest or go visit with your in-laws."

"Speaking of covering your butt and my in-laws . . ." Alicia said with wide eyes and a little giggle.

"Oh shit. You heard about that?" Claire's face heated up again.

"Yeah, Mary came in a little while ago. She wanted to get my impression of you. I told her how terrific I think you are and that you're very professional and very good for Cole," Alicia answered.

"Oh, thank you, Alicia." Claire let out a big sigh. "I feel sick about what happened. Just sick."

"It's okay. She'll get to know you over the next couple of weeks, and she'll see what you're made of," Alicia said, hugging her back.

"I owe you big time. Anything you need, just ask," Claire said.

"Well, there is one thing . . ."

"Name it. Anything," Claire answered.

"I just really want to find out how you lost your panties." Alicia grinned.

Claire burst out laughing and covered her face with her hands. "Without going into too much detail, let's just say someone got a little overzealous yesterday afternoon when we checked into the hotel."

"Say no more. I get the picture." Alicia laughed. "You two have some heat going on, hey?"

"If it got any hotter, I'd get scorched," Claire said. "He's perfect. I just can't get enough of him. I want to be with him constantly, even just to talk with or look at him. Each minute apart feels like an hour."

"Sounds like the real thing," Alicia smiled at her. "I'm so glad. You would be my dream sister-in-law."

"You too," Claire said, "but I doubt I'd be Mary's dream daughter-in-law."

"Give it time. She'll come around when she gets to know you."

"I hope so. Now, you get out of this kitchen and get some rest!"

"Will do." Alicia grabbed her phone and headed for the door. "See you later!"

* * *

Claire spent the afternoon listening to the radio and cooking up a storm. She decided to go for simple home cooking with her own little elegant twists. She thought anything too fancy would be a mistake. For appetizers, she made grilled shrimp skewers with a touch of red chili pepper to add a bit of heat, as well as her signature hummus with a veggie platter and soft pitas. The main dish would be roasted carrots and potatoes with garlic and rosemary, grilled steak and mushrooms, and grilled asparagus. She made spinach and strawberry salad with candied pecans, goat cheese rolled in cinnamon, dried cranberries, and an Asian sesame dressing. Dessert would be chocolate mousse served in wine glasses with a dollop of whipped cream and shaved chocolate on top.

"Well," she said as she surveyed the results of her afternoon's work, "if this doesn't do it, nothing will."

"I'm sure it's going to do the trick," Cole said.

Claire started in surprise. "Oh, Cole, how long have you been standing there?"

"A couple of minutes. You seemed so lost in your work that I didn't want to disturb you. I also like the view." Cole crossed the room and kissed her on the lips. Claire felt herself melt into him, closing her eyes.

When he pulled back, she sighed happily and said, "Is it weird that I've been missing you all afternoon?"

"Not really. I am pretty amazing," he said with a mischievous grin.

"You are indeed, Mr. Mitchell," she said, resting her hand on his chest. Suddenly, her smile faded, replaced by an anxious look. "So, I made pretty much the worst first impression possible on your parents today."

"Well, it could have been worse, actually," he said, dipping a carrot in the hummus and popping it into his mouth. "You could have been smoking a crack pipe while I groped your ass."

Claire laughed at the image. "Good point. Okay, well, crack pipes aside, have you talked to your parents about me?"

She slapped the back of his hand, which was reaching for another carrot, then proceeded to smooth the hummus with the back of a teaspoon.

Cole smiled at her. "I may have. I can't really remember right now."

Claire lifted one eyebrow, clearly getting annoyed. "Cole, seriously. I need to know where I stand."

"I'm too hungry to think. Maybe if I had something more to eat I could remember." Cole grinned.

"Oh, fine, have a few veggies if you must," Claire replied, giving him an exasperated look, even though she was feeling more turned on than irritated by his teasing.

"Thanks!" Cole said, helping himself. "I told them I'm crazy about you and that I'm pretty sure I want to marry you even though I've known you for only two months."

Claire's heart pounded. "Really?" she asked quietly. "Did you really say that?"

"Yes, I did." He watched her, trying to read her reaction. "Do you think I'm crazy?"

"No," she said, her voice thick with emotion. "I think it makes perfect sense."

Cole lowered his head and gave her a lingering kiss. "I suppose we should go on a few dates before we decide for sure, though."

Claire laughed. "Are you asking me out on a date?"

"Yes. Are you up for it?"

"I'll get back to you. I have lots of other offers right now, so I should really weigh my options carefully." Claire turned back to the counter to finish the salad she was working on.

Cole walked up behind her, wrapped his arms around her waist and kissed the nape of her neck, then moved up to her earlobe, taking his time. He waited for Claire to make her little moan and then he asked, "How are my chances?"

Claire's voice came out in a whisper. "Pretty good."

Suddenly, she snapped out of her haze. "Ack! I have to get this supper on the table for your family, or I'll never redeem myself."

"How can I help?" Cole asked.

"How are your barbecue skills? I need to grill these shrimp skewers and then get the steaks cooking."

"I'm on it."

"Thanks, sexy." Claire's anxiety had been replaced by pure joy.

After Cole walked out to start the barbecue, Claire smiled to herself. *He wants to marry me.*

A few minutes later, Claire brought the shrimp out to the barbecue. Cole was scraping off the grill.

"You did it again, Cole," she said, putting the tray down on a small table next to the barbecue.

Cole looked up confused. "Did what?"

"You took a crappy situation and you made it better," she said, standing on her tiptoes to kiss him on the cheek.

"I better have. I'm the one who caused the situation in the first place," Cole answered.

"And here I thought it was my fault for being irresistible."

"Good point. I guess it is all your fault."

* * *

Dinner started off well. Claire had set up a long table on the restaurant patio so they could eat outside and enjoy the lake view. Everyone complimented her on the food, and as the evening wore on, Claire started to relax. It felt like a nice family dinner to her, something she hadn't realized she'd been missing out on for a long time. Around the table sat Jake, Mary, Ben, Alicia, Cole and Claire.

By the time Claire brought out dessert, she was feeling much more relaxed, having had a couple of glasses of wine before dinner and one with the meal. The sun was starting to set, and as everyone dug into the chocolate mousse, the view became the topic of conversation. The table went quiet for a moment, everyone taking in the sunset while enjoying the creamy flavours of the mousse.

Mary put her spoon down and cleared her throat. "So, Claire, have you been married before?"

Claire looked up in surprise, feeling her cheeks flush. "Um, no, I haven't, actually. I was in a long-term relationship for four years, but it didn't work out," she replied, hoping to put an end to the discussion.

"Oh, so were you giving the milk for free to that guy, too? You know they never marry you if you do that." Mary gave her a cold, hard look.

"Jesus, Mom!" Cole snapped. "That's enough."

"It's okay, Cole," Claire said, not breaking eye contact with Mary. "She's your mom, and she has the right to worry about you." She paused and took a sip of wine, fortifying herself. "I would worry, too, if the first time I met my son's new girlfriend she had her assets on display. I've been here only a couple of months, and it's a big gamble for us to be romantically involved since I'm your chef and you're trying to make a somewhat risky change to the ranch. Am I right so far, Mary?"

"That's about it," she answered, watching Claire carefully.

"I'm from Seattle, a big city on the ocean, so maybe I'll get sick of living in the country near the mountains and just up and leave. Maybe that concerns you too?"

"Should it?" Mary answered in an even tone.

"I can see why it would. You don't know me at all. Cole has known me only a matter of weeks, and he's putting a lot of faith in me. I can tell you I love it here, I feel alive here, and that running my own kitchen has always been my dream. I can also tell you how much I love your son." Claire paused as she poured herself another glass of wine. "But only time will tell, right? Give me a chance, though. I will prove that you can trust me and that I'll be good to Cole."

Jake spoke up. "Claire, I like you. You took the high road just now, which shows me two things. First, it shows me you're smart, because you can see the bigger picture and how getting drawn into a fight tonight would have hurt things long term. It also shows me that you care a lot about Cole, because it matters to you if things are good for the long haul. Besides, this was one of the most delicious meals I've had in a long time, so you get my vote right there."

"Thank you," Claire said quietly, giving him an appreciative look.

Jake smiled at her and then turned to his wife. "Besides, honey, maybe Cole takes after his old man, and he will actually buy the cow after getting the milk for free."

* * *

When Cole and Claire got into bed that night, Cole leaned over and beamed at her. "You know what? You impress me—and I mean *really* impress me. The way you handled my mother tonight was amazing. Most women would have either wilted under that kind of pressure or would have gone on the attack. But not you. You stood up for yourself without being unkind or sarcastic in any way. I hope this doesn't sound condescending, but I was really proud of you tonight."

Claire turned on her side to face Cole, leaning on one hand. "I know, right? I actually surprised *myself* with how I handled that. It was what you said this afternoon about being pretty sure you want to marry me that did it. I had a snippy retort on the tip of my tongue and then I thought 'this woman might be my mother-in-law.' I tried to put myself in her shoes, and I could imagine that if it were my son with some no-panty-wearing floozy, I would have some tough questions, too. And making what you and I have work, and making your life easier, after everything you've done to take care of me, is far more important than telling your mom that you don't buy a car without test driving it first."

"Oh, so I'm the car in this scenario, now?" Cole asked, trying to look hurt. "I tell you I'm proud of you and I want to marry you, and you compare me to a car you could either buy or leave on the lot?"

"Well, I can tell you the test drive has gone really well up to this point, so there is only a very slim chance I'll leave you on the lot," Claire said with a grin.

Cole reached around behind her and slapped her on the ass. "You're a bit mean, Ms. Hatley, you know that?"

Claire laughed. "I never claimed to be nice, Cowboy," she said, climbing on top of him, straddling his waist. "But I think I should go for a test ride again just to be sure."

"Oh, I see. So you think you can just climb up onto me and go for a ride whenever you want?"

Claire lifted her shirt over her head and tossed it on the floor, leaving herself fully nude. "Pretty much," she said as she moved her hips in a long, straight line back and forth over his erection.

Cole's eyes shifted to her breasts and his hands soon followed. "I'll let it go tonight, but the next four nights, forget it," he said, lifting his head up to give himself access to her luscious curves.

Claire giggled. "So, you're putting your foot down? I can't have you while you're on a cattle drive?"

Cole paused from sucking on her nipple, giving her a sexy little half grin. "That's right. A man's got to have some self-respect."

With that, he rolled them both over in one swift move, making Claire gasp of pleasure as he landed on top of her, the full weight of him pressing into her. His body felt warm and smooth and hard in all the right places as he lowered his mouth to hers. He nipped at Claire's top lip with his teeth, causing her eyes to fly open in surprise as he sucked the place he had bitten, to soothe her. Lifting himself onto his knees for a moment, he used both hands to take hold of Claire's hands, bringing them up over her head. He kissed her mouth, then moved his lips down to her breasts again, now heavy with desire. He took hold of both of her wrists with one hand and kept them over her head while he settled back onto her, her legs opening wider, almost of their own accord, to welcome him in.

Claire rested her feet on the back of his ass,

with her outer thighs resting on the mattress, and she tilted her hips as he rocked his hard length up and down her sex. She was wet with arousal and this slow movement felt so good and yet made her so urgently need to have him inside her that it was almost taunting in nature. She tried to reach down with one hand to steer him inside her, but he held her wrists firmly.

"Not yet, gorgeous," he murmured, causing her to whimper in spite of herself. He smiled a little as he kissed her long and hard, thrusting his tongue into her mouth and then pulling out. She nipped at his lip, trying to urge him to come back, but he moved his mouth over to her earlobe again, sucking on it in the most deliciously slow way, flicking it carefully with his tongue.

Claire tilted her body up and tried moving in circles to bring him inside her, but each time, he pulled back or moved forward, avoiding her attempts. She felt desperate with need, her sex throbbing so hard she could barely take it.

Cole propped himself up on the arm he was using to hold her wrists and used his other hand to trace her collarbone and then move down to her hips while he kissed her neck. He moved his hand back up lazily, brushing against her with the tips of his fingers and then gliding them over to her nipple to tug on it a little and then lick it. She arched her back at his touch, begging for some small relief from this torture. He moved over to the other nipple and gave it the same careful treatment.

The whole time, he continued moving with the same long, slow drags, feeling her become wetter and more engorged. Claire moaned and whimpered again. She had lost all restraint now. Cole was in complete control of both of their bodies and was taking his time in getting them to the end. He was so turned on by how shamelessly she wanted him and how she responded to each touch to her body. He was thick and hard with the pleasure of it all, getting wetter and wetter from rubbing against her ready sex.

Claire finally managed to grab hold of him, using tiny back and forth and side to side motions to bring the head of his length into her. "Yes," she moaned at the feeling of it. "Please, Cole, now," she whispered, looking at him with such yearning and pleading that he couldn't deny her any longer. He pushed his way inside her, bringing her the relief she so desired.

As he rocked back, Claire tightened around him in a vise-like grip in case Cole decided to slip out again. He pulled out almost to the tip and then plunged in all the way again. Claire could feel her orgasm coming on in one strong wave as he pushed into her farther, grinding his hips into her core when he was in all the way. Claire squeezed him with her tight sex as she locked her feet around the inside of his thighs, holding him firmly with her powerful runner's legs.

Cole watched her face as she came—first she bit the bottom lip of her beautiful, kissable mouth and then held it open, breathing heavily. He had never seen anything sexier in his life. Her eyes opened and locked with his as she came again. She lifted her head up, trying to reach him. He lowered his mouth over hers, closing his eyes as their tongues and lips joined. He had to fight with all his willpower not to come just then. He could feel her tremble with each wave of her climax.

When she was finished, she opened her eyes again, trying to catch her breath. Cole let go of her wrists and she moved her arms down, gripping his back and pulling him down to rest on her, embraced by her legs and arms. Cole's erection twitched inside her, still hard and ready. He pulled out, kissing her on the mouth as he did, and then lay beside her, giving her a moment to breathe. He caressed the length of her body with his fingers as he kissed her shoulder and arm.

Claire looked him up and down, seeing his erection waiting. It was her turn to torture him now. "Well, that was definitely passable. Thanks for that. Good night, Cowboy," she said, giving him a quick peck on the lips as she rolled over away from him and settled into her pillow.

Cole groaned even though he was enjoying her

playfulness. "If that was only passable, I better keep going."

He slid his hand between her legs and lifted the top one, holding it up and bringing his body in line with hers. He brought his top leg between hers and rubbed her sex with his thigh, rocking her back and forth. He took hold of his shaft with his hand, guiding it back inside her, still with one leg between hers and their bodies interlaced. Leaning on one hand, he shifted his body so his chest and head were angled over hers, giving him access to her mouth and breasts while he continued to push himself into her from behind.

He watched Claire, taking in the sight of her, with her long, brown waves of hair falling just to the top of her breasts, brushing against them. Her cheeks were pink with arousal, her eyes were closed and she panted in time with his movements.

"You're so beautiful," he said as he used his hand to brush her hair off her neck so he could plant kisses from her ear to her shoulder. Her eyes opened as he spoke, and she watched him, reaching behind his neck with her hand to pull him into her even further.

She suddenly felt a preview of the longing she would have over the next few days while he was away. She wouldn't be able to touch him or feel him inside her, and it made her heart ache and made her desperate in her lust for him all at the same time.

Cole seemed to sense the shift in her. It was as if he could read her mind. "It's going to be so hard for me to leave tomorrow, knowing exactly what I'll be missing."

Claire kissed him. "I don't think I could ever get enough of you."

Their bodies moved together, hungrily, full of passion, perfectly in sync. Cole held her face with his hand, locking his mouth over hers as he drove himself inside her over and over until he finally gave in to his need for release.

"Oh, fuck, Claire, you're so sexy," he growled as he felt his orgasm rip through his body. Claire tensed her muscles around him as she felt him coming inside her, the sensation of it bringing on another climax. Cole reached down and pressed firmly on her sex, making her tighter and causing her to come so hard everything went black for a second. They lay there, bodies intertwined and holding each other until they fell asleep with Cole still buried inside her.

THIRTEEN

The next morning seemed to greet the pair too early. The sun poured in through the window as they lay naked, still touching one another. Cole woke up and watched Claire sleep. The thought of riding off that day brought a sense of dread. He wanted to stay here in this bed with her and shut the world out forever. He smiled as Claire stirred and opened her eyes.

"Good morning, gorgeous," he said with his sexy grin.

Claire gave him a look of pure adoration. "That might be the best way ever to wake up," she said, her voice a little raspy from sleep.

Cole pulled her into a warm embrace. "I was just thinking about how I would like to stay in this bed with you forever," he said, kissing her shoulder.

Claire grinned at the thought. "That sounds nice. How could we arrange that?"

Cole thought for a moment. "Lottery tickets?"

She laughed. "Dare to dream."

Cole held her closer. "This is the first time in my life that I haven't wanted to go on a cattle drive. You're the only woman who has ever done that to me. It's almost physically painful that I have to leave for even a few days."

Claire caressed his arm with her hand. "You mean you're worried about blue balls?"

Cole laughed out loud at her crudeness. "No, I mean because I've got it so bad for you that I feel like I have to be near you at all times."

Claire shook her head. "Me too. The thought of it is so sad, which is just silly, because in five days, we'll be right back here. And yet, I have this crushing feeling in my chest when I think of you getting on your horse and leaving."

"Plus, you're such a nympho, how will you manage to go more than a day without sex?"

It was Claire's turn to laugh. "Oh, don't worry about me. I'll just wait for the UPS guy to show up."

"I hate that guy," Cole teased. "I could just kill him." He kissed her on the forehead and got out of bed.

Claire watched him cross the room. He looked like an athlete in the locker room, casually walking around, utterly unaware of his own nakedness.

"Well, in the meantime, do you want to join me for a shower? Your breasts look like they could use a lot of soap."

Feeling bold, Claire threw off the covers and looked down at her breasts. "They do like the feeling of your big hands soaping them up," she said. The sight of her nude body and the thought of his hands on her had him hard again.

They made love in the shower, losing track of time. As they hurried to get ready for the day, Claire asked, "So, Cole, how do I handle things with your parents while you're away?"

Cole pulled his T-shirt over his head. "Just be yourself. You won my dad over already, so that's easy. My mom might take a little longer, but I think she gained a lot of respect for you last night. They won't be here the whole time anyway. They're going to ride out with us today, camp for two nights with the group, then ride back."

He walked over to her, fully dressed, and gave her a kiss on the forehead. "I wish I could be here the whole time. You'll be okay, though. You're so wonderful, Mom'll figure it out soon enough."

Claire had thrown on her jeans and the button-up shirt from last night. "Thanks, Cowboy. I feel better," she said, pressing her hands to his muscular abs. "I better run back to my place and get dressed."

"You know, you should just move all your stuff over here. It's silly for you to be going back and forth all the time."

"Why, Cole," she said as she smiled coyly "are you asking me to move in with you?"

Cole looked down at his feet and then raised his eyes to hers. "Too soon?"

"Logically? Yes. But it does feel right, doesn't it?" she said, wrapping her arms around his neck and kissing him hard on the mouth.

When they broke their kiss, she said, "Let's wait until your parents leave. I don't think it would play out well if we did it now."

"If that makes you more comfortable, okay. But you know, Claire, we're grown-ups, and I don't let them make my decisions for me. It seems a little silly pretending you aren't sleeping here when we all know the truth."

"I know. Of course you're right, but I'd rather just wait anyway. Just in case your mom doesn't warm up to me, okay?" Claire replied.

"Okay. As long as you won't stop sleeping here in the meantime," he said, locking his arms around her waist.

"Sure. Does that include with the UPS guy while you're away, or should I take him to my place instead?" she asked with a wicked grin.

"Grr . . ." He nipped at her lip and squeezed her bottom. "You could drive a man crazy."

"That's my goal," she said, winking at him. "See you at breakfast?"

"Not if the UPS guy is there."

Claire laughed and rushed down the stairs, calling back, "Don't worry! He's scheduled to deliver the package sometime between three and five!"

* * *

The next few hours were a flurry of activity, with everyone preparing for the arrival of new guests. Three families were meeting for a reunion of sorts. They had all been to the ranch before, so they were going to saddle up on the same horses they had the last time they stayed and head out right after lunch.

Claire had made a large fruit tray with a yogurt dip, a salad, burgers and sweet potato fries with an aioli dip for lunch. She and Alicia had all the camping food packed up before the meal was served.

Cole was busy greeting the guests, taking care of the logistics and making sure all the cattle and horses would be ready to go on time. By lunch, he and Claire were both feeling sad for having to say goodbye for a few days.

Cole's mom had been busy as well, getting herself packed and her own horse ready for the ride. She had been very polite to Claire at breakfast, but things were definitely awkward between them.

At lunch, Claire and Cole ate alone on the patio in the shade after she had served all the guests. When it was time for the group to head out, Claire walked down to the stables with Alicia and Ben to see them off. Claire went over to Cole as he got ready to mount Dudley. He looked down at her and smiled as she approached, pulling her in for a long hug, pressing his lips to the top of her head.

"I'm going to miss you," he said softly, "but at least I'll have the memory of last night and this morning to hold me over until I'm back."

"Me too," Claire said. "No man has ever made me whimper or beg before."

"Good," he replied, smirking a little. "What are you going to do with yourself while we're gone?" he asked.

"Probably run and swim a little and maybe head into town. See if I can find a Victoria's Secret store. I need some new panties. Someone wrecked my favourite pair." She rolled her eyes, trying to look annoyed.

"Oh, now *that's* a shopping trip I would gladly go on." He smiled down at her and gave her a light kiss on the lips. "How am I supposed to sleep with that thought on my mind?"

"You can lie awake in your tent, knowing that I'm in bed thinking of you and touching myself," she said very quietly so no one else would hear.

Claire could feel his erection straining against his jeans, and she liked knowing she had this effect on him. Cole's face looked almost pained. "Okay, gorgeous, take it easy. If I get on my horse with a raging hard-on, I could break something."

Claire giggled. "That won't do. I'll need your something when you get back."

Cole gave her a big, tight hug and another gentle kiss. "I'd better go. I love you."

"I love you too."

As she watched him ride away, leading the group, she was certain he was just about the sexiest man she had ever laid eyes on, and she couldn't believe he was hers.

* * *

That evening, as Cole kept the campfire going, Mary came and sat beside him on a fallen log. She put an arm around him and sighed. "Oh, my sweet boy. You and Ben are the only things that make me not want to travel. I miss you both so much when we're away."

"Us too, Mom. But I'm happy you and Dad get this time to travel together. It's what you've always dreamed of doing."

They sat for a moment staring at the fire.

"So, Cole, I imagine you think I was pretty unfair to Claire last night," she said.

"Yeah, I do. I was really disappointed you decided to go after her like that, especially in front of everyone. That was uncalled for. If you have concerns about choices I'm making, I'd much prefer you to talk to me privately," Cole responded.

"You're right. I'm sorry about how I handled things."

"You need to make that apology to Claire, Mom. Not to me."

"Okay, I can do that for you. But I'm worried, Cole. She's got you so you aren't even thinking straight. Carrying on in the parking lot in broad daylight with the chef, of all people! And no panties? Come on, Cole! You're supposed to be smarter than that."

"Alright, calm down. I know that wasn't the best choice, but it's not exactly a habit of ours. And anyway, it wasn't her fault she wasn't wearing any underwear. It's a long story, just trust me on that."

"I raised you better than to fool around with an employee. What do you really even know about her?"

"I know a lot, actually. I know she is kind-hearted and honest and smart as hell. She has a great sense of humour and always tries to see the positive side of things. She's not afraid of hard work either, which I know you respect. In fact, in her interview, she didn't even hesitate when I told her the job included cleaning up. She just said she was happy to be a part of building something from the ground up, even if it meant scrubbing counters. She's a *chef* and yet she goes in every day and cleans without complaining. She's excited about the potential the ranch has, she wants to be a part of it and I want to share it with her."

Mary watched him talk. "You just haven't known her long enough to understand what she's really all about. That takes a lot of time. You talk about her being the chef as if it's okay for you to be involved with someone who works here, but it's not! I'm just shocked that you would jump into bed with her as soon as she came along. If you two have a falling out, it's not just you who will get hurt. The ranch will suffer along with you."

"Don't you think I've thought of that? Of course I have. But Claire and I are both professionals. If it doesn't work out between us, we'd make things work long enough to find another chef. I've made good choices as far as the ranch is concerned. Nobody is more committed to it than I am, so you'll just have to trust that I know what I'm doing."

"I do, Cole. Just promise me you'll slow down a bit with Claire. Take the time to really get to know her, and not just how she is in bed. There's more to life than that."

"I *have* gotten to know her, Mom, and honestly, I can tell you I've never felt this way about anyone before."

"I seem to remember you saying you had never felt that way when Gabriela came along, too. You didn't really know her either before she suddenly moved in with you. I didn't say anything that time, even though we could all see what she was about. A year later, she broke your heart. I'm not going to stay silent this time and watch you get hurt again."

Cole sighed heavily. "Claire is nothing like Gabriela. They couldn't be more different. Claire and I have so much in common—she loves riding and being out in nature, and she has this sweet way of talking to Nellie and Otis. Otis just follows her everywhere, he might as well be her dog. Gabriela never even so much as glanced at him. She's so . . . I don't know . . . real, and the way I feel about her, and about myself when I'm with her, is completely different. She loves me for who I am, Mom. She doesn't want me to be anyone other than myself. I'm enough for her and so is the ranch life. I'm at my best when she's around, which is not at all what it was like with Gabriela."

"How can you possibly know if the ranch life will be enough for her after only two months? It might seem pretty good to her right now when you two are hot and heavy, but a few years from now, if the economy takes another turn and things get tough, will she really be here?

Cole sighed in defeat. "You done?"

"No, I have one other thing to say, and I know you won't want to hear it. But you need to consider the possibility that she might be after your money. She might be one of those women who tries to attach herself to a man, hoping for a big windfall."

Cole burst out in a sarcastic laugh at hearing this. "You just couldn't be more wrong. She has her own money. Her parents died and left her some big inheritance. Big enough that her ex showed up with an engagement ring trying to get her back so he could start his own business." Cole reached down to pick up a log and toss it onto the fire. "Stop jumping to conclusions, alright? Gabriela was a *huge* mistake. I know that better than anyone, so you can quit throwing it back in my face. It doesn't mean I'm incapable of making good choices for the rest of my life." Cole stood up. "I'm going to bed. I'm worn out."

*   *   *

The next day Mary and Jake said goodbye to the group after breakfast. As they were about to depart, Cole walked over to his mom. He was still angry about their conversation the night before.

"Mom, I need to know that you're going to give Claire a chance. I want you to be kind to her, especially while I'm gone, and try to get to know her. If you mess this up for me, it will be hard for me to get over."

Mary looked up at her son and sighed. "I promise, Cole. I'll put my best foot forward. I would never stand in the way of your happiness. I just want the best for you and that includes the best wife."

"I know, Mom."

Mary got on her horse and looked down at him. "Cole, I've thought a lot about what you said last night and you're right. I need to trust you more. And if Claire really is the kind of woman you say she is, I'm going to *want* you to marry her. Just give it some time."

* * *

Back at the ranch, Claire had nervous knots in her stomach about Mary's return. She didn't want to face her without Cole, but she knew she couldn't exactly avoid her for the next couple of days either. Claire did the only thing she could in the situation—she cooked. She spent the afternoon making turkey chili, salad and homemade rolls for supper. For dessert, she made strawberry shortcake.

In the late afternoon, she was walking to her cabin when she saw Mary and Jake riding back. Her stomach dropped at the sight of them. She went inside and plopped herself down onto the couch, grabbing her cellphone to check for messages. There was a text from Cole.

> Hey, gorgeous! I hope you're having a great day.
> I had a big talk with my mom last night about us.
> I think she gets it now. How are you?

She texted back:

> Pretty nervous about spending time with your

parents but otherwise okay. Thanks for talking to
your mom. You're the best.

Claire decided to go for a swim before supper
to calm her nerves. She put on a modest tankini in
a deep purple, a casual wraparound black cotton
dress over it and slipped on a pair of flip-flops.

When she got to the pool, she sank into the hot
tub. It was a warm day and the late afternoon sun
gave the world a slow, relaxed feel that reminded her
of lazy summer days when she was a girl. Her mind
wandered to the first time she had been in this hot
tub—it was the first time she had seen Cole nearly
undressed. Her pulse quickened at the thought of
him showering in front of her.

Her thoughts drifted to Cole's parents and then
her own. She would have loved it if they could have
known Cole. It seemed strange and sad to her that
they would never get to meet the man she wanted
to spend her life with or see the place where she
wanted to spend it. Her thoughts were interrupted
by Mary approaching the hot tub in a black one-
piece swimsuit. Mary looked great for her age and
had obviously kept herself in good shape.

"Mind if I join you, Claire?" she asked in a
soft tone.

"Of course not." Claire gave her a smile. "It's
your hot tub."

Mary took a moment to get settled in across

from Claire, "Ahh, that feels good. My bones don't take to riding for two days like they used to. Getting old is not all it's cracked up to be."

"Although two days on a horse would be a lot for most people, I imagine."

They sat in silence for a long moment. Claire started thinking maybe she should go when Mary looked over at her. "You know, Claire, being a mom is a tough thing. You want the best for your kids, and no matter how old they get, you want to protect them from any hurt. But the other night, I was out of line with what I said to you and I'm sorry," she said with a grim expression.

"That's okay. I know I made a horrible impression on you to start with. I was absolutely mortified. I also realize how completely unprofessional it is for me to get involved with my boss at all, especially so quickly. It's risky, too—if it doesn't work out, I lose my job *and* my home. Cole and I both realized that right away, and we tried to stay away from each other. We just couldn't." She paused for a moment, sighing and looking out at the mountains. She turned back to Mary. "For what it's worth, I've never had a relationship with someone I worked with before."

Mary looked over at her. "I'm glad that you share my concerns, and I really am sorry I attacked you like that in front of the family. I expect that I embarrassed you and hurt your feelings. I'm the one who made a bad first impression. You mean a lot to Cole, and if I stood in the way of that relationship, I'm not sure he would ever forgive me."

"He means the world to me too," Claire said, her eyes glistening with tears, both from Mary's apology and from hearing again how Cole felt about her. "I've never met anyone like him. He's so honest and caring. He's just so good to me. If you could have seen how he looked after me after I was in the accident, or even just how he was so concerned with making sure I felt welcome when I got here. I haven't felt so loved or protected since my parents were alive. I would do anything to make him happy, and I would never hurt him."

"That warms my heart to hear, Claire. I just want you to be cautious. I love my son with all my heart, but Cole has a habit of falling fast and hard without really considering compatibility. I know it's not the most romantic quality in a relationship, but it's certainly one of the most important. His relationship with Gabriela was a disaster in the making. She was all wrong for him, but he just dove right in without seeing the signs."

Claire looked out at the lake, not wanting to meet Mary's eyes. It would be too embarrassing to admit she had never heard of Gabriela. "Well, I really think Cole and I are compatible in all the most important ways," she said, returning her gaze to Mary. "We are both really passionate about our work, and I love his vision for what this ranch could be. We work really well together, and we have a lot of respect for each other. So I think we'll be just fine. Every relationship is a risk, but with Cole, it's a risk worth taking."

Mary smiled at Claire. "I sure hope so, Claire. Just take your time. There's no real rush, is there?"

"That's probably good advice," Claire said, nodding and smiling back. "Now, I better go get changed. Supper is already prepared, but I need to get it served. The guys will be getting hungry soon."

Claire got out of the hot tub and wrapped the towel around herself, slid into her flip-flops and started to walk away. She turned back to Mary after a minute. "Mary, thank you for this chat. I feel so much better. I've been really worried about us getting off on the wrong foot. See you at supper?"

Mary smiled. "You bet."

* * *

Claire hurried back to her cabin with a sinking feeling. She knew she should be feeling happy about how her conversation with Mary had gone, but she wasn't. *Cole has a habit of falling fast and hard.* What did that mean? Was Claire just another one in a succession of lovers he had gotten involved with too quickly? Why hadn't he mentioned Gabriela yet?

Claire brushed out her hair and put it up in a ponytail, then changed into jeans and a black V-neck T-shirt and rushed down the path to the restaurant. She decided she needed to play it cool. She would resist the urge to ask Alicia about Gabriela. She would try not to jump to any conclusions over the next two days and would find a time to ask Cole about it when he got back.

That evening as she made a mug of tea for herself, she got a text from Cole.

Planning a big date night for us after this group leaves. Everything is booked for Saturday night. Can't wait to see you.

She smiled at his thoughtfulness. Can't wait! Miss you lots! XOXO

When she switched off her phone, an unwelcome question entered her mind. Was the date he had planned a repeat of one he had had with Gabriela? She shook her head and turned on the TV to distract herself from her destructive thoughts.

* * *

On Friday the group returned before supper. Cole rushed to get the horses taken care of before heading over to see Claire in the kitchen. As soon as the door flew open, Claire rushed into his arms.

"Hey, Cowboy!" She grinned, taking in the sight of him. He had stubble covering his normally smooth face and looked sweaty and tired.

"Hey yourself." Cole scooped her up into a big hug. "I need a shower. Sorry, I'm a bit sweaty."

"Well, you somehow manage to smell good anyway," she said, kissing him on the lips.

"I missed you so much." He smiled, softly kissing her on the cheek. "How's it been here with my parents?"

"Really good. I had a great conversation with your mom when they got back, and it's been very nice since then. We've had some meals together and shared a few laughs, even." Claire rested her forehead on Cole's chest. "Mmm, I'm so glad you're back."

"Me too," Cole said. "I'm surprised you're in jeans, though. I thought you went lingerie shopping the other day. I was hoping you'd have on something small and lacy."

Claire laughed. "I thought better of it, since I'm still trying to get your parents to forget that I'm a complete harlot."

"Oh, right. Am I at least going to see it on you later?"

Claire grinned. "Well, if you play your cards right, Cowboy." She gave him a wink as she walked over to the counter to peel some garlic.

"How about if I start with a shower and then we eat together?" Cole responded.

"Sounds like a plan. I'll see you back here in a bit."

She fired up one of the burners on the gas stove as she heard the door shut behind him. Dinner would be spaghetti and meatballs, sure to be a hit with the children staying at the ranch. For the adults, grilled shrimp would serve as a succulent appetizer and a spinach salad with feta cheese, cherry tomatoes, olives and her signature balsamic vinaigrette would balance out the meal nicely. Thick slices of buttery garlic toast would adorn each plate as it left the kitchen, creating a picture-perfect dinner. Dessert would be homemade apple pie and ice cream, a classic crowd pleaser.

Grinning to herself, Claire placed a large pot on the burner, added olive oil and crushed the garlic, letting it drop into the pan. Inhaling deeply, she let the delicious aroma fill her nostrils as she pushed the garlic around the sizzling oil. Wiping a bit of oil off the stovetop, she turned down the burner before crossing to the fridge and removing the meatballs she had baked earlier. Simple comfort food for the guests and ranch hands after a long ride. What could be better than that?

As she added strained tomatoes to the pot, she realized how completely happy she was, knowing that the man of her dreams was back again and they would soon be sitting across from each other sharing a meal she was preparing at this very moment. Even though the oven had seen better days and some of the equipment could use upgrading, she had never enjoyed cooking as much as she did here. Claire thought of her father and how much he would have loved seeing her work here at the ranch in her own kitchen. Both of her parents would have loved Cole; they would have known he was perfect for their little girl. He respected her, supported her and took care of her the way they would have wanted. That might be better than comfort food.

* * *

After cleaning up the post-dinner mess, Claire locked up the kitchen and went over to Cole's cabin with Otis in tow. When she walked in, Cole was sitting on the couch in a fitted white T-shirt and grey lounge pants, watching sports highlights. He turned off the TV and strode over to her, giving her a long hug. When he pulled away, he said, "What can I get you to drink?"

"I would love a beer, actually." Claire grinned and flopped down onto the couch.

"Coming right up," Cole said, walking over to the kitchen. He called back over his shoulder, "So, what have you done to my dog anyway? I was a bit put out tonight when I left the restaurant and he wouldn't come back here with me."

"Really?" Claire laughed. "I guess I'm just generally better than you. Dogs can sense these things."

"Oh, is that so?" Cole said, handing her a beer. He settled himself next to her on the couch and reached into the pocket of her jeans when she lifted the bottle to her mouth. He pulled out a small plastic baggie with dog treats inside.

"Aha! Found it!" he said, feeling satisfied. "You have been bribing my dog so he'll like you better!"

"I have done no such thing! Those treats are for me. You know, in case I need a little protein," Claire said with her most convincing look. Otis walked over and sat down, wagging his tail and staring at the bag in Cole's hand.

"Oh, well, maybe you should have one now. You're probably tired from all that hard work in the kitchen today," he said, taking one out of the bag.

"No, no. I couldn't right now. I ate too much at supper. I'll save those for tomorrow when I need them."

Otis nudged Cole's hand and Cole gave him the treat. "Nice try, lady, but I'm on to you."

Claire snatched back the bag and stuffed it into her pocket, looking over at Otis. "That was supposed to be our little secret, dog."

Cole laughed and took a long swig of his beer. "It's so nice to be home with you. I can't wait to get into bed. I'm a bit sore from sleeping in a tent for four nights."

Claire smiled, curling up her legs under her and

turning to face him. "I'm so glad you're back. My bed has been so empty without you."

Cole wrapped an arm around her and drew her to him. "So, no UPS guy?"

Claire laughed. "He never made it to the bed. I just had my way with him and sent him off in his brown truck."

Cole chuckled. "You're lucky you're so bendy, or I wouldn't put up with that."

Claire smiled and gave him a long kiss and then sighed happily.

Cole nuzzled her neck. "So, I've kind of been waiting for the Victoria's Secret fashion show to start."

"Oh, have you?" Claire laughed. "I seem to recall requesting that someone put on his hat, belt and boots and give me a little show . . ."

"I never said yes."

"Good point. All my new lacy things are at my place, except what I'm wearing under these clothes."

"Mmm," Cole murmured, kissing her neck. "I'm intrigued."

Claire gave a soft little sigh. "Cole, I have to ask you about something your mom said."

Cole sat straight up, giving her a questioning look. "Does it have to be right now, Claire?"

"I'm sorry," she said, touching his cheek with her hand. "But it kind of does. Something has been bothering me, and I really need to get it off my mind."

Cole took his arm from around her and placed it on his knee. "Okay . . . What's up?" he asked in a tentative voice.

"Your mom told me you have a habit of falling in love fast without really knowing the woman you're with. She also mentioned a Gabriela, who apparently lived with you?"

Cole let out a big sigh and reached for his beer. "I'm not sure what you want me to say. I had a life before you got here. I'm sure you would expect that. I'm thirty-two."

"Yes, of course. I'm not trying to start an argument with you. I was just hoping to understand what your mom meant about you making this a habit," Claire said in a soft voice.

"She's exaggerating to make a point," Cole replied, taking her hand in his and moving it over to his leg. "I think she must have given you the same speech she gave me about slowing down. My last relationship was with a woman named Gabriela. I did get involved quickly with her, and things didn't work out. Now my mother seems to think I need her to oversee my love life in order for me to get it right."

"Hmm, yeah, she did talk to me about us taking it slow. I don't know, maybe she has a point. We were all set to move in together and there are obviously some things we don't know about each other," Claire said, pausing to take a sip of her beer.

"What?" Cole asked, shifting himself away

from her on the couch and letting go of her hand. "Are you seriously going to let a conversation with my mom dictate how we're going to do things? She doesn't even know you."

"You're right, she doesn't, Cole. But I don't know how well we really know each other either. Until a few minutes ago, I didn't know you had lived with anyone before."

"So, is that what this is about? Gabriela?" Cole asked, sounding exasperated.

"Partly." Claire nodded. "I mean, it sounds like a significant relationship to me. Those things shape who we are. They are important to talk about."

Cole sighed. "This is *not* how I expected this evening to go. I missed you, and I'm tired as hell. Do you *really* need me to go through my complete dating history right now?"

Claire raised her eyebrows at him. "Cole, I'm not trying to piss you off here, but the fact that you are avoiding telling me anything about Gabriela is, frankly, a bit off-putting for me."

"I'm not trying to put you off. I just don't see the point in dragging up the past when it's over. But if you really need to hear about her, fine." He drained his beer and stood up. "I'm just going to grab another drink first."

He walked into the kitchen and opened the fridge. Claire sat waiting on the couch, feeling very uncomfortable all of a sudden. Had Gabriela lived here in this cabin? Had they made love in the same bed or on the couch she was sitting on?

Cole came back and flopped down into an armchair off to the side of the couch. "Gabriela and I met in Las Vegas about two years ago. She's from Brazil and was travelling around the US with a few of her girlfriends. We spent several days in Vegas together, and then she and her friends decided to come here for a couple of weeks so we could spend more time together. We did get involved really quickly, mostly because she was set to go back home so soon. It felt like we had to make a decision right away to either be together or forget the whole thing.

"She ended up staying and moving in with me when her friends went back. Her parents showed up after a few months to try to bring her home. They didn't like the idea of her living with some cowboy out in the sticks. I found out she had a fiancé in Brazil who was waiting for her. She hadn't told me about him or him about me. Her family had been covering for her, but they were out of patience and wanted her back. They own a large chain of hotels, and her fiancé's family owns a bunch of resorts or something that they wanted to merge. Gabriela refused to go home, and I decided to overlook the fact that she had neglected to mention her fiancé. She made it sound like an arranged marriage, and she assured me that she loved me and wanted to stay in Colorado. She was here for almost a year, and then one day her mom called and told her that her dad had had a heart attack. She flew home the next day and never came back. She called me a couple of weeks after. Her dad was fine; he'd never had a heart attack—her parents just knew that would get Gabriela to return home. When she called to tell me, she made it clear I had been a fun diversion from her real life but nothing more. She told me she did love the guy in Brazil and was getting married to him. So, that was a rough lesson for me."

He took a long swig of his beer and then sighed heavily. "Looking back, I can see how wrong we were for each other, you know? But at the time, I thought our differences would make it work. I ignored all those things that were staring me in the face."

"Wow," Claire said softly. "That is quite the awful story. I'm so sorry that happened to you, Cole." She stood up and closed the distance between them, kneeling down in front of him, holding his face in her hands. "She shouldn't have used you like that." Claire brushed her lips on his forehead.

"Yeah, well, it's over, and I'm sure you can see why I don't like my mom throwing it back in my face," Cole answered.

"I definitely understand that," she replied as she took his hands in hers. "What do you want to do now? Do you want to just get some sleep?"

"I want to forget," Cole said, leaning down to kiss Claire's lips. "You can help me forget."

Claire kissed him back tenderly, running her hands up his thighs. They stayed like that for a long time, kissing and touching each other. Cole felt a wave of relief wash over him, almost like Claire could mend his scarred heart with her touch. She was the complete opposite of Gabriela—perfect for him in every way that Gabriela had been wrong for him.

Claire kissed and touched him with such love and genuine care, hoping she could erase, a little bit at a time, with each caress, the imprint Gabriela had made on him. Together they could heal each other from the pain caused by their former lovers and learn to trust completely again.

"I love you, Cole," she whispered, hugging him and pressing her head to his chest. "I'll stay as long as you want me to be with you."

Cole pressed his lips to the top of her head. "I'll never stop wanting you to be with me."

"Then I'll never leave."

Their lips met in one sweet, long kiss, full of love. Claire pulled back for a moment. "I have a crazy idea. Come with me," she whispered, getting up and holding out her hand.

Cole stood up and took her hand. "I'm all yours."

"Good, get your shoes."

"What?" Cole asked. "Going out right now is not really what I had in mind."

"Trust me, Cowboy. You'll like this," she said with a grin.

She slid into her ballet flats and grabbed her keys. As she opened the door, she told Otis to stay, pulling Cole out the front door with her and shutting it behind them.

* * *

The path toward the lodge was lit only by moonlight as Claire hurried along it with Cole. The grounds of the ranch and the pool were completely deserted and the sky was clear, giving them an amazing display of the stars above them. Stopping when they reached the gate to the pool, Claire quickly unlocked it.

She led Cole over to the hot tub and turned on the jets. Soft blue lights turned on under the water. She kicked off her shoes and turned to Cole. He pulled her to him and gave her a long, hard kiss, wrapping his arms around her. "You're right. I am going to like this."

Claire ran her hands over his chest and then pulled his T-shirt up over his head. He finished taking it off and then tossed it onto a lounge chair. He reached for her shirt, but she grabbed his hands and stopped him.

"Just you," she said, raising her eyebrows a little.

Cole gave her a confused look and then decided to go with it as Claire untied the drawstring of his pants and slid her fingers in, lowering them along with his boxer briefs. She ran her lips down his chest and stomach as she lowered her body to remove his pants. He stood in front of her, completely nude, becoming fully erect next to the hot tub. Claire moved her hands up his thighs and then lifted herself to standing, giving him a lingering lick as she began to straighten up. A shudder went through his body at her touch. After she stood, she turned suddenly and walked over to the other side of the hot tub, leaving him standing, looking a little frustrated.

"Get in," she ordered.

Cole obliged and sank into the hot, swirling water, curling his lips into a little smile in anticipation of what was coming. Claire stood opposite him and started unbuttoning her shirt slowly, swaying her hips from side to side as she did.

"I believe I promised to finish this . . ." she said with a sexy grin.

She made a slow circle as she pulled her shirt out of her jeans and then unbuttoned the last couple of buttons, turning to face him. She bit her lip and looked down for a moment, feeling a brief twinge of embarrassment. When she looked up, Cole's expression emboldened her, and she continued to sway as though there were a slow, sexy beat playing.

With her shirt open, he could see she was wearing a lacy red push-up bra. It made her breasts look even bigger and perkier than they were. Cole couldn't peel his eyes off her chest as she slid her shirt off her shoulders and let it drop to the ground. He spread his arms wide, resting them on top of the hot tub, thoroughly loving the show along with the feeling of the warm jets on his back.

Opening the top button of her jeans, Claire swivelled so her back was to Cole again as she unzipped her zipper. She slid her thumbs into the sides of her pants, then wriggled her hips from side to side, lowering the waistband to reveal a thong in the same lacy material as her bra. When she got the waistband just below her bottom, she lifted it up again, gingerly pulling her jeans back up. She heard a low groan from her audience and she turned, smiling. Lowering her jeans again, she revealed the front of her panties and then made another circle, stopping with her back to him, before bending forward to give Cole a clear view of her ass as she slid her pants down to the tiled floor.

Cole let out a sigh. "Wow."

Claire lifted herself back to standing in one quick snap, then stepped out of her pants, one foot at a time. She turned back to face him again, swaying her hips as she lifted her hands up her sides, caressing them with her fingertips. When she reached her neck, she lifted her hair up, raising her arms above her head. She turned her back to him one last time, bending forward with straight legs and a flat back, placing her palms on the ground. She slowly brought her hands to her toes, then slid her fingertips up her body as she lifted herself back up. Bringing her hands behind her back, she reached her bra clasp and flicked it open before letting the scrap of lacy fabric slide off her shoulders ever so slowly, leaving her standing in only her panties now. She swivelled back to him and tossed her bra right at him. He caught it with one hand, grinning at her as he threw it as far from the hot tub as he could.

Shaking her head at him with an exasperated smile, she crossed her arms over her breasts, pushing them up a bit and caressing her upper arms with her fingers as she gazed at him with her lips slightly parted. Tugging her panties down past her hips, she let them fall to the ground, stepping out of them with a little spin.

Cole sat in front of her, hard as a rock, feeling conflicted. Part of him never wanted the show to end and the other part needed her to get into the water with him so he could touch her.

Claire stepped into the hot tub, still covering her breasts as she lowered her body into the water, feeling liberated and sexy. She sat opposite him for a minute, smiling. His expression was completely carnal as he stared back at her. She knew without looking that when she crossed the tub, he would be rock hard and ready for her. She let her arms float straight out to her sides as she stood up, her fingertips skimming the water's surface as she crossed to him. The view of her coming toward him with her wet, naked breasts exposed fulfilled the fantasy he'd had of her the first night they met.

His hands moved to her waist as she stood in front of him. He looked up at her as he drew her to him, opening his mouth and taking her right breast in. He swirled his tongue around her hard nipple and then sucked it with an intensity that showed her exactly what effect she had on him. Drawing in a sharp breath at the feeling of his mouth sucking so hard, Claire grabbed his head with her hands and lowered her lips to kiss his forehead. Cole brought his mouth up to hers, kissing her lips with hard, short, passionate motions.

Spinning her body away from him, she slid onto his lap and lifted her arm up and behind her to touch his cheek. Cole turned his face to hers and continued kissing her while he ran his hands up to her chest and then down to her hips in long strokes.

"You are so fucking sexy, you know that?" he murmured into her ear.

"Only around you. I've never been this way before," she said, kissing his mouth tenderly. He pulled her body closer to his and pressed his chest against her back, sucking gently on her neck.

Claire could feel his erection pressing into her bottom as she sat on his lap with him cradling her in his arms. She shifted her core backward and up against him, drawing him inside her. As she pushed down with her body, he was finally inside her after so many nights apart. Cole moved his hands to her hips and lifted her body up and down, back and forth with his powerful arms. Claire tightened her muscles around him and moved her hands down to touch the sides of his thighs. They stayed like this, rocking slowly and tenderly, bodies pressed together in the swirling heat of the water for a long time, until the momentum seemed to take over.

"I love you, Claire," he whispered in her ear. "I love you so much."

Claire turned her face to meet his again, kissing his lips. "I am so in love with you," she whispered, her voice thick with emotion.

Cole reached his hand in between her legs and firmly held her sex against his erection as they moved together. With his other hand, he reached up, covering her breasts with his arm and holding her to him as she lifted and lowered herself over his cock. Finally, they both came in tender, quiet swells of bliss.

When it was over, Cole lifted her off him and turned her around to face him. Claire wrapped her legs around his waist as they kissed and caressed each other for a long time before either of them spoke.

"I've never been loved like this before, Cole. You're everything I've been waiting for my whole life," she said as she rested her forehead against his.

Cole kissed her lips gently, cupping her face with his hands. "That's exactly how I feel about you. I just want to be with you every minute of every day." He smiled warmly at her and then hugged her tight.

As they left the pool, after drying off and dressing, Claire took Cole's hand. "Can we sleep at my place tonight? We could go grab Otis so he won't be alone."

Cole raised his eyebrow, looking confused for a moment, and then a wave of understanding crossed over his face. "Sure, if that makes you more comfortable."

He raised her hand to his lips and kissed her fingers. "Are you feeling strange about Gabriela having lived with me?"

"I am," she sighed. "I know it's in the past, but somehow, I just feel weird about it right now. Can you give me a bit of time to adjust?"

"Of course, Claire," he replied. "I don't think I would necessarily love being in the bed you shared with Antonio. Let's go get Otis and get some sleep."

FOURTEEN

Just after breakfast the next morning, the guests said their goodbyes and left for the airport. Alicia walked over to Claire. "Grab your purse. You're coming with me. Ladies' day out."

"Oh, fun! What did you have in mind? I have to be back by about five to get ready for a mystery date with Cole."

"I know. He has our day planned, too. We'll be back in plenty of time."

"Really?" Claire smiled. "This is intriguing. Am I dressed for what we're doing?"

"Um, wait . . . you'll need a button-up shirt and flip-flops," Alicia said with a smile. "I will, too. Meet me at my car in a few minutes?"

"Deal!"

As Claire started for her cabin, she saw Cole leaving in his truck with Ben in the passenger seat. He gave her a wave as he pulled out.

Fifteen minutes later, Claire was sitting in

Alicia's Ford Escape on her way to the city. "I'm excited, and I don't even know what we're doing! Can you tell me where we're going now?"

"Yup! We are going for a spa day. Manis, pedis, massages, lunch, makeup and hair!" Alicia grinned at her as they sped along the highway.

"Really? Wow! So fun!" Claire had a huge smile on her face.

"Cole called and booked everything and paid for it all already."

"Wow, he is just so thoughtful. You know it's our first official date?"

"I know, he told me. He's pulling out all the stops."

"He's the best. How did I get so lucky?"

Claire sent Cole a text as they neared the salon.

Just found out what Alicia and I are doing today! SO excited! You must be the sweetest man on the planet. Can't wait to see what we're doing later!

The day was pure luxury for both Alicia and Claire. First they were treated to massages. Then they were each taken to a private room lit only by candles for a soak in an aromatherapy bath with rose petals floating on the water. They met up again for lunch afterward, wearing bathrobes. They ate on the enclosed terrace of the spa under a large umbrella.

"This is the most relaxed I've ever felt," Alicia said, smiling.

"Me too. I could do this every day," Claire agreed, taking a bite of her salad.

After lunch, it was time for manicures and pedicures. Claire chose a soft, light pink for both her fingers and toes. Then it was off to have their hair washed, blown out and styled, and then, makeup.

It was after four thirty when they left. Claire had her hair pinned in an off-centre bun at the nape of her neck with a few pieces of hair falling in waves around her face. Her makeup gave her the look of flawless skin and lush pink lips. Her eyes had a slightly smudged, smoky look, and her lashes were full and long.

Alicia looked gorgeous, with her hair falling in curls around her shoulders and beautifully applied makeup on her already glowing face. They walked out of the spa feeling every bit as amazing as they looked.

When they got back to the ranch, Cole's truck was there. Claire hurried back to her cabin to get dressed. She texted Cole to let him know she was back.

A few minutes later, she got a message.

I'll be over at 6 to pick you up. Can't wait to see your beautiful face.

Claire looked over at the clock. She had forty minutes to get ready, which was plenty of time. She showered quickly to freshen up, being careful not to wet her face or hair. She rubbed body butter all over releasing a faint fruity and floral smell. Then she selected a pair of diamond drop earrings and a diamond necklace that had been her mother's. She had worn these only once before, at her sister's wedding. Tonight felt like a special enough occasion.

She sat in her robe for a few minutes, admiring the work of the stylist and makeup artist before wandering over to the kitchen and pouring herself a glass of water. She put on some music, deciding on Enigma's *Love Sensuality Devotion* CD to set the mood. Back in the bedroom, tugging her suitcase of shoes out from under the bed, she selected stilettos in nude with an iridescent finish.

Humming along to the music, Claire slid into a new navy-blue push-up bra and matching thong before finally slipping on her dress. It was a navy-blue silk cheongsam dress with a delicate cherry-blossom pattern in a muted gold thread. It had a mandarin collar and was fitted through her chest, waist and hips, and it fell to her mid-calf with a long slit up one side. She fastened the knotted butterfly buttons, smoothed the dress along her sides and took a long look, feeling satisfied with what she saw. It was two minutes to six when Claire touched up her lip gloss and slid into her stilettos. She was just putting her cellphone and lipstick into her clutch when she heard a knock at the door.

* * *

Her heart skipped a beat as she opened the door
and saw Cole standing in front of her in a sexy
European-cut suit. The black jacket and pants fit
him perfectly and managed to display his build
despite covering his body completely. He had on
a crisp, white fitted shirt and a silver tie with thin
stripes in black, white and light blue. His face was
freshly shaved and he'd had a haircut. In his hand
was a bouquet of eighteen red roses.

The pair stood staring at each other for a
moment, both wide-eyed. "Wow!" they exclaimed in
unison. A moment of awkwardness fell upon them
before Cole leaned over and gave Claire a soft kiss
on the cheek. "You look amazing," he murmured,
handing her the flowers.

"Thank you," she replied. "So do you. I mean,
serious *GQ* material . . . And these are beautiful
roses." She took his hand and led him into her cabin.
"I better put these in some water," she said, taking a
long whiff of the flowers. "Mmm, thank you."

Cole watched her as she walked over to the
kitchen to find something to put the flowers in. "That
is some dress you're wearing. And your hair and
makeup—you are stunning. I'm going to have to fight
off all the other men who see you tonight."

Claire turned to him. "And I'm going to feel
sorry for all the women who see you tonight because

they won't ever get to sleep with you. Lucky for them, they won't know *everything* they're missing."

Claire quickly took care of the flowers, setting them on the kitchen table to admire them. "There! Perfect!"

She smiled at her date. "You are so thoughtful, Cole. Thank you for such an amazing spa day today. Alicia and I had the best time. You picked a wonderful place. They totally pampered us," she said as she picked up her clutch and walked over to him. She gave him a kiss on the lips, lingering for a moment. "I can't wait to see what you've got planned for tonight. Can you tell me yet?"

Cole smiled down at her. "I'm going to keep it a mystery just a little bit longer, if you don't mind." He looked down at his watch. "We'd better get going. I think our ride should be here by now."

They walked out of the cabin together and Claire locked the door. "Our ride?"

Cole took her hand and walked down the path with her. When they reached the parking lot, a long, black limousine was waiting for them. A driver stood beside the back door, smiling at the pair. "Hello, I'm William. I'll be your driver this evening."

Cole introduced himself and told William where they were going. Claire stepped into the back of the limo first, surprised by how elegant it was. The cream-coloured leather seat wrapped around two sides, creating enough seating for several people. There was a full bar, a TV and opulent lighting.

Cole climbed in after her. "So, what do you think?"

Claire looked over at him with wide eyes as he seated himself next to her. "It's wonderful! I mean the whole day has been perfect—more than I ever could have imagined. But really, it's too much, Cole. First the spa and the roses, now a limo? This all must have been so expensive. I would honestly have been happy with burgers and a movie."

"That's one of the things I love about you. I already knew that you'd be happy with a simpler date. But I wanted tonight to be something we'll always remember. Besides, with all those other offers you have to consider, I need to pull out all the stops to make sure I'm still a contender." He looked down at her with his sexy grin.

Claire smiled back. "Well, you are off to an amazing start, Mr. Mitchell. Things are definitely looking good for you so far," she replied, gazing into his hazel eyes. Her eyes flicked down to his mouth. "You know, I don't normally kiss on a first date, but with you, I'm willing to make an exception."

"Well then, I made the right choice with the whole romance package today," he said, leaning into her.

They shared a lingering embrace. Cole held her cheek with his hand, feeling her soft skin on his fingertips. She smelled of delicious perfume and tasted of strawberries. Claire moved her hand along his abs as they kissed. She could feel his muscles under the smooth, cool fabric of his shirt. It was all she could do to restrain herself from climbing onto his lap at that moment and ripping his shirt open. Instead, she pulled away from him and straightened herself next to him on the seat, picking up her clutch. "That's all you get, Cowboy," she said, digging out her lipstick.

Cole let out a sigh and ran a hand through his hair.

"I wouldn't want you to think I'm easy." Claire looked over at him with a wicked grin.

"I really only asked you out because I thought you might be easy," Cole said, snatching the lipstick out of her hand and kissing her hard on the mouth as he held the lipstick just slightly out of her reach. She tried for a moment to retrieve it but gave in, choosing to hold his face with her hand instead. They stayed like this, snuggling and touching, for a few delicious minutes. She could smell his cologne, and it made her wet with desire. Cole pulled his mouth away and kissed her neck and her earlobe, causing her to moan softly. Then he stopped suddenly and handed her back her lipstick. "That's all *you* get."

Claire gave him a sultry look. "I could get more if I wanted to. I'm just not in the mood for more, actually." She plucked her compact out of her clutch, opened it and carefully applied her lipstick.

"That's not possible. No woman can resist me," Cole retorted, shaking his head. "You're just saying that because I put the brakes on." He leaned into her ear and lowered his voice. "I know how badly you want me. You're so wet right now, your panties are probably soaked."

Claire looked over at him, snapping her compact shut. "Who says I'm wearing panties?"

Cole groaned in defeat just as the limo slowed to a stop in front of the Broadmoor, an expansive resort property. It was majestic, with a large fountain in front and mountains behind it.

"We're here," Cole said, watching Claire's reaction. Her mouth fell open in surprise, and she had that excited look he loved to see.

"Wow!" she said under her breath, biting her bottom lip.

William opened the door and Cole exited the car first. He held his hand out to help Claire get out.

"I'll be here waiting for you," William said, smiling at them. "Enjoy your dinner."

They both thanked him, and Cole pressed his fingertips to the small of Claire's back to guide her into the hotel. The lobby was as impressive as the building's exterior. It had vaulted ceilings and was lit by intricate crystal chandeliers. Claire's heels clicked on the marble floor as they crossed the room toward the elevators. When they got in, Cole pressed the button for the top floor. He kept his hand on her back, just above the curve of her derrière. Claire smiled up at him and wiped a trace of lipstick off his bottom lip with her thumb.

"You're amazing," she whispered as the elevator doors opened.

They stepped out into a classically designed restaurant with floor-to-ceiling windows on three sides. A large balcony surrounded the restaurant. The tables were intimate, with white linens and comfortable high-backed chairs in rich gold and cream stripes. A trio including a pianist, a violinist and a cellist played a romantic song. The host stood behind a podium, wearing a black tuxedo.

As they approached, he greeted them with a gracious smile. "Welcome to the Penrose Room. Do you have a reservation?"

Cole answered in the affirmative, and they were led to a table for two near the corner windows. The view was amazing. It overlooked a large lake and the mountains to one side, with the other window showing a spectacular view of the city. Claire gave him a wide grin. "This must be the best table in the entire state."

"I think you might be right. I've never been here before, but I'd heard it had the best view," Cole said.

A tiny flicker of relief passed through Claire as she realized that he hadn't brought Gabriela here.

The host pulled out Claire's chair as she sat

and then handed them each a menu. "Naomi will be your server. She will be here in just a moment to go over the specials and take your drink orders." With that, he quickly turned and walked back to his post.

Claire sat for a moment with her hands under her chin, thoroughly entranced by the view out the window as Cole opened his menu and began scanning it. Naomi appeared, dressed in a white button-up shirt and a black fitted skirt that showed off her lean legs. She had long blond hair and was young and beautiful. She smiled at them and her eyes grew wide as she took in the sight of Cole. She introduced herself and went over the specials for the evening. Claire watched her closely, feeling irritated at the server's obvious attraction to her date. She looked at Cole as a feeling of jealousy brewed inside her. It was exactly the type of scenario in which Antonio would have failed miserably. He would have spent the entire meal flirting with Naomi, ruining the evening and, likely, the next day as well. Claire was pleased to see how impassive Cole's face was as he listened respectfully to Naomi and how quickly his gaze became warm when he looked back at her.

"Sweetheart, have you decided on an appetizer yet?" he asked.

Claire grinned at him. "I need another minute to decide."

"Of course," Naomi said, quickly glancing at her and then back at Cole.

Cole smiled. "We're celebrating tonight. Could we start with a bottle of the Louis Roederer champagne, please?"

"Certainly. I'll be right back with it," Naomi replied and turned to leave.

Claire looked up from her menu at Cole. "I have to warn you, champagne makes me get a little crazy."

"I'm counting on it."

Naomi returned with the champagne, two flutes and an ice bucket with a stand. She popped the bottle open and filled their glasses, setting them down in front of Claire and Cole.

"Have you decided on appetizers?" she asked Cole.

"Yes, I think we're ready to order. Go ahead, honey," he said to Claire.

Naomi's face turned to slight boredom. Claire ordered her meal. She was going to start with the Moroccan spiced artichoke soup and, for her main course, she chose the butternut squash and prawn ravioli with truffle butter sauce. Cole ordered the Maine lobster bisque to start and the braised beef tenderloin with gnocchi to follow.

Claire thought she saw Naomi touch Cole's hand as she took the menu from him, making eye contact. He gave her a polite half smile and returned his gaze to Claire as he leaned across the table and reached for her hand, which was resting on the stem of her champagne flute. Naomi walked off.

"I think she likes you," Claire said.

Cole rubbed her fingers with his thumb. "It's the suit. I've been told I look like I stepped out of the pages of *GQ* in this," he replied with a teasing grin.

Claire laughed, resting her other hand on top of his fingers. "It *is* a highly fuckable look on you."

"My, my, Ms. Hatley, you are a bit forward for a first date. It must be the champagne."

"No, it's you. It's the main reason I'll probably go out with you again."

"Speaking of fuckable, have I told you how hot you are in that dress?" Cole replied. "If I could, I'd clear this whole restaurant out and have my way with you on the table."

"I was thinking of the piano over there." Claire picked up her champagne and took a long drink.

"You are the only woman I've ever met whose mind is as sexy as her body," Cole said. "I never know what you're going to say next, but I'm always excited to hear what's going to come out of that pretty mouth of yours."

"Okay. I've decided. I'll go out with you again," Claire replied.

Another server approached the table with their appetizers. The pair sipped their soup, enjoying the scenery and the flavours.

"This is so delicious." Claire closed her eyes as she took a spoonful of soup.

Cole put his spoon down and observed her for a moment. "Watching you eat could become my new pastime. I love how enthusiastic you are."

Claire tilted her head to the side. "Well, when you take me somewhere with food like this, I definitely can't help but be thrilled." She slid her bowl toward him. "Try some?"

He dipped his spoon into her soup and took a sip. "Mmm, that is good. I think I like mine better, though," he replied as he slid his bowl toward her.

"You need to have at least two bites of something. The first one just mixes the new flavours with the last thing you were eating."

She took a sip of champagne and then tried his soup. She took two spoonsful, making a little moan of pleasure at the second one.

"Yup, yours is better. Good choice, Cowboy."

"Trade with me," Cole said, moving her bowl closer to him.

"I couldn't do that. Mine is delicious, too. I'm happy with it," she said, sliding his bowl back toward him.

"The bisque made you moan. I live for that sound. Swapping a bowl of soup is a small price to pay," Cole said, pushing his bowl back over to her.

He dipped his spoon into the artichoke soup and took another sip. "Funny that a lowly cowboy would choose a far superior soup than a chef."

Claire laughed a little too loudly at his joke and

then covered her mouth with her hand. "I think the bubbles are going to my head. You're going to have to stop being witty, or we'll get kicked out of here."

"I wasn't being witty," he said with a suspicious look. "I'm just wondering if you even are a chef. Maybe you're a beautiful line cook who goes around pretending she went to culinary school."

Claire giggled. "You are the first man who's figured out my game. I travel the country to get hot guys into bed since no man can resist a culinary-arts graduate. It's the only way I can score super-sexy men."

Cole's face turned serious. "Don't do that."

Claire pulled back in surprise. "Do what?" she asked, feeling her face turn pink with embarrassment.

"Don't put yourself down like that, even as a joke. The more you do that, the less you will trust what we have," Cole said softly. "I need you to trust this for it to work."

"Sorry, Cole," she said, blinking back a tear. "Bad habit."

"It *is* a bad habit. You've spent your whole life feeling not good enough, which is just garbage. If you keep thinking like that, you're always going to believe that *you* are lucky to have *me* and not that *we* are lucky to have *each other*. If that's the case, you're always going to be waiting for the other shoe to drop. You'll look for signs that I'm losing interest in you or that I'm going to cheat on you with Naomi over there. As far as I can tell, that's the only thing that could tear us apart."

Claire dabbed at her eyes with her napkin, hoping her makeup wasn't smudged. "Okay, Cole. I'll work on convincing myself that I'm a sex goddess instead of a chubby nerd."

"Good," he said. "And I'll always be here to remind you of how completely perfect you are when you forget."

Claire nodded and pursed her lips, trying not to cry. Cole slid his chair over to the other side of the table so that he was sitting next to her. He took her chin in his hand and drew her to him, kissing her softly on the lips. Then he wiped her tears away with his thumb and rested his forehead against hers.

"You okay?"

"Yeah," she said softly as her voice broke. "It's just that you can read me like a book. I *am* always waiting for the other shoe to drop. When my parents died, I realized that the people you love the most can leave you without warning. Maybe that's why I ended up with Antonio. Somewhere inside I knew we didn't really love each other, and so I wasn't going to be cut too deep when it was over. This thing with you is terrifying for me. We're only at the beginning, and I already think I would be destroyed if it ended."

"Let's not end it, then," Cole said, kissing her

again. "We get to decide, Claire. You and I. Let's decide to stay together."

Claire nodded and kissed him back. "Okay, Cowboy. You've got yourself a deal."

"Good," he said, moving his place setting over so he could stay close to her. "Now, eat my soup before it gets cold."

They ate in silence for a moment with Cole resting his hand on Claire's knee.

"Wow, your soup is so much better than mine," Claire said as she finished the bowl.

"Isn't it, though?" Cole said, making her laugh again.

Before their main courses came out, they each ordered a wine that would pair well with their meals. When the food arrived, they each tasted the other's dish and ate quietly, smiling into each other's eyes from time to time, both thinking about their earlier conversation.

When their dishes had been cleared, Cole took Claire's hand. "Come with me."

He led her out through the open French doors onto the balcony. It was dark outside now, and the city's skyline was a perfect backdrop as they stood alone in the warm night air. The trio was playing a version of Bryan Adams's "Have You Ever Really Loved a Woman?"

Cole turned Claire toward him and held on to the small of her back with one hand, holding out his other hand to the side in an invitation to dance with him. Claire obliged, and he pulled her close, leading her in a waltz with surprising grace. She could smell his cologne as she pressed her face close to his neck. With her heels on, she was several inches taller and she was grateful for the extra height. Their bodies moved together perfectly in sync, with no space between them. When the song ended, Cole wrapped his arms around her and kissed her, lips parted. Claire tucked her hands inside his jacket and wrapped them around his back, feeling safe and warm and loved. As they kissed, she slid her hands down over his firm ass. She could feel him becoming erect. He pulled his mouth away from her. "Ms. Hatley, this is a respectable dining establishment. There is no groping allowed here."

She grinned at him and reluctantly moved her hands back up. "Sorry about that. It's this suit. It makes me want to do very naughty things to you."

"Oh, great," he said. "How am I supposed to walk back in there with a raging hard-on?"

Claire giggled. "Too bad there isn't somewhere out here I could help you relieve that. I would really love to undo your pants and suck on your huge cock right now." She slid one hand around to his lower abs and caressed along his waistband with her finger.

Cole let out a groan. "Stop that!" he commanded teasingly, grabbing her hand and holding it firmly in his.

"Sorry, but I did warn you about giving me champagne. You might as well have just propped me up on the table, poured it all over me, then licked it off, because that's how wet I am right now."

"I can't take you anywhere, can I?" he said in a strained voice.

"Not really. You'd be better off just chaining me to the bed in my lacy panties and keeping me as a sex slave."

"Oh Christ, you are really naughty," he said, pulling at his shirt collar.

"Only around you. You might have to spank me to get me to stop."

"You're enjoying this," Cole said in exasperation. "You're a little bit evil, Ms. Hatley."

Claire laughed and nodded, wrinkling her nose. "A little bit, yes."

He smiled warmly and kissed her again. "You know, if you weren't so damn hot, I wouldn't put up with this."

"If you weren't so damn hot, I wouldn't act like this," she said, kissing him back. "So, essentially, you are responsible for my bad behaviour."

"I should apologize to myself. I've been putting me in an awkward position this whole time."

"I was thinking the same thing. You really shouldn't put up with that crap from you."

They laughed for a moment and then Cole said, "I think I can make my way back to the table now."

"Would you like to share a dessert?" Claire asked as they walked back inside, holding hands.

"If by 'share a dessert' you mean get two spoons and watch you devour it while we both pretend that isn't what's happening, I'm in."

Claire used her free hand to gently slap him on the stomach. "A true gentleman doesn't discuss such things. He goes to his grave allowing his lady to believe she has fooled him."

"I'll try to remember that," Cole said as he held her chair out for her.

"Good. You do that and don't shush me again, and we're going to get along just fine."

"Deal."

They ordered the blueberry financier for dessert, with two spoons and two glasses of ice wine to go with it.

When the dessert arrived, Claire picked up a spoon and handed it to Cole. "You have to at least hold the spoon for a while and pretend for the people around us. Also, if you could take at least one bite, then your spoon will be used."

"For the benefit of the person busing tables, I assume?"

"Exactly. And now you know everything you need to about women," she replied, taking a sip of her ice wine and then scooping up a bite of delicate cake along with some lemon-berry compote.

"Thanks for the tips. I had no idea you women

were so easy to understand" Cole answered, taking his obligatory bite.

"Now you know," Claire paused. "I have to admit one more thing. I'm a little bit tipsy right now, which is a total faux pas on a first date. Now you're going to think I'm a lush as well as easy."

Cole chuckled. "Well then, you're my favourite type of girl."

*　*　*

Later, as they settled back into the limo, Claire rested her head on Cole's chest, feeling completely content. Cole put his arm around her, sighing happily.

"This has been the best day of my life. You are unbelievably romantic. Thank you, Cole," she said, nuzzling into his neck.

"You're welcome, gorgeous," he said, caressing her arm with his fingertips. "It was my pleasure. I always have so much fun with you. I'm either laughing or turned on."

Claire kissed the nape of his neck, inhaling his irresistible scent. "Me too. We're kind of perfect for each other," she murmured as she gently tugged at his earlobe with her teeth.

Cole turned his face to hers and kissed her. "I love you, you know."

"I love you too. You were definitely worth the wait."

Cole pulled her onto his lap, planting a long, hard kiss on her mouth. Her lips parted as she slid her tongue into his mouth. Their kisses became more eager as they left the city limits and the inside of the limo grew darker.

Claire pulled her face away from Cole's. "Is the privacy screen up?"

They both looked.

"Yup," Cole said as he slid his hand between her thighs and up her dress. "This may be my new favourite way to travel," he said.

"Mine too. Let's go everywhere by limo," she said, undoing his pants and pushing her hand into his boxer briefs. He strained against the fabric as her fingers stroked his smooth skin.

Cole's hand found its way to her panties through the slit in her dress, causing him to pull back from her. "I thought you said you weren't wearing panties?"

"No, I said, 'who said I'm wearing pant-ies?' which leaves it open to either possibility. Disappointed?"

"Never," he replied, pulling her thong to one side and pressing his fingertips to her warm, wet core. He thrust two fingers inside, causing her to gasp. Cole lifted his other hand and pressed a finger to her mouth. "I don't want to shush you, but we have to be quiet if we're going to do this."

"Oh, we're doing this," she purred, pulling her

mouth up to draw his finger inside, sucking on it slowly.

Cole let out a low groan as he watched her full lips sucking on his finger. Turning her entire body away from him, she sat on his lap, her back to his chest. Claire used her thumbs to push his briefs out of the way. Cole lifted his hips to help her, before he pulled the hem of her dress up to her waist.

Moving her thong out of the way, he used his hand to guide himself inside her. Pushing down hard with her hips, she started rocking back and forth, rubbing herself over his length, groaning as she moved. Cole put his hand up to her mouth and she bit down on his finger to stop herself from making noise. Cole's other hand was pressed against her sex, massaging her as she moved. They needed to move slowly and quietly to prevent the driver from hearing them.

The limo took a curve on the highway, causing Clair to lose her balance momentarily; catching her quickly around the waist, Cole steadied her before taking advantage of his grip to press her down onto him and then back and forth. Back and forth, harder, deeper, over and over. Claire held one hand up to the roof of the car to give herself more leverage, and her other hand was behind her, pressed between her ass and Cole's lower abs. He continued to grind her body into his lap, their breathing becoming rapid, their skin becoming moist with sweat.

The alcohol removed Claire's inhibitions. She was wild and free, riding her magnificent cowboy. She could feel her thong rubbing on her skin as she moved, and it made her feel naughty. She turned her head and whispered, "I love the feel of your huge cock inside my panties."

Cole let a low moan escape his throat, turned on by her dirty words and the feeling of her silk dress in his hands as he pushed and pulled her over his lap. He leaned his head against the seat back and closed his eyes, taking in all the physical sensations, the motion of the limo smoothly moving over the road, the smell of Claire's body mixed with her perfume, her tight, wet muscles squeezing him as he moved her easily over his lap. They were fucking, giving in to their most primal need, with no regard for where they were.

Suddenly, he felt Claire's nails dig into his thigh and her body jerk over his as she started to come. Sitting forward, Cole put one hand over her mouth and pressed his arm over her chest, pushing her down hard onto him, thrusting himself deeper inside her. She bit the side of his finger hard to keep herself from crying out as she came undone. Thrusting down hard on him, she shifted her hips from side to side in quick, small movements, bringing on his release.

"Fuck, fuck, fuck," he whispered into her back.

Claire tightened her muscles around Cole,

feeling each wave of his orgasm deep inside her. He held her firmly as they let a sense of pure satisfaction overtake their lust. Their breathing slowed to normal as Claire let her body relax against his strong chest. He closed his arms around her body, holding her to him, caressing her neck with his lips.

"You are a wild one, aren't you?" he asked in a low voice.

"I never used to be," she replied. "Something got switched on when I saw you showering by the pool that first night at the ranch."

The limo slowed and turned off the highway onto the road out to the ranch. Claire lifted herself off Cole and reached for some tissues from a box on the bar. Cole took the tissues from her and wiped her gently with them, then put her panties back in place and helped her return her dress to a more decent state. He wiped himself down and tucked the tissues into his suit pocket, then zipped up his pants.

"I'm sorry the ride is over," Claire said, smiling lazily.

"Me too," he said as the limo turned into the ranch parking lot. "But I have one more surprise for you."

Claire smiled, her eyes glowing with love. "More? How is that possible? You've already made this the most incredible day and evening in the history of dating."

The limo stopped, and William walked around to open the door for them. Cole gave him a large tip and the pair thanked him.

"Come on," Cole said, taking her hand and starting over toward his cabin. "I've been impatient to show you this surprise since I thought of it. I can't wait!"

As Claire wandered down the path with him, waking her up from her post-sex haze, the air felt cool on her skin. She shivered a bit as they walked. Cole slid his coat off and wrapped her in it, rubbing her shoulder and pulling her close.

She looked up at him. He was beaming with excitement. "You've got me so curious!" Claire said, enjoying his enthusiasm.

"Let's go, gorgeous!" He grinned, jogging up the front steps. Once he had the door open, he swooped her up in his arms and carried her inside, shutting the door behind him with his foot. He headed straight up the stairs.

"Close your eyes," he said.

Claire grinned with anticipation as she obeyed him. When they reached the top of the stairs, he put her down carefully, saying, "Don't open your eyes yet. I need one minute." He grabbed the black silk sleep mask he had tucked in his jacket pocket earlier and placed it over her eyes. "So you don't cheat."

She stood at the top of the stairs and heard him

crossing the room and lighting a match. A moment later, she felt his hands on her face as he lifted the mask off.

"Okay, you can look now . . ." he said.

Claire stood completely still and took in the surprise, then turned to him and gave him a huge hug and a kiss. "Cole! I can't believe you did this! It's perfect!"

Then she turned back to the room and took another look around. He had replaced his old double bed with a king-size one with white linens and throw pillows. Red rose petals were sprinkled around the duvet. The headboard was made from rustic cedar logs and a large wrought-iron, rectangular mirror hung above it. New night tables with candles flanked either side of the bed, and a new cozy white armchair and ottoman sat off to the side of the room.

"Do you like it?" Cole asked. "Because it can all go back tomorrow and you can pick out whatever you like."

"I absolutely love it. This is exactly what I would have picked if I had every bedroom set to choose from," she said, standing on her tiptoes to kiss him again. "How did you do this all in one day?"

"I got the guys to move my old bedroom set out of here while I was in town shopping with Ben. He helped me load everything on my truck, and I got Dustin to help us bring it all up here and get it set up. The hardest part for me was picking stuff, but Alicia showed me some pictures on the Internet to give me some ideas."

"You're amazing, Cole. Though I feel a little silly about the guys helping with this. You didn't tell them it was because I was feeling insecure about Gabriela, did you?"

"Of course not," Cole replied. "I told them the truth. That you're like an acrobat, and I needed a much larger bed or I was going to end up in a wheelchair."

Claire laughed, covering her mouth with her hands. "You didn't!"

"I did. I'm a little bit scared of you," he teased.

Claire giggled and then gave him a sultry look. "You should be scared. If you think I was wild before, wait until you see what I'm going to do to you in this room." She loosened his tie and pulled it off him. "This tie should come in handy later," she said, tossing it onto his bed.

"Mmm, I like how you think, gorgeous," he said, pulling her to him for a kiss.

He moved away for a moment. "Listen, about the room, you should add whatever you like to it. I left it white so you could choose colours for throw pillows or paintings or whatever you ladies like in bedrooms, okay? Then I thought we could go pick out a new couch and other furniture. I want this to be our place together, not just mine."

"Oh, Cowboy, you are about to get so lucky right now. You have no idea," Claire said, unbuttoning his shirt.

When she reached the last button, she stopped for a second. "Wait, I have a surprise for you too. Nothing on this level, but I think you'll like it. Why don't you go relax on the chair for a moment?"

Claire walked over to his closet and pulled out a bag from Victoria's Secret. "Be right back," she said as she went into the bathroom and shut the door.

Cole waited for a few minutes and then walked over and tapped on the door. "I'm just going to run downstairs for a minute, okay?"

"Okay," she called back as she quickly freshened up and brushed her teeth. She pulled on black thigh-high silk stockings and a red-and-black lace garter slip, clipping the suspenders to the stockings and sliding her feet into stilettos. She put on some glossy red lipstick and took the pins out of her hair, letting it fall over her shoulders in curls left by the bun.

When she opened the door to the bedroom, Cole was sitting in the chair with two glasses of champagne on the table beside him. His shirt was unbuttoned and his pants were still on, but he had bare feet. She stood in the doorway for a moment, giving him a sexy look and biting her bottom lip.

Cole let out a long breath when he saw her. "Oh, yeah. That is a great surprise," he said, feeling himself becoming aroused again. "Any chance you'll do a little spin and let me see the rest of it?"

"There's every chance that I'll do whatever you want right now," she said, crossing the room toward him.

Claire picked up his cowboy hat on her way over, placed it on her head and did a slow spin, one hand on her hip and the other on the brim of the hat. Continuing across the room, she stared at him with pure lust. When she reached him, she took off the hat, placed it on his head and then bent forward to pull his knees away from each other. She took two more steps until she was standing between his legs. Cole gently ran his fingertips along her outer thighs and up to her breasts. She turned again, and he let his fingers glide over her back and down her legs. He groaned when he reached her ass and realized she wasn't wearing panties. She walked over to the bed and picked up a pillow, then came back, dropping the pillow on the floor in front of him. She picked up the champagne glasses, handing one to Cole and taking a long drink from hers and setting it back down on the table. Cole drained his glass with a smirk.

Claire bent forward, kissing his neck as she lowered herself to her knees on the pillow in front of him. She hooked her fingers under his shirt and slid it off his shoulders. Next, she stared at him as she undid his pants and started to pull them down along with his boxer briefs. He sat in front of her, completely nude, with his thick length at attention. Claire planted delicate kisses on his lower abdomen, leaving traces of red lipstick as she did. Circling his navel with her tongue, she worked her way down to the base of his shaft. Gazing up at Cole's face, she licked him as if he were a delicious ice cream cone.

"Mmm," she moaned. "You have the most perfect cock. It's so thick and long and hard and smooth," she said, licking him between each word. She reached up and picked up her glass, taking another swig of champagne, then lowered her mouth over him again, giving him the sensation of the cold bubbles inside her warm mouth.

Cole groaned with pleasure as he looked down at her. Her position on her knees made him feel powerful as he watched her. She was beyond sexy, with her large breasts barely contained and her red lips covering him as she slowly lowered her mouth over his full length. The expression in her eyes was hedonistic, as though sucking on him were the most pleasurable thing she had ever done. She let a little of the champagne escape her lips, soaking his shaft completely. As she lifted her mouth off, she swallowed the rest of her champagne and then returned to his base again, licking up the liquid that she had spilled on him. She ran her lips along his shaft, sucking gently as she moved up and down. Placing one hand firmly on his lower abdomen, she gripped the base of his length with her thumb to hold it in place. She massaged him with both hands in time with her mouth, working slowly for several drags, followed by a few quick, hard thrusts before slowing down again. Cole reached his hands down and slid the straps of her slip off her shoulders and was rewarded when the top lowered slightly to reveal more of her breasts. He slid his hands in and filled them with her silky soft skin. He used his thumbs to rub her nipples, his excitement building as they responded to his touch.

Claire pulled her mouth off, leaving her lips parted and slapping his cock on her tongue and bottom lip as she stared into his eyes with an erotic look. She swirled her tongue over the head of his penis again, then plunged her mouth over it, releasing it finally with a wet caress.

"I love sucking on your cock. You taste so good," she said in a breathy voice.

A guttural sound erupted from Cole. She opened her mouth over him again and moved over his length, first slowly, then with quick motions.

"Wait, Claire," he blurted in a strained voice. "I'm close. We should stop so we can make love."

She lifted her mouth off him. "We *are* making love, Cole. I *want* this," she said before she plunged her mouth over him again, taking him deep into her with one long move.

Cole squeezed her breasts as she lifted her

mouth back up until he was almost all the way out, and then she pushed her head down again and back up with four fast thrusts. The next slow drag brought on an intense orgasm for Cole. He came in her mouth with a violent force. Claire felt him tremble as the waves hit him. She held him in her mouth until he was completely satisfied. Speechless, Cole sat recovering before reaching for her shoulders.

"Wow," Cole said with a wide grin. "That was the best . . . I've never . . . That was just . . . Wow."

Claire laughed. "That was my goal—to render you unable to complete a sentence."

"Mission accomplished," he said, refilling the champagne glasses and handing one to her.

Claire stood and took a long drink while Cole grabbed her bottom and pulled her to him. He brought one hand back through her legs and rubbed her with his fingers, surprised to find her so wet.

Claire looked down at him. "You see? I really was enjoying myself just now."

Cole pushed two fingers inside her and ran his other hand over her chest, pulling down her slip to reveal her breasts. Claire leaned in toward his mouth, giving him access to them. He sucked hungrily on each nipple, taking his time. Bringing his hands to her hips, he stood, picking her up off the floor so she could wrap her legs around his waist. Kissing her greedily on the mouth, he crossed the floor to the new bed. He put her down on the edge and then leaned back with her across it with their mouths locked together. After a few moments, he pulled his mouth away and picked up a rose petal off the bed and brushed it over her cheek, lips, neck and down to her breasts. He used it to trace her curves and circle her nipples. The sensation for Claire was pure bliss. The soft, cool rose petal along her skin gave her little goosebumps as it passed over her.

Cole lowered his body down so that he was the one on his knees now. He brushed her sex with the rose petal slowly and brought his mouth down, licking her from centre to front in one long drag. Claire lifted her hips and spread her legs wide in response to his touch. This time, he didn't torture her but instead parted her with his fingers and plunged his tongue deep inside her throbbing, wet heat. Claire moaned as he thrust his tongue in and pulled it out again, ending each motion with a flick. He sank the tips of his thumbs into her as he pushed his tongue into her harder and flicked it back and forth quickly and deeply. Claire caressed her breasts with her fingers and tugged on her nipples as he worked his magic. Finally, Claire succumbed to her fiercely intense orgasm, coming in delicious waves. He continued pressing his mouth to her, circling her with his tongue as she came.

When it was over, she reached down and encouraged him to join her on the bed. Cole lay down beside her, brushing his fingers over her lush curves and sucking on her nipples again.

"You are *so* good at that," Claire said when she had finally recovered her senses. "Okay, you win. I'll go out with you again," she said, taking his chin in her hand and kissing him on the lips.

"Well then, I did what I set out to do tonight," Cole said, smiling.

FIFTEEN

Cole woke up with the sun. It was a crisp October morning, and he was too excited to sleep. He and Claire finally had a day off together for the first time in a month. The restaurant and the ranch had been growing busier as some of their marketing plans had started to pay off. They had had more guests over the past two months than ever before. They had hired a sous-chef, Lauren, several weeks earlier, but it was still hard for them to keep up.

Cole got up quietly and went downstairs to prepare coffee, fruit and toast for them. He grabbed a tray and brought the food upstairs, placing it down on the centre of the bed. He kissed Claire gently on the cheek, rubbing his face against her soft skin for a moment.

"Good morning, gorgeous," he said as she blinked.

"Mmm, good morning, Cowboy," she sighed. "Is that coffee I smell?"

"And toast and berries."

"I see you're still going with the whole being perfect thing."

"If something works, you should stick with it." He laughed.

They ate their food and sipped their coffee together in bed. Claire looked out the window. "It looks like a beautiful day for our ride!" she said.

"Yup! It's my favourite type of day. Crisp air and warm sun." Cole grinned.

"Let's get out there," she said, wiping her mouth. "I'm going to have a quick shower and then run over to the restaurant to get our picnic put together."

"I can't wait," Cole said. "Now, don't get caught up checking on Lauren. She'll be just fine serving lunch and supper tonight without you. She's been here long enough now to know her way around."

"I know that," Claire said, crossing the room to the closet and picking out some sexy jeans, a black tank, and a royal-blue button-up shirt. "I promise not to spend any more time than I have to in the kitchen. I just want to get away with you for the day."

* * *

An hour later, they were at the stables walking their horses out toward the pasture. When they got outside, Cole helped Claire mount Nellie and then he got on Dudley.

Cole smiled over at her as they got going. "I want to take you up the mountain today. There's a spot with an amazing view where I thought we could stop for our picnic."

"Really? That sounds wonderful!" Claire grinned back, then grew quiet for a moment. "I've been missing you lately. We haven't had nearly as much time together as I'd like."

"Me too, which is crazy in a way, because we're never far from each other."

"I know," Claire replied. "I'm so greedy when it comes to you. I want to be right with you every minute. All day at the restaurant, there's a part of me that is waiting for you to come walking through the door. I've got it bad for you, Cowboy."

"I'm glad it's not just me. I must look at my clock one hundred times every morning, waiting for lunch, just so I can see you." He rode his horse close to hers and took hold of Nellie's reins. He stopped both horses easily and then leaned over to her to kiss her.

Claire lifted her hand to his cheek as they kissed for one beautiful, lingering moment. When they stopped, Cole looked at her, his hazel eyes shining with love. "God, you're beautiful," he said. "I will never get tired of looking at your face." He paused to stare at her. "Although, I do like your ass, too."

"Who could blame you? I've been told it's flawless," Claire replied, laughing.

They rode for a long time and Claire took in the beautiful view of the blue sky set against the rugged mountain, the sounds of the gurgling creek, the birds singing and the feeling of the fresh, crisp air on her face. She felt completely at peace and in love as she turned back to look at Cole.

He had been watching her for a while. "You know one of my favourite things about you, Claire, is how you enjoy the simple things. You never miss out because you are always open to life."

"I get that from my mom." Claire smiled as she thought of her. "She could never walk past a lilac bush without stopping to smell it. And she never seemed to be in too much of a rush to let us pick dandelions or chase butterflies when we were little."

"I wish I had met her. Your dad, too," Cole said.

"Me too, Cole. It sometimes seems hard for me to believe that my parents will never meet the most important man in my life," she said, her voice breaking. She rode for a moment and then turned back to him. "They would have adored you."

"I hope so," Cole said. "I hope I can be everything they wanted for you."

"You are," Claire said. "This might sound nuts, but sometimes I think they hand-picked you for me."

"That doesn't sound nuts to me. I hope they did," Cole said.

They turned onto a trail that led up the mountain.

Claire asked him, "Is this one of the trips you make on trail rides?"

"No," Cole said. "Some parts are pretty steep and the weather has to be just perfect. If it's at all wet, it can be a bit dangerous. We're okay today, though. I checked the forecast and there's no sign of rain. I'll stay behind you on the way up and go ahead on the way back, just in case."

"So you can stare at my ass on the way up, and I can stare at yours on the way back?"

"I get the better end of that deal," Cole replied, chuckling.

"I don't know about that. Have you ever seen your ass?" Claire asked.

As they rode along up the mountain, Cole became quiet.

"You okay back there?" Claire asked.

"I'm great," Cole replied. "Just mesmerized by the view."

Claire stood up in the saddle and gave her hips a little wiggle.

Cole gave a low whistle. "You better stop that, Ms. Hatley, or you're gonna get us lost."

Claire laughed, turning her head to face him. "Maybe I should try a little striptease, horse-back-style?"

"On second thought, knowing where you're going is highly overrated."

A few minutes later, they reached a grassy

clearing on the mountainside. A small waterfall trickled down, leading to a crystal blue pool which fed more falls. Claire stopped and turned her horse back to Cole. "Please tell me this is where we're stopping for lunch. This might be the most beautiful place I've ever been."

"Yup. We're here," Cole replied, getting off Dudley in one powerful move. He dropped the reins and walked over to Claire, holding his hands out to ease her down from her saddle. He untied the rolled-up picnic blanket and the cooler bags from Dudley before selecting the perfect spot to set up their picnic. The horses followed, stopping to drink from the cool, clear pool.

Claire unloaded the food, first taking out two bottles of Strongbow cider, followed by brie and crackers, two apples, a knife and a small cutting board. She handed the knife and board to Cole. "Would you mind slicing the apples for us?" she asked.

"Not a bit," he said.

Claire took out two plates and some cutlery and then a small container of red pepper jelly. She arranged the crackers and apple slices on the plates in an artful display, then cut the brie and placed it on the crackers, topping them with the red pepper jelly.

"Your appetizer, sir," she said, handing Cole a plate.

"So, this lunch has more than one course? Good

thing I wasn't in charge of food. It would have been a can of baked beans and some potato chips."

"Damn, that's the next two courses."

Cole tried to open the bottle and realized it wasn't a twist-off.

"Oh crap," Claire said. "Those aren't twist-offs? Sorry, babe, I didn't even think of that."

"No problem," Cole said, grabbing a butter knife and popping the tops off. "Good thing I'm here, or you'd be thirsty all day."

"Oh no, I'd be fine. I can open a bottle with my eye socket, but I don't like to do it around men I'm dating. I've been told it's not that sexy."

"What! Seriously?" Cole asked.

"No, not seriously!" Claire laughed. "That would be gross. I would have been thirsty all day."

He took a long pull on his drink and then leaned over and gave her a lingering kiss, sucking a little on her bottom lip as he moved away.

Claire opened her eyes. "Um, where are you going? You can't just give a girl a kiss like that and then expect her to go back to eating."

"That was just a sex appetizer. I made it myself. You'll get the main course later."

"You're like a sex genius. You definitely know how to whet a girl's appetite," Claire said, licking her lips suggestively.

Cole groaned. "Don't give me that look. I'm really hungry."

"Then don't give me a sex appetizer if the main course isn't going to be ready soon." Claire pouted, getting out the muffaletta sandwich she had made. She unwrapped it and put a quarter onto Cole's plate.

Cole laughed, then took a bite of his sandwich. "Good lord, Claire, this is delicious!" he said.

"I had a feeling you'd like it," Claire said, taking a bite of her part of the sandwich.

They sat together quietly eating, feeling the sun warm their skin and enjoying the romantic setting and the feeling of being in their own world.

Claire got two more bottles out and handed them to Cole to open. He popped the tops off and passed one back. He took a swig of his and then set it down, staring at her.

"I want to meet your sister and her husband," he said suddenly.

"Yeah? Where did that come from?" she asked.

"I should meet the family of the woman I want to spend the rest of my life with."

Claire gave a big grin and leaned in to kiss him. "You want to spend the rest of your life with me? You sure? I'm a bit of a nightmare. All I think about is food and sex."

Cole nuzzled her neck. "Well, when you love someone, you try to overlook their flaws."

"True. I totally try not to let it get to me that you wear clothes most of the time," Claire replied in a strained voice as Cole gently nibbled on her earlobe. "When could we take time to go to London?"

"Hmm, well, things are usually pretty slow in November and January. Could we plan a trip then?" he asked as he unbuttoned her shirt.

"Sure. It's not the best time of year to see London, though," Claire said, putting one finger in the top of his shirt and sliding it down in one quick move to undo his snaps.

"Well, I want to go soon and I'm not really going there to see the sights. I want to get to know your family." He slid her shirt off her shoulders, leaving her tank top and bra to contend with.

"Dessert time," Claire announced as Cole lifted her shirt over her head and started to unbutton her jeans.

"Exactly what I was thinking," he said, lowering his mouth over hers.

She pulled away. "No. I meant, I made dessert for us."

She stacked the plates, putting them and the empty bottles into the cooler bag as Cole took off her boots and socks. He took off his own boots and socks and then shrugged his shirt off, watching her take a container of whipped cream and another of strawberries out of the bag. She folded their shirts, making them into a pillow and placing it on the blanket. "Here, lie down for a minute."

"You lie down," Cole said. "I know how I want

to eat my dessert," he said, taking the containers from her.

Claire laid her head down, her hair falling over the makeshift pillow. She watched him open the containers. He took out one strawberry and dipped it into the cream, then brought it over to her lips and dabbed the cream onto them. She licked the cream off, then he offered her the strawberry. She took a bite, then he popped the rest into his mouth.

He put both hands on her jeans, hooking both the waistband and her panties with his fingers, then pulling them off, leaving her lying on the blanket in her bra. He looked her up and down, sighing with satisfaction. Leaning his body over hers, he teased her with his mouth, coming close to kissing her but backing away a little each time she tried to meet his lips with hers. She shivered with pleasure as he ran his big hand down her body and then back up. Next he took her wrists in his hands and pulled her up so she was sitting. Then he kissed her neck and collarbone, sliding his hands behind her and unhooking her bra. He laid her back down and let his eyes run over her naked body again.

"Much better," he said, his voice thick with lust.

Claire reached for his jeans and undid them. "You're overdressed, Cowboy." She tugged them down, along with his underwear, pushing them off with her feet as he moved to hover over her. He kissed her before pushing himself back up onto his knees. He grinned, picking up another strawberry, dipping it into the cream and then placing it into her mouth. He took his finger, dipped it into the cream and dabbed it onto one nipple. Then he took more cream for her other nipple. It felt cold and soft on her skin. He looked her in the eyes as he lowered his mouth to lick off the fluffy, sweet dessert.

"Mmm." He swirled his tongue around her nipples one at a time until the cream was gone. He picked up more cream with two fingers and covered her smooth sex with it. "This is how I want to eat my dessert from now on."

Claire was so filled with desire she could hardly speak, her voice coming out as barely a whisper. "Sure, honey."

"Honey—we should try that next time," he said as he added some whipping cream to her navel. He took his hand up to Claire's lips, gently pushing one finger into her mouth for her to suck. The sight of her luscious lips sucking on his finger made his already-hard length twitch with desire. He moved back to her breasts, sucking on them for a long moment before moving down to her navel. Sucking the cream off, he licked in long, slow swirls, taking his time. Claire's legs quivered with anticipation, knowing what was coming next. She was surprised when he picked up another strawberry and dipped it into the cream, and she watched him as he carefully slid it into her sex.

"Oh," she exclaimed at the new sensation. The strawberry and cream felt cold and smooth inside her.

Cole brought his face down between her legs and gave her a long, careful lick. He looked back up at her, smiling. "I can taste you with the whipped cream. I can't decide which is sweeter."

Giving her another lick, he allowed the tip of his tongue to touch the strawberry. "I'm going to have to stay here a while until I figure it out."

Claire felt lightheaded with erotic pleasure. She was powerless to do anything except give a little moan. She moved her hands over her breasts, caressing her nipples with her fingers as the sun shone down on her, warming her body.

Cole licked and then sucked on her soft, velvety skin. He brought his fingers up and parted her, opening her wider for his tongue. He looped his tongue around behind the strawberry and then pulled it out partway, pressing his lips to it and taking a nibble. Claire could feel his mouth sucking and nibbling. The feeling of it was a little bit taboo and completely sexy at the same time. He looped his tongue behind the berry again, pulling it out a tiny bit more, biting a piece off gently. Claire gasped, her breathing growing heavy. When Cole pulled out the last bit of strawberry, Claire grabbed his hair with both hands, pushing his mouth into her.

"I want your tongue inside me," she breathed.

Cole groaned, thrusting his tongue into her hot, creamy core. He flicked his tongue back and forth before plunging in and pulling out with force. In and out. Harder. Faster. Over and over. Claire grabbed his hair and pulled him against her forcefully as she started to come, crying out as she did. She held him there until the last spasm was long over. When she released his hair, Cole continued to lick and suck on her for a long while, thoroughly enjoying the taste and feel of her.

He lifted his head and brought his body up and over her with one strong move, lowering his weight onto her and thrusting himself inside her. Claire's legs spread wide to the side and then she wrapped them around his upper back, her hips tilted out to the sides as he pounded her with his core. His moves were quick and urgent at first, then he slowed down to make each thrust long and deep. They stared lustfully at each other in the warm glow of the autumn sun as their bodies moved in perfect unison. Claire could feel another orgasm building inside her as she looked down, watching his body where it joined hers.

Cole started gathering an unstoppable momentum, slamming himself into her. The hard ground under her allowed him to get in deeper than he ever had, filling her completely. He watched as Claire closed her eyes, mouth open, her head turned to the side, moaning and breathing fast. He could feel her muscles tighten around him as her orgasm began. Cole started to come with her, lifting her ass up off the ground as he gave one last, hard thrust.

"Oh God!" he cried out. "Oh, Claire!" He pressed himself in even farther, circling inside her as he felt another wave pulse through him.

He somehow managed to hook his arms underneath her body, sitting back onto his knees and pulling her onto his lap. Claire kissed him wildly on the mouth as she started to grind herself into him as hard as she could. She moved her hands up to his face, holding him as they kissed and their bodies continued to shudder with what was left of their orgasms.

She finally pulled her mouth away and leaned her forehead against his. "Oh God, Cole . . . That was just . . . Christ . . ." was all she managed to say.

"Yeah," he smirked. "Look who's speechless now."

"I am going to remember that for the rest of my life."

"Me too. I'm pretty sure you're the sexiest woman on the planet," he said, kissing her neck. "But I still can't decide about the whipped cream. I definitely prefer how you taste, but I'll have to run more tests to determine which is actually sweeter."

"Of course. I'll make sure the fridge remains stocked for your experiment."

"I'm sure you will."

They lay back down on the blanket, bodies intertwined, under the warmth of the sun. It was a quiet and beautiful spot, and it felt at that moment as though no one and nothing else existed. They kissed and cuddled for a long time, feeling completely lost in each other.

Cole gave her a lingering kiss. "You're it for me, Claire. I am done looking. You're the only woman I want to be with for the rest of my life."

Claire kissed him back. "I knew all that yoga would pay off someday."

Cole narrowed his hazel eyes at her. "I'm serious. I won't ever stop being in love with you."

"I'm going to love you forever, too," Claire said. "And it fucking terrifies me."

"I come from a long line of people who live happily ever after, and I know we're going to be fine. Nothing is going to happen to us, Claire. I promise."

"I believe you, Cole," she said, closing her eyes and pressing her forehead to his.

They lay there together for a while longer before the sky started to cloud over, making it feel suddenly chilly.

"I don't like the look of those clouds," Cole said, suddenly getting up. "We'd better get going."

"Yikes! Where did those come from?" Claire said, looking at the sky. Over the mountaintop, a huge mass of black clouds was moving slowly in their direction.

They quickly got dressed and packed up. Claire took one last look around. "I don't ever want to leave this moment. This day has been perfection. Thank you for bringing me here, Cole."

"Thank you for coming with me. Let's promise each other to come back again soon, okay?" he said, wrapping his arms around her and pressing his body to hers.

"Deal," she said smiling at him. "It can be our secret hideaway from the world."

A clap of thunder pulled them away from each other. Cole helped Claire hoist herself onto Nellie before mounting up and starting down the trail. Claire looked over her shoulder at their beautiful spot one last time, feeling a sense of sadness closing in with the black clouds.

"Cole," she said, "let's soak in the hot tub after supper and then make love, okay?"

Cole turned to look at her. "You okay, gorgeous? You seem sad."

"I am a bit sad. This has just been so incredible. I want something to look forward to."

"This is just the beginning, Claire. We have our whole lives to look forward to."

They picked up the pace as they descended the steeper switchback part of the trail. Cole looked behind them at the sky, concerned as he saw the black clouds rolling in quickly behind them.

"Sorry, babe. We're going to have to hustle to

stay ahead of this storm. I didn't bring any rain gear," Cole called back. "Can you keep up if I go faster? I don't want to push you to ride quicker than you're comfortable doing."

"I can do it, Cole. Let's go!" Claire called to him.

Cole gave Dudley a little kick to get him moving. Claire did the same to Nellie and was surprised by how nervous she felt. The combination of speed and the steep angle of the trail made her feel out of control, but she didn't want to slow them down. She held on tight with her legs and tried to lean back a bit in her saddle.

"If we start seeing any lightning strikes or if that thunder gets closer, we'll have to find a low patch of trees and dismount, then get all the gear off the horses. The metal on their bridles could attract lightning."

Claire looked at him with wide eyes.

"It's okay, Claire, I've made it through much worse storms than this. I won't let anything happen to you."

Claire nodded, taking comfort in his confidence.

He continued leading them quickly down the path as rain started to fall. As the large drops hit Claire's face, she muttered, "Shit, that's cold!"

A moment later, the rain started to pour down so hard it was difficult to see in front of them. Claire wished she had worn her cowboy hat instead of worrying about hat hair; between the rain and her mascara, her eyes were starting to sting. She was soaked through to her bra by now and was starting to shiver. She looked ahead at Cole in his cowboy hat as he guided Dudley down the path with an expert touch.

They were just reaching the steepest part of the path when Cole stopped and turned to Claire, calling back, "This part is going to be a bit tough! It's steep, and now that it's wet, it will be slippery. Let me go ahead a ways so Nellie can have a better view of the path. Don't pull tight on her reins, she needs to move her head to keep her balance. You'll want to lean back but don't. It makes it hard for her to move her hindquarters, and she'll need all the help she can get. Try to sit up straight. Concentrate on keeping your body lined up with the trees—they grow straight, okay?"

Claire nodded, looking worried.

"You're doing great, Claire. Really great. We'll be through the worst of it in a few minutes. Trust Nellie. She's a good horse." He nodded and then turned ahead.

Cole could tell Claire was scared by the lack of smartassed comments coming out of her mouth. He wanted to get her the hell off that mountain and away from the storm. He felt stupid for not having rain gear and was regretting bringing her up there in the first place. It was his job to keep her safe, and at this moment, he felt like he had failed miserably.

Dudley started sliding a bit, losing his footing, lowering his hindquarters to the ground for balance. Cole relaxed his body, trying to calm himself and let Dudley find his feet again. "You're okay, buddy," he said in a low tone.

When they got to a flatter part of the trail, Cole stopped and turned to check on Claire. She was a long way back, looking terrified and stiff as she rode down in the rain. Nellie started to slide in the same spot as Dudley had. Claire pulled her body back hard and lost her balance, falling off Nellie before sliding off the trail. She hit the mud hard and slipped over the bank and out of sight.

"Shit!" Cole exclaimed, dismounting in one quick move. He whipped Dudley's reins around a nearby tree and hoisted himself quickly back up the hill along the side of the trail toward Nellie, giving her room to manoeuvre. As she slid past him, he hopped out of the way behind a tree, knowing the horse would be better off making her way down the steep, slippery slope without his help. He couldn't see Claire, and panic set in as he realized he had no idea how steep the embankment was.

"Claire?" he yelled. "Claire! Can you hear me?" He ran to the spot where she had fallen off the path and frantically scrambled down, sliding partway. His heart stopped when he saw her lying motionless on the ground below.

He saw her lift her head and sit up. Claire

turned to look up at him as he approached. She was drenched and covered in mud from head to toe. His heart twisted at the sight of her, soaked and cold and trying not to cry.

"Oh, shit, Claire. Are you alright?" he asked, crouching in front of her and wrapping her in his arms.

She looked up at him, blinking fast. "I'm fine. I think I'll have a nasty bruise on my right butt cheek, though."

"I am so fucking sorry, Claire. I never should have brought you up here. I could have gotten you killed," he said, his voice thick with emotion as he pressed her to him.

"Are you kidding me? Up until the last few minutes, this has been the most romantic day of my life. I wouldn't change a thing. Well, maybe the whole falling-off-the-horse thing, but that's it," she replied, lifting her face up to meet his. Just then a loud clap of thunder overhead caused them both to flinch.

"We should get out of here. Can you walk?" Cole asked, rising to his feet and pulling her up with him.

"I'm fine. I can't wait to get into that hot tub, though!"

Cole climbed up the hill with Claire in front of him so he could catch her if she started to slide. Just as they got up to the trail again, another clap of thunder boomed. Cole turned his head in time to see Nellie taking off down the mountainside at breakneck speed.

"Looks like we're going to have to share a horse," Cole said.

"Will she be able to get home?" Claire asked.

"Yup, she's heading there right now," he answered. He was touched that her concern was for the horse rather than for her own comfort. He smoothed her hair with both hands and then turned her chin up so she was facing him "You had me worried there when you fell. I need to take better care of you than this."

Claire sighed and gave him a thoughtful look. "This isn't your fault, Cole. You do take care of me," she replied, swiping her finger over his nose, depositing some mud in the process. "I bet I look pretty, though, with mud all over me and makeup running down my face."

"You look beautiful," Cole said, "in a really dirty way."

He wiped his hands on his shirt and then tried to wipe off the makeup under her eyes, spreading it around instead.

"Oh. Shit. I should not have done that," he said with wide eyes, covering his mouth with one hand and trying not to laugh.

"My mascara is all over my cheeks now, isn't it?" she said, looking annoyed.

"I had no idea you had so much on. It's just . . . everywhere," he said, stifling another bout of laughter. Recovering quickly, he said, "You still look hot, though."

He stood and took her hand, starting down the trail to Dudley, who was waiting in a small clearing below them. Cole looked over at Claire, suddenly overwhelmed with gratitude that she was okay. He kissed her, getting mud on his face and losing his balance at the same time. He brought her down with him as he fell but caught her at the last second so she landed on his lap as they slid down the hill a few feet. He dug his heels into the mud to stop their fall. They sat for a moment staring at each other in the rain. Claire lifted her hand to Cole's jaw, holding his face still so she could plant a hungry kiss on him.

When she lifted her face away, she smiled. "Looks like I rubbed off on you. Now you're as dirty as me." They helped each other get up, laughing a little.

"Now I know I have to marry you." He wrapped his arms around her and pulled her in to him tightly. "You're the only woman in the world who would find this funny. Most women would be really upset or angry right now." He gave her an adoring smile and kissed her hard.

"I'll marry you on one condition," she said. "You lend me your hat until it stops raining. All this makeup in my eyes is stinging like crazy."

"My hat?" he replied, and then he shook his head. "Forget it. That's a deal breaker."

Then he turned his eyes up as though he was considering her offer. "On second thought, you do give award-winning blow jobs, you're really bendy and you can cook," he said, taking his hat off and placing it on her head.

They started down the hill, this time sliding a little but managing to stay on their feet. When they reached the clearing, Cole looked over at her. "That's a contract, you know. You agreed to marry me if I gave you the hat. That's a binding verbal agreement."

"I'm okay with that. You are super sexy and built and smart, and when you aren't trying to kill me on dangerous trail rides, you take pretty good care of me," she said, giving him a grin. "I also love how you eat strawberries and whipped cream. I have never seen anyone do that before. If you agree to keep eating them like that, I'll definitely marry you."

"You can't keep adding stipulations. You agreed to marry me if I lent you the hat. The deal is made, gorgeous," he said, slapping her on the ass. "I'm going to keep eating strawberries and whipped cream out of your tight little pussy, but only because I like it."

She reached up with her mouth and gently bit his bottom lip. "Even better."

They reluctantly pulled away from each other and walked over to Dudley. Cole untied the horse's reins and swung himself up into his saddle.

"Sorry, Dudley," Claire said, petting his side. "I bet you're tired and now we're asking you to give us both a ride."

Cole smiled down at her and moved his foot out of the stirrup, making room for her to hoist herself up. He grabbed her hand and pulled as she hoisted herself up, securing her in front of him on the saddle. Their bodies were pressed together as they rode. Claire lifted off Cole's hat and reached behind her to pop it back onto him, then rested her head against his shoulder. "We can share."

Cole held her tightly as they rode in the rain to the bottom of the mountain, the heat from his body warming Claire's back now, making her feel safe and slightly dizzy with love. The rain let up as they crossed the meadow and soon the sun came out again. Cole took his hat off and held it on his thigh with one hand to let it dry out. He held the reins in the other hand, which was firmly wrapped around Claire's waist. He gently ran his nose along her neck and then planted soft kisses along it.

Claire sighed happily. "You keep doing that and I'm going to make you take me straight to bed instead of eating supper."

"I had a big lunch. I can wait."

"You also had a lot of sex already today."

"When I'm around you, everything else can wait. Food and sleep have never mattered less."

Claire turned her head to face him, letting her mouth hover over his. Each time he moved toward her, she pulled back a bit, changing the angle of her face slightly. He chased her with his mouth over and over, finally groaning in frustration. A wicked little grin spread across her face as she finally let him catch her. He kissed her greedily, thrusting his tongue into her open mouth.

When he stopped and pulled back, he looked at her. "I love you, Claire. I didn't know it was possible to love someone this much."

Claire leaned into him. "It's wonderful, isn't it?"

A few minutes later, the ranch came into view. The sight was beautiful, with the late-day sun shimmering off the lake. The world smelled fresh and new. They were both completely content as they rode through the gates. When they reached the stables, Cole climbed off Dudley and then put his hands on Claire's waist, lifting her down carefully. They could hear some rustling in the far end of the stables and they looked in to find Ben saddling up his horse frantically.

"Ben, what's wrong?" Cole asked.

Ben turned and when he saw the pair he let out a breath of relief. "Thank Christ you two are okay. Nellie got back here a few minutes ago. I figured Claire must have been thrown." He paused for a moment, taking in the sight of them covered with mud. "Looks like Cole took you up the mountain," he said to Claire.

"He did," she said, smiling up at him. "It was quite the date."

Ben walked over and took Dudley's reins from Cole. "I'm just glad you two are alright. You go have a shower and get warmed up. I'll take care of old Dudley here."

"Thanks, bro." Cole smiled, wrapping his arm around Claire's shoulder lazily. "Let's go get back in the shower," he said to her in a low voice. They sauntered out of the stables, arms wrapped around each other. Cole lifted Claire's hand up to his lips.

Suddenly he stopped dead in his tracks, his entire body frozen in place. Claire stopped and looked over to see what he was staring at. In front of them was one of the most beautiful women Claire had ever seen. She had long, perfectly straight black hair and was wearing a short flirty dress that showed off her incredibly curvy body and tiny waist. Her tanned legs went on for miles until they reached her strappy red high heels. On her hip was a baby, sitting up, gripping onto her dress with his tiny hand. He had sandy-blond hair and a big smile on his little face.

The woman's eyes flicked over Claire in an instant of jealousy. She recovered quickly, giving Cole a sultry smile. "*Meu amor*, I want you to meet your son, Tomas Cole Ferreira."

PART TWO
She Leaves

SIXTEEN

Claire sat in her seat with her head pressed against the window. It was dark outside, and a soft rain fell on the plane as the last of the passengers finished boarding. She waited impatiently for the cabin's bright lights to be turned off so she could hide the tears streaming down her cheeks. Although the air was hot and stale before takeoff, Claire pulled her dark grey cardigan tighter around her. People were getting settled into their seats, taking off their coats and stowing their bags, chatting happily. Claire was completely disconnected from her surroundings, wishing she could just melt into the seat and disappear.

She had booked herself into business class in the hopes of avoiding people travelling with babies. She didn't need any more reminders of what she'd left behind at the ranch. So far, the seat next to her was empty, and she hoped it wasn't too much to ask that it stay that way. She was incapable of small talk and wanted to be alone with her misery and exhaustion.

Even though she had left Colorado earlier that morning, it seemed like several days ago. She was plain worn out by the time she arrived at JFK. She would be in London in a little over seven hours, although she didn't really care how long it took to get there. Nothing would bring her any joy now that she and Cole were through for good. Only two weeks earlier her new life with Cole had been well on its way, and for one brief moment, everything had been perfect. Then in a split second, her bubble had burst, just as it always did for her. Maybe she just wasn't meant to live happily ever after.

A flight attendant stopped at Claire's row, leaning over quietly to address her. "You okay, sweetie?" she asked with concern.

Claire turned and nodded with a weak smile.

"Are you a nervous flyer or is it man trouble?" she asked. She looked to be about fifty years old, with warm green eyes and greying brown hair pulled back in a tight bun.

"The second one," Claire whispered.

"Thought so. Whoever he is, I'm sure it's his loss," she said, handing her a pillow and blanket.

"Thanks," Claire said, folding the pillow and placing it on her shoulder, then resting her forehead against the window again.

A moment later, she noticed a man settle in beside her. *Shit*, she thought, hoping he would ignore her. She didn't want to look directly at him but could just see his arm out of the corner of her eye. He had a light-blue dress shirt on, and she could tell he was taking off his tie. He carefully folded the tie and placed it into his blazer pocket, then stood up to put the blazer into the overhead bin. She could see he was tall with a lean but muscular build.

He sat down quietly, turning on his tablet to read the newspaper. Claire could feel him look at her, and she was relieved when he didn't say anything. Soon another flight attendant appeared with a pillow and blanket for him. He ordered two glasses of white wine in a slight French accent.

Oh great, thought Claire. *Hopefully he gets drunk and becomes really obnoxious. That's all I need right now.*

When the wine arrived, he tapped Claire on the shoulder, holding a glass out to her. "For you. You look like you could use a drink."

Claire looked into his face with confusion. He smiled at her kindly. "Take it, please. I hate to drink alone."

Claire gave him a small smile and took the wine. "Thanks."

"*Je vous en prie*," he said graciously as he tilted his head to her and took a sip of his drink. He had classic French good looks, with a bit of stubble and a definite sense of style. He looked to be close to forty and obviously had money, based on his expensive-looking suit and watch. He had black hair and his eyes were the colour of dark chocolate. He was the type of man that exuded power and confidence and was obviously used to getting a lot of female attention.

Claire drained her glass of wine and set it down on the armrest. The man flagged down a flight attendant. "My friend could use another wine when you have a moment." He paused. "Me as well."

The attendant nodded, returning with two full glasses and removing their empty ones. The captain's voice came over the speaker, advising the passengers that they would be delayed by twenty minutes from getting onto the runway. Mutters of complaint could be heard throughout the cabin.

Claire took a large gulp of wine and turned back to the window, watching the rain splash off a puddle on the ground outside. Her mind wandered back to the moment she first saw Gabriela and Cole's baby, Tomas. She had been covered with mud and her makeup was all over her face as they walked around the stables to go to their cabin. Even though she was a total mess, Claire was happier than she had ever been. She could feel that moment as though it were happening all over again—Gabriela's words as she introduced Cole to his son, then her little smirk as she looked Claire up and down like a bug she could squash. The feeling of Claire's knees going weak as her entire world was ripped apart by one sentence spoken in Gabriela's sexy Brazilian accent.

Claire had stood frozen for what seemed like an eternity, the scene not registering. The blood was pumping so hard through her ears that it made it impossible to hear what Cole and Gabriela were saying. She excused herself in a whisper and hurried to the other side of the stables, then stood bent over, feeling as though she would vomit. She somehow ended up in the shower back at the cabin, sobbing violently as the hot water rushed over her body and mud washed down the drain.

Claire's thoughts were interrupted as her empty glass was gently taken from her hand. Mr. Suave was replacing it with his untouched, full glass. "You obviously need it more than I do."

"I suppose I do," Claire said quietly. "Thank you again . . ." Her voice trailed off as she realized she didn't know his name.

"Luc," he said, handing her a napkin to wipe away her tears.

"Claire."

"And, Claire, what do you do when you are not crying on airplanes?" he asked with a serious look. It was a forward question, but he appeared to be the type of man whose life had taught him he could get away with such boldness.

"Lately, I cry in cabs, at airports and wherever else I am," she said, starting to feel numb from the wine.

"Ah, I see. I'm guessing you made the classic

mistake of the American woman. You believed all the fairy tales you were fed as a little girl, and now you're devastated to discover they don't always come true."

Claire gave him a dirty look. "I'm guessing you're used to getting away with being such a patronizing ass since you're good-looking and rich." She drained the rest of her wine and set the glass down, turning back to the window.

Luc's lips curled up in amusement. He opened his mouth to respond but was interrupted by the captain's voice announcing that they were finally ready to depart. The plane started to back up and then turned toward the runway as the flight attendants took their positions in the centre aisle to give the safety instructions.

Claire covered her lap with the blanket and rested her head against the pillow again, closing her eyes. The third glass of wine was taking effect, causing her to feel warm and wonderfully detached from her miserable reality. Her last thoughts before she drifted off to sleep were, *Wine. That's the answer. If I stay a little drunk for the rest of my life, I can get through this.*

She woke five hours later. She felt cozy, and for one dream-like moment, she thought she was sleeping pressed up against Cole's body, although he had changed his cologne. She tightened her arm around his chest and made a soft moaning sound. Then reality hit her. She would never see Cole again.

Her eyes flew open, and she discovered that she had been sleeping curled up with her head on Luc's shoulder and her arm wrapped around him.

She jerked her body away from him in shock. He was awake, reading a book on his tablet. He looked at her with playfulness in his eyes. "Good morning, sweetheart."

"Oh my God, I'm so sorry," she apologized, putting a hand over her face. "Have I been sleeping on you for very long?"

"About an hour. It's fine, really. I thought it better to let you sleep. You seemed to like me more than when you were awake."

Claire's mind flashed back to calling him a patronizing ass. And now she had been sleeping on him. "Shit. I hope I didn't"—she searched for a more appropriate word than *grope*—"do anything inappropriate."

"Not at all," Luc replied with a little smirk. "You distracted me from my reading, though, by making the most adorable little sounds in your sleep."

"I was snoring?"

"No, no," he said with a laugh. "Little sighs and happy moans. You are a very sensual woman when you are asleep."

Claire blushed at his words. Realizing she must have dragon breath, she excused herself to go to the washroom, bringing her carry-on bag with her. Luc stared at her ass as she stepped over his feet to the aisle. His face wore an expression that could only be described as appreciative.

Claire stood in the bathroom trying to steady herself as she brushed her teeth and washed her face. She rooted around in her makeup bag for her face cream and lip balm. When she looked in the mirror, she saw how puffy her eyes were. She was a frumpy mess in her grey oversized cardigan, and her hair was beyond fixing, looking somehow greasy and frizzy at the same time. She sighed heavily, putting her cream back into the bag and zipping it up. She felt very awake after having finally slept for more than a couple of hours for the first time since she had booked her flight. When she stepped out of the tiny washroom, her eyes scanned the cabin of the plane and fell on Luc. He was reading again, but he glanced up at her as she approached. He held her gaze for a moment and then moved his legs to the side to allow her to pass by him.

As she sat down, she saw that two glasses of wine were waiting. She smiled at Luc and thanked him.

"Are these both mine?"

"I thought I would have one as well, if you don't mind."

"Of course," she said, raising her glass and taking a long drink.

"Claire, I owe you an apology for what I said earlier. It was one of those comments that make people think the French are arrogant."

"In that case, you should apologize to French people, not to me," she said, smiling at him. "I called you an ass and had a nap on you. Let's call it even."

"A fair resolution." He nodded, taking a sip of his wine. He stared at her for a moment. "You know, my shoulders can be used for things other than sleeping on. If you need to unburden yourself, I can listen without being an ass."

Claire finished her wine and caught the eye of a flight attendant, signalling for another. "Thanks. My story is close to what you thought, though. Only I didn't completely believe in the fairy tale until the last page. Right before it ended."

"I'm sorry to hear that," Luc said. He paused, waiting for Claire to say more. When she didn't, he continued, "This is why I don't believe in marriage. Life is long and we are meant to experience love for as long as it is good. People aren't supposed to chain themselves to one person and spend the rest of their lives wishing they hadn't. Life is meant to be lived with pleasure. If you know *that* going in, love won't destroy you when it ends."

"You might be right . . . I don't know," she said, holding her glass up for a refill. She thought for a moment. "I have seen love last for other people, and I thought I had it. But it wasn't meant to be. No one's fault."

"Surely, someone is to blame!"

"Well, it wasn't his fault, or mine, anyway, which actually makes it worse. It would be so much easier to get over him if he had done something really rotten to hurt me. Then I would have my anger to get me through this."

Luc shifted his body to face hers, propping his knee up casually on his seat. "Hmm, that does sound difficult. In that case, there is only one way to get over it: pleasure of every kind."

Claire raised her eyebrow at him.

"Not right now. You cry now. Give yourself a week, or two, even, then you start seeking out every type of joy you have denied yourself. Food, wine, sex with lots of different men or women, dancing . . . whatever you like that will remind you life is meant to be enjoyed."

Claire stared at him, unconvinced. "Well, Luc, you've certainly given me something to think about. For now, I will enjoy as much wine as I can."

"It's a good place to start," he said, nodding with approval. "But not too much of this wine. It's shit."

Claire laughed out loud for the first time in days. "It really is awful, isn't it?"

He nodded, studying her face as she smiled. "Tell me what you do for work. I have a few guesses, and I want to see if I'm right."

Claire was surprised he had taken the time to wonder about her. She thought for a moment. "I'll give you five chances to see if you can guess. If you can't, I won't tell you."

"Oh, she likes games, does she?" he asked, looking impressed. "*Bien*. But I may ask one question after guess number four, and you must answer it truthfully."

"You're on."

"Teacher?"

"Nope."

"Nurse?"

"Oh, please. Are you just going through the most stereotypical careers for women?"

"Librarian?"

"It's the sweater, isn't it?"

Luc laughed out loud. "A little bit, yes. Answer the question."

"No."

He gave her a long look, searching for some type of clue in her blue eyes. Finding nothing, he decided to try to make her laugh again. "Porn star?"

Claire blushed. "Obviously not."

"Why would that be obvious? I'm sure porn stars wear ill-fitting sweaters and cry sometimes, too."

"One more guess left."

"My question first. You must answer truthfully."

"Yes, I remember."

"What do you do for a living?"

Claire rolled her eyes. "Of course that's your question. You don't seem like the type to play fair."

{339}

"You agreed to it," Luc answered with a little smirk.

"I'm a chef."

"Hmm," he replied. "I can see that. You have a deeply sensual side when you sleep, so it must be there when you are awake, at times, too."

"I don't know about that, but I do love food, anyway."

"I would love to taste your food sometime," he said, his eyes falling to her lips for a brief moment.

Claire blushed at his suggestion and looked down at her hands. "Well, maybe I'll get a job in London while I'm here."

"I don't live in London. I live in Paris most of the time. I've been in New York on business and have business in London now."

"What do you do?"

"Five guesses."

"Lawyer."

"No."

"Some type of businessman."

Luc laughed again. "Yes."

"Got it in two," she said, looking satisfied with herself.

"I own a few nightclubs here and there."

"So, pleasure is your business."

"In a sense. Making money is my real business, but I suppose I provide a diversion for people at the same time," Luc replied.

"A diversion. I can see how you would make

money that way. People need to be distracted from life sometimes," Claire said, glancing out the window. It was light outside now as they neared London. It would be mid-morning when they landed.

Luc's gaze followed hers to the window. "A new day is starting."

"That it is," Claire said, staring at the clouds.

The plane began to descend, and as it lowered beneath the cloud cover, she could see the River Thames running through the city. The familiar sight didn't bring with it the excitement it normally did. She felt exhausted and empty inside, each passing mile taking her farther away from Cole. Her heart felt seared with pain at the thought of him.

As they got off the plane, Luc handed her a business card. "In case you need a diversion or a job."

Claire put it into her pocket. "Thank you, Luc."

"Do you know your way around London or would you like a hand to get where you're going?"

"I'm all set. My sister lives here, so I'll be well taken care of. Thank you for everything, Luc. I haven't slept that well in weeks."

Luc leaned over and kissed her on both cheeks. "Until we meet again," he said as he started to walk away. He took a few steps and then turned back to her. "I do mean for you to call me, Claire. You make me laugh, which few people can do."

Claire grinned and saluted him, then turned to go find the baggage claim area.

* * *

Twenty minutes later, Claire had a huge pile of luggage on two carts. She stared at the sum total of all her belongings, packed up again so she could move on with her life. This time, most of her things were in tightly packed boxes rather than garbage bags. Cole had reluctantly helped her pack, bringing several empty boxes up to their room for her. "I didn't think your things would make the plane ride in garbage bags," he said.

A porter came over to offer Claire help, which she gladly accepted. "If you could help get my stuff over to that pub on the other side of the arrivals section for now, that would be terrific. I need a beer."

The young man helped get her things tucked into a corner of the pub and waited while she ordered a pint. She gave him a tip and thanked him, then sat down at a small table. She checked the time and realized she had a couple of hours to kill before her brother-in-law would be awake if he had had a gig the night before. Her sister would be at work for at least another six hours. She decided not to call her. She knew Janet would insist on cancelling her meetings and rushing to her, and there was no point in burdening her more than Claire would already be doing.

SEVENTEEN

Colorado Springs—Two Weeks Earlier

Cole stood rooted to the ground. He was in a state of shock that made his skin go clammy and his legs feel like cement. A strange feeling of calm came over him, as though he were just observing, from the outside, what was happening. Gabriela was telling him he had a son and then she was walking toward him and handing him the baby. She took out her cellphone and took a picture of the two together. Cole wasn't sure what expression he had on his face as the first photo of him with his son was taken.

Cole wasn't aware of the moment that Claire disappeared, but he suddenly realized she was no longer standing with him. He heard himself say something about getting Gabriela settled into one of the larger guest cabins, and he started walking over to the lodge to get the keys. He was carrying a baby in his arms. The little boy touched Cole's cheek, bringing him back to his thoughts again, the feeling of calmness leaving him, replaced by panic and a deep sense of building rage.

His mind was racing now. What would this mean for him and Claire? Where had she gone just now? How could Gabriela not have told him she was having his baby? How could she have kept this from him for so long? Was this even really his baby?

It was far too much for him to make sense of as they walked into the lodge. He handed the baby back to Gabriela and went behind the front desk for a set of keys. He called Trey's cellphone, forgetting he had left for college two months earlier. When the voice mail picked up, he remembered and dialed Ben's cellphone. He asked him to come up to the lodge to find the playpen for guests' babies.

When Ben got to the lodge, he stopped short, staring at Gabriela and the baby. She walked over, hugging him briefly and introducing him to his nephew. Ben looked at Cole's face, wet with sweat and pale under the mud, his eyes full of panic as he looked at his brother.

Ben said hello to Gabriela and the baby and repeated his name. "Tomas?"

"Yes. Tomas Cole." Gabriela looked cautiously at him. "I know this will be a shock for everyone here. I'm sorry that I've kept him a secret for so long."

Ben looked back at Cole, who was leaning against the front desk for support.

"I'm sure you had your reasons, Gabriela," Ben replied, looking confused. "You must be tired. I'll take you over to your cabin and then bring the playpen and your luggage over in a few minutes." Ben looked over at the several large suitcases sitting on the floor near the front door. "Are these yours?"

"Yes." Gabriela nodded, with a look of gratitude at Ben's thoughtfulness. "Thank you, Ben."

Ben took the keys from Cole. "You should go have a shower, little bro. You're a mess."

Cole nodded, his face expressionless. "Yeah, I am," he mumbled. *In more ways than one*, he thought.

Cole walked slowly back to his cabin, trying to sort out what had just happened and think about what to do next. He could hear the shower running upstairs when he closed the front door behind him. On autopilot, he walked over to the kitchen and grabbed a beer from the fridge. He sank down into a chair, opening the bottle and draining it in long gulps. He rested his forehead on his hand as he sat, trying to process everything. A few minutes later, he heard the water turn off. He moved slowly up the stairs, his body feeling like lead. As he reached the top, Claire opened the bathroom door. She had a towel wrapped around her head and was wearing a bathrobe. Her eyes and nose were red from crying.

She started at the sight of him looking so pale and wide-eyed with shock. "Cole, I'm sorry, I think I used all the hot water."

"That's okay. It doesn't matter," he replied quietly. Neither of them were ready to face the elephant in the room. "I'm going to shower now anyway." He silently made his way into the bathroom and shut the door.

* * *

Claire collapsed into the armchair, letting her body go limp. Today had gone from the best day of her life to one of the worst in a split second. Only a couple of hours earlier, she and Cole had been talking about getting married and had been making plans to go to London so he could meet her family. Their lives had been so uncomplicated. Now their world was completely upside down and she had no idea how to get her footing again. She sat in the chair for a long time, waiting for Cole to finish his shower and come out, finally deciding to go downstairs and make something for them to eat. She took the towel off her head and combed out her hair, then put on some yoga pants, a bra and a long-sleeved black T-shirt.

In the kitchen, she reached into the fridge and pulled out a carton of eggs, then cracked them into a bowl. She cut up a few mushrooms and chopped some red pepper to add to the eggs before heating up a pan and buttering it, then put the kettle on to make them some tea as the omelettes cooked.

A few minutes later, she set down two plates with omelettes, sautéed cherry tomatoes and toast on the kitchen table, then brought over the pot of tea and two mugs. Cole came down the stairs just as she was pouring the tea.

He stared at her for a moment before he walked over. She looked so lovely with wet hair and no makeup. It made his heart ache to see her sitting there, looking so confused and sad.

"Smells great down here," he said, coming over to her. He had a light grey T-shirt and jeans on. He kissed her lightly on the forehead and sat down opposite her. "Thank you, sweetie, this looks delicious," he said, picking up his fork.

Claire smiled weakly. "You're welcome."

They both ate slowly. Claire pushed the food around on her plate, taking only a few bites. It was almost impossible for her to swallow the food past the lump that had lodged itself in her throat.

"Is your hip okay where you fell? I imagine you've got some bruises," Cole managed after a few minutes.

"Oh, yeah, a few," Claire replied. "No big deal. I'm lucky it wasn't worse."

They seemed to have an unspoken agreement that if neither of them mentioned the baby, they could have a few more minutes pretending things hadn't changed. It was no use, however. They were both in shock; all feelings of romance from earlier in the day were long gone by now. Cole finished dinner and wiped his mouth with his napkin, staring out the window. Claire continued to poke at her food with her fork, eating tiny bites here and there until she gave up and pushed her chair back from the table. She got up and went over to stare out the large living room window so Cole couldn't see her tearing up.

A moment later, she felt his hands on her shoulders and his lips pressed to the back of her head. "Christ, Claire, I can't believe this is happening," he said quietly.

Claire sighed, her heart breaking. "Me too. I'm in shock. I feel like everything before was just a wonderful dream, and now I've woken up to a nightmare."

"Same here," Cole replied, walking over to the couch and collapsing onto it. "I don't know how to feel. I never imagined I would react with rage to seeing my first child, but I've never been this angry in my life, and I also feel like shit for being angry."

Claire came over and sat next to him. "Oh, Cole, of course you should feel angry. She hid the entire thing from you, let you move on with your life for a year and a half, and then showed up unannounced with a baby she claims is yours. What else could you feel? You can't expect yourself to be happy about it."

Cole rubbed his face with his hands and then rested his head on the back of the couch, trying to stop the tears that were welling up in his eyes. Claire wrapped him in her arms and brought his head onto her shoulder. "It's okay, Cole. Let me take care of you right now like you've taken care of me."

She held him for a long time before he pulled back and took a deep breath. Claire went over to the kitchen and grabbed a bottle of Jack Daniel's and two shot glasses. She poured each of them a drink and handed Cole one. They each did their shot. Claire's burned going down her throat, and she remembered how much she hated whisky. She poured another round anyway.

"What do I do, Claire?" he asked, looking at her.

"Well, what are the options? Maybe the first place to start would be to find out for sure if he's really your son."

"Claire, he looks exactly like me when I was a baby. Unless she slept with Ben before she left, that's my kid."

"He still might not be. You should insist on a paternity test. It's only fair after what she's done. It's not like you can blindly trust her."

"I know. You're probably right, but it doesn't change the fact that he's a dead ringer for me."

Claire sighed, not wanting to allow his words to register in her brain. "Did she say why she didn't tell you until now?" she asked, her voice rising with anger. "It's all so unbelievable! I just can't under-stand it at all."

"Honestly, I can't remember much of what happened after she said I had a son. I know she said something about needing to wait for his passport and being overwhelmed, but the rest I didn't catch. I'll need to have a long talk with her to find out what the hell she was thinking this whole time. As far as I'm concerned, there's no excuse for what she's done."

"Well, whatever she says, take it with a grain of salt. I don't think you can trust her. The only thing we can trust for sure is that she wants you back."

"Too fucking bad for her. I'm with you, and that is never going to change. What she wants is irrelevant to me."

"It's going to become relevant fast if she decides to go back home with your son. She doesn't seem like the type to play second fiddle. She looks more like the all-or-nothing type."

Cole sighed. "You're right about that. I think tomorrow I'll need to talk to a family lawyer and find out about the steps to gaining parental rights. She holds all the cards right now."

Claire let the gravity of the situation sink in. She was suddenly exhausted from the long day and the shocking news. She knew Cole was the type of man who would insist on being a real dad to his child. His sense of honour was one of the things she loved most about him. And she knew it would also be their undoing.

They sat quietly for a few minutes, then Cole took Claire in his arms and hugged her for a long time. "I'm in love with you, Claire, and nothing is going to change that. We're going to figure this out together, okay? We aren't the first people to have to make a situation like this work. There are ways to do this, and we'll find them."

* * *

The night passed slowly. Claire and Cole both lay awake for hours at different points during the night. Cole was up long before the sun, researching paternity and custody laws on the Internet.

Claire woke at five to an empty bed. Putting on her robe she went downstairs and found Cole at the kitchen table in front of his laptop. He had dark circles around his eyes and looked exhausted. She started a pot of coffee and walked over to him, leaning over his shoulders to wrap her arms around his chest and give him a kiss on the cheek.

"What have you figured out so far?" she asked.

"Well, right now she can obviously take off if she wants, and I can't do a thing about it. There are two ways to gain parental rights in Colorado: genetic testing or signing an admission of paternity form in front of a notary. The admission form would mean I gain rights a few weeks faster than through the genetic-testing method. I can also petition to have my name put on his birth certificate if it isn't there already. I'm not sure how that works, though, since the birth certificate was issued in Brazil. It's going to be complicated."

Claire walked over to the counter and poured two coffees and brought one back to Cole before making some toast. She knew she should eat something, even though she felt completely nauseous.

"So, which way are you leaning?"

"I think I should just sign the admission of paternity form. It's my best shot at keeping him. If I insist on the genetic testing, I'm going to waste valuable time I don't have. If I do it this way, it shows trust in her, and I can get it on the books that I have parental rights. By the time she figures out she can't break us up, it will be too late for her to threaten to take him back to Brazil."

"So, you're just going to jump right in and accept that she's telling the truth after everything she's done?" Claire asked. "That's insane, Cole! How can you even consider that? What if he's not your child, and you're saddling yourself with the two of them for the rest of your life when it's got nothing to do with you?"

Cole put his hands up, palms open. "Whoa, take a minute to think about what I've just said. I know it's hard to digest, but it's the logical thing to do. We have got to stick together here, Claire, or we are going to be in real trouble."

"Well, you know what else will cause trouble? Trusting her word about anything! I'm telling you, this is a bad idea."

"It's easy for you to say," Cole countered, raising his voice a little. "I'm sure you would love it if that baby weren't mine! Part of me would love it, too. I could be rid of Gabriela forever, and you and I could pick up where we were yesterday morning. But the reality is that he *is* my son, and I have to fight to keep him here with me. I can't push her away and then never see him again. I just can't. He belongs with his father. If I let him grow up with her and her horrible family, what kind of man does that make me, Claire?"

"Well, you certainly don't want to be the kind who ruins his own life accepting responsibility for some other man's child!"

"He's not going to ruin my life, Claire! He's an innocent baby, for God's sake!"

"Yeah, a baby who comes with a real piece of work for a mother! You *cannot* trust her. Don't be so naive!" Claire stormed up the stairs, leaving her toast in the toaster and her coffee untouched. She got dressed in her running clothes and walked down the stairs and out the door without a word.

Claire didn't see the sunrise lighting the top of the mountains as she ran. It was a cold morning, but she hardly noticed the wind on her face or how icy her hands were as she propelled herself forward with increasing force. She ran as fast as she could, hoping to release some of the rage she felt toward Gabriela and Cole. How could he have let this happen? How could he have loved such a person before her? She stopped when she reached the end of the path, breathing so hard she felt like she might vomit. She leaned her hands on her knees, allowing herself to cry for a long time, tears spilling onto the path. When she was ready, she jogged back toward the cabin, trying to centre herself and come up with a plan for how to handle this. When she got there, Cole was gone. It was still so early she figured he must have gone down to the barn or his office.

By the time she was in the shower, Claire decided the only thing she could do was play a supportive role for Cole right now. She would try to be logical and think of how she would want him to handle things if the roles were reversed. She would only push him away with her anger, so she needed to find a way to keep those feelings in check. Underneath that anger was fear. If she could remind herself that she was scared, she could stay calm and convey her fear to Cole instead. Fear wouldn't push him away, it would pull him toward her. He had such a strong protective nature, and she needed to trust that he would never want to hurt her.

When Claire was dressed and had dried her hair, she went to find Cole. She found him in the stables with little Tomas in his arms. He was standing in front of Dudley, and Tomas was touching the large horse's face and squealing with laughter when Dudley licked his fingers. Claire watched them for a brief moment, her heart breaking, wishing he was her little boy instead of Gabriela's.

She walked up beside them. "I'm amazed he isn't scared. Dudley's so huge compared to him."

"I know, right?" Cole replied. "He's a brave little guy, I think."

Claire swallowed to push down the lump in her throat. "I'm sorry about this morning, Cole. I'm really tired and really, really scared."

Cole gave her a kiss on the cheek. "I'm sorry, too. Neither of us slept last night, and this whole thing is a shock. We'll have to muddle our way through together, okay?"

The moment was interrupted by a voice behind them.

"Oh, there are my boys!" Gabriela breezed across the wood floor as though it were a catwalk, her gaze set on Cole. She wore a tight white turtle-neck sweater and fitted jeans tucked into tall brown leather riding boots. Her hair was pulled back in a high ponytail that swung behind her as she strode over to them. Claire felt suddenly very plain in her favourite navy V-neck sweater and her boot-cut jeans.

Gabriela acted as though Claire didn't exist.

"Thank you, *meu amor*. To shower without worrying about our son was absolutely delicious!"

Claire cleared her throat. "Good morning, Gabriela. I'm Claire. I don't think we've officially met," she said, extending her hand.

Gabriela glanced her up and down and then gave her a weak little handshake. "Oh, yes. I saw you yesterday, but you were all covered in mud so I did not recognize you today. Are you one of the ranch hands?"

Cole spoke up. "Claire is my girlfriend, and she's the executive chef at the ranch as well."

"Oh, how nice of you to give your girlfriend a job," Gabriela replied with amusement.

"I had the job first. My goodness, you look great for someone who just travelled so far with a baby."

Gabriela gave her a phony smile. "Oh, she's sweet, Cole. I can see why you like her. Come here, my little angel," she said, holding her hands out for Tomas. Cole handed him over to her. "Did you like Dudley? He's a nice horse, isn't he?" she asked the baby.

"He really likes him. He's pretty brave," Cole said.

"Just like his daddy." Gabriela smiled at her son and back to Cole. "I'm going to go feed him now. He also has his daddy's appetite." She waved Tomas's little hand at Cole. "Bye-bye, Daddy!"

It was all Claire could do not to roll her eyes. She

and Cole watched them depart, Gabriela's ass and ponytail swaying behind her.

"She's not going to make this easy, is she?" Cole said.

"I guess not. She came all this way for a reason, and I'm in the way of her getting what she wants."

"Well, too bad for her," Cole said, giving Claire a big kiss on the lips, "because you're my girl and that's not going to change."

* * *

A little while later at the restaurant, Claire got a text from Alicia. It was her day off, and she invited Claire to come by for coffee after the breakfast service was over. At nine thirty Claire knocked gently on Alicia and Ben's door. She was surprised when Ben opened it.

"Hi, Ben. I came to have a coffee with Alicia."

"Mind if I join you?" he asked.

"Of course not." Claire smiled at him. She would have loved having him for a brother-in-law, but she doubted that would happen now.

Alicia was sitting at their kitchen table. There were three plates with cinnamon rolls on them. Ben poured coffee. Claire flopped down into a chair across from Alicia.

Alicia looked over at her friend. "Holy shit, Claire! I can't believe that bitch is back."

"I can't either. This is just a fucking nightmare," Claire said, tears starting to well up in her eyes.

Ben grabbed a box of tissues and placed it down in front of her along with her coffee.

"I'm sorry," Claire said, blowing her nose. "I'm just a complete wreck. Neither of us slept last night, and we had a huge fight about her this morning. I have no fucking clue what to do here."

"Neither do we," Alicia said. "But we're pretty sure Mary will. Ben called her last night. She and Jake are on their way back from Arizona as we speak."

Claire's eyes widened with surprise. "What? What will Cole say?"

"He might be pissed at first, but he'll get over it." Ben shrugged. "Mom could always see through Gabriela's bullshit, so the sooner she gets here, the better."

"In the meantime, maybe you could call your sister for some advice. She went to law school here in the States, right?" Alicia asked.

"Yes, she did, but I can't get a hold of her. She's on a vacation in Bali with Ted right now. I won't be able to reach her for another couple of weeks."

"Well, we can ask around to see if we can get a recommendation for a good family lawyer here," Ben said.

"Thank you, but Cole said he was going to find

someone first thing this morning." Claire had a sip of her coffee. "I can't believe you called Mary and Jake. How did they take it?"

"My dad didn't say much. He seemed shocked and worried for the two of you. My mom, on the other hand, had a lot to say—none of it nice. She never cared for Gabriela, and she doesn't sound at all convinced that this is even Cole's child."

"I'm not either," Claire said, "but Cole seems so certain of it. This is my absolute worst nightmare. She came into the stables this morning—looking gorgeous, of course—and treated me like a bug she could just squash into the ground. It was humiliating, actually. And if that's what is in store for me, I don't know how long I'll be able to handle it."

"Hang in there, Claire," Alicia said. "We're all on your side, and Cole's no dummy. He knows what she's about."

"I know he does, but he's also a good man. He'll want to raise his son, and she comes with the package, unfortunately," Claire said, sighing heavily.

"You have nothing to worry about," Ben said. "I know my brother better than anyone. He'd never leave you for her. He's completely in love with you, and if Tomas really is his son, he'll find a way to make it work."

Claire gave him a worried look. "I hope you're right, Ben. He was in love with her once, too, and now it seems they have a child together."

* * *

That afternoon, as Tomas napped, Gabriela nervously paced the tiny living room of the cabin. She knew Cole would show up soon and that he would have a lot of questions for her. She had spent weeks imagining how the whole conversation would go, and now that it was about to happen, she felt sick with worry. She had known there was a chance Cole would have moved on with another woman and was more than a little annoyed to find out he had indeed done that. Claire's presence complicated things for Gabriela at a time when she desperately needed things to go smoothly. She wasn't worried about the pudgy chef, though. She could sense Claire would be easily driven off by the way she had fled when she first saw Gabriela and the baby. She was obviously insecure, and Gabriela knew exactly how to play on those insecurities. She would do whatever she had to do in order to give Tomas a proper family with a good father. The trick would be to make sure Cole didn't see that she was intentionally running Claire off.

That evening, just after she got Tomas to bed for the night, Gabriela heard the knock she had been waiting for. She smoothed her hair and took a deep breath before opening the door.

"Cole," she purred, smiling warmly. "Come in."

"Is this a good time?" Cole asked politely, stepping inside and shutting the door behind him.

"I came all this way to be with you, Cole. It will always be a good time. I'm sure you have many questions for me," she replied, sitting down on the couch.

"That I do," Cole said, planting himself in a chair opposite her. "Obviously I can't understand why you kept this from me all this time. Didn't you think you should pick up the phone and tell me when you found out you were pregnant?"

"The horrible truth is that I didn't know until he was born that he was definitely yours. I wasn't going to call you until I knew for sure," Gabriela said, looking Cole in the face, her heart filled with regret.

"When I got back to Brazil, Evandro was waiting for me at the airport. I found out my parents had set it all up to get me home. Both families were intent on us getting married. He made all sorts of promises and declared his love to me and told me how much he regretted being so inattentive before. I believed him. I wanted the life he was offering—full of excitement and luxury. I was so stupid, a little girl chasing an easy life."

Gabriela paused, letting her head hang down for a moment and sighing heavily. She didn't look up again until her eyes were glistening with tears. "I didn't realize what was important. I am ashamed to say I slept with him within days of returning home. A few weeks later, I discovered I was pregnant. I *hoped* it was his child. I even told him there was no way it was yours so that he would stay with me. When Tomas was born, it was clear he was your son—his blond hair and blue eyes gave away my secret. Evandro left me at the hospital as soon as he saw his little face for the first time. He just stared at him and said, 'We are done,' then turned and walked out of my life. Of course, I deserved it.

"My parents were outraged. I had ruined everything. Evandro sent all of my things to their house, but they refused to allow me to come home. I had to ask my sister if I could stay with her. She agreed to let me stay until I got on my feet again, but she couldn't help me with the baby. You remember how busy she is with her children and her clothing store. I was so tired and humiliated. The wedding was cancelled, and I realized Evandro had never loved me. If he had, he would have tried to make it work, no?"

Cole said nothing but continued to stare at her, searching for the truth.

Gabriela went on with her explanation. "I know I should have called you right away, but I was exhausted and so overwhelmed with trying to look after Tomas. I couldn't think of anything but taking care of him. I was so big and felt so ugly. I wouldn't have wanted you to see me like that, especially after how I left you. It took me this long to get back on my feet again."

Gabriela's voice shook with emotion. "I am so, so sorry, Cole. I wish I could go back in time. I would have come right back as soon as I realized my parents had tricked me. We would have been together, you could have had the excitement of knowing you were going to be a father and been there when your son was born." She was sobbing now, her face in her hands.

Cole sat across the room watching her come undone, not sure what to do. No part of him wanted to comfort this deceitful woman, and yet he had not been raised to be cruel, which was how he felt, sitting silently, watching as she cried. He got up and walked over to the kitchen, poured her a glass of water and grabbed some tissues from a box on the counter. Returning, he sat down beside her, holding them out to her and setting the water down on the coffee table. She took the tissues and hung her head, continuing to sob. Cole put one hand on her back and patted her stiffly.

Finally, she looked up at him. "I took it all away from you, Cole. I robbed you of your son for so long, and I will never forgive myself for that. I don't expect you to forgive me either."

Cole leaned back against the couch, letting his body slump down. "I'm not going to lie to you. I've never been this angry with anyone in my life, and this is not going to be easy to get over, Gabby. We'll figure things out somehow, but it's going to take time."

Gabriela looked up at him, a surge of relief

flooding through her. Here was the man who would look after her and her son. He was kind and forgiving. He was a good man and he could give them a good home, even if it was on a ranch in the middle of nowhere interesting. She threw her arms around him and buried her face in his neck, sobbing. Cole put one arm around her and rubbed her arm for a moment, then tried to pull himself away from her carefully. Gabriela raised her face to his, looking into his eyes with longing.

She wanted him to kiss her but instead he gently unwrapped her arms from his body and placed them carefully on her lap. He got up from the couch and crossed the room, picking up his coat. He turned back to her.

"Why did you leave in the first place, Gabriela?" Cole had fought the urge to ask her, but in the end he gave in.

"I left because I was told my father had had a heart attack. You know that."

"Yes, but when you got home and found out he was fine, instead of getting on a plane and coming right back here, you decided to stay with Evandro. Why didn't you want to come back to me?"

Gabriela paused, looking uncomfortable for a brief moment. "I was so lonely here, waiting for you to finish work every day or to come back from long trail rides. I missed my home and my old life. I was always going out with my friends, travelling, spending days at the beach. I was so stupid. I didn't know what was important in life. I was chasing fun like a dumb, young girl." Gabriela's eyes glistened with tears. "I never should have left, Cole."

Cole gave her a hard look. "It's the exact same life here that you hated before, Gabby. But there are two major differences—now we have a son, and I have Claire. No one has ever loved me the way she does. Certainly not you."

"But Cole, I never stopped loving you when I was in Brazil. I know you won't believe me now, but in time you will see. We had something so wonderful and full of passion. From that came our son. He is here because you and I are meant to be together. I made such a horrible, horrible mistake, but I can't believe it's too late. I will spend the rest of my life making it up to you if you will let me."

Cole sighed. "Gabby, I'm in love with Claire. In time, I hope you'll see she is a good person and maybe even accept her as part of Tomas's life. We'll figure out a way to make this work so he can have both his parents, but you and I aren't going to get back together. I need you to know it's not going to happen, okay?"

Gabriela sobbed into her hands, hoping he would take pity on her. For now she just needed to gain his sympathy; reminding him of his lust for her would have to wait. "Okay, Cole. However it has to be. I gave up my say when I left here."

"We'll work this out. We just need time," Cole said as he put his jacket on. "I'll be back tomorrow morning before work to see Tomas, if that's okay. Maybe I can take him each morning for a little while so you can shower or get some sleep. We could start there."

"Okay," Gabriela acknowledged. "And Cole, I haven't thanked you. Tomas is the best part of my life by far, and you gave him to me."

Cole stared at her for a moment and then turned and walked out the door. He had no response to her gratitude, having never intended to give her this gift.

EIGHTEEN

The next day, Gabriela woke up feeling refreshed. She brushed her teeth and applied just enough makeup to give her a natural-looking glow. She knew she could win Cole back. Claire was a chubby, boring little cook. She was no match for Gabriela. She would be patient for now, biding her time until she could move her out of the way. It would be a delicate operation to get what she wanted. She would need to push Claire just hard enough to make her leave but not so hard that she would dig her heels in and decide to stay.

Gabriela had the one thing that would bring Cole back to her—Tomas. It was only a matter of time before she would have her man back, and Claire would be searching for a new job and a new man. Cole would get over his anger toward her, and they would pick up where they had left off. There was no way he could have forgotten how much heat they had when they were together.

That afternoon, Gabriela took Tomas for a

walk to the barn. She found Dustin there, working alone. He had already heard the news about her and the baby.

"So, this is the little guy everybody's talking about?" he said, taking Tomas's hand gently in his. "Hello, buddy."

Tomas smiled at him. Gabriela greeted him warmly with a kiss on the cheek, and the two chatted for a few minutes.

"Well, I should let you get back to work," Gabriela said, starting to walk away. She turned back casually. "Where is that brother of yours? I haven't seen him around yet."

"Oh, you mean that ugly mutt, Trey? He went to college this fall. We had a team of female volleyball players here a few months back, and he realized what he was missing out on."

Gabriela felt a wave of relief that the women were long gone before she laughed at Dustin's joke. "Good for him. Hopefully he'll actually make it to a few classes while he's there. Which school did he go to?"

"He's at the University of California in San Diego. I'm thinking he's working on his tan and learning to surf more than he's studying, though."

"Well, I'm happy for him. You must miss him."

"Yeah, a little. We don't hear from him much. He's not really an email or phone call kind of guy. But he'll be home at Christmas for three weeks, so that's coming up."

* * *

Cole's parents arrived in the late afternoon. They went to find Cole first. Then he took them over to Gabriela's cabin to meet their grandson. Mary was simmering with rage at what Gabriela had done to her son. She chose to ignore Gabriela completely and pay all of her attention to the sweet little boy who looked so much like her side of the family.

When they left the cabin, Mary put her hand on Cole's arm. "How's Claire doing with all this? It must be awful for her."

"Yeah," Cole agreed, nodding. "She's taking it pretty hard, but who could blame her? It's really driving a wedge between us right now. I honestly don't know how we'll get through this."

"That poor girl. I can only imagine how she must be feeling. How could you have let this happen, Cole?"

"We took every precaution, but I guess nothing is a hundred per cent. To be honest, I'm having trouble understanding it myself."

* * *

As the days dragged on, Claire became increasingly lonely and insecure. Cole would leave early each morning to be with Tomas before starting work and go back over after work to bathe him and give him his bedtime bottle. Claire felt uneasy while he was in Gabriela's cabin. She knew that Gabriela was using each moment they spent together as an opportunity to erase the mistakes of the past and regain his trust, even just a little. Things were different now. Gabriela was no longer just a woman who had abandoned Cole. She was now the mother of his child, and she would be able to show him a nurturing, kind side of herself that came in that same sexy package.

Claire could feel her insecurities bubbling to the surface. She barely made it through work each day, getting through meals without even noticing what she was doing. By the time evening came she was a mess, often drinking half a bottle of wine while she cleaned up the supper dishes at the restaurant. She and Cole hadn't made love since Gabriela had arrived. Claire was suddenly self-conscious about her body again and oscillated between feeling sympathy for Cole, feeling jealous and feeling complete rage at him and Gabriela for ruining everything.

Each time she saw Cole holding the baby, it was as though someone was squeezing her heart; he was so tender and careful with him. At night, she would go to sleep with a sick feeling in the pit of her stomach. Come morning, she would wake up lying next to Cole, and for the briefest moment she would think everything was perfect only to have the crushing feeling settle over her chest again.

Cole barely slept at all. He would lie awake for

hours, thinking or watching Claire sleep, with an ache in his heart. He missed their feeling of closeness that was now absent. He wanted to make love to her so much it hurt, but he knew he couldn't. It was obvious Claire couldn't be intimate with him right now because of the huge problem they were facing and all the tension between them. She fell asleep each night with her back to him, as far away from him on their large bed as possible. He would doze off for a while, then wake again suddenly and go downstairs to have a glass of Scotch to numb his nerves before attempting to sleep again. He was still in shock and furious at Gabriela for what she had done. Every time he saw her, he grew more resentful. He didn't want her back in his life—this woman who had robbed him of the first several months of his son's life.

When he was around Gabriela, he tried to act as though nothing was wrong, knowing he needed to tread lightly. A few days after her arrival, he discovered that his name was not on Tomas's birth certificate. She could easily take Tomas back to Brazil, leaving Cole with little chance of obtaining custodial rights.

During the time he and Claire did have together, they argued about how to proceed with the legalities of Cole gaining custody. He still didn't see the point in having the paternity test done, and Claire still couldn't understand the upside of not doing it.

The evening after Mary and Jake arrived, Mary brought out Cole's baby album. She, Jake, Cole and Claire all pored over it, agreeing that Tomas looked a lot like Cole had at that age. A moment Claire should have enjoyed—seeing Cole's baby pictures for the first time—was ruined. It should have been a "what could be" event but instead felt like the beginning of the end. Mary watched the pair with her lips set tight, clearly hurting for them both.

* * *

It was a cool afternoon ten days after her arrival when Gabriela managed to find Claire on her own in the restaurant after lunch. Mary had taken little Tomas for a long walk by the lake in his stroller so she could have some time alone with him. Gabriela breezed into the kitchen as though she owned the place. She gave Claire a shrewd look and asked if they could talk. Claire agreed and told her she would be finished up in a minute.

"Why don't I wait for you in the dining area?" Gabriela said.

Claire nodded. "Okay." She exhaled sharply as she heard the door to the kitchen close.

"Fuck," she said under her breath. She had no idea what to say to Gabriela, or "Gabby," as Cole called her.

Claire finished up the dishes and took a compact

out of her purse, putting on some lip gloss, although she knew there was no point. Her eyes in the mirror were full of defeat and she knew Gabriela could sense it. She was moving in for the kill. Claire's feet felt like lead as she walked out to the dining area, carrying an open bottle of wine and two glasses. She sat across from Gabriela, who looked fresh and composed as usual.

"Wine?" Claire asked her as she poured.

"Please," Gabriela answered.

They sat in uncomfortable silence, sipping their drinks. Claire looked out at the lake, knowing she would not see this lovely place at Christmastime, something she had been looking forward to. They were planning to put up a large tree in the restaurant and lights all around the lodge before Thanksgiving. She knew she would be gone by then.

"Claire, I want you to know I'm sorry about what this has done to you. I can tell you are really attached to Cole, and if it were me, I would want you and the baby to disappear."

Claire kept her gaze over the lake, taking a long sip of her wine before answering. It would require everything in her not to respond to the insult. Saying how attached she was to Cole clearly indicated that Gabriella didn't believe him to be attached to Claire in return. This woman knew how to dig subtly enough that she could pretend, after the fact, that the comment had been innocent.

Claire chose her words carefully. "I'm sure you wanted to find Cole alone when you got here."

"You're right. I was fool enough to think he might not have moved on yet."

"If you wanted him back, why did you wait so long?"

"At first I wasn't sure if it was his baby at all. I got pregnant very close to the time I left here. I slept with my fiancé almost as soon as I returned home, so I was hoping it was his baby. I told him there was no chance it was Cole's child, and he was humiliated to find out that was not the case, so he left me. By then, I was as big as a house and my whole world just fell apart. My parents were furious with me, I was humiliated after having to cancel my wedding, and I was devastated."

Gabriela's eyes shone with tears as she looked up at Claire. "I don't say this to make you feel sorry for me. I am only trying to explain, okay?"

"I know. I'm the one who asked."

"Of course," Gabriela said, blinking back tears. "Anyway, it took me this long to get myself back in shape for Cole and to pull myself together. I could hardly return to him so huge and with big bags under my eyes from no sleep."

Claire scoffed. "You are mistaking him for someone shallow, which just shows that you don't know him at all."

"That's not true. I'm speaking only of my own insecurity," Gabriela replied quietly.

Claire forced herself not to raise an eyebrow in disbelief. This was the most self-assured woman she had ever met. She never seemed to have a hair out of place, and Claire had yet to see her lose her composure, even when Mary had arrived with hatred in her eyes.

"Claire," Gabriela continued, "I plan to leave. You and Cole want to be together. I will take Tomas back to Brazil and get out of your way for good. There is no life for me here on this ranch, in a tiny cabin, alone. I could hardly be happy like this."

"What about Cole? Doesn't he deserve to have a relationship with his son?"

"He can know him still. There is Skype, and when Tomas gets older, he can spend summers here, maybe. Cole could come and visit him in Brazil from time to time."

"Doesn't Tomas deserve to be raised by both his parents?"

"Of course, but not if both of his parents are miserable. That is no life for a child either. He will be happy with my family. He has lots of uncles, and someday, I will find a man to look after us both."

"You act as though it is all up to you, Gabriela. But what about Cole? He doesn't get to have some say in all of this?"

"Yes. I have given him time to make his decision. It seems he is choosing you."

Claire rolled her eyes. "You make it all sound so simple—it's me or his son. But until ten days ago, he didn't even know he was a father. It's hardly fair to expect him to figure out his whole life in less than two weeks!" Claire's voice rose. "What did you think would happen? He would magically be overcome by your beauty and whisk you away to marry him, after what you've done to him?"

Gabriela turned away, a hitch in her breath. "I've been such a fool." She got up and rushed out of the restaurant, letting the door slam behind her. Claire sat at the table, her heart hard as stone. She wasn't buying any of it.

* * *

That evening Cole got back to the ranch after a long day at the vet with one of the horses. He was exhausted as he made his way to Gabriela's cabin to see Tomas before his bedtime. It was obvious that Gabby had been crying before he got there. As Cole put Tomas's sleeper on him, he wondered if Gabby was going to take off with his little boy. After he gave him his bottle, he sat in the armchair, holding him for a long time, tracing his index finger along Tomas's face until he fell asleep. Cole carried him over to the playpen they were using as a temporary crib and settled him snugly under his blanket. He stood for a long time watching him sleep, his heart melting as it did each time he looked at his sweet little baby.

When he left the room, he walked over to the couch where Gabby sat curled up under a blanket, her eyes red. He sat in the chair opposite her. Neither of them said anything for some time.

Finally, Cole spoke up. "It looks like something happened today. Anything I should know about?"

Gabriela looked up at him. "I had a talk with Claire. It didn't go well."

"I see," he answered quietly. "How did you think it would go?"

"I don't know," she said, shaking her head and looking down to inspect her fingernails. "I guess I hoped we would start to sort out this mess I got us all into. I think Tomas and I should go home for good. We are in the way here."

Cole gave a big sigh. "So, if something is hard, you just run away?"

"I can't stay here like this. Waiting all day for you to show up so you can spend an hour with our son before he goes to sleep. Constantly being around people who despise me. What kind of a life is this for me?"

"What did you expect?" Cole responded, sounding a little angrier than he intended. "Did you think you could show up with our son, whom you've kept hidden from me, and I'd say, 'Oh, that's okay, Gabby. No big deal. Let's start over'?"

Gabriela tucked her knees under her chin and folded her arms around her legs. She rested her head on her knees.

Cole softened his voice. "Look, we're all trying to adjust here. I'm trying to put Tomas first, and you need to do the same. It's not about what you want or what I want. It's got to be all about him now."

"He needs happy parents. If my being here is making you miserable and I'm miserable too, it's no good for him."

"Just give it some time. You can't simply cut and run whenever things don't go your way."

Gabriela shook her head. "I don't know. I can't see things getting any better, Cole. I want to go home. You can see Tomas as much as you like on the computer and whenever you want to visit. When he is older, he can stay here during his school breaks, maybe. I think that would be best. Then you and Claire can go back to how things were, which is what I know you both want."

"Go back to how things were? You think I can just forget I have a son and go on with my life? What kind of man do you think I am?" Cole raised his hands up in the air and then let them drop to his sides in exasperation. He exhaled sharply and said in a very slow, even tone, "I will not be a stranger to my own child."

"Cole, I am giving you an out. Take it," Gabriela

said, getting up and walking into her bedroom. She shut the door, ending the conversation.

Cole sat for a while, unsure of what to do. In the end, he left and walked back to his cabin.

* * *

He found Claire sitting at the table with a faraway look in her eyes. She was drinking a beer and there was an empty bottle sitting beside her. She didn't look at him when he came in. She knew he had just been at Gabriela's and that he would have gotten her version of things by now.

Cole walked over to the fridge and pulled out a beer for himself, then dropped into the chair opposite her. He took a long swig and put it down, staring at her. Her face was expressionless. She seemed dead inside, with no trace of the fun, vibrant woman she was.

"So, I hear you and Gabriela had a talk today."

Claire nodded slowly. "She came to find me at the restaurant. I'm not too sure what she wanted to accomplish, but I don't think she was successful."

"Well, maybe don't worry about what she wants and start thinking about what I want. I want to be part of my son's life. Whatever you said to her made her want to up and leave, which is exactly what I asked you not to do." Cole's jaw was set and his eyes were cold.

"So, you're just going to trust her word without even having the consideration to ask me what happened? She is a manipulative liar, Cole. I cannot believe you don't see that!"

"I know she can be that way, but she's also scared. You have to try to put yourself in her shoes. She fucked up and she knows it. But look at her—she lost her fiancé, her parents won't have anything to do with her, she's raising a baby on her own and now she's come thousands of miles from home only to find I'm with someone else."

"And now you're just completely on her side? I'm so glad you can be sympathetic to *her*," Claire retorted, sarcasm oozing out of her pores. "Have you stopped to think what this whole situation is like for me? You seem to be forgetting I had nothing to do with creating this shit show! I didn't fuck her, and I didn't hide that I was having your baby from you either! I'm doing my best to keep it together here, but of the three of us, I'm really the only one who doesn't get any say in what's going to happen next! Now you're accusing *me* of making things hard for *her*?"

Cole drew a deep breath before speaking. "Look, I'm not trying to make you the villain, Claire, but I thought we agreed we have to tread lightly with Gabriela right now. If she leaves with Tomas, I'll never gain custody. I can't have you going off on her."

Claire's eyes met his now with an indignant rage.

"So, she tells you I've been mean to her and you *believe* it? That is rich, you know that? Rich. How *dare* you take her side over mine without even having the courtesy of finding out what really happened!"

Claire got up from the table and walked out of the kitchen, not really sure where she was going. When she reached the bottom of the stairs, she turned back to Cole. "I just realized Gabriela achieved exactly what she wanted today. She wanted to get between us, and we both fell right into her trap. She's got you questioning me and me pissed right off at you."

"You know what, Claire? This is the *last* thing I need from you right now. Don't you think I have enough shit piled on my plate already? You need to scoop some more on?"

Claire snapped her head back, feeling like she had just been slapped in the face. "I'm not the one with the scoop, Cole. I've been the one trying to clear your plate for you. You're just too pigheaded to see it."

"I'm pigheaded? You're the one who won't believe that Tomas is my son! You're completely set on chasing them off before I can gain custody of him! I knew I was making the right decision a few days ago."

Claire's heart felt like it had stopped. Her voice became icy as she looked at him. "Exactly what decision are you talking about?"

"I went to see the lawyer to sign the admission

of paternity forms. I knew it was only a matter of time before you two got fighting and she'd threaten to take off," Cole said in a low voice as he looked her in the eye.

Claire felt like the wind had been knocked out of her. She stood silently for a few moments, reaching for the wall to steady herself. "You did what?" Her voice was almost a whisper.

"It was the day after we were looking at the baby photos with my parents. I've been waiting for the right time to tell you. I was hoping you'd start to accept the reality that he's my son, but it hasn't happened so far. I knew Gabriela would rub you the wrong way and you'd say something to chase her off. I couldn't live with myself unless I knew I had done everything in my power to keep Tomas here."

Claire scoffed. "So *I'm* the bad guy here? This is fucking unbelievable! You've been lying to me for days!" Claire was screaming now, tears pouring down her cheeks. She was completely filled with rage and a deep sense of betrayal.

Cole raised his voice so he could be heard over her. "Believe me, I am sorry, Claire, but I have to do what's right for my son. He has to be my first priority now. If you can't understand that, we've got an even bigger problem than I thought."

"No, Cole, the bigger problem began when you started *lying* to me," Claire said, growing numb with the shock of what she had just learned.

"I didn't mean to keep it from you. I was just waiting for the right time to talk to you about it."

"You didn't mean to keep it from me?" She shook her head with disgust. "That's *exactly* what you meant to do. You either choose to tell me what you're doing or you choose to hide it from me. It's not a fucking accident. It's a choice!" Claire raised her voice again, looking at him with complete disdain for the first time in their relationship.

Cole exhaled sharply. "Alright, just calm down, Claire."

"Do NOT tell me to calm down. You know what? You can try to spin it however you want to make yourself the hero, but I sure as shit am not the villain here! I'm just the sucker who fell in love with you and got screwed over!"

Claire started to walk up the stairs, then turned back, realizing she wasn't done yelling. "You know what else? These past days have been an absolute hell for me! I've been doing my best to stay calm and not add any pressure on you, but inside I'm dying here! Gabriela is my worst fucking nightmare come to life! She has your son, Cole! Your son! Forget how drop-dead sexy she is. How the fuck can I compete with the mother of your child? And within days of her arriving, you've started lying to me on top of all that!"

Cole yelled back, "This isn't about you, Claire! It's about a little boy who needs both his parents in his life!"

He stood up and stalked over to the counter to grab his keys. "You know what? You're acting exactly like Gabriela right now. She can't see past the nose on her face either!"

"Fuck you!" Claire screamed. She watched as he stormed past her to the front door. "And just where the hell do you think you're going?" she yelled.

"Out. I've had enough of selfish women for one day," he growled, slamming the door behind him as he left.

Claire sat down hard on the bottom of the stairs, tears welling up in her eyes. She stayed there for a long time, tears of fear, indignation and anger pouring out of her as she hugged her knees. Otis walked over and licked her face, wagging his tail. Claire leaned her head on him as she let the emotion out.

When she couldn't cry any longer, Claire finally stood and dragged herself up to bed, her body heavy and her mind shutting down. Exhaustion overwhelmed her as she lay down in their bed without bothering to get undressed. She pulled the covers over her head and closed her eyes. Her head pounded, and she needed to rest before she could face what would come next. The clock beside the bed read 8:45 p.m. as she fell immediately to sleep.

* * *

Claire woke at 2 a.m. She sat up and slowly swung her legs over the side of the bed, sitting for a moment to get her balance. She felt sickeningly too hot, having slept in her sweater and jeans too long. Her head was still hurting from all the crying she had done. Turning, she saw that Cole had not come to bed yet. She got up and quietly made her way to the bathroom. After she came out, she crept down the stairs, feeling the walls with her hands to help guide herself through the darkness. She could see the outline of Cole's body lying on the couch. She walked over and sat on the end of the coffee table nearest his head. She could see his face faintly in the moonlight. His eyes were open and he was expressionless.

"Does she know?"

Cole sighed. "I needed her to sign the form."

"I see," Claire said. "Does she know you've been keeping this from me?"

Cole sat up and faced her. "I told her I would need to find the right time to tell you, so I asked her not to say anything."

Claire let out a long sigh. "Wow," she whispered, more to herself than to him, "the hits just keep on coming." She got up and started toward the stairs.

"Claire?" Cole called out quietly.

She didn't answer him but continued up to bed. Cole didn't follow her, knowing that trying to chase her with an apology right now would be a mistake.

There was nothing he could say that would ease the sting of humiliation and betrayal she must be feeling. They both lay awake, separated by far more than the physical space between them.

* * *

Claire didn't go back to sleep that night. She tossed and turned, knowing she had to leave. If, within a matter of days, Cole and Gabriela were already keeping a secret from her, what would be next? It wouldn't take long before Gabriela completely erased the pain of the betrayal Cole had suffered. Maybe Cole's willingness to believe that Tomas was his son was a sign that deep down he had wished she would come back to him. He had violated Claire's trust and she wasn't going to look the other way this time and allow herself to be made a fool of again, like she had with Antonio.

At five in the morning, she emailed a colleague of hers from Seattle, a chef named Peter. He was an excellent cook and loved to move around, always looking for a new adventure. She told him about the ranch and her need to leave right away, asking if he might be interested in taking over for her. She then booked a flight to London leaving in two days. After that, she got dressed and quietly left for the restaurant to get an early start on the day's work.

Cole had finally dropped off to sleep around

3 a.m. and didn't hear her tapping away on her keyboard upstairs or hear the door close behind her when she left. He woke after four hours with a sick feeling in his gut, knowing how badly he had screwed up. He had a horrible feeling he had just dealt the final blow to his relationship with Claire.

NINETEEN

London—Present Day

After her second pint, Claire decided it was time to try to find her way to her sister's house in Richmond. Her brother-in-law might be home, as he often was during the day. Usually gigs with his band ran late into the night, so he would sleep in the next day. She figured if he was home, he would be awake soon. She got another porter to help her bring her luggage outside and get it all loaded into a cab. She was quite tipsy as she handed the porter a twenty-pound bill and stumbled into the back seat.

She gave the driver the address to her sister's townhouse and asked him to stop at a grocery store on the way. Picking up some flowers for Janet, a bottle of whisky for Ted and a six pack of Bulmers Original cider for herself, she got back into the cab. Pointing her finger forward, she yelled "Tallyho!" at the driver, giggling hysterically.

When they reached Janet and Ted's, the driver helped Claire unload all of her boxes and luggage onto the steps of the townhouse. Claire buzzed a few times, but there was no answer.

"Say, my good chap, what is the time?" she asked the cabbie.

He gave her an irritated look and then checked his watch. "It's twenty past one."

"Thank you," she said, handing him her credit card to pay for the ride.

Once he had driven off, she settled onto the top step, along with her things, before cracking open a cider with a grin.

"Let's keep this party going," she muttered to herself. It was an unusually warm day for London in November, and Claire was grateful for the sun shining on her and the numbing effects of the alcohol as she sat waiting for Ted to show up. She felt pleasantly detached from the pain that had brought her there.

* * *

Two hours later, Janet's assistant put a call through from her neighbour across the street, Mrs. Gladstone.

"Hello? Janet? I'm sorry to bother you at work. I know you're terribly busy."

"I'm sure it's important. What do you need?"

"I wondered if you knew there is a young woman on your front step. She looks a lot like you and has a lot of boxes and luggage."

"What? That could be my sister, Claire. She lives in the US, though, and I'm not expecting her."

"Does she have long dark brown hair and a love of cider?"

"Yes to the hair, but not really to the cider. Is she drinking?"

"Quite heavily, I'm afraid. She has lined up five tall cans on the step while I've been watching my shows this afternoon."

Janet looked at her watch. It was three thirty, and she still had two more clients coming in before she could go home. "I'll call Ted and get him to come home right away. If that is Claire, something must be horribly wrong. Can you do me a favour and keep an eye on her until he gets there?"

"I will definitely do that."

Colorado Springs

In Colorado, it was eight thirty in the evening. Cole was in his cabin taking a shower. He stood under the spray of hot water, feeling emptier than he ever had. He let a loud sob escape and tears flowed, mixing with the water. He had blown it with the only woman he would ever love, and now she was gone for good. He sat down heavily on the shower bench and held his head in his hands. He let the water rush over him until it started to run cold.

He turned off the shower and got out, wrapping a towel around his waist and heading to the kitchen for a beer. His cellphone was sitting on the kitchen counter. He checked it for the hundredth time to see if Claire had tried to reach him. She had made no contact. Crossing the living room, he leaned against the window to look out at the lake. He saw the lights on in Gabriela's cabin and could see her standing in front of the kitchen window, at the sink washing dishes.

He sighed and went to bed to read a book. He kept reading the same paragraph over and over, not taking in any of it, finally putting the book down on his night table and looking around the room. Claire's half of the closet held only empty hangers. This place that had only a matter of days ago felt so warm and full of love was now cold and lonely.

A memory of her sitting in the armchair in the corner of the room flooded his thoughts. It was evening, and they hadn't spoken since their horrible fight the previous night. She was wearing her cozy bathrobe and waiting for him to come out of the shower. She gave him a serious look and asked him to come and sit down. He pulled on a T-shirt and some pyjama pants and sat on the ottoman near her.

Her voice was quiet and she didn't meet his eyes as she started to speak. "Cole, I've booked a one-way flight to London. I leave on Thursday morning."

Cole felt like he had been punched in the gut. "Claire, don't do this. I know I fucked up, but we can work it out. I know we can."

"No, we can't," she said, shaking her head. Her voice was quiet and full of defeat. "I can't be with you if you're going to lie to me, and I honestly can't handle having Gabriela in our lives. I'm not built that way."

Cole sighed heavily and rested his face in his hands, elbows propped up on his knees.

Claire waited for him to say something, and when he didn't, she continued. "I've given this a lot of thought. As long as I'm here, you'll have to worry about Gabriela taking Tomas away from you. She holds all the cards and she knows it. It could be a long road getting parental rights through the court system, maybe years, even. The quickest way would be to marry her, and then she'll gladly sign all the paperwork you need to make sure she can't just disappear with him."

"Are you kidding me? I'm getting married to you, Claire. Or have you forgotten that you made me a promise? Was that all bullshit?"

"Come on, Cole. That's not fair and you know it. *Of course* I wish we could still get married. But now everything's changed, and it won't work." Claire shook her head. "Think about it. Tomas will grow up without you, and when he gets older, I will be the woman who was more important to you than he was. He'll have a huge hole in his life because his dad chose me over him. You'll have an emptiness that would otherwise be filled with your son's love. After a while, you'll grow to resent our relationship. You'll wonder if it was really worth losing your son over. Whether I leave now or you grow to hate me later, it's going to end badly. We've only been in this for six months. It's nothing compared to the lifetime commitment you have now. I won't get in the way of that."

"Don't do this, Claire. Please," Cole begged, his voice breaking. "I know I messed it all up, but I'm going to make it up to you. I won't ever lie to you again. I promise."

"It's not just about that, Cole," she replied sadly. "It's the right thing for me to do, and we both know it. I've found you a chef, Peter McPherson. I used to work with him in Seattle. He's emailing you his resumé, and he can be here next week. He's really great, he'll fit right in and he does excellent work. So, at least no one will have to worry about the restaurant."

Cole covered her knees with his large hands. "Claire, just wait. Give me time to figure this out. I can fix it. Just give me a few weeks, okay? I promise things will feel better by Christmas. I can make this work."

"Oh, Cowboy, you can't fix this. No one can," Claire lamented, a tear streaming down her cheek.

"You owe it your son to give it another shot with Gabriela. Maybe things will work out this time. I hope for all your sakes that they will."

Cole pulled her to him, wrapping his arms around her tightly. "Just stay, Claire. I can't do this without you. I need you," he whispered.

"I just can't. It's already done," she whispered back.

Claire let him hold her for a long time, drinking in the scent of him and feeling his warm, strong body surrounding her. She would not allow herself to hug him back for fear of not being able to let him go. She allowed her hand to rest on his chest, feeling his taut muscles as he held her close.

Cole leaned his forehead on hers. "What about you? What are you going to do?"

"I'll stay with my sister for a while, maybe find a job there. Move on. After a while, I'll be fine. Really, I will," she responded, trying to sound sure of herself, but there was nothing convincing in her words as they came out of her mouth. Cole pulled her onto his lap and held her close.

* * *

The next night was to be their last together. They hadn't spoken much during the day as they both began silently grieving their relationship. In the afternoon, Cole had rounded up some boxes to pack

Claire's things. "Here, I didn't think your things would make the trip as well in garbage bags."

Later as they lay in bed beside each other, the realization that this was the end for them sank in. There was no chance to salvage things now, and they both knew it. Claire was getting on a plane the next morning and would never return. Cole reached his hand out and wrapped his arm over her, pulling her to him. They lay together, skin touching for the first time in two weeks. She could smell his aftershave and feel his amazing body—two things she would soon be missing. Cole pressed his forehead to the side of her face. A single tear ran down Claire's cheek as she turned her face to his. Cole looked into her eyes and kissed the tear away, then ran his lips along her mouth ever so gently, not sure if she would allow it.

"I'm sorry, Claire," he whispered, closing his eyes to fight back his own tears, burying his head into her neck. "I'm so sorry."

"So am I, Cole," she whispered back as she wrapped her arm around him and hugged him tight. She closed her eyes and kissed his cheek, then gently pulled his face to hers with her hand. She kissed him again, parting her lips a bit to invite more. She was desperate for time to stop so she would never have to leave. As it was, her impending departure hung over them like a black cloud.

They kissed for what seemed like hours. Finally,

Cole let his hand move from the small of her back down to her bottom. He caressed her with his fingertips slowly and then moved his hand up and over the curve of her hip and up to her waist. As he reached under her shirt, he stilled his hand suddenly. "Is this okay for you?" he asked.

"Only if you don't stop," Claire whispered, managing to smile at him. Cole smiled back, remembering the first time they had made love, when they had each said those same words. He would give anything if only they could start over again and relive it all, except this time, he would change the ending.

Cole skimmed his fingers up from her waist to her breast. She had no bra on, and was dressed only in panties and one of his old T-shirts she had claimed as her own. He cupped her breast with his hand, tracing her nipple with his fingers. Claire moved her hand from his back to the waistband of his boxer briefs. She hooked one finger in and slid it around to the front of his body, tugging the fabric away from his waist and then down, freeing him with one move of her hand.

Cole propped himself up on one arm and used his other hand to carefully slide her panties off, caressing her leg as he did. He brought his body back in line with hers, then lifted her shirt up. Claire pulled her shirt over her head as Cole took in the sight of her naked body one last time.

"I love you so much," he sighed, leaning down to kiss her neck.

He took his time working his way down with his lips until he reached her breasts. He kissed and sucked on her nipples until they were hard. Claire could feel herself becoming wet as she caressed his powerful back and his sculpted ass with her fingertips. She put her hands in his hair and tugged, drawing his face up to kiss him hungrily. She wrapped her legs around his waist and pulled him toward her. Cole pressed his body against her, making small circles with his hips to guide himself inside her tight warmth. They both let out a sigh of pleasure as he entered her. The past two weeks of not touching had felt like torture, but it was only a glimpse of the lonely hell that was about to come.

Cole made love to her with long, slow drags as he kissed her with such intensity it was almost too overwhelming for both of them. They were saying with their bodies what they couldn't with words: they would always love each other, always have an endless yearning for each other. They were saying goodbye. Cole was filled with both the most beautiful love and the most horrible regret as he moved over her. He was desperate for her to know how sorry he would always be for the way things had turned out and for how he had lied to her. She was the only woman he would ever love and always need. And even though no part of him could accept it, he understood why she had to go. She was doing it for him and for his son, and it made him love her even more than he had thought possible. Claire was giving up her job, her new home and love itself in order to give him a chance to be a father to his little boy.

Claire gripped Cole with her legs and arms as firmly as she could, willing every single cell of her body to show him how much she loved him. She held his face in her hands and kissed him, showing him she was sorry for all of her harsh words and anger. Claire could feel the fervour in his body, how much he wanted her and needed her. She knew they would always be connected, even if they never saw each other again. She had finally known real love, the unconditional kind, and although she had to leave, she would leave knowing what that felt like and would never settle for less.

They made love like this long into the night until finally they both gave in to their bodies' need for release, clinging to each other as they came. Tears streamed down Claire's cheeks as Cole collapsed onto her. He could feel his eyes welling up as he heard her trying to stifle a sob. He moved off her and lay beside her, pulling her into his chest to cradle her body in his as she cried. Silent tears rolled down his cheeks as he held her. He didn't know what to say—it would be meaningless to say it would be alright, because it wasn't going to be.

Finally, after a few long minutes, he found his voice again. "Claire, I'm always going to love you. Always. I'm so sorry. I'm just so sorry for everything."

"I am too, Cole," she said in a whisper. "I wish I could have been stronger and handled this whole thing differently."

"You wish *you* could have been stronger?" he asked in disbelief. "Claire, between the two of us, you are the strong one. I was a coward not to tell you what I was doing, and I never would have been strong enough to leave you, even for my son's sake. You made the choice we both knew needed to be made, and you did it selflessly for my little boy and me. You're the most incredible woman I've ever known, and it makes me wish I could keep you here forever."

They both struggled to stay awake for as long as possible, knowing that sleep would bring the morning in an instant. They kissed and caressed each other for hours, making love again. Around four in the morning, they could fight sleep no longer and drifted off, their bodies intertwined.

Less than two hours later, Claire's alarm rang. She shut it off with a feeling of doom. It took every ounce of her strength to slip out of Cole's arms and leave the bed. As she crossed the floor, she turned back to watch him sleep for a brief moment. Her perfect cowboy would soon be nothing more than a memory. She stepped quietly into the ensuite to shower.

A horrible emptiness crept over her as she dried off and slid on her jeans and a white long-sleeved T-shirt. When she walked out of the bathroom with her makeup bag, Cole was no longer in bed. She could hear him downstairs making coffee.

Reaching the kitchen, her heart broke at the sight of him making her breakfast. He looked up at her, his expression grim. Claire's face twisted as she tried to fight back her tears. She blinked quickly, looking up at the ceiling. *Come on, Claire, keep it together*, she told herself.

Cole walked over and wrapped her in his arms, pressing his lips to her forehead. "You sure you want to do this?"

"Every fibre of my being is begging me not to, but I have to," Claire said, resting her head on his chest and pressing her hands to his abdomen.

"I don't think I can let you go, Claire," he said, squeezing her tighter. "Even if you leave, I won't be able to stop loving you."

Claire nodded her agreement, unable to speak.

"Can I at least drive you to the airport? I don't want to miss a minute with you."

"No, I can't handle a terminal full of people seeing me say goodbye to you. As it is, I'm feeling bad for the unlucky cab driver who will be here in a few minutes."

They stood holding each other until Claire's cellphone rang to notify her the cab had arrived.

"Let me take your stuff out. You have a coffee."

"I'll grab one at the airport. I need to get some fresh air."

The pair silently loaded up as many of Claire's things as they could carry and headed out of the cabin together. It was still dark outside, and the air was cold enough for them to see their breath. The world seemed completely still and devoid of life— the only sound was their feet crunching in the snow. Cole went back to the cabin for the rest of the luggage while Claire helped the driver arrange things. Once Cole had brought out the second load and everything had been packed into the cab, the driver got in and shut his door, giving them some privacy to say goodbye.

Claire stood beside the back door to the cab. "Well, this is it then," she said, wishing she could think of something better to say.

"I guess so." He pulled her to him, holding her close. "Claire, I . . ." his voice trailed off as he felt a lump in his throat again.

"I know," she whispered. "Me too, Cowboy." With that, she gave him one final kiss and stepped quietly into the cab. She was grateful it was still dark out so the driver would not see what a complete wreck she was.

Cole stood in the cold air, with the first signs of light appearing in the sky. He watched as the cab disappeared around the bend in the road, taking her out of his life forever. He turned and noticed a light on in Gabriela's cabin. He walked slowly over to go get Tomas. He needed to see his little smile right now to remind him why this awful pain was worth experiencing.

TWENTY

London—Present Day

Ted arrived at the townhouse thirty minutes after Janet texted him. He taught music at a high school nearby and had just wrapped up his last lesson for the day when the text arrived.

He saw Claire sitting on the front step, now wrapped in a blanket over her clothes, singing softly to herself what sounded like Maroon 5. Her eyes were closed, and she was swaying back and forth. Her words were largely unintelligible, but he caught something about the daylight and holding him so close. Ted was shocked, but he pretended nothing was unusual.

"I had no idea you could sing, Claire. Those aren't the words, but you have the tune anyway," Ted said, smiling at her.

Ted was tall and wiry with long blond hair pulled back in a ponytail. He had on a dark grey wool coat with a purple, black and white striped scarf tucked in and black dress slacks.

"Teddy! Theodore!" Claire screamed. "My favourite brothhherrr! Come here, you," she slurred, pointing at him with her last can of cider, causing some of the liquid to spill onto her shoes.

Ted climbed the steps two at a time and gave Claire a big hug as she teetered on the top step. "Well, this is a surprise, Claire. How are you?"

"Teeerrific. Never better!" she answered as he unlocked the door and pushed it open.

Claire slung her purse over her shoulder, picked up the nearest box and carried it into the house. "Oh, shit—I forgot . . . Surprise! I'm here!" She giggled.

"Why don't you go sit down? I'll bring your things in for you."

"Sure, my balance is a bit off. I haven't got my land legs yet."

"I thought that was only after a long time at sea."

"Right. Then it must be because I am hammered." She was talking in a loud voice and over-pronouncing each word as she flopped onto the couch.

She sat humming to herself as Ted brought her luggage and boxes inside and placed them in the front hall. He quickly pulled his phone out of his pocket and sent a text to Janet.

Claire is here and is wasted. From the amount of luggage, it looks like she's planning on staying.

By the time Janet got home, Claire had managed to drink a good portion of her gift to Ted. She got up when she saw her big sister come through the front door. Claire stumbled over to her.

"Janet! Surprise!" She then turned back to Ted. "I remembered to say it that time," she said in a stage whisper, winking at him and giggling to herself as though she were a genius.

Ted and Janet exchanged stunned glances. Janet had seen Claire this drunk only once in her life, during Claire's senior prom. She had managed to down a ridiculous amount of rum and Coke on her way to the dance. She had partied hard for about thirty minutes before spending the next twelve hours vomiting.

After giving Claire a long hug, Janet walked over to the kitchen, got a cleaning bucket from under the sink and brought it into the living room.

Claire watched and shook her head and her finger at her. "Oh no. You think I'm going to puke, but I'm not. I'm fine, sista! Just a little welcome-to-my-new-life party I'm having. You two are invited . . ." Her voice trailed off as she stumbled over to the kitchen in search of two more glasses. Janet and Ted followed her.

"Claire, honey, what's going on?" Janet asked finally.

"Nothing, I just can't remember where you keep the ice. I wanna make you a nice drinkaroo for celebating . . . brating . . . celebrating . . . the freezer! Same as in America!" she exclaimed, tapping her head and nodding. "Oh! You meant why I am in England! I had to get away from Gabriela. Did you know Cole has a son? Weird, right?" she said, opening random drawers.

"He has a son named Gabriela?" Ted asked.

"No, silly. That's his ex. Do you have a lemon zester? I want to make you a Cuban. Mmm, Cubans . . ." she answered, stumbling over to the liquor cabinet and rooting around for some peach schnapps and gin. "So, you want to know why I'm here, and I'm gonna go ahead and Dr. Phil it for you." She paused, trying to remember what she was looking for.

Ted gave Janet a confused look. "Dr. Phil it?"

"She's gonna tell it like it is," Janet said quietly to him.

Claire looked up at them. "I'm gonna make you supper tonight. Something delishish . . . delisus— shit— something yummy. It's the least I can do since you're letting me stay here for a while." Claire paused. "Thanks for that, by the way," she said, winking at them and making guns out of her fingers and thumbs and pointing at them. "Now, I was going to tell you something. Why I'm here . . . I flew here to get away from Mr. Perfect and his adorable baby and his sexy Brazilian ex-lover."

Claire put on a terrible imitation of a Brazilian accent. "*Meu amor*, here iz your baby. Doesn't he look just like you? And my body iz exactly as amazing as before. I can resume my career as a swimsuit model, escept I don't need to work cuz I'm really reech."

Ted and Janet stood staring at her with their mouths gaping.

"You prolly think I'm bitter, but I'm not. Lemons are bitter, though, and I need one for our drinks."

"Um, lemons are actually sour . . ." Ted started to say, holding up one finger to Claire.

Janet put his hand down. "Nope. No point, babe."

Claire rambled on, not noticing them. "I can't believe it's taking me so long to make these Cubans. *Ridiculous.* How are you guys doing? I haven't even asked you yet. Rude, Claire, just rude."

"Fine. We're doing fine," Janet answered, nodding.

"Good. Good. You know what? Fuck it. Let's just go out, and I'll buy you dinner. Quite honestly, I don't think I should operate the stove right now."

Claire closed her eyes and pointed one finger up in the air. "I'm just gonna say one more thing about Cole and then I won't ever mention him again, okay?"

With that, she turned her head and vomited into the sink.

* * *

The next afternoon Claire woke up in the spare bedroom, lying on top of the bed rather than in it. She was still wearing the clothes she had put on almost two days earlier, except now they reeked of vomit, booze and body odour. The smell caused her to gag as she sat up. She had spent most of the night in the bathroom, either with her head in the toilet or lying with her face pressed against the cold tile floor. Now she felt like someone had driven an axe into her skull, and her abdominal muscles quivered as she stood up. Her throat burned and her mouth tasted like something had died in it.

"Fucking hell," she mumbled as she opened the door to the hallway, allowing the light to come in. She looked ahead to the embarrassment she would feel as soon as she stopped being so ill. It wasn't going to be pretty. She wandered down to the kitchen, where she found Ted and Janet having a late lunch.

"She lives!" Ted said, grinning at her.

Claire gave him a deadpan look. "Barely," she croaked.

"Mimosa? A little hair of the dog might do the trick," he said.

Claire gagged and turned back down the hallway. "Shower. Must shower."

* * *

Over the following week, Claire spent most days sleeping. She would come out of her room in the late afternoon to cook for Janet and Ted. She drank glasses of wine back to back and barely ate more than a few bites at each meal. At night, she would lie awake crying or staring into space, restless.

Janet hadn't brought up the subject of Cole, waiting for Claire to be ready to talk. She watched her sister with concern; by the time Janet arrived home each evening, she found her sister already three sheets to the wind. She could see Claire spiralling down at a furious pace, almost as if she *wished* to self-destruct.

On Friday night, Ted had a gig. He left early to get set up, allowing Janet and Claire to have the house to themselves for the first time since she had gotten to London. Claire had been feigning enthusiasm about getting out for the evening, but it was obvious her heart wasn't in it. As the two got ready in Janet's large bathroom, Janet decided to approach the subject that was so clearly being avoided.

"So, Claire, when do you think you'll be ready to talk about what happened?"

Claire looked in her makeup bag, rooting around for her mascara. "Never."

"Okay. I want you to know I'm here if you need to talk. I'm worried about you, sweetie. I've never seen you drink like this, and you don't eat. Ted said you haven't gotten up before two in the afternoon all week, and you somehow manage to be drunk by the time I get home."

"It's fine. I just can't sleep at night right now. I think it's the time difference. I'll get it together, though." Claire could feel Janet's eyes on her but she refused to turn to her.

"You know you don't have to handle this all on your own. Ted and I are both here for you. We love you so much, and you know you can always talk to either of us. It might help to get it off your chest."

Claire's shoulders drooped suddenly as she dropped her eyelash curler onto the counter, tears pouring down her cheeks. She sobbed into her hands as Janet wrapped her arms around her, letting her cry into her neck. After a few minutes, Janet led her over to the loveseat in her bedroom. She helped Claire sit down, still holding her as she cried. Claire let tears of humiliation and anger pour out of her as she started talking, spilling the entire horrible story. Janet listened without saying much.

"Shit. Now I've made us miss Ted's gig," Claire sniffed, blowing her nose.

"They have another gig tomorrow," Janet said with a shrug.

Claire nodded. "Thank you. I needed that."

"I know. I'm so sorry you've had such shit luck with men, Claire. Seriously, this is just fucking awful."

"I know, right? It just sucks so hard. We were perfect together, and now I don't know what it will

take to get over him. I don't know how to do this."
Claire sighed heavily.

"I don't know either, sweetie. I wish I knew what to tell you."

"You want to hear something weird? I met this French guy on the plane over here who said to give myself two weeks to get over Cole and then to seek out every pleasure life has to offer. Lots of sex with lots of people, food, booze, dancing, whatever."

Janet considered the notion. "Maybe he's right. Hanging around here won't help. Whatever you do, you need to start eating more and drinking less."

"I will. I just don't have an appetite these days."

"Well, for tonight, why don't I make a huge bowl of buttery popcorn and we could snuggle up and watch a movie?"

Claire nodded. "Sounds good."

Colorado Springs

It was mid-afternoon as Cole sat in his office waiting for the day to be over. He stared out the window, watching the snow fall in swirls, wondering where Claire was at that moment and what she was doing. His chest felt the crushing weight of anguish every time he thought of her. He had never in his life felt this type of pain before; it was nothing like when Gabriela had gone back to Brazil. That time he had been hurt, but part of him had taken comfort in the fact that they weren't really right for each other. Other than in bed, they had little in common. This time, there wasn't even a hint of relief for Cole, knowing Claire was out of his life for good. He felt somewhat less worried that he would lose Tomas, but other than that, he felt an overwhelming sense of grief.

Gabriela, meanwhile, had been struggling to contain her pleasure. Her smile was a bit wider, she wore more perfume, a bit more makeup, and her clothes seemed to get tighter and more low cut as the days wore on. Cole knew she considered it only a matter of time before she was back in his bed for good. She was being patient and showing respect for his losing Claire. He knew she was waiting for him to start over. That evening, when Cole went over to give Tomas his bath and bottle before bed, Gabriela answered the door in a tight red tank top and black yoga pants. The combination showed off her curves perfectly.

"Cole," she purred as she opened the door, "you look tired. Come in and sit down. I made some seafood jambalaya. I remembered it was your favourite. Tomas had a long nap, so he's not ready for bed just yet."

"Oh," Cole said, taking off his boots and coat. "That sounds nice, thank you."

Tomas was sitting in his ExerSaucer, with a

huge grin for Cole. He cooed and laughed when Cole walked over and crouched down to him.

"You're still wide awake, buddy? How's my boy?" he asked, picking him up in the air and blowing a raspberry on his chubby little neck. Tomas squealed with laughter and grabbed Cole's nose. Cole played with him and chatted happily for a few minutes before sitting down at the table in front of a heaping bowl of jambalaya. Gabriela poured two glasses of wine and brought over a basket of buns.

Tomas sat contentedly on Cole's lap, playing with a napkin as Cole picked up his spoon and started eating. Gabriela beamed, watching the domestic scene unfold in front of her.

"This is delicious. Thank you for inviting me, Gabby," he said, having a sip of wine.

"You don't need an invitation. You are welcome here anytime, Cole, day or night," Gabriela said, her eyes locked on his. Her meaning was unmistakable.

Cole looked quickly back down at his meal, feeling trapped. Gabriela took no notice and continued to chat as they ate. She told Cole about some of the cute and funny things Tomas had been doing lately, and asked him about how the ranch was doing. Cole didn't say too much about it—just enough not to be rude but not enough to bore her. Gabriela somehow managed to eat her entire meal without smudging her lipstick. When they were finished, Cole stood up with Tomas in one arm and cleared his plate and wine glass with his free hand.

"Well, I should get this little guy into the bath," he said, walking out of the kitchen. "Thank you for dinner."

Gabriela watched him enter the bathroom, feeling rather satisfied with herself. It was their first real meal as a family, and in her mind it had gone very well. She hadn't been positive that he would even accept her invitation to dinner, but he had. She had managed to remind Cole that Claire wasn't the only one who could cook, and soon she would remind him of all the other things she could do. She quickly tidied up the kitchen and warmed up Tomas's bottle. She brought it to the baby's bedroom and leaned against the door watching Cole attempt to get their child into his sleeper while he squirmed around.

"He's always on the go, isn't he?" she said.

Cole looked up at her. "That's for sure. I don't know how you keep up with him all day."

"He helps me stay in good shape. Better than the gym!" She laughed. "You are really wonderful with him. Such a natural at being a dad."

"Well, I guess we're figuring it out as we go," Cole said, snapping up the final snap. He picked Tomas up off the change table and rubbed his nose to his son's. "Isn't that right, buddy? We're figuring it all out."

He took the bottle from Gabriela and sat down

in the rocking chair. Gabriela grabbed a blanket and brought it over to Cole, letting her fingers linger on his hand as she passed it to him. She leaned down to give Tomas a big kiss, knowing Cole would get a nice view of her cleavage and lacy black bra if he bothered to look.

"*Boa noite, meu amor*," she whispered to Tomas as she rubbed his little forehead with her hand. She glanced at Cole to see if he was looking at her chest and was disappointed to see that he was staring at Tomas instead. She walked out of the room, flicking her long, straight hair behind her as she went.

When Cole left Tomas a little while later, Gabriela was sitting on the couch with her legs curled under her. She had two glasses of wine on the coffee table in front of her, and the lights were low.

She patted the seat next to her. "Come and sit a while. Have a drink with me."

Cole walked over and sat down. "I want to talk about the next steps in my gaining parental rights and getting Tomas his American citizenship."

Gabriela reached down to the coffee table and picked up the glasses. She handed him his wine and took a sip of hers. "Of course, we should do that right away. First, I want to thank you again for putting him to bed. He gets so excited to see you. I think he gets bored of being with just his dull old mom all day."

Cole ignored her obvious fishing for a compliment. "It's what I want to do, Gabriela. He is my son, and I want to take care of him."

"And you do it so well." She gazed at his lips. "Cole, I know this has been such a difficult time for you. You must be so lonely now, and I want you to know I'm here for you. If you need to talk or anything . . ." She traced his shoulder with her fingertip.

Cole swallowed the wine in his mouth and shifted a little away from her on the couch. "You know, I bet you could use a break. Maybe one night soon, Tomas could stay at my place for a night or the weekend so you could go out or get some sleep or whatever."

"I'd love that! How thoughtful of you!"

"Do you think he'd be okay without you for a night?"

"I'm sure he'd be just fine with you."

"Okay, great. Just tell me when, and we'll set it up." He drained the rest of his wine and stood up, deciding that leaving was the safest choice that night. "I should go. I need to get some sleep. Thanks again for supper."

Gabriela sat on the couch pouting for a long time after he left. Part of her had thought she could get him into bed that night. She wasn't used to having to work so hard for a man's attention—certainly not for Cole's. After a while, she realized she could use the sleepover to her advantage. She sent Cole a text later that evening.

Maybe Tomas can stay at your place next Saturday afternoon and night? I could use some time to go shopping. x

Sounds great. I'm free.

Cole felt a hint of contentment; having Tomas there would be the best way to distract himself from how miserable he was. He sat on the couch with Otis asleep at his feet. Sports highlights were on, but he wasn't really taking any of it in. He wished it were warm out so he could go swimming to help alleviate the restlessness he was feeling. Picking up his cellphone, he checked for a message from Claire, but nothing had come. He scrolled through his phone so he could look at pictures he had taken of her. Seeing her image was torture for him, yet he couldn't stop himself. He needed to see her beautiful face. He came to a picture he had taken of her in the hot tub one evening. He could feel himself getting hard as he stared at Claire in her little blue bikini. He could remember the feel of it under his fingertips. How they had made love late into the night.

He regretted promising not to contact her. He would never break his word no matter how badly he yearned to hear her voice. She was the only one who could comfort him right now, but he had to do without that and he knew it. He had to let her forget.

Turning off the TV, he wandered restlessly around his cabin and finally went to bed.

When he turned the light off, he laid his head down on Claire's pillow like he had every night since she had left. It still smelled like her. He knew he should stop doing that, but he just couldn't bring himself to wash her pillowcase yet. He lay awake, hoping to dream of her so he could feel happy for a while, even if it was while he was asleep.

Cole wondered how long it would take for this pain to go away. The thought that Claire was feeling as utterly hopeless as he was haunted him. He wanted her to be happy and move on with her life, even though the thought of another man touching her made him physically sick. His mind wandered to Gabriela, alone in her cabin. She was certainly beautiful and sexy, but he had no interest in being with her again. Any love they had shared was over, and he just hoped he could find a way for them to coexist peacefully. Maybe someday he would want to be with her again, but for now, he just couldn't think about another woman in his life or in his bed.

He rolled over and turned his phone back on, finding the picture of Claire in the blue bikini. He gazed at her image for a long while, letting his mind drift back to that night. He moved his hand under the covers and into his underwear, pulling them down. He was hard from the sight of her pouty lips and her eyes staring back at him. He could hear her voice in his mind and see her mouth moving as she begged him to make love to her. He was moving over her, teasing her, coming close to entering her and then moving away. *Fuck me, Cole, please, now.* He gripped his shaft, moving his hand up and down its length as he heard her little moan, felt her mouth on his and her tight core wrapped around him, drenching him. He continued moving his hand as he imagined her riding him, rubbing herself over him, arching her back as he pulled down her bikini top to reveal her breasts. He could feel his mouth sucking on her nipples and them growing hard under his lips. He let his mind wander until he finally came, releasing all the pent-up lust he had for Claire.

TWENTY-ONE

Over the next week, Cole was swamped with preparations for Thanksgiving. The ranch was fully booked for the holiday, and although he needed to oversee the creation of a winter wonderland, his heart was definitely not in it. He worked quietly and quickly, without feeling the joy that this time of year usually brought him. His parents had left for a week to visit friends, making things lonelier for him.

Peter, the new chef, was working out as well as Claire had said he would. He knew his way around the kitchen and had created an excellent menu for the Thanksgiving holiday. He was enthusiastic and kind. Cole was grateful Peter was there so he didn't have to worry about that end of things, at least.

Cole repeatedly caught himself wanting to talk to Claire about how much he liked the new chef only to remember that Peter was there because she was gone. Each day seemed to bring with it a new realization of just how much he had lost when

Claire had left. She wasn't just the woman who had shared his bed—she was the one with whom he had shared his dreams and his life in its entirety. In a very short period of time, Claire had helped him develop the vision for the future of the ranch. They had become partners in the truest sense of the word. And now she was gone. He knew without a doubt that Gabriela had no interest in the ranch other than maybe its potential revenue and what type of lifestyle it could afford her. She would never love it; it would never really be her home.

Gabriela had invited him for supper several nights that week. He made excuses a couple of times and ate with her twice. He wanted to be around Tomas as much as possible without leading her on.

* * *

Saturday afternoon found Gabriela making last-minute finishing touches to her makeup and clothes. She spritzed on some of the perfume that used to drive Cole wild and inspected herself in the mirror. It was definitely harder to make a sexy impression in the winter. She had put on a fitted ivory blouse, with the buttons open to reveal a hint of her perky breasts, which were held in place by a light-pink, lacy push-up bra. The colour of the shirt showed off her olive skin tone, still dark and creamy in spite of the past few cold weeks. Her shirt was tucked into dark skinny jeans, and she wore tall black leather boots. She decided to go with a glossy red lipstick and pulled her hair up into a maze of twists at the back, giving herself a polished look.

Cole knocked on the door right on time to pick up Tomas and bring his things over to his cabin. Gabriela flashed him her best smile as she opened the door.

"Hey, you," she said, leaning against the door so he had to brush against her to get inside.

"Hi, Gabby," Cole answered. "Where's my little guy?"

Tomas was sitting on a blanket on the floor of the living room, surrounded by toys. He turned when he heard Cole's voice and grinned at him. Cole took his shoes off and walked over to Tomas, crouching down to say hi.

Gabriela came over, holding a necklace in one hand. "Can you help me with this?" she asked.

Cole stood and took the necklace from her as she turned her back to him and tilted her head to the side a little to reveal her long neck. "I got so excited about a day out that I might be a little over-dressed for shopping."

Cole managed to close the tiny clasp. "There you go. All ready?"

"Yes, I have all of Tomas's things packed," she said, turning back to him as she put her earrings on.

"Great!" Cole said, grabbing Tomas's winter coat off the top of his diaper bag and going over to get him dressed to go outside. "You ready to go, little man? You get to stay at Dad's house tonight! Just you, me and Otis. What do you think of that?"

Tomas grabbed Cole's chin and tried to eat it. Cole zipped up his coat and then attempted to gently put a fleece hat onto his little head while Tomas squirmed in irritation.

"Here, let me help you," Gabriela offered, sliding the hat onto Tomas's head. "There. Now, if you take the playpen and my little sweetie, I'll bring his diaper bag. All the bottles are in there, plus some rice cereal and jars of baby food."

"I can easily carry everything. You get going. Enjoy your freedom." Cole ignored the look of disappointment on Gabriela's face. He continued to smile politely at her as he slung the bag over his shoulder and picked the playpen up with his free hand. "Okay, Tomas, say bye to your mom."

Gabriela stepped over and gave the baby a big kiss and said goodbye in Portuguese. She smiled at them both and said, "I hope my two favourite guys have a terrific time!"

"Thanks, we will," Cole replied as Gabriela opened the door for them.

* * *

That night, Cole got into bed content for the first time in weeks, feeling as though he had done well with his little boy. Cole had taken Tomas for a long walk, played with him and read him a few board books while they sat together in the armchair in Cole's bedroom. He enjoyed feeding him his meals and giving him his bath and bottle. To Cole's relief, Tomas didn't seem to be upset about his mother not being there. Cole decided to have him sleep upstairs on the other side of his bedroom, in case the baby woke up in the night. Cole went to sleep without having a nightcap—another thing that hadn't happened in a long while.

Drifting off quickly, he dreamed about Claire. It was a hot summer day and they were sitting outside together on a picnic blanket, playing with a baby. The baby looked like Tomas but was Claire's child. Cole watched Claire lovingly as she lay on her back with the baby sitting on her tummy. She held the baby's hands and talked and laughed. She seemed so happy it filled his heart with warmth.

She looked into his eyes with a smile and said, "Let's get this little guy to bed early so we can have some grown-up time together."

"Oh, just how grown-up are we talking?" he asked.

"NC-17–rated stuff." She grinned.

"My favourite kind," he said, leaning over and kissing her.

Suddenly, they were in bed together. It was nighttime. Claire was dressed in a black bra and panties. She was straddling his body, massaging his chest and arms. She leaned her face down and kissed him seductively, parting her lips and letting her tongue glide across his mouth. He reached up and cupped her breasts in his hands, loving their fullness. She kissed his neck and moved her body down slowly over his, finally reaching his rigid length. She looked up at him as she held him in one hand and traced the head of his shaft with her tongue.

"I want you to come in my mouth," she purred. There was something strange about her voice but he couldn't quite figure out what. She pushed her lips over his length, drenching him. He lay on his back, excited by her firm sucking.

"Oh, Claire, yeah," he heard himself say.

She suddenly lifted her mouth off him. "*Meu amor*, there is no Claire. There is only us."

Cole woke with a start. He suddenly realized there really was a woman under his covers. He scrambled out of bed and flipped the light on. Gabriela was there, completely nude, and looking annoyed and lustful at the same time.

"Gabby, what the fuck?" he exclaimed, grabbing his boxer briefs and pulling them on.

Tomas woke with the light and the noise and started to cry. Cole rushed over and patted his back, pulling his blanket up over his shoulders and shushing him. Gabriela quickly turned the light off and lay back with a frustrated sigh. After a minute, Tomas fell back to sleep.

Cole put on a T-shirt and his pyjama pants and motioned for her to get up and meet him downstairs.

He crept down to the kitchen, turned on the light above the stove and leaned against the counter. He was fuming, feeling both manipulated and guilty at the same time. Gabriela came down the stairs a moment later in his bathrobe, clearly thinking she could convince him to let her stay. She had a naughty grin on her face.

"Cole." She laughed. "I'm sorry I startled you. It is just that you have been so sad, and I can make you feel *so* good." She crossed the kitchen as she spoke, reaching out to touch his lower abs with her fingertips. Cole took her hands and removed them, then placed them firmly by her sides and let them go.

"I didn't invite you into my bed. I'm not ready for any of this, Gabby, and we woke Tomas. He was right in the room with me, for God's sake!"

"Cole, he would have slept through the whole thing if we had been quiet. But if you aren't comfortable, we could just stay down here for a while. I seem to remember us making good use of this counter before." She undid the belt on the bathrobe, letting it fall open to reveal her nude body.

Cole took a deep breath and then reached out and closed the bathrobe. "Thank you for trying to cheer me up, Gabby. But I just can't. Give me some time, okay?"

Gabriela sighed and looked down at the ground. "Am I different to you now that I've had a baby?"

Cole looked at her with surprise. "Of course that's not it. You look exactly the same, but you have to think of what the last month has been like for me. My whole life has been turned upside down, and I need time to sort everything out and to learn to trust you again."

"Okay," she said, tearing up with embarrassment more than remorse. "I'm so sorry, Cole. I hope someday you will forgive me for what I've done. I just want you to know that I'm here waiting for you."

She wrapped her arms around his neck. "You've forgotten how good we are together." She kissed him full on the mouth. Getting no response, she turned to go back upstairs and dress. She took long enough that Cole knew she was waiting for him to change his mind and follow her. When he didn't come upstairs, she returned to the kitchen, fully clothed.

"I'll come by and get Tomas first thing in the morning," she said stiffly.

"You can leave him here as long as you like, really. I have the day free and we had a lot of fun together. I could bring him by in the evening if you want."

"Well, maybe lunchtime, then," she answered with a little nod, walking out the door and closing it behind her. She hurried back to her cabin with a feeling of panic in her chest. She needed to have Cole wrapped around her little finger before Trey came back for the Christmas holidays. If she couldn't do that, everything would be ruined.

TWENTY-TWO

On Monday at 9 a.m. sharp, Janet's assistant put a call through to her office. "It's a Cole Mitchell. He said it's about your sister, Claire."

Janet put down her pen. "Really? I have a few things to say to him. Put him through."

A moment later the phone clicked and she was on the line with Cole. "Janet Hatley speaking," she answered with a distinct edge to her tone.

"Janet, it's Cole Mitchell calling. I'm so sorry to disturb you at work. I promised Claire I wouldn't try to contact her, but I had to know if she's okay."

Janet had been pissed right off at Cole until she heard his voice. He sounded so worried that now her anger dissolved into pity. He had just taken all the fun out of being mean to him.

"Hi, Cole. She's not too great, actually." She heard him sigh heavily on the other end of the line.

"Right. I guess that makes sense. I just had to know if she was safe. All this time, I assumed she had made it to your place, but then tonight the horrible thought occurred to me that maybe she hadn't arrived, and you wouldn't have known she was coming, even. I can't believe I didn't think about that possibility before."

"She made it here two weeks ago," Janet replied, not sure how much she should say. "What time is it there anyway?"

"Two a.m." His voice was quiet and thick with emotion.

"Can't sleep either? Claire's having the same problem."

"Is she eating, at least? She wasn't eating at all the days before she left."

Janet was annoyed he wasn't giving her a reason to lay into him. "Not really. She seems to have replaced food with booze for now."

"Oh shit. I am so sorry," he answered. "I can't believe how badly I screwed up what we had. I keep replaying the last two weeks before she left in my head, wishing I could change so much of them."

"Well, you were dealt a rough hand, but you definitely didn't play your cards right either."

"Oh, I know I didn't. I don't think I'll ever stop regretting that. I just can't stand the thought of her being angry at me."

"Oddly enough, she's not angry with you. If she was, it would actually be a lot easier for her to move on."

"Janet, I would do just about anything to make this better for her. I just wish there was *something* I could do."

"If I could think of anything, I'd tell you. But not contacting her is a good plan. It would be much harder for her to hear you like this, sounding all considerate. I don't think I'll tell her you called."

"Thanks, Janet, I appreciate it. I would hate to make things any harder for her than I already have. I just needed to know if she was okay. I'm sorry to have bothered you at work. I'll let you go."

"Okay. Goodbye, Cole."

"Goodbye, Janet. Janet, wait. Please take care of her."

"I will, Cole. You take care, too."

"Thanks."

Cole hung up the phone, wishing he could stay on the line with Janet a little longer, to somehow have some connection to Claire. He wandered over to the window. It was snowing out and the moon's reflection on the fresh snow lit up the night, giving the sky a reddish glow. He watched the snowflakes falling softly onto the deck, his heart breaking. Standing there for a long time, he resolved to find a way to help Claire.

London

On Wednesday morning, the day before Thanksgiving, Janet and Ted got up early to catch a flight to New York. They had booked the trip to visit Ted's family for the holiday several weeks earlier. They had planned to surprise Claire in Colorado as well but were now staying on in Syracuse, New York, for a few extra days. Claire got up to see them off, having not slept again.

"You look like shit, Claire," Ted said, giving her a hug. "You have got to get out and have some fun. And for God's sake, eat something."

"Thanks, Ted, but I already know how I look," she replied. There were dark circles around her eyes, and her face looked gaunt and pale. Her hair hung down limply around her shoulders, needing to be washed.

"Are you sure you're going to be okay on your own?" Janet asked, giving Ted a dirty look. "You really are welcome to come with us, or I could easily stay home."

"Thank you, but I'll be fine, I promise. You should definitely go. You haven't been across the pond for a while, and I need to stay. I'm not in any condition to go visiting people right now."

Janet gave her a look of concern. "I could just stay here and feed you all day for the next few days."

"I'll eat. I'll eat. I promise. Just go already so

you don't miss your flight," Claire replied, giving her a big hug.

* * *

Later that day, Claire wandered around the house, looking for something to do. An unbearable loneliness had set in as soon as her sister and Ted left. She took a shower and then decided to find ways to keep busy. She had already cleaned the fridge, washed the floors and put away her laundry. She decided to walk down to the grocery store to buy some fresh buns and the ingredients to make minestrone for supper so she would have leftovers for a few days. The cold weather made her want soup.

Her cellphone buzzed just as she was returning to the townhouse. She dropped her keys and the grocery bags onto the counter, then dug her cellphone out of her coat pocket. Swiping the screen to read the text, she felt the breath leave her body. It was a message from Cole, but it wasn't for her.

It read: Hey, babe, last night was terrific. Can't wait to see what you have planned for tonight . . .

Colorado Springs

Cole sat in his office, his heart pounding. He was immediately filled with regret upon pressing Send.

It had taken him two days to decide to go ahead with his plan, hoping it would help Claire move on without him. It was all he could do not to call her right then and tell her why he had sent the text. He sat at his desk, his eyes trained on the cellphone in front of him. He hated playing games, and this seemed like an awful one. His fingers drummed restlessly on his knee as he watched and waited for some response.

London

Claire sat on a stool at the kitchen counter, draining the last drop from the bottle of wine she had opened an hour earlier. She stared at the message for the fiftieth time since she had arrived home. The wine was numbing the pain by now, and her initial shock had turned to rage. She could picture him, sitting at his desk, smiling smugly to himself because he was going to get laid again tonight.

She hit Reply and tried to draft a message that would cut him to the core. Coming up blank, she put her phone down on the counter and picked up the bag of buns she had bought earlier. She pulled one out of the bag and slowly ripped off tiny pieces, eating them one at a time. She weighed her options carefully. She could call him over and over again until he picked up, then scream and swear at him.

That would certainly feel good and would hopefully ruin his day. But it would be completely devoid of dignity, so that was out. She could go to a bar, pick up some random guy and pretend to pocket dial Cole while they made out. Too obvious. She could take the high road and do nothing, which would feel like shit for now but would make her proud later. Fuck that.

> I see you and Gabriela are making it work. Congratulations. Maybe don't rub it in my fucking face, though. Delete my number from your contacts. It's Claire, by the way, in case you forgot who I am.

She read it over a couple of times. "Fuck him," she declared as she pressed Send. She turned her phone off and went to her room to put on her coziest pyjamas. She added a fluffy bathrobe and pink fuzzy socks for good measure and then went back to the kitchen to make her soup.

The next two days, Claire neither showered nor dressed. She had taken to sleeping on the couch and left the TV on all day and night to keep her company. She drank wine from the moment she woke up until she passed out at night. No reply came from Cole, which didn't surprise her. Part of her burned with anger at his thoughtlessness, but a tiny part knew he would feel very bad about sending that text to the wrong woman. She hoped at the very least she had managed to wreck his Thanksgiving. He had moved on within a few days of her leaving and it hurt like hell. Everything they had said and done together, the promises they had made, the dreams they had had—she, herself—meant nothing to him. He was back in Colorado with his new little family, and she was an ocean away, devastated and utterly alone.

The third morning, Claire woke up with a splitting headache and an aching body from lying around so much. Her eyes refused to open completely as she tried to focus on the clock across the room. She walked down the hall, feeling a little off balance as she trudged slowly to the bathroom. When she got there, she flicked on the light and stood for a moment with her eyes closed, preparing herself to see her own reflection. Finally, she opened her eyes to see a pale, thin face with sunken eyes and greasy, matted hair. She hardly recognized the woman she saw in the mirror. How could she have let herself spiral down so far?

"You done?" she asked the woman staring back at her.

She knew she had to stop feeling sorry for herself. It was time to let go and move on, to find her strength. She couldn't let losing a man destroy her like this. So what if he was with Gabriela already? Big fucking deal. There were people in the world with much worse problems. She had survived losing her parents as a teenager, she had started her life over twice in six months and somewhere inside that pathetic-looking woman was someone strong and sexy and vibrant.

Claire stripped off her pyjamas and stepped into the shower. She stood under the spray of hot water for a long time, washing away her self-pity along with the vile build-up she had accumulated over the past forty-eight hours. Thirty minutes later, she was clearing out all the empty wine bottles and cleaning up her mess. She wouldn't sit around wallowing for another minute. She needed to be productive and useful and find a purpose to her life.

TWENTY-THREE

Colorado Springs

Back in Colorado, Gabriela was in her cabin, folding laundry on the couch with the TV on in front of her. Tomas was playing on a blanket near her. She realized that up to now Cole had been the one making all the moves to be named Tomas's legal father and that she should have been pushing things forward as quickly as she could. If the paperwork was done before Trey got back, there would be a better chance she could convince him to stay quiet about their one-night stand.

It had happened three days before she went back home to Brazil and was one of the reasons she had left. Cole was out on a week-long cattle drive, and she was feeling miserable and bored to tears. Trey invited her out with a group of his friends on a pub crawl. She decided to go along, thinking Cole wouldn't mind if she was out with his younger cousin. Trey's friend picked them up on his way into town and they met up with a large group, going from nightclub to nightclub, dancing and drinking heavily.

Trey had kept a careful eye on Gabriela, fending off the advances of the many men who hoped they would have a chance to take her home that night. As the evening wore on, Gabriela started to get a little thrill that Trey was watching over her. By the time they reached the third bar, the pair found themselves pressed together on the crowded dance floor. What had started out as innocent fun turned quickly into a dangerous flirtation.

When Trey's friend had dropped them off back at the ranch, Gabriela overheard him as he grabbed Trey's arm before he got out of the car. "Buddy, you better cool it with your cousin's girlfriend before you do something you'll both regret."

Trey brushed it off. "What? Her? Don't worry about it man, she's like a sister to me." He stumbled out of the car after Gabriela.

She turned to him as the car pulled away. "Walk me home, my big, strong bodyguard."

Trey stared at her for a moment, weaving from side to side a little. "Oh, you are trouble."

Gabriela gave him a sexy smile. "You have no idea."

When they reached the door to Cole's cabin, Gabriela unlocked it and pulled him inside by his shirt. "I think I will turn you into a man tonight."

"Gabriela, it's not my first time," he said.

"But I'm your first real woman. Those little girls you've been with don't know what they're doing," she replied, pulling his T-shirt over his head and undoing his jeans.

Not liking the idea, Trey stopped her from taking his pants off. She raised an eyebrow at his attempt to resist her and slid the straps of her dress down, allowing it to fall to the floor. She stood in front of him in her lacy bra and panties and high heels, giving him a sultry look. She was excited by the challenge he presented. Reaching behind her back, she took off her bra, revealing her perky breasts.

Trey grabbed her by the waist and pulled her to him, kissing her with pent-up lust. His hands were everywhere, his tongue exploring her urgently, as though he knew he needed to hurry to get what he needed. Gabriela gripped his muscular arms and let her fingers glide over his chest, basking in his adoration. It was the most powerful aphrodisiac—being wanted. And she had been wanted by every man who had seen her that night, including this one. The challenge of getting him to sleep with her was the next best thing to being wanted. She could make a man like him forget his morals, forget his family, just to be with her, and the thought of it made her feel powerful. Gabriela pulled away and went over to the couch, sitting down and stretching her arms out to the sides. She stared at him, her lips curling into a little smile.

"Get undressed," she told him in her thick accent as she crossed one long leg over the other slowly. She watched as he pulled his boots off, then his jeans and underwear in one frenzied move. He stood naked before her, with an eager look on his face and his erection straining. He crossed the room and all but lunged at her breasts with his hands. She spread her legs out wide for him as he groped her wildly and sucked on her nipples.

Gabriela pushed him off, and for one moment, Trey thought she was about to kick him out. Instead, she flipped herself around on the couch, propping herself up on her knees, lightly placing one hand on the back of the couch and sticking her ass up in the air for him. She pulled her panties to the side with one hand and rubbed herself as she looked back at him.

"You can fuck me now," she ordered.

Trey was more than happy to comply, leaning over her and guiding himself into her sex with one quick thrust of his hips. He had never seen a woman so sexy, so in command of herself. The girls he had been with before had been willing but had lacked confidence. Gabriela knew what she wanted and how to get it. He watched her from behind as he fucked her. He could feel her fingers pressing against her sex, rubbing herself as she pushed her ass up toward him. It didn't take long before he felt her body tense with her climax, and he quickly followed. It was fast, and it was fun while it lasted, but the second it was over, he was filled with guilt. Even though he was quite drunk, he knew better. Trey got dressed quickly and left, mumbling a goodbye to her.

The next morning, he tried to look casual as he walked over to Cole's cabin, hoping no one would see him. Gabriela ushered him through the door with a look of concern. She had spent the last few hours trying to figure out how to spin this. She had no idea if Trey had told anyone yet. The past several weeks she had grown increasingly bored and lonely and had started to want to leave. Her time with Cole was never supposed to have been more than a sexy adventure before she settled down with Evandro, and she had never intended to stay so long. This wasn't how she wanted to leave Cole, but it was too late now. Gabriela knew when she saw the look on Trey's face that she would need to get out of Colorado as fast as possible.

Trey was a complete wreck. He looked both lovesick and guilty as hell. They talked for a long time—Trey confessing that he had been in love with her for months now and Gabriela dismissing it as a meaningless crush, telling him it was just sex and that it really meant nothing. He was insisting they tell Cole the truth so that he and Gabriela could be together. Gabriela finally had to be mean in order to get through to him. She told him he meant nothing to her and he was going to ruin his life if he told anyone, especially Cole. She told him she had booked a flight back home and would be leaving the next day.

She left as she said she would, inventing the story about her dad's heart attack to help soften the blow to Cole. She cared about him and didn't want to hurt him more than she had to. Trey had emailed her regularly for a few weeks, suggesting he come and visit her. In the end, she had called to tell him she was getting married and that their time together had been fun but it would never be anything more than a one-night stand. Before she decided to bring Tomas to the US, she had searched for Trey on Facebook, planning to contact him. He didn't have his own account, but she saw that he had been tagged in some photos at a frat party in San Diego and she knew he would be out of the way for the time being.

*　*　*

Now, as Gabriela sat on her couch putting Tomas's little onesies and tiny socks into the laundry basket, her stomach churned at what lay ahead. She knew it had been a huge risk coming back here and that there was a good chance Trey would come clean about their night together. She would have to work fast in order to make sure he kept his mouth shut.

If she could get to Trey first, she would be able to convince him that she and Cole belonged together. Surely he wouldn't want to give up his freedom and education to become a father, especially at the risk of ruining his relationship with Cole and the rest of their family.

Gabriela hadn't realized what she had when she and Cole were together. She had been arrogant, thinking that good, honest men were easy to find. Now that she was a mother, her perspective had changed entirely, and she knew without a doubt that a man like Cole was exceedingly rare. He was kind, smart and tender, in addition to being incredibly hot. He was also going places, turning this ranch into a thriving business. Gabriela wouldn't take Cole for granted again. She knew what he had offered her the first time around had been love at its best. This time she would do whatever it took to get him back and keep him, even if it meant living away from her home and family. He would take care of them in ways Trey never could.

TWENTY-FOUR

London

It was a week after Thanksgiving. Claire woke to the sound of her alarm clock for the third day in a row. She dragged herself out of bed just after 7 a.m. still exhausted from another restless night. Dressing in her winter running clothes, she left for Richmond Park. She loved it there, with the long, paved paths winding through the expansive green park. It was cold and cloudy when she left the townhouse, and she was grateful that it wasn't raining. She put in her earbuds and walked briskly for a few blocks before reaching the park. Once she hit the path, she started to run, feeling alive again.

After twenty minutes, she was startled by someone tapping her on the shoulder. She turned, then stopped, surprised to see Luc beside her in his running gear. He was covered with little beads of sweat and had a wide grin.

Claire took out her earbuds and smiled. "Luc! What are you doing here?"

"I've been trying to catch up with you for a few minutes. You're fast."

"That's a little creepy, Luc, I have to say," she said with a grin.

Luc chuckled. "You are mistaking friendliness for creepiness—I think your English is not so good. I wanted to see how you are doing. Can I run with you?"

Claire shrugged. "If you can keep up, sure."

"I'll do my best, but I did a thousand push-ups before this, so I'm a little fatigued."

Claire laughed. "I'll slow down for you, then, knowing it has nothing to do with your age," she replied, starting a light jog.

"Just how old do you think I am?"

"Um, over forty?"

"Yes, but barely. I'm still in my prime, believe me," he said indignantly, jogging alongside her. After a couple of minutes, he asked, "So, how are you?"

"Not so great. I've been allowing myself to wallow in self-pity for the past couple of weeks. The last few days, I've been forcing myself to get up with the rest of the humans and go for a run."

"Have you slept, or do you need me to come over and sit beside you for a few hours?"

Claire laughed again, feeling her face grow hot with embarrassment at the memory of waking up on the plane with her arm wrapped around Luc. "Actually, sleeping is about all I've done lately."

"So, are you ready to move to phase two?"

"You mean the carnal-pleasure phase? No. I'm going to try to get a job instead. I think that will serve me better."

"You can do both, you know."

"I suppose that's true. Okay, I'll go buy myself a cake later and eat the entire thing in one sitting."

They jogged along until they reached the park gates. They both slowed to a stop and Claire began to stretch.

"This is me, here. My sister's place is a few blocks away."

Luc nodded, a little out of breath. "I have to go back through the park to get to my hotel."

"By that do you mean wait until I'm out of sight and then hail a cab?"

Luc laughed, running his hand through his hair. "No, no. I'm going to sprint the whole way now that I won't have you to slow me down."

Claire grinned. "It was nice to see you again, Luc. Maybe we'll run into each other again sometime."

Luc gave her a very direct gaze. "Come out with me tonight. I will take you to a place with one of the best views of London, where we can drink some very good wine together."

Claire was taken aback. When she had woken up that morning, she hadn't expected to be asked out on a date. It was the furthest thing from her mind right now, but maybe it was exactly what she needed. "You wouldn't be talking about your hotel room, would you?"

"Of course not. I'm talking about a restaurant I know. You aren't quite ready to come to my hotel room. But you will join me for drinks, yes? It will be good for you."

Claire gave him a skeptical look, not sure how she felt about his cockiness. "You seem to think you know what I need better than I do, which is odd, since we are basically strangers."

"It's only because I *do* know what you need. Even though I'm only a tiny bit older than you, I have a lot more experience," Luc replied.

"A *tiny* bit older? I think you might be the one who misunderstands English. A decade is big," Claire retorted, wrinkling her nose at him.

Luc couldn't help but laugh. "Ouch. You're going to give me a complex. You keep implying that I'm an old man."

"If the orthopedic shoe fits . . . " Claire grinned.

"Okay, young lady, now I'm not sure I even want to take you out. You are as mean as you are beautiful."

"You still want to take me out." Claire grinned. "I can tell."

"Yes, I do. Unfortunately, we men are weak when it comes to beautiful women."

"It's sad, really," Claire answered, nodding. "I

still have your business card. I'll text you later *if* I decide to come."

"You'll come. You can't resist the chance to make fun of me," Luc replied, leaning over and giving her a quick peck on the cheek.

"It *is* amusing," she said, giving him a playful look. With that, she turned and jogged up the street and out of his view.

* * *

As Claire propelled herself up the hill, she could feel Luc's eyes on her. She wasn't sure how she felt about his proposition. He was definitely sexy, and she enjoyed verbally sparring with him, but she really didn't think that a man was necessarily a good idea right now.

When she got back to Janet's, her sister was just about to leave for work.

"Good morning, sunshine!" Janet called out when she saw her. "You're up and at 'em early again today."

"Yeah, I decided to join the rest of the humans. Enough wallowing," Claire said, peeling off her running shoes and walking into the living room to stretch.

"I'm glad for you. There is much fun to be had," Janet replied. "Wanna go to yoga with me this evening?"

"I would love that, but I sort of have a date tonight . . . If I decide to go," Claire responded.

"Really?" Janet asked, raising her eyebrows. "I'm intrigued."

"I ran into that French guy from the plane just now. He asked me out for drinks, but I'm not sure if I should go."

"Why not?" Janet asked, slipping into her coat.

"Well, I don't know if dating is such a smart move for me right now. I went straight from Antonio to Cole without any break in between. Maybe I should take some time to be alone, you know? Be man-free for a few months or a year, even."

"That's not a bad plan. But would there really be any harm in having a little fun and then sending him on his merry way?"

Claire laughed in surprise. "That is *not* what I was expecting to hear from you! Is that what you would do if you and Ted broke up?"

"Oh, honey, I'd shag everything that moved." With that, Janet picked up her briefcase and walked out the front door. "Have fun deciding!" she called out as she shut the door behind her.

Claire shook her head as she walked down the hall to the bathroom. After she had showered and eaten breakfast, she sat staring at her cellphone and Luc's business card sitting next to it.

She was attracted to him, but it was nothing like the craving she had for Cole. Her regard for Luc would never bring her to her knees like her love for Cole had. There was something liberating about the idea of having sex with a man just for the sake of sex, with no threat of falling in love or getting hurt. Maybe she *should* call him. Have some fun based on mutual respect and desire, then they could shake hands and part ways. Claire wasn't sure if she could actually go through with it, but she decided to throw caution to the wind and at least go have a drink with Luc. It wasn't as if she needed to make a decision at that very moment about where things would go with him.

She picked up her phone and sent him a text before she could change her mind.

> You're right. I can't pass up the chance to amuse myself at your expense. Where and when?

A minute later she heard her phone vibrate.

> In front of the Savoy at 8 p.m. Dress up.

* * *

At five minutes after eight, Claire stepped out of a cab to see Luc standing in front of the lobby entrance to one of the most exclusive luxury hotels in England. He was dressed in a black suit with a classic white shirt open at the collar. He had a striped scarf wrapped casually around his neck, making him look extra French. He let his eyes fall on her, admiring what he saw.

He strolled over to her, kissing her on each cheek. "You look stunning."

"You look surprised."

Luc broke into a wide grin. "This is going to be fun," he replied as he held his arm out to lead her into the hotel lobby. "I booked us a table at the seafood grill," he informed her.

As they entered the lobby, Luc helped Claire remove her coat. She was wearing a snug-fitting royal-blue minidress with three-quarter length sleeves. She had put her hair up in an off-centre bun and had borrowed a diamond necklace from Janet.

"That is a beautiful dress," Luc commented. He walked behind her toward the restaurant, enjoying the view of her curves moving gracefully under the blue fabric. "You look fantastic."

"Thank you. This is the first time you've seen me not a complete mess or totally sweaty."

"Yes, but you are beautiful all three ways, actually."

Claire raised her eyebrows at him.

"All three are looks men can't resist. The first time I saw you, you were vulnerable, which makes a man want to protect you. The second time, you were working out, which makes a man think of how you would look after a long, vigorous night of sex. Tonight goes without saying."

"A girl could learn a lot from you, Luc. You're a wealth of knowledge."

"Then stick with me. There are many things I can teach you that I know you would like."

The restaurant was luxurious yet comfortable, with art-deco decor and round-backed blue leather chairs. When they reached their table, Claire stopped short. The view was everything Luc had promised. She could see the River Thames and the London Eye.

"You weren't kidding about the view. It's wonderful!" Claire remarked as Luc pulled a chair out for her. She caught a hint of his cologne. She felt that frisson of attraction and immediately found herself unsettled by it. She knew this was a mistake. She couldn't sleep with Luc, even if he was sexy, even if it was just for fun, even if Cole was already with Gabriela. As ridiculous as it was, her heart and body still belonged to Cole, and she knew she would not give any man a fair chance until she had gotten Cole out of her system. And even if she did muster up the courage to have sex with him, Luc deserved better than to be used by her so that she could forget her pain. She scanned the menu quietly and for much longer than she normally would, trying to figure out how she could get out of the date gracefully.

"Claire? Claire?" Luc asked. "Are you really

that engrossed in the wine list, or is there something on your mind?"

"Oh, sorry, Luc. Were you saying something?"

"I was saying something very charming and witty, in fact, but you missed it because you were thinking of your former lover."

Claire winced at his accurate assessment of her. "I was, Luc," she replied, nodding her head, "which is just stupid of me when I'm somewhere this perfect with someone like you."

"But I am not him, and this is a very romantic place. A place to go to with someone you are in love with, yes?"

"Yes." Claire sighed. "I have to make a confession, Luc. I have been very selfish. I came here tonight to get you into bed, to help me forget. But I didn't take your feelings into consideration. As soon as we sat down, I realized that what I am doing is very unfair."

"Claire, this would be totally fair to me," he replied with a grin. "As you have so aptly pointed out, I am an experienced older man and am certainly not naive. I can sleep with someone without expecting it to turn into anything more."

Claire gave him a serious look. "But would you really want to sleep with someone who just wants to forget another man?"

"You are struggling with your conscience. Let's say, for a moment, that I want only one night with you, that I would love it, in fact. To go to bed with you and then get up in the morning, satisfied, and happily part ways as friends. Would it feel right to you then? If that's what I wanted?"

"But is that what you want, Luc?" Claire asked.

Just then the server came up to see if they had any questions about the menu. Luc ordered a bottle of Chassagne-Montrachet Premier Cru and a plate of calamari to go with it.

When the server walked away, Luc turned back to Claire. "You were asking me what I want. Of course I want to sleep with you. But you need to think about what is best for Claire. What would Claire do if she could have her way completely right now?"

"I . . . I don't honestly know."

"You do know. You just don't want to say it. My guess is that you aren't used to being forthcoming, because you're afraid of what people will think of you if you say something they don't like. So tell me what you would do if you could do anything at this very moment."

"I would get on the next plane to Colorado, where he is, and I would get into bed with him and never leave."

"So why don't you?" Luc asked tenderly.

"He's with the mother of his child, trying to start over, and I can't get in the way of that. I could never do that to a little baby."

"I see. So, did he leave you to get back together with her?"

"No. I left him so he could. He didn't know about the baby until about two months ago. She showed up with their son and things got really complicated really fast. She threatened to leave and take the baby back to her home in Brazil. He didn't have any legal rights and couldn't stop her, so I left. It's for the best anyway. I could never handle having a woman like that around."

"A woman like what?"

"She's a goddess. The kind of woman every man fantasizes about. Gorgeous. Confident. Self-assured. Sexy. Your basic nightmare if you're competing with her for a man."

"Competing?" Luc asked as the server brought the wine for him to taste. He gave it a quick swig and nodded. The server poured two glasses and quietly walked away.

Claire stared out the window at the view, feeling suddenly detached from the beautiful surroundings.

Luc had a sip of wine. "That is such a silly notion, that you were in competition with her. You women make problems where there aren't any. It is simple. Your man either loves you or he doesn't. If he loves you, he isn't available to any woman, no matter how beautiful. If he doesn't, he will wander—and again—it won't matter if the woman is a goddess or very plain."

Claire listened carefully, not appreciating being called silly or his know-it-all attitude. "So, you don't think it's possible for a man who is in love to fall prey to an irresistible woman who pursues him?"

"No, I do not. There are beautiful women everywhere you look. If we were so weak as to fuck every beautiful girl we saw, not one relationship in history would have lasted for more than a few days."

"Huh. I never thought of it that way," Claire replied, taking her first sip of wine.

"I know. I'm not sure why, but for some reason, women see each other as threats even if they are in a good relationship with a good man. The truth is, you are competing only with your own demons. It is insecurities and fears that tear relationships apart, not other women."

The calamari arrived at the table. Luc scooped some sauce onto Claire's plate, followed by several pieces of the squid. He then did the same for himself.

"You know, Claire, you need to consider the possibility that everything you did, you actually did to protect yourself, not this baby. By leaving, you took control of the situation and stopped yourself from being the victim, even though you have been looking at things through the eyes of one."

Claire could feel anger rising in her chest as she stared at Luc. "That is really not fair! You're saying I acted out of selfishness when I literally gave up everything to give their family a chance."

"A chance that won't work. If he really is in love with you, he won't be able to just shut that off and find happiness with this woman. You know that. You cut the ties before *you* could get hurt. Your ego was maybe too fragile to handle being rejected in favour of this goddess."

Claire's eyes stung as she fought back tears. She was filled with a sense of indignant rage. How *dare* he tell her she was selfish after what she had done for Cole and Tomas?

Her voice came out as an angry whisper. "What the hell do you know about it anyway? You're making all these snap judgments based on almost no information, and now you're insulting me. I certainly didn't come here to be told I'm silly and selfish."

"No. You came to have your ego stroked. To prove to yourself that you are indeed beautiful and attractive. To make yourself feel better. And that's okay, Claire. It's okay to want to feel better." Luc's voice was impassive.

"I think I should go before I say something very unkind."

"So say it." He shrugged. "There is nothing you can say that will shatter me."

"Okay, then. You are an arrogant prick. I thought so when I first met you, but I decided to see if there was anything else to you. I should have followed my first instinct." Claire opened her purse and threw some money down on the table, then got up to leave.

Luc reached up and grabbed her hand. "Please sit down, Claire. Let's not end things like this. You're right about me. I am arrogant. But I'm also right about you. That's why you are so upset. If none of it were true, you would be able to laugh it off. I've hit a nerve because I'm saying things you don't want to admit to yourself. But please don't go. Since I've met you, I've only wanted to help you."

Claire had tears streaming down her face as she pulled her hand away. "You want to help me? If you see me again, run the other way."

With that, she turned to walk out of the restaurant. Luc watched as she retrieved her coat from the host and stormed out without looking back. Regret that he would never sleep with her settled in. He picked up his fork and began eating.

* * *

Claire rode home in the back seat of a cab, simmering with rage. Who the hell did he think he was, analyzing her like that? He didn't know the first thing about her or Cole or women, for that matter. She had had no choice but to leave Cole. She had done it to give Cole a chance at raising his son. Luc's words were meaningless drivel spoken by an arrogant prick.

"Asshole," she muttered under her breath.

"Pardon me?" the cab driver asked.

"Oh, sorry! I didn't mean to say that out loud. Not you. I was thinking about someone else," Claire explained quickly.

"Bad date?"

"Very."

"Well, love, let's hope the next one works out for you," he said as they pulled up to Janet and Ted's.

She paid the driver and apologized again, then walked up the steps to the townhouse. As she took her keys out of her purse, a shadow of self-doubt crept over her. She saw Janet and Ted in the living room, watching a movie. They looked over at her as she entered the house and took off her coat. Ted paused the show.

"That was fast," Janet said with a worried expression. "Everything okay?"

"Yeah. Turns out he's an ass. I decided to come home instead of wasting any more of my time."

"Did something happen, Claire?" Ted asked.

"Not really. Just an uncomfortable conversation. I'm going to go to bed. I'm worn out."

"You sure you don't want to join us? Maybe tell us what happened?" Janet asked.

"There's really not much to tell. Don't worry about it. You two enjoy your movie. Good night." Claire managed a smile as she turned and went down the hallway.

She got into her pyjamas and went straight to bed. As she lay there, tossing and turning, Claire was haunted by Luc's words. Had she *really* left to protect herself? She thought back to the moment she had decided to leave, to how she had been feeling when she had booked the flight. She had been angry at Cole for lying, and she had felt completely threatened by the fact that he and Gabriela shared not only a son but a secret as well. She had felt betrayed. She had also felt as though Gabriela had them backed into a corner. She hadn't thought she had any choice but to go.

Getting up, Claire put on her bathrobe and made her way down the hall, glad to find Janet and Ted still awake. She flopped down onto an armchair and watched the last few minutes of the movie with them.

As soon as the closing credits rolled across the screen, Ted turned off the TV. He and Janet both looked over at her.

"Well?" he asked. "What happened?"

"He said I left Cole solely to protect myself from being hurt, that my ego couldn't take it if Gabriela won out over me. He made it sound like I was being completely selfish."

"Selfish isn't the same thing as self-protective," Janet said.

"Do *you* think that's why I left?" Claire asked, giving them a hard look.

"You know, Claire, I'm not sure how much you

remember about our first conversation when you got here. You talked about 'the goddess' and how you needed to get away from her," Ted replied.

"I don't remember that, actually, but just now I was thinking back to when I left Cole," Claire responded, nodding slowly. "I was really angry and hurt, and I knew I couldn't take it if Cole left me for her. I think Luc might be right. I convinced myself and Cole that I left for him, to give him a chance to raise Tomas, but that story is full of shit. I did it for me."

Janet spoke up. "I think it's more complicated than that. You had to protect yourself. You had just been cheated on by Antonio and then Cole started lying to you. You would have been a fool to stick around for that. But I also know you were worried about him and his son. It's not an either/or thing. It's a both/and thing."

"Luc saw so clearly that I've been lying around moping like some kind of martyr when really I left Cole for my own reasons. What does that say about me?"

"It says you aren't as weak as you thought you were. You did what you had to do. You were in a no-win situation and you took control of the outcome so that you wouldn't be the victim again. You made a tough call, and it took strength to do it."

"Maybe . . . I don't know," Claire said, wrapping her robe tightly around herself. "Wouldn't it have been stronger to stay and fight for what was mine?"

"I don't think so, honey," Janet answered softly. "The writing was on the wall. If you had stayed, you would have just been dragging out the inevitable."

Claire's face suddenly went pale as the realization of what she had done struck her for the first time. "Oh my God, Janet, I gave up the best thing that's ever happened to me because I was scared. And he wouldn't have given up on me. No matter what."

TWENTY-FIVE

December in London brought cool weather off-set by festive Christmas lights that brightened the evenings. Claire was still grappling with her new insight about why she had left Cole. She wished she could call him and tell him the truth. It didn't seem right to have him thinking she was here only for his sake when really she knew that Luc was right. This was a self-imposed exile to protect her own fragile ego. She had cut the ties before he had even had a chance to prove that he wouldn't leave her. The question of what would have happened if she had stayed haunted her. She had to remind herself repeatedly that Cole had indeed taken up with Gabriela already, which meant she had made the right choice. If he could move on so quickly, surely their love hadn't meant much to him.

She did her best to put the whole thing out of her mind. She started going to yoga classes with Janet in the evenings and ran most mornings. In her quiet, private moments, Claire still ached when she thought of Cole. Sometimes she could almost hear his voice or smell him. When she went to sleep at night, she would dream of him, sometimes happy, wonderful dreams in which they were still together and everything was perfect again. Other times she slept restlessly, dreaming they were on the mountainside again, making love, and then a huge dragon came along and picked her up, dropping her into the valley below. She would wake up just before she hit the ground.

One evening, Claire and Janet went for hot chocolate after yoga. Feeling peaceful and invigorated after the class, Claire smiled at Janet. "I think I should find my own place in London, maybe make this my home."

Janet beamed at her and gave her a big hug. "Oh, I've always wished we lived closer to each other!"

"My biggest problem will be finding a source of income."

"Yeah, that could prove tricky," Janet agreed. "With the immigration laws, it would be very difficult to get a work visa . . . But you could start your own business."

"I was thinking maybe I should use my inheritance to open a café. I think Dad would have wanted me to do that."

Janet's eyes filled with tears. "I know he would

have, and I think that sounds like a wonderful idea. You'll finally run your own show, Claire. I can put you in touch with the right people to help you find a great location."

"Thank you, Janet. You're so good to me. I don't know how I can ever repay you."

"Your moving to London is enough. I've missed you so much all these years. You know what? Forget getting your own flat. You should stay with us until you get all set up."

"I don't know, Janet. It'll take me a long time to get everything up and running. I should find my own place. Let you and Ted have your privacy back."

"We've both really enjoyed having you stay, Claire. You're welcome to live with us as long as you like, honestly."

"Thanks, sis. I appreciate that."

"Tomorrow morning, I'll get a hold of a realtor I know to help you search for a space you can lease. I also have a friend who invests in small businesses. He'll have some good advice."

Later that night as Claire lay in bed, she felt excited for the first time since she had left Colorado. A new life lay in front of her, and it was full of possibilities. She could start over, with people who loved her in her corner. She could move on with her life, and this was the perfect way to do it.

Colorado Springs

At that moment in Colorado, Dustin waited impatiently at the airport arrivals gate for his brother. Trey finally stepped through the doors and the two greeted each other with a brief man hug, which included hearty pats on the back.

"Hello, Ugly," Dustin said.

"How the hell are you, you little turd?" Trey asked.

"Same as always—lookin' for trouble before it finds me," Dustin said, handing him a winter coat. "Here, Mom thought you wouldn't have brought one with you. She couldn't stand the thought of her little boy being chilly on the way home from the airport."

"She's a good woman. I do hate being cold." Trey held the coat in one hand as they walked over to pick up his luggage.

"Well, you've been living in the right place, then. That's quite the tan you've got. You ever make it to class?"

"I'll have you know I've made it to all of them. Turns out your brother is a bit of a genius. My GPA is in the top ten per cent of all the business students'."

Dustin looked at him with wide eyes. "You serious, man? Good for you."

"Who knew, right?"

Trey grabbed his duffle bag off the conveyor belt and the pair exited the airport.

"You wanna grab a burger at The Dive?" Trey asked.

"We can't tonight. We're expected out at the ranch for a big supper, so we better not show up full. Mom and Dad will be there along with all the relatives. You'll get to meet Cole's baby boy."

"You mean *Ben's* baby, you moron. Claire wasn't pregnant, Alicia was."

"Nope, I meant Cole's, dipshit. It's not Claire's baby. Gabriela showed up last month with his son. Shocked the shit out of everyone."

Trey stopped in his tracks for a moment, his stomach doing a flip.

Dustin stopped alongside him and stared at him. "What?"

"I'm just shocked is all," he said, trying to brush it off.

On the ride out to the ranch, Trey couldn't hold two thoughts together. He found himself sweating and his heart racing. He could hear Dustin talking and hoped his own responses made sense.

"Trey. Trey!" Dustin said, staring at him as they sat parked at the ranch. "You sure you don't have something on your mind? You've been acting weird since we left the airport."

"Nah, I'm fine. I've been studying and party-ing pretty hard for the past week," he replied. He paused for a moment, trying to sound casual. "I guess I'm in shock about Cole, too. That's gotta be hard for him and Claire both."

"Yeah, a little too hard. Claire left. It was like watching a train wreck. I think he's trying to make a go of it with Gabby, but I can't see it working."

Trey exhaled loudly. "Shit. That sucks," he said, getting out of the truck.

He felt as though his feet were moving toward the restaurant of their own accord. He had never thought he would see Gabriela again, and now, without any real warning, he was about to come face to face with her. Was it possible the baby was his and not Cole's? A horrible mistake that should have been left in the past was about to smack him in the face.

When they walked into the restaurant, the fireplace was warm and festive sounds filled the air. The entire family was there to greet Trey. He hugged his parents and his aunts and uncles. Ben brought him a beer as he chatted with everyone. It was several minutes before he spotted Gabriela standing over by the Christmas tree with her back to him, holding her baby. His mouth went completely dry as he watched them.

Fern, his mom, walked up beside him, seeing him staring at Gabriela. "That's quite the situation Cole's in now," she said under her breath.

"No kidding," Trey said.

"Have you met Tomas yet? He's such a cute little guy. He sure takes after our side of the family. Reminds me so much of you and Dustin as babies."

Trey swallowed hard. "Really?" he squeaked out.

"It's uncanny, actually. Makes me nostalgic," she replied. "I'll have to wait years to get a grandbaby out of either of you boys, but seeing that little guy makes me hope you'll hurry it along a bit."

Trey practically choked on his beer at her words. *You might not have to wait at all*, he thought.

They watched as Cole walked over to Gabriela and took Tomas from her. He carried him over toward them. "Hey, Trey, I guess you heard by now that I'm a dad. This little man is Tomas!"

Tomas smiled at Trey, shaking the little plush toy car he was holding. Trey stared from Cole to Tomas, feeling his body go clammy. He was going to have to come clean with Cole about what he had done, and things were about to get ugly.

Gabriela looked on with absolute panic. She saw the expression on Trey's face and knew she was going to have to act fast and work hard to prevent him from ruining everything. She tried to look relaxed as she crossed the floor in their direction.

"Here, Cole, I should change him before we all sit down to eat," she said, reaching out to take Tomas.

"Oh, I got it, Gabby," Cole replied. "You haven't

had a chance to say hi to Trey yet." He walked away with Tomas, grabbing his diaper bag and heading toward the bathroom, leaving them alone.

"Trey, I know what you're thinking, but stop," she hissed at him. "This is definitely Cole's baby. There is no way Tomas is yours, so don't even think about telling him."

"How can you be so sure? Did you have DNA testing done?" Trey asked quietly, putting on a fake smile for anyone who might be watching, although his eyes were filled with terror.

"There is no need. Cole has no doubt that Tomas is his son." Gabriela matched his phony smile. "We are starting over and things are going very well. We will soon be a proper family, so just leave well enough alone."

They didn't notice Mary watching them from across the restaurant. She could tell something was up, and it didn't take a genius to realize what it might be. Just then, Trey's dad asked everyone to take their seats for dinner, ending their conversation. Mary kept a close eye on both of them throughout the meal, seeing them each glance at each other from time to time.

After supper, Mary caught Gabriela and Cole, jackets on, saying their good nights to everyone. Cole was walking beside Gabriela carrying a bundled-up Tomas and the diaper bag. The three looked very much like a happy young family.

"Can I help Gabriela tonight, Cole?" Mary asked, pulling on her coat. "You should stick around and visit with your cousins a while, and I need to spend as much time as I can with this little guy."

Gabriela gave her a wary glance. Cole looked over at Gabby. "Is that okay with you, Gabby? I wouldn't mind sticking around."

"You should both stay. Spend time with your family while everyone is here," she replied smoothly.

Mary's mouth was curled up in a smile, but her eyes were full of ice. "I insist," she said in a crisp voice, taking the diaper bag from Cole.

"Okay, great!" Cole agreed without noticing the body language of either woman. He gave Tomas a kiss on the forehead before he handed him to Gabriela. "Good night, little man. Love you. Night, Gabby," he said as he held the door open for them to make their exit.

The women walked along the path to the cabins without a word to each other, their feet crunching in the freshly fallen snow. The tension between them rose as they neared Gabriela's cabin. She could feel her heart pounding throughout her body as she realized her carefully laid plan was about to unravel. She knew that Mary was on to her. If Cole found out she had slept with Trey, it was all over. She would never be able to regain his already wavering trust. Even if Tomas turned out to be his son, he would never forgive her.

Gabriela unlocked the door and turned on the interior light, stepping inside the warm living room. "You know, Mary, I can get Tomas off to bed. You go back and enjoy the party."

"Aren't you thoughtful? I'll join them soon enough. I need to have a talk with you first," Mary answered in a clipped tone. She closed the door behind her and took off her coat.

Gabriela put Tomas down on the floor of the living room with some toys to play with. She did her best to look casual, but Mary could see the fear in her eyes. "What do you need to talk about?"

"I saw you with Trey tonight. Do you want to tell me what that was about or should I ask him?"

Gabriela looked Mary straight in the eye, trying to appear utterly confused by the question. "I have no idea what you think is going on. We said hello. We talked about Tomas for a minute. There is nothing to know."

Mary snorted in disgust. "Okay, Gabriela, if that's how you want to play it, I'm sure my nephew will be more forthcoming."

With that, she picked up her coat and walked out the door. Mary marched back to the restaurant, a woman on a mission. She had never liked Gabriela, and now she knew she was right not to have trusted her. Every instinct she had told her that her suspicions were about to be proven correct. Even though she hadn't gotten Gabriela to admit anything, Mary could lead Trey to believe that she knew the truth. She didn't want to hurt her nephew, but if she was right, he had betrayed her son in the worst manner, and he needed to accept responsibility for it. There was no way she was going to allow Cole to saddle himself with a lying, cheating woman for the rest of his life.

Mary took a deep breath and tried to look calm as she walked back into the restaurant. She spotted Cole sitting with Trey and Dustin on one of the couches by the fireplace. Cole and Dustin seemed relaxed and were sharing a laugh, while Trey was staring into the fire as though lost in thought.

Mary walked up behind the couch and put her hand on Trey's shoulder, bending down to his ear. "I know everything, Trey. Come to the kitchen with me. We need to have a talk."

She could feel his body stiffen under her hand and when he turned, his red face and wild eyes told her all she needed to know. Cole and Dustin stopped talking and watched them, looking confused. Mary decided to have them come along.

"Cole and Dustin, can you help Trey and me in the kitchen for a minute?"

The four walked through the door to the back and found the kitchen empty. Mary stared at Trey for a moment before she spoke. Dustin and Cole leaned against the counter opposite her and exchanged glances. Trey stood close to the door, keeping his eyes aimed at the floor.

"Dustin, I thought you better be here in case we need you. Trey, you better tell Cole what he needs to know."

Trey took a deep breath and closed his eyes for a moment before speaking. His entire body felt weak as he looked up at his cousin and confessed. "Cole, I don't know how to say this, but there is a chance that Tomas might not be your son."

Cole swallowed hard, glaring at him. His voice came out as a growl. "And just how would you know that, Trey?"

Trey's reply came out in a quiet, strained voice. "Because he might be mine."

Cole stared at him, rage filling his brain like a heavy fog. Betrayal. Lies. Losing Claire. Now the threat of losing Tomas. His veins coursed with red-hot anger as he clenched his fists, staring at his younger cousin—the boy he had taken under his wing and taught to ride and rope and fight. The cousin he had given a job to and cared for had fucked his girlfriend and pretended it had never happened. Bitter disappointment. Rage.

Trey looked up with a mixture of fear and guilt in his eyes. "I'm so sorry, Cole. I'm so sorry. It happened one time right before she went back to Brazil. We were both very drunk. I swear I had no idea about the baby until I got home today! I would have told you sooner if I had known."

Cole crossed the kitchen in one swift move,

grabbed Trey by the shirt and shoved him to the ground. He pinned him to the floor with a knee on his chest and had one arm pulled back, ready to strike a vicious blow to Trey's face. Somewhere in the distance, he could hear his mother and Dustin shouting at him to stop. Cole looked at Trey's face; he was wincing with his eyes closed. Unable to bring himself to punch his cousin, he let go of Trey's shirt and got up with disdain, as though being near him made him want to retch. He didn't notice his Aunt Fern, who had heard the commotion, walk into the kitchen.

"You little piece of shit," Cole swore under his breath. "Get the fuck off my ranch before I beat you till you're dead."

Cole strode away, rubbing his face with his hand. He stormed out the back door of the kitchen. A garbage can near the back door took the hit that had been meant for Trey. Cole cut his knuckles badly as he punched it.

"Fuck!" he shouted. He knocked the can onto its side and continued on to his cabin.

He looked over at Gabriela's place as he passed by. The fleeting thought went through his mind to go over to order her off the ranch too, but he thought better of it. He knew he was too angry to keep his voice down, and he didn't want to scare Tomas. He went back to his cabin instead, slamming the door behind him so hard the walls shook. Otis scooted over to his bed with his tail between his legs and lay down instead of greeting him.

Mary watched Cole from the back door of the kitchen, feeling sick to her stomach. She held on to the frame of the door to steady herself. Her son was in so much pain, having been betrayed by Gabriela and his own cousin. He had lost the love of his life and now might be about to lose the boy he had started to love as his son. She felt no pleasure in revealing Gabriela for the liar she was or in finding out her own nephew was of such low character. For the moment, she felt only a hint of relief that the truth had been exposed.

TWENTY-SIX

The next morning, Cole went to Gabriela's just as he had done for weeks. She had insisted he stop knocking, so he just walked in. Gabriela was already dressed and waiting for him in full makeup that hid the dark circles around her eyes. She had been awake all night but could think of no way to spin this so she wouldn't come out looking awful.

Cole stood in the small entryway giving her a long, hard look before he said anything. Tomas crawled over to him with a big grin. Cole scooped him up in his arms and kissed him on the cheek. His heart ached as he realized he wouldn't be able to do this much longer. Even if Tomas was his son, Gabriela would know there was no way they could start over now, and she would run back home to Brazil as soon as she could.

Cole got right down to business. "I want to get the genetic testing done today. Trey and I can both provide samples so it'll be quicker to determine who the real father is. We should know within the week. In the meantime, I'll continue to pick Tomas up in the mornings to take him back to my place to play before work, and I'll come in the evenings to put him to bed. I'd appreciate it if you don't talk to me unless it's absolutely necessary. It won't do any good."

Gabriela nodded, tears rolling down her cheeks. Cole dressed Tomas in his little red snowsuit without looking at Gabriela again. She sat at the kitchen table, sobbing quietly into her hand.

Just as Cole and Tomas were about to leave, she spoke up. "Cole, for what it's worth, I'm so sorry."

"It's worth nothing to me." With that, he closed the door.

* * *

The next few days seemed to drag on forever as they waited for the test results. It was less than one week until Christmas, and by the time Tomas had his first visit from Santa, they would all know who his father was. Cole wasn't sure what to hope for. If Tomas wasn't his son, he would finally have Gabriela out of his life for good, and he might have a chance to get Claire back, but he would have to grieve losing this little baby he had grown to love so much in such a short period of time. He would worry about Tomas, knowing that his cousin Trey was too young and immature to be a good father. He also didn't want such a selfish, dishonest pair of people to have the privilege of raising this little boy and teaching him their messed-up version of right and wrong.

Things were extremely tense around the ranch. Cole's mom and her sister, Fern, were fighting, Dustin was extremely uncomfortable around Cole when he came in to work and Trey was staying away from the ranch completely. Trey and Cole had met at the lab four days earlier to provide the DNA samples. Cole would not look at him and said nothing while they were there. Trey knew Cole well enough to know there was no point in trying to talk to his cousin. It would be a long time before Cole would be ready to hear anything he had to say.

Cole had spoken with his lawyer about the new developments. He had found out that even though he had accepted legal responsibility for Tomas, that could easily be undone. It would have been much harder if Tomas were older and Cole had taken on the role of father for more than a few weeks.

* * *

Ben and Alicia came into Cole's office on Friday morning and found him doing payroll.

"Hey, Cole, how are you?" Alicia asked.

Cole looked up and put his pen down on his desk. "Alright, I guess. I keep waiting for the email to come. Could be anytime now. How are you feeling?"

"Wishing this baby would just come already. I am so sick of being pregnant," she replied, easing herself into a chair.

"I bet. Three weeks max?"

"Apparently. So, have you figured out what you're going to do if Tomas isn't your son?"

"You mean about Claire?" Cole asked, leaning back in his chair and sighing.

"Yes." Alicia nodded.

"I can't even let myself think about that yet. I don't know what to hope for. I want Tomas to be my son, but I also want to drop everything and go get Claire."

"And would a part of you like Gabriela to fall off the face of the earth?" Ben asked.

"Yup. That wouldn't be so bad either. Trey, too, for all I care," Cole answered bitterly.

"You have every right to be angry, Cole," Ben replied, shaking his head. "What they did was unforgivable."

Cole sighed. "I just can't believe I didn't listen to Claire. She tried to warn me, but I just pushed her away, trying to give Gabriela the benefit of the doubt. On top of that, I lied to her. I don't know what I was thinking. Now Claire is gone and, honestly, I wouldn't blame her if she never wanted to see me again."

"Don't give up, Cole. It's been only a few weeks since she left. Claire loves you and once she knows what happened, she'll come back," Alicia replied.

"I don't know if she will, Alicia. In the meantime, I just have to sit and wait for the email from the lab to let me know if I'm a father or not."

* * *

Later that afternoon, Cole was out in the stables brushing Dudley. It was cold, and he could see his breath as he quietly stroked the large horse's black hair, a ritual both Dudley and Cole found soothing. Cole's cellphone vibrated in his pocket. He stood still for a moment and took a deep breath, putting the brush down. Reaching into his pocket, he took out the phone and swiped the screen to see what the message was. It was from the lab. Cole sat down on a stool in the stall and opened the attachment.

He scanned the report quickly to find the paragraph he was looking for.

> Cole Mitchell is excluded as the biological father of Tomas Cole Ferreira. This means that Cole Mitchell cannot be the father of Tomas Cole Ferreira because the analysis shows they do not share a paternity relationship.
>
> Trey Johnson is not excluded as the biological father of Tomas Cole Ferreira. This means that Trey Johnson is considered to be the father of Tomas Cole Ferreira because

the analysis shows they do share a paternity relationship.

He let out a long exhale, relieved to know the truth at last. He sat for a long time rereading the words and reliving the past six weeks in his mind. He realized how many dreams of fatherhood had already crept into his brain—teaching his son to ride a horse, taking him fishing and camping, playing catch. None of these things would happen now, and it hurt like hell to lose that.

* * *

Gabriela sat on the couch, her laptop on the coffee table, watching Tomas play with some blocks. She was numb. She had read the results over and over in the last hour, letting the tears flow. Whatever flicker of hope she had had that she and Cole would spend their lives together had now been extinguished. She had gambled and lost. The father of her child was little more than a boy himself, someone she had never loved and never would. She placed the computer on her lap and began searching for a flight back home. If she was very lucky, she would be there in time for Christmas. She doubted Trey would fight her on it.

* * *

Trey sat alone at a table in the back corner of a bar. He had been at the gym when the email came. He had gotten showered and dressed, then had walked across the street to have a stiff drink. He was a father. He would forever have a reminder of how he had betrayed his cousin. Trey had no idea what to do. He had no money and wouldn't be welcome to work at the ranch anymore. He doubted he would be able to finish school now. A feeling of nausea washed over him as he stared at the results again on the screen of his phone. After half an hour, he put some cash on the table and walked out, leaving his drink untouched.

* * *

Cole walked back to his office. He sat at his desk and forwarded the email from the DNA lab to his lawyer, along with instructions to revoke the admission of paternity filing. He sat staring out the window, thinking about Claire. He wouldn't be able to go anywhere until after the Christmas holidays were over. The ranch was fully booked over the next two weeks, and he couldn't leave Ben and Alicia right now, in case she had the baby early.

He looked at the clock to see what time it was. It would be the middle of the night for Claire. He wanted so badly to call her and tell her the news. They could start over, and this time, nothing and no one would be able to get in their way.

He locked up his office and walked over to Gabriela's cabin. He wasn't going to just disappear from Tomas's life. This time when he reached the door, he knocked. When Gabriela opened it, Cole was surprised to see Trey was already there, playing with Tomas. His heart dropped as he walked in.

"I guess we have a few things to sort out," Cole said, taking off his boots and coat.

Gabriela nodded and sat down on the couch. Trey looked up with fear in his eyes as he watched Cole cross the room and sit in an armchair. Tomas crawled over and used Cole's pant leg to pull himself up. He lifted the baby onto his lap and gave him a little peck on the head.

Cole spoke first. "I've emailed my lawyer to have me removed as Tomas's legal father. Trey, I can send you his contact info so you can go through him to have an admission of paternity form filed with the courts. You still have to do that. The DNA test isn't considered proof of paternity. He said it would be quicker and cheaper for you than starting over with a new lawyer."

"Thank you, Cole," Trey said quietly. "I'd appreciate that."

"I'm not doing it for you. I'm doing it to make sure you don't try to skip out on Tomas."

Trey nodded, saying nothing.

Gabriela looked from one man to the other. "I have decided to go back to Brazil. I came here looking to make a family for Tomas, but that isn't going to happen. Trey, you need to go to school right now, not raise a family. Maybe you can come and see him sometime soon."

Trey nodded his head. "You're probably better off with your family than with me. I'd like to send you some money when I can. It won't be much for now, but eventually it might be something. I do want him to know me, though, Gabriela. Can we manage that?"

Gabriela looked at him, relieved he wasn't going to make it difficult for her to go home. "Yes, Trey. Definitely he will know you. You can spend as much time as you like here in the next two days before we leave. That would actually let me get all my preparations done." She gave him a sad little smile, feeling sorry for him.

"Well, that settles it, then," Cole said, standing up and pressing his face to Tomas's little cheek, feeling its softness against his skin. "Here, buddy, go see your dad." Cole handed Tomas to Trey. Trey held the baby awkwardly as he squirmed around in his arms.

Gabriela watched the scene unfold, her dreams dissolving in an instant. "How can you not yell at us, Cole?"

He looked over at her. "What would be the point? You both know what you've done. I just hope you can raise him to have higher morals than either of you have. Do that for me." He put his boots and coat on and walked out the door with a lump in his throat.

He made his way straight over to Ben and Alicia's cabin to give them the news. The pair sat quietly while he told them what had just happened. He blinked back tears for a moment and sighed, looking over at Alicia's tummy. "Well, at least I'll have a little niece or nephew to spoil soon."

"You're going to be a terrific father someday, Cole," Alicia said. "And it will be with the right woman, which will make the whole thing that much better."

Ben handed him his laptop. "Speaking of the right woman, let's find you the next flight to London so you can go get Claire."

"There is no way I can go right now. We're going to have a full house here for the next two weeks."

"Like hell you can't," Ben declared. "You think you're the only one who knows how to run this place? I may not like it in the office, but I know what to do when I'm in there. Dad and Mom are here as well, and if you remember, they ran this place when you and I were still in diapers."

"You have to go, Cole. Now. Don't leave it another minute," Alicia urged, handing him a piece of paper. "This is the address for Claire's sister. I emailed Claire for it so I could send her tax forms when they come. Go get her."

"What if your baby comes early? I need to stay here at least until after the Christmas holiday is over," Cole said, looking at her doubtfully.

"We'll be just fine. The doctor said there is no way this baby is coming for at least another two weeks. Gabriela's wasted enough of your time. Now get your head out of your ass and go get her already," Ben said.

Cole smiled at him. "Okay," he answered, opening the computer and turning it on. "Let's find me a flight."

TWENTY-SEVEN

London

In London, Claire was sitting up in bed. It was 2 a.m., and she had just woken up from another bad dream. She turned on the lamp and sighed, mentally calculating the time of day back in Colorado. It was early evening there, and she imagined that Cole and Gabriela were probably together, maybe snuggled up on the couch watching a show or making love. Claire tried to shake the thought out of her head. Cole was in her past as much as Antonio was. Neither would be a part of her life again, and she had to find a way to forget Cole, as he had forgotten her.

She needed to focus on her future. Claire thought about the new year; it would be a fresh start for her. This past year had completely depleted her emotional energy—finding out Antonio was cheating, starting over in Colorado, falling for Cole only to lose him, ending up heartbroken in another new place. Her heart and mind were exhausted from all of it. She needed something new to fill her with hope and purpose again.

She wanted the next year to be a chance for her to develop her independence. Finding a commercial property she could lease was proving difficult. She had seen several strong possibilities, but none of them were exactly what she wanted. The reality Claire didn't like to admit was that nothing would be perfect if Cole wasn't there to walk through the door and taste what she was preparing, smile at her or wrap her in his arms. She needed to find a way to get excited about her life without him, and she had no clue how she would do that.

TWENTY-EIGHT

Cole boarded the early morning flight with nervous knots in his stomach. By the time he arrived in London, it would be late evening local time on Christmas Day. He hadn't let Claire know he was coming but planned to get a cab straight over to her sister's house. He felt horrified every time the thought that she might already have fallen for someone else crossed his mind. Logically, he knew it wasn't likely, but he couldn't help considering the possibility.

He tried in vain to watch the movies offered, feeling too anxious to take in any of them. He fidgeted, staring out the window and checking his watch every ten minutes. *Come on, come on*, he thought to himself. He finally saw the lights of London as the plane descended. The city seemed to go on forever, brightly lit with reflections glowing off the river. He had never seen a sight more thrilling. This city held his Claire, and he was about to go find her. He could only hope she would be willing to give him a second chance.

He got his backpack and left the airport, heading straight outside to find a cab. As it drove along the streets of London, he barely took in his surroundings, thinking about Claire, wondering how she was spending Christmas Day, praying he would find her at home. The house was dark when he got there, except for the outside light.

"You want to wait here or shall I drive you somewhere else?" the cabbie offered.

"I'll wait here."

"You sure? There are no buses running, and the Tube is shut down for the night. It'll be hard to get another cab from here tonight."

"Thank you, but I want to wait here."

"Grand romantic gesture?"

"Something like that." Cole nodded.

"Good luck with that, mate. I hope it works."

Cole paid the driver the fare and took his backpack out of the trunk. He jogged up the steps of the house two at a time and rang the bell, just in case someone was home. After a moment, he knocked and then had a seat on the cold steps to wait.

* * *

Claire had been invited to Christmas dinner at friends of Ted and Janet's, including some of

Janet's colleagues from the law practice. She sat quietly in an armchair by a window in the living room, where the party had gathered after their meal. She felt very out of place in a house full of couples. On top of that, her feet were freezing. She had worn nude tights and heels with a merino-wool, knee-length dress. She hated having cold feet. She wished she was snuggled up under a blanket on the couch back at their place watching movies. This felt nothing like Christmas to Claire. There was nothing peaceful or cozy about this day. She sipped at her wine, watching the clock and wondering what time they could leave.

Ted came over and sat on the chair next to her, leaning over and speaking in a low tone. "Here's a fun fact you may not know—this party has been nominated for the *Guinness Book of World Records* in the Dullest Evening category."

Claire giggled quietly, covering her mouth with her hand. "I thought I was the only one who felt that way."

"Are you kidding me? If I hear one more of these pretentious snobs go on about his portfolio, I'm going to smash him in the face with that disgusting Christmas cake."

Claire tried to stifle another laugh. "It was gross, wasn't it? When do you think we can go home?"

Ted looked at the clock on the fireplace mantle.

"I don't think we have to stay much longer. I'll try to give Janet the signal."

"Perfect. I just want to curl up on the couch and watch *Elf*."

* * *

An hour later, the three were pulling up to the town-house. Claire was sitting in the back seat of Ted's car, half asleep. She heard Janet say "Holy crap."

Janet looked back at Claire from the passenger seat, seeing her sister's eyes closed. "Claire, honey, I think Santa left something for you on the steps. Or maybe for me. Dear God, I hope that's for me. No offence, sweetheart," she added, looking at her husband.

Claire opened her eyes and looked at Janet. "What?" She looked out the window and took in the sight of Cole sitting on the top step, looking like the sexiest man on the planet in his jeans and a dark grey wool overcoat.

Janet handed her a mint. "I take it that's your cowboy?"

Claire was speechless as she nodded and took the mint. She sat staring at him through the window of the car in complete shock. Cole got up and walked down the steps with a look of uncertainty as he peered through the glass at Claire.

"Claire, I think Janet and I are going to go for

our traditional Christmas evening drive around London for the next hour or so," Ted said, grinning at her.

"Is that okay with you, Claire? Or do you want us to stay?" Janet asked protectively.

"Mm-hmm . . ." She nodded keeping her eyes on Cole. "Have fun."

"Claire, get out of the car," Ted ordered. "There's a dreamy guy standing there waiting to talk to you, and if you don't get out, my wife is going to."

"Right," she said, nodding. She could feel her heart pounding in her chest as she wrapped her red pashmina around her shoulders and opened the door. She stepped out and gazed at Cole, who was on the other side of the car, his face full of emotion.

Janet unrolled the window and said, "Welcome to London, Cole. We have to run, but we'll catch you later."

"Okay, nice to meet you, Janet," Cole replied, without taking his eyes off Claire.

Ted slowly pulled the car away and down the empty street, leaving a large space between them. Snow began to drift gently down from the sky, as if it had been cued by a movie director.

Claire stood in the middle of the street, not completely sure this moment was really happening. She had dreamed of Cole appearing out of nowhere since she had gotten into the cab at the ranch so many weeks ago. She had convinced herself it was never going to happen, and yet now that he was here, she wasn't sure how to feel. Her first instinct was to run to him and jump into his arms, but something was holding her back. Feelings of fear, anger and guilt muddied the desire she felt for him.

Cole stood on the sidewalk searching her eyes for some sign that she wanted him there. The past days of planning and travelling and then waiting on the step had been like a roller coaster, filled with moments of absolute exhilaration that they would be together soon to complete uncertainty that she would even want to see him. His heart ached just looking at her, so beautiful and delicate in her dress and red wrap. She looked too skinny to him, her cheeks too defined—a sign of the toll these past weeks had taken on her.

He pulled something out of his coat pocket. "You left your gloves in the barn." He held his hand out to her but stood still, waiting for her reaction.

Claire gave him a faint smile and looked at the gloves in his hand. "It's a good thing you brought them. My hands have been really cold this whole time."

"I was worried about that. I realized I better get them to you as soon as I found them."

Claire laughed a little and then gave him a hard look, still not sure what to do.

"It's over, Claire. Gabriela's gone. You were right about everything. Tomas isn't my son. I should have listened to you in the first place instead of being such a jackass and trying to do things my own way."

He paused and looked down at her gloves in his hand. When he looked back up, his eyes were glistening with tears. "The thing is . . . the thing is, I need you, Claire. My life doesn't mean anything without you. I don't want any of it, not even the ranch, if you aren't there with me."

Claire's eyes welled up. "Really? But Cole, you moved on. What about that text?"

He sighed. "I sent that to you on purpose to piss you off. I thought it would help you forget about me. I never started up with Gabriela. How could I when I won't ever stop loving you? I came here hoping you'll give us another shot. But this time, it has to be forever, Claire."

Claire nodded, trying to blink away the tears. "I think I can do that. Yeah. In fact, I'm pretty sure about it." She took a few steps toward him.

As soon as she started to move, Cole rushed to her, wrapping her up in his arms and lifting her off her feet. He kissed her full on the mouth. Claire kissed him back, pressing her hands to his cold face. Their embrace expressed everything they felt for each other—the longing, the love, the regret, the passion.

Cole gently set her back down on the ground, their mouths never parting as she wrapped her arms around his neck, shivering from the cold. He pulled back from her a little.

"You're freezing. Let's get you inside." He brushed some snow off her hair gently as he smiled at her, his eyes shining with love.

"Oh, I'll be fine now that I have my gloves back. But you seem chilly," she said as they turned back to the house. Claire reached into her clutch and found the keys. They made their way up the steps slowly, stopping to kiss along the way. Cole picked up his backpack and slung it over his shoulder. When they reached the door, Claire unlocked it as Cole pressed his body against her back and snuck his arms around her waist. As the door swung open she swivelled around to face him. Their lips met with quick, passionate kisses. Cole backed her into the house with his hands on her hips and then put his foot against the door and swung it shut behind him.

He brushed his lips along her neck, leaving tender kisses from her ear to her collar. "Merry Christmas, Claire," he murmured.

"Merry Christmas, Cole," she whispered. Suddenly pulled back into reality, Claire leaned back to look him in the face. "I still don't know how you ended up here, Cole. What happened?"

Cole gazed down at her. "It's a long story. Can we curl up together while I tell you everything?"

"Of course. I'll put the kettle on. Hang up your coat and turn on the fireplace."

A few minutes later, the two were snuggled up under a warm blanket on the rug in front of the fireplace, sipping cocoa while Cole told Claire all the details of the last six weeks of his life. Claire listened quietly. Her heart broke for his loss of the little boy he had believed was his son and for how he had been betrayed by Gabriela and Trey. His face wore a pained expression when he spoke of little Tomas and anger as he described how things would never again be the same between him and his cousin.

"I'm so sorry, Claire. I should have listened to you from the start instead of being so stubborn. I thought you were just being insecure instead of logical. You were looking out for me the whole time, and I couldn't see it. And I'm so sorry for that text. It was a rotten thing to do, but I hope you know that in my own stupid way, I was trying to help you."

Claire stared at him for a second before replying. "Misguided, maybe, not stupid. I was devastated at first, but afterward I *was* angry enough to try to move on, so in a way, it worked as you intended it to. It was still shitty, though."

Cole pulled her to him and held her against his chest. "I know it was, and I feel like a total asshole, Claire. I wish you could know how much I regret all of it. These past weeks, thinking I would have to spend the rest of my life without you, have been the worst time of my life. I don't ever want to be apart from you again."

They sat quietly for a long time watching the fire as Cole held her and ran his fingertips up and down her arm. He whispered in her ear, "Are you sure you can give us another chance?"

Claire looked up at him. "I am. Just tell me one thing first—do you have any more ex-girlfriends who might show up with children of yours?"

Cole laughed and kissed her. "God, I hope not. If you want, I can make a list and get a hold of each of them to make sure."

"Is it a long list?"

"Not really. It wouldn't take that long, but it would be a little awkward."

Claire grinned. "Let me think about it."

Cole gave her a long kiss. "I should probably go check in at my hotel. I don't want your sister and her husband to spend Christmas night driving around, thinking they can't come home. Would it be presumptuous if I asked you to spend the night with me so we can have a little privacy?"

"No, it would be wonderful, but it's going to be almost impossible to get a cab tonight."

"I booked a hotel near here. It's supposed to be about a ten minute walk."

Claire gave him an admiring look. "I'll go pack an overnight bag and text my sister that it's safe for them to come home now."

A few minutes later, Claire emerged from her bedroom, dressed warmly in jeans and a wool sweater. She had taken a quick shower to freshen up and had taken out the bun she had worn at the party. Her hair fell in waves around her face. Claire found Cole standing by the front door with his coat on, ready to go. He helped her into her coat and handed her the gloves he had brought. Claire wrapped a royal-blue scarf around her neck and then pulled on a matching wool hat.

Cole stared at her for a long moment, admiring her. "You are so fucking beautiful. You have no idea how much I missed your face and those blue eyes."

"I think I do, Cowboy."

Cole picked up his backpack. "You ready?" he asked.

"Ready." Claire nodded.

Outside, the snow was beginning to accumulate on the ground, giving a soft, peaceful look to the deserted street. Cole reached for Claire's hand and they walked side by side in the direction of the hotel. Claire leaned her head on his arm for a minute and squeezed his hand.

"I'm just checking to see if you're real," she said.

"It's hard to believe this is happening, isn't it?" Cole said, smiling down at her.

"Almost impossible. If this is a dream, I will kill the person who wakes me up."

They made their way to the Bingham Inn, which turned out to be a very romantic hotel that backed onto the Thames. When they walked into Cole's suite, they were both impressed by its grandeur. It was large and had high ceilings, with French doors that led out to a balcony overlooking the river and the park. Off to the right, there was a sitting area with a dark grey leather couch and matching armchair, and to the left, a king-size canopy bed with white linens. A large crimson poinsettia decorated the coffee table, adding a festive warmth to the otherwise cool decoration of the room.

Cole put down his bag, unzipping it and pulling out his shaving kit. "Mind if I go get cleaned up a bit? I need to get the plane grunge off me."

"Of course," Claire said, giving him a lingering kiss on the lips. "You must be so tired."

"Not really," Cole said, caressing her cheek with his hand. "I've been waiting so long to get here, I'm not going to waste my time sleeping."

"Good, but you will be exhausted when I'm done with you," Claire replied with a playful look.

"I'm counting on it," Cole said, pulling himself away to go shower.

As Claire watched him walk into the bathroom and close the door, she smiled to herself with a sense of pure contentment. Cole was here, this was really happening. Through some divine intervention, they had been given another chance at love. Claire took off her coat and tossed it onto the chair, then made her way over to the bed and sat down. She looked around restlessly as she waited for him to emerge from the shower, soon realizing she had to brush her teeth. In the past, she would have just walked into the bathroom while he showered, but tonight that level of intimacy wasn't there. Things felt strangely formal, and she wasn't entirely sure how to proceed.

Cole was in the shower, quickly rinsing himself off. He hastily towelled dry and then filled up the sink with hot water to shave. He stared at his reflection in the mirror. He looked tired. The past two months had put him through the wringer, and he was relieved to be in London so he could be with Claire and have a real break from everything. Things were still tense back at the ranch, with his mom and her sister angry at each other, and everyone, including himself, being so disappointed in Trey. He was glad Trey would be back at school in the new year so he wouldn't have to see him for a long time.

Cole's thoughts wandered to the woman waiting for him on the other side of the door. There was nowhere else he wanted to be other than with her. He anticipated touching her, kissing her, feeling himself inside her very soon. He hummed happily to himself as he slapped aftershave onto his face.

A minute later, Cole opened the bathroom door and walked out wearing nothing but a white towel. His hair was still wet, and as Claire took in the sight of him, she was reminded of the first time she had seen him like this, at the pool. She felt exactly the same way now as she had then, completely turned on at the sight of his rippling muscles but also so unsure of herself. The sexy vixen she had become at the ranch seemed to lie dormant somewhere deep within, and she wasn't sure how to bring her out just now.

Cole looked a bit surprised to see her sitting on the bed fully dressed. He smiled at her warmly and gave her a thoughtful look as he crossed the room to her. He sat down on the bed and leaned against the headboard. "Either I'm underdressed or you're overdressed."

Claire tilted her head to the side and looked at him. "Is it weird that I feel a bit uncomfortable?"

"No," he replied, shaking his head. "We've been apart for almost two months, and we both thought this was over."

"Yeah. I just feel like so much has happened, and I need some time to adjust, okay?"

"It's totally okay, Claire. It's enough for me just to be able to look at you and hear your voice again. I would never like anything to happen if you weren't absolutely sure you wanted it to." Cole smiled and took her hand in his and lifted it to his lips, giving her a little peck on her knuckles.

Claire smiled gratefully at him. "Thank you, Cole. I'm glad that you aren't too disappointed."

"Even if I were disappointed, Claire, that wouldn't be a reason for you to have sex with me.

{504}

And you know what? I'm just so happy you were even willing to talk to me when I got here. I really thought you might just kick me to the curb after everything that happened."

Claire kissed him on the cheek. "I would have, but I really wanted my gloves back."

Cole laughed. "God, I missed your sassy little mouth."

He gave her a kiss on the lips, then pulled back a bit. "Now, why don't we throw on some pyjamas and watch a movie? Maybe order a little room service, if the kitchen is still open."

"Sounds like a perfect evening," Claire answered. They both got up off the bed and went over to their respective bags. Cole put on his grey, low-slung pyjama bottoms and a fitted white T-shirt. Claire rooted around, realizing she didn't have loungewear.

Cole tossed her a T-shirt of his. "Here. It'll look better on you anyway."

"True. Your shirts always look better off you than on," Claire said as she picked the shirt up and walked over to the bathroom to get changed. She came out a few minutes later in Cole's T-shirt and a hotel bathrobe and slippers.

Cole was sitting up with his legs tucked under the covers, channel surfing. "*Love Actually* is starting in a few minutes. I thought you might want that one?"

"You thought right. Now, shall I see if we can get some food brought up?"

"I already called. Is ham and mushroom pizza and beer okay? I can call back and add something else if that doesn't sound good to you."

"That's just what I was in the mood for," Claire replied, climbing into bed.

* * *

Two hours later, the movie ended. Claire had a lump in her throat as she always did watching the final scene with all the families and lovers greeting one another at Heathrow airport. She was unbelievably content, with her head leaning on Cole's chest and her arm wrapped over him. He had her snuggled in his arms and was fighting to stay awake after having travelled so far. Claire looked up at his face, seeing how exhausted he looked. She found the remote and turned off the TV, leaving the room in the darkness. They snuggled themselves under the covers and held each other close.

"Good night. I love you," Cole whispered, drifting off to sleep.

"I love you too. I'm so glad you're here."

Lying in bed, waiting for sleep to come, Claire realized something had changed in these last weeks. She was different. Stronger. Before Cole, she had never allowed herself to love with abandon. When she had fallen for him, she had given herself over to Cole completely and then had survived losing him. The realization that she hadn't broken into a million pieces gave her a confidence she'd never had before. She was different than the wounded, vulnerable woman who had found herself on the ranch last spring. She didn't need to rely on his being a good man. She knew she could rely on herself to be strong enough to love, to lose and to live on.

TWENTY-NINE

The next morning the pair slept late, both finally having had their first restful night since Gabriela had shown up at the ranch. It was after ten o'clock when Cole woke. He lay on his side, watching Claire, overcome with gratitude for being allowed to be near her again. Her face was so peaceful and beautiful as she slept beside him, with her hand still entangled in his.

A few minutes later, she stirred and her eyes opened. She looked at him and smiled. "Good, you're still here. I thought I dreamed you."

"I'm really here," he replied, tracing down her cheek with the back of his fingers. "God, your skin is so soft, and you are just so beautiful. I could lie here and watch you sleep all day."

"But if we did that, we'd be really hungry by evening. How about if you come with me to Janet and Ted's so I can introduce you to them properly."

"That sounds good, too. Breakfast first?"

"Let's eat at their place. We were going to have a big brunch this morning."

* * *

A little while later, Cole found himself in the kitchen at Janet and Ted's, with the four of them preparing brunch together. He had been assigned to fry the pancakes. He liked Claire's family immediately. He was surprised to find them both welcoming after everything he had put Claire through. They made him feel comfortable by including him in the brunch preparations and by teasing Claire.

Claire stood beside him at the stove, preparing scrambled eggs and sausages. She grinned at him, feeling exhilarated that her sister was finally getting a chance to meet the man she loved.

"So, what don't I know about Claire that I should?" he asked as he looked up from flipping a pancake.

"Well, lots of things really," Janet said. "Starting with the fact that, according to her, that pancake is overcooked."

"Uh-oh, overcooking the food will definitely get you dumped, my friend," Ted added.

"This pancake?" Cole said, feigning shock. "This is perfectly prepared."

"Oh, please," Claire said sarcastically. "Pancakes are not supposed to be chocolate brown. You are so dumped, Cowboy."

"Hey, I don't seem to remember you liking me for my cooking abilities," Cole said, pausing to flip another pancake. "But, Janet and Ted, have you noticed how Claire objectifies me like that? As though I'm just another easily replaceable cowboy in a long succession?"

"That's because you are, buddy," Ted said. "You and me both. These Hatley girls are players. You gotta stay on top of your game if you're going to keep one."

The four found many reasons to laugh as they finished cooking and shared the meal. Claire was pleased to see that Cole seemed to fit so well into this part of her life She smiled, taking in the moment.

"So, what do people do on Boxing Day in England?" Cole asked.

"Go shopping or watch sports," Janet replied.

"We have tickets for a local rugby match later this afternoon, actually," Ted replied. "You should come with us. It's a bit chilly, but we drink a lot, so after a bit, you don't notice the cold."

"That sounds like a great way to get to know London. Claire, you up for it?" Cole asked.

"I was already going, to scope out hot rugby players," she said, shrugging, "but I guess you can come along."

"Oh, so you're into rugby players these days?"

Claire laughed. "I wouldn't worry if I were you, unless I can find one who can also rope a cow. Then you're history, I'm afraid."

Cole looked at Janet and Ted for support. "She's a little bit mean, right?"

They both nodded. Ted replied first, "It's a family trait. I'm telling you, man, run, before it's too late."

Janet gave Ted a little punch on the arm.

Cole looked over at Claire. "I'm afraid it's definitely too late for me already."

"Poor bastard," Ted said, shaking his head sadly.

* * *

That afternoon, Claire and Cole sat in the stands cuddled up under a blanket, drinking coffee with Irish cream. It was a cool day but surprisingly sunny, and the snow that had fallen the night before had already disappeared. Claire wore the gloves Cole had brought for her. They flirted and laughed with each other, at times forgetting there was anyone else there, even though they were surrounded by thousands of people. It felt very much like a date between two people who were just getting to know each other.

At one point, toward the end of the match, Claire looked up at Cole. "This is fun. I'm so happy you're here with me."

She leaned in, giving him a lingering kiss, letting

her tongue slide ever so slightly between his lips. Cole moaned a little, feeling himself immediately react to the slightest touch from her. It had been way too long. Claire's hands were under the blanket that covered them, and she moved her fingers to rest on his upper thigh.

Cole pressed his forehead to hers. "Ms. Hatley, you seem to be getting a little fresh. You do realize that we are in public."

"You make it sound like it's all my fault. If you don't want to get groped in front of a stadium full of people, you shouldn't be so hot."

"Hey, I am not to blame for your lack of self-control. You're the sexiest woman I've ever met, and I don't have my hand up your shirt right now."

"Is that where you want your hand?"

"Among other places."

"That sounds fun . . ." Claire said, giving him another kiss.

Ted, who was sitting next to Cole, cleared his throat loudly. "Claire, you are distracting Cole from learning about the intricacies of rugby."

Claire straightened up. "Sorry, boys. I'll let you get back to your very important business."

* * *

After the game, the four went for dinner at a pub near the stadium so Cole could have his first authentic English supper. He had a plate of bangers and mash, washing it down with a pint of bitter. The pub was busy and warm with a lively atmosphere, many of the patrons having just come from the rugby match. Claire laughed as Cole told the story of their first horseback ride together and how she had fallen into the river. She was overcome by how genuine he was in his regard for her and how his eyes sparkled when he looked over at her. She was remembering how loved she had always felt around him.

Janet watched her sister and Cole as they ate dinner. She noticed how they laughed together and how they seemed to know what the other was thinking. She smiled, feeling happy for her sister in a way she never had when Claire was with Antonio. She thought back to Cole's phone call a few weeks earlier and how concerned he had been for Claire. This man was worthy of her sister. He would take care of her and be a good partner to her for life.

Suddenly, feeling more than a little tipsy, Janet spoke up. She looked Claire in the eye and said loudly, "Claire, this man has my one-hundred per cent approval. You should marry him right away and make lots of gorgeous little cowboy babies."

Cole and Claire both blushed with embarrassment. Cole stared down at his beer while Claire gave her a wide-eyed look that unmistakably said *stop it*.

Ted moved Janet's beer away from her and said, "Well, you're cut off, my dear," with a wide grin.

Cole gave Janet a grateful look. "Thank you, Janet. Your approval means a lot to me, even if it is soaked in alcohol. I would marry your sister today if she'd have me."

"And I'd marry you today, Cole, but not in this outfit," Claire said, pointing at her sweater.

Cole leaned over and gave her a kiss. "You look beautiful to me. A little too skinny maybe, but beautiful."

* * *

Later that night at the hotel as they climbed into bed, Claire looked over at Cole. "What you said at the pub, Cole, about marrying me today, would you really have?"

Cole turned to her with a serious expression. "Yes, Claire, in a heartbeat. If these past few weeks have shown me anything, it's that I don't want to waste another minute not knowing we are together for good. I want to start our life together."

He gave her a long kiss on the lips and then let go. "But I also don't want to rush you. I understand you need some time to trust me and trust this again, so I'll wait as long as it takes for you to get where I am."

"Today has been so amazing, Cole," she answered, touching his cheek with her fingertips. "It feels like we picked up where we left off on the side of the mountain. But I still have a few questions."

"Okay," he said hesitantly. "What kind?"

"I wish it didn't matter, but I really have to know if you and Gabriela did anything physical."

"She did. I didn't," Cole said.

Claire sat up in bed and tucked her knees in to her chest. "What does that mean?" she asked quietly.

Cole sighed, sitting up and leaning against the headboard. "It was a few weeks ago. I had taken Tomas overnight so she could have a break and I could spend some time with him. In the middle of the night, I woke up with her in my bed, pawing at me. I got really pissed off and made her leave. It was awful. I felt like I was cheating on you, and I felt so manipulated at the same time. She didn't try anything again."

"Wow. That is terrible. The thought of her touching you like that is *so* not good for my rage," Claire replied, trying to make a joke. After a moment, she added, "And what did she think would . . . Don't answer that—I already know."

"The good thing is that she's out of our lives forever. And I never felt anything for her the entire time she was back. Not even for a minute, Claire. I just kept missing you and wishing I could come get you. I was pathetic. I didn't even wash your pillow-case, so I could smell you every night."

Claire smiled, touched and secretly thrilled. "Thank you for telling me that, Cole. Until yesterday,

I was certain you had moved on with her and forgotten all about me."

"That's just not possible, gorgeous. You're as much a part of me as the ranch is."

"Do you mean that?"

"More, even."

Claire leaned into his shoulder for a moment, her gratitude crowded out by guilt. She needed to tell him why she had really left. She needed to be as honest with him as he was being with her. She hesitated, nervous about how he might react. She was so close to having everything she ever wanted, and she was suddenly terrified that she might be about to ruin everything.

"Cole, there's something I need to tell you too. I went out for drinks one evening with someone. I met him on the plane over here, and he was kind to me. We ran into each other at the park, and he asked me out. As soon as I was on the date, I wanted to leave. I felt like I was cheating on you."

Cole looked surprised for a moment, and then said, "Claire, you don't owe me an explanation. I had to expect you were going to move on with your life. I practically pushed you to."

"There's more to it that I need to explain. When we went out, I told him a little bit about what had brought me to London. He decided very quickly that I had left you for my own selfish reasons—to protect my fragile ego, as he put it."

Cole wrinkled his nose in surprise. "What? That's bullshit. There is nothing selfish about you, Claire. How could someone you just met possibly know what your reasons were anyway?"

"At first I thought he was dead wrong. But then as I started thinking about it, I realized he was kind of right. I mean, my decision to leave was *in part* for you and Tomas to be together, but it was just as much because I couldn't stand the thought of having you choose Gabriela over me. I didn't think I could survive that, so I left. I was so angry and so insecure, Cole. I gave up on you, and I'm sorry."

Cole stared down, thinking about what she had just said. He sat quietly for a minute and then spoke up. "Claire, I already knew why you left. When you told me you were leaving, the first reasons you gave were because I had lied to you and because you couldn't handle being around Gabriela the way things were. But then, when you started talking about it being the right thing for Tomas, I knew there was no changing your mind. If you had been leaving *only* for you, we could have worked it out. And you know what? I don't think anyone could blame you, under the circumstances. You were put in a shitty situation; I wasn't listening to reason. I was keeping a secret from you, and Gabriela was stirring the pot. What were you supposed to do?"

"I don't know, Cole. I've been thinking about that over the past couple of weeks, trying to figure it out. Maybe I should have stood my ground and stayed."

"The way I see it, it's not that cut and dried. As far as you knew, staying would have meant I would lose my son. There wasn't much choice in the matter. You did what you had to for me and to protect yourself. No one could fault you for that."

Claire let out a big breath of air. "I'm so glad you see it that way, Cole. I've been so scared you would think less of me when I told you the truth about why I left."

Cole pulled her to him and gave her a kiss on the lips. He looked down at her. "Not a chance, gorgeous. It would have been a lot easier to let me think the whole thing was for my benefit, but you told me the truth. That's who you really are, Claire. You are an honest and caring person."

Claire put her hand on his chest and looked into his eyes. "I won't ever run like that again, Cole. No matter what happens. I'm going to stay and fight for us. I promise you."

Cole grabbed her around the waist and pulled her on top of him so she was straddling him. "I won't ever give you a reason to run again."

Claire kissed him hard on the mouth, her hair falling around him. Cole gently tucked her hair behind her ears as he opened his mouth to slide his tongue between her parted lips. Claire moaned softly at his touch. Lying on his back, he ran his fingertips up and down her body slowly. He let his hands glide over her bottom and then gave her a little squeeze.

She pulled her mouth away and then moved over to his earlobe, sucking on it gently, then biting it carefully. Cole groaned with pleasure as she moved her hand down to his chest and then over his tight lower abdomen.

"Yup, still hard as a rock," she said, pressing her hand to his body. She reached down lower over his boxer briefs, finding him thick and ready for her. "This is still hard as a rock too, just how I like it."

"Careful, Claire, we might be moving past cuddling here."

Claire gave him a sultry look. "We better be . . . "

"Well, if you really want to, I suppose I could be persuaded to have sex with you," Cole replied, lifting his hips off the bed to quickly slip out of his underwear.

Claire giggled and kissed him. "You should know I've been doing a lot of yoga lately, so you might have trouble keeping up with me." She pulled her T-shirt off, leaving her body nude except for a pair of lacy, red French-cut panties.

"You should know I have a lot of pent-up energy, so this might take all night," he said, cupping her voluptuous breasts with his hands. Claire could feel herself becoming wet in response to his touch. Since she had left Colorado, it was as though the sexual side of her had been in hibernation. Cole had woken her up with one touch, bringing back the wild, uninhibited woman she harboured inside.

Cole lowered his mouth to her breasts. He slowly kissed them, one at a time, savouring the feeling of her skin in his mouth. "You have the best tits."

Claire rubbed herself over him in one long drag. There was nothing but a tiny strip of lacy fabric between them now, and the feeling of his hard length against her panties excited her like nothing else could. Cole gripped her around her hips with both hands, flipping her onto her back and tugging her panties off. His gaze was hungry as he lifted himself to lie over her. They kissed each other with an urgent passion now, mouths melding together as Claire parted her legs and wrapped her ankles around Cole's waist. She held his firm ass in her hands, squeezing him roughly with her fingers. She had never wanted anything as much as she wanted him inside her right at that moment. It was a desperation she had never known before. Cole moved his face down, kissing her neck and then her breasts, one at a time. Then, coming back up to hover over her, he gave her a loving smile.

"You are so fucking sexy, Claire Hatley," he said as he lowered himself to her body. The head of his length pressed against her centre and he could feel how wet she was. He shifted his hips from side to side slowly, finding his way inside her.

Claire moaned, lifting her bottom up to bring herself closer to him. Their bodies joined together, leaving no space between them, bringing them both the most delicious relief from the despair of being apart. They were here, in a moment neither of them had allowed themselves to believe possible. Claire opened her eyes and saw Cole watching her, his face full of desire as he moved his body easily over hers. Their eyes locked as he rocked back and forth, thrusting a little harder each time.

"I missed you so much it hurt," Cole said.

"I missed you too. All of you," Claire said, moving her hands up to his hair and pulling his head down to kiss her. She tugged gently on his bottom lip with her teeth and then let her mouth drift to suck on his neck. Claire could feel him circling inside her tight sex, filling her completely. Their breathing became ragged as Claire moved her hands down to Cole's ass and urged him to move harder and faster. Harder. Faster. She let out a groan that showed him how much she loved the feeling of his body on top of hers, his smooth skin rubbing against her soft curves.

Cole opened his eyes again. He could see Claire was close to coming by the expression on her face. Her breasts were full, and he could feel her erect nipples against his chest as she moved in unison with him. Her mouth was open, and she licked her top lip as she smiled seductively up at him, gripping his body even tighter with her legs.

"Just like that, Cole . . ." she breathed. "Right there. Yes," she moaned.

Cole could feel her squeezing him with her sex, and he watched as her body jolted with the force of her orgasm. He could feel her nails digging into his back as she let the waves of her climax roll through her. Pressing his forehead to hers, he came with one final thrust of his body. Claire smiled at him as she felt him thicken and release inside her. She was overcome by the love she felt for him and the pure ecstasy of being with him again. He was hers, and he loved her and wanted to marry her.

Cole stayed on top of her for a long time after they finished, kissing her face, mouth and neck, letting his lips linger over her. He breathed in the smell of her perfume and took in the feel of her silky smooth skin, an irresistible combination.

"There hasn't been a moment since I first saw you that I haven't wanted you, Claire, and there never will be. Being apart from you was absolute hell."

Claire hugged him tightly, her eyes filling with tears. "I still can't believe you're really here with me. I thought I would never see you again, and I didn't know how I would ever get over you."

"You won't ever have to, Claire. You're mine. All mine, for the rest of our lives."

THIRTY

The next morning, they stayed in bed making love and talking, needing to savour the bliss of being together again. It seemed hard for either of them to believe they were in each other's arms after everything they had been through. They showered together, exploring each other's bodies with enough tenderness and desire to erase the past weeks. Somewhat reluctantly, they got dressed and went for lunch at Janet and Ted's.

After the meal, Ted spoke up. "I'm going to steal Cole away for a while this afternoon, if you don't mind, Claire. I was hoping to catch the Ashes on TV down at the Olde Ship and thought I would introduce Cole to cricket."

"Sure," Claire said, grinning. "Just have him home in time for supper. I was going to make everyone a special treat tonight."

That afternoon as she chopped vegetables, she smiled, thinking about how well Ted and Cole got along. Everything felt so natural with the four of them. She had never felt this way the few times Ted and Janet had met Antonio. It was always strained, and Claire felt like she was often making excuses for something he had said or done, or for his noticeable absences.

Janet sat at the kitchen table, tapping away on her computer. She had taken time off between Christmas and New Year's but needed to respond to a few urgent emails in the meantime. Claire poured two glasses of red wine and brought one over to Janet, setting it down in front of her.

"Here. So you don't forget you're supposed to be on vacation."

Janet glanced over at the wine and smiled. "Almost done. I just have to finish this reply and then I want you to spill all the juicy details of you and your man."

Claire walked back over to the sink and started washing some kale. When she turned off the water, she heard the sound of Janet's laptop closing and looked up to see her sister crossing the kitchen and sitting down on a bar stool at the island.

"So? What are you willing to dish?" Janet said, eyes wide.

Claire laughed. "Where do I even start? He is just . . . Wow, you know? Kind and caring and fun all wrapped up in that delicious body of his. I am absolutely head over heels."

Janet smiled at her. "You know what? It is so wonderful for me to see you like this. You're happy. I haven't seen you smile this much since we were kids."

"What?" Claire asked, wrinkling her nose in surprise. "No way."

"It's true, Claire. I've been worried about you since Mom and Dad died. You just never seemed to find your groove. You were always fun to be around, but I could tell something was missing, and I think it was your cowboy."

Claire took a sip of her wine, digesting what her sister had just said. "I think you're right. I haven't really experienced pure joy since they were alive. Not until I met Cole. I certainly didn't feel good when I was with Fuckwit."

"No, you didn't. You were completely missing that sparkle you had as a kid. You seemed to have lost your confidence. Now it looks like you have it back."

Claire leaned against the counter. "When I met Cole, I started to see myself through his eyes. He makes me feel so beautiful and has so much respect for me. I've finally realized what my own worth is. It's like for the first time, I know how a man should treat a woman, and I would never settle for less. I think that's why it was such a huge hit for me when we broke up. I have never loved anyone like this, and to lose him was like having my heart ripped out and put through a paper shredder. It was completely different than when I found out Antonio was cheating on me. I was humiliated and upset about being betrayed and about losing my home, but I didn't feel anything close to the same pain as when I lost Cole."

"I can see that. Cole is a wonderful guy, Claire, and I am absolutely rooting for you two to make it . . ." Janet's voice trailed off hesitantly.

"But . . . ?"

"But I'm worried that if things don't work out this time, you'll fall apart again. You were a mess when you got here."

"I know. I kind of went off the deep end there, but then I started to pull it together. I realized something when Cole showed up here—I survived losing him. I got hurt, but I was moving on with my life. I feel like I'm stronger now, more confident. Before, I was so insecure and jealous, you know? Every woman was a threat. Now I know different. Also I know that it won't *literally* kill me if things don't work out."

*   *   *

That night, as they walked back to the hotel, Cole looked down at Claire with a serious expression. "You know, I've been assuming that you're coming back to Colorado and we'll live there. I just realized I haven't asked you if that's what *you* want."

Claire stopped walking and looked up at him in surprise. "Of course I want that, Cole. I want to be with you. Besides, you can't leave the ranch, it's your home."

"No. The ranch is where I live. *You're* my home. That became clear to me when you left, and I could hardly stand being there. The only thing I wanted was to get on a plane and get to you. I can start over anywhere, Claire, but not without you. We can build a life anywhere that will make you happy," he replied, wrapping his arms around her waist and kissing her.

"I'll be happy on the ranch. That's the life I want to build with you." She kissed him back, her heart swelling at the thought that he would give it all up for her.

"I want you to know that if you ever change your mind, I'll go with you wherever you need to be. I'm serious about that."

"Thank you, Cowboy. That means a lot to me. For now I want to get into that warm bed waiting for us at the hotel."

He grinned at her. "Done."

THIRTY-ONE

New Year's Eve was unusually warm for that time of year. Janet and Ted had invited Claire and Cole to a party at a swanky club, Rain. Since the women had gone shopping and were having their hair done, Ted had taken Cole along to the tux-rental shop.

It was early evening when Cole got showered and ready to go at the hotel. Cole had rented a black suit with a white shirt and a black silk tie. On his way to the house, he took a detour to see if he could buy some flowers.

He found a flower shop a few blocks away and bought a bouquet of red roses for Claire and white ones for Janet. The ladies in the store gawked shamelessly at him as he made his purchases. The cashier tittered, commenting that he looked like James Bond come to life, which made him smile as he left.

He walked along down the street, taking in the sights as night fell over London. He sighed, realizing he would have to leave in two days, and that Claire wouldn't be with him. There had been no seats left on his flight, so she wouldn't get back to Colorado until January fifth. He wished he could stay so they could travel together. He had spent enough time away from her for one lifetime. But if everything went well tonight, he would be leaving England an engaged man.

When he reached Janet and Ted's, he jogged up the steps, his heart racing with a nervous energy. He knocked on the door, and it was opened almost immediately by Ted, dressed in his tux.

Ted looked at the two bouquets of flowers. "For me, Cole? You shouldn't have."

Cole laughed. He stepped inside and took off his overcoat.

"You ready, buddy?" Ted asked him quietly.

Cole tapped the breast pocket of his jacket. "I'm all set. Thanks again for running me around town to find a ring the other day, Ted. I really appreciate it."

"Glad to do it. Ought to score me some points with the wife when she finds out how romantic I can be," he said with a wink.

"I'll make sure I put in a good word for you. So, are the ladies almost ready?"

"Who knows? They've been in the bathroom giggling away for an hour now. I seriously can't imagine what could possibly take so long, when they already had their hair done at a salon."

"Women are a mystery for many, many reasons," Cole said, nodding in wonder.

"You can say that again," Ted said in agreement. He then turned and yelled down the hall, "Ladies! You were already beautiful when you went in there. If you don't come out soon, Cole and I will need to shave again before we can leave!"

A moment later the door to the bathroom opened, and Janet and Claire came walking down the hall.

Ted let out a puff of air. "I take it back, you're worth the wait." He gave Janet a kiss.

Cole swallowed hard, unable to take his eyes off Claire. "Wow, Ms. Hatley, you look amazing," he said as she stopped in front of him.

She was stunning in a strapless minidress in peacock blue with a contrasting high-cut overlay in black lace. Her dress showed off her curves perfectly without being revealing. From her hair falling softly around her shoulders to her strappy black heels, she had a classic, romantic look. Cole stared at her, trying to memorize every detail of how she looked at that moment. Best of all was the expression on her face. Her eyes were smiling as she took in the sight of him in his black suit. Cole reached down and picked up her hand in his and lifted it to his lips, giving her a gentle kiss on the back of her hand. His smile said everything he was thinking. He was completely in love with this beautiful woman standing before him.

He lifted the two bouquets off the table and handed each of the sisters their respective gift. "Happy new year," he said.

"Flowers? Look, Ted. Cole bought me flowers," Janet said, opening the top of the package. "Roses, even. I can't remember the last time anyone gave me roses. Can you, Ted? Can you remember the last time anyone gave me roses?"

Ted gave Cole a dirty look.

"Sorry, man," Cole said. "I'm the new guy here, so I'm still trying to impress everyone."

Cole's eyes grew wide as he glanced over at Claire. "Not that I'm going to stop trying, Claire."

Claire reached up for a kiss. "Consider me impressed. Don't let Thoughtless over there worry you about some non-existent bro code."

"Thoughtless? Thoughtless?" Ted replied, looking shocked. "If it weren't for me, Mr. Perfect over there would be wearing jeans and a T-shirt."

"True. Thank you, Ted," Cole said, holding his arm out for Claire. "Shall we go?"

"Yes," Janet and Claire replied together.

* * *

The party was in full swing by the time the foursome arrived. The women in the club were dressed in all manner of evening wear, from elegant to wild. The nightclub shimmered with silver and gold decorations. The music was pumping out of the speakers as the two couples checked their coats and found their way through the crowd to their table. Several of Janet's colleagues sat around the table already, deep in conversation. Claire recognized most of them from the Christmas dinner. They greeted the newcomers, and Janet made introductions. One of Janet's work friends, Cindy, couldn't keep her eyes off Cole. Her mouth practically hung open as she stared at him. Claire couldn't help but laugh to herself. She really couldn't blame her.

Glasses of champagne were being passed around by waiters dressed in white tails. Cole took two and gave them to Janet and Claire, then grabbed two more for himself and Ted.

"To new beginnings," he toasted, lifting his flute to them.

The three repeated the toast, and they all downed their champagne.

A remix of Daft Punk's "Get Lucky" started to play, and Claire pulled Cole onto the dance floor to take a spin. "We've never danced at a club before. I want to check out your moves."

"That's a lot of pressure for a guy," Cole answered, leaning into her ear so she could hear him.

Claire grinned at him as they moved their bodies along with the beat. She was pleasantly surprised by how comfortable he seemed on the dance floor. He held her hips lightly with his hands and swayed with her. He spun her around and moved in close to her, keeping things just this side of indecent, his hands sliding down her bottom and to the tops of her thighs.

He could feel that she had garters holding up her thigh-high silk stockings, and he gave a little groan. "I really want to see what's under that dress."

"Play your cards right and I might let you," she teased.

Cole grinned and then kissed her. They stayed on the dance floor for a few songs, flirting and letting the music ignite a feeling of excitement in them.

"Let's go get another drink," Cole called to her as they made their way through the crowd.

Claire flagged down a server with a tray of cocktails. Cole spied the buffet table. "Let's go get you something to eat. We need to fatten you up a bit. You're still too damn skinny."

Claire slipped her hand into his as they walked over to the buffet table. Suddenly, she stopped short as she spotted Luc ahead of them. He was standing near the table, talking with a group of well-dressed partygoers. He stopped speaking when he saw her, his eyes smiling at her as he looked from her to Cole. He excused himself and strode over to the pair.

"Claire, you look lovely," Luc said, kissing her on both cheeks, "and this must be the man you couldn't get off your mind." Luc extended his hand to Cole. "Luc Chevalier. It is a pleasure to meet you."

Cole shook Luc's hand, looking slightly confused. "Cole Mitchell."

Claire spoke up, feeling very awkward. "Cole, Luc is the friend I met on the flight to London. He has some interesting insights into the female mind."

"One could say I am a student of human nature, but that my observations are not always welcome," Luc added.

Cole remembered the conversation he had had with Claire about why she had really left Colorado. He suddenly felt very uncomfortable knowing this man was aware of their breakup. The three stood in awkward silence for a moment.

"So, Luc, is this one of your clubs?" Claire asked.

Luc nodded. "It is my most successful one, actually. I'm very happy with how it's doing." He paused and then shook his head a little. "What a strange coincidence that we keep running into each other."

Claire smiled. "I think it must be because I owe you an apology. I'm sorry I stormed off on you. A lot of what you said was true."

"Please, do not apologize. I was being brash." Luc shrugged. "But more importantly, it looks like things have turned out the way you hoped."

He turned to Cole. "I am happy for you both. Cole, you are a lucky man. Claire is an extraordinary woman."

Cole reached around her waist with his arm and

pulled her to him. "That she is, Luc. Thank you. This is a great place you've got here, by the way. I've never seen anything like it."

"I can't take credit for it. I have an excellent team . . ." He paused. "And I see one of them trying to get my attention right now. I must excuse myself. It's not all pleasure for me at an event like this. Happy new year to you." Luc smiled warmly and patted Claire on the arm. Turning to Cole he said, "Take care of her."

"I will," Cole replied.

As Luc walked away, Claire looked up at Cole, trying to gauge his mood. He smiled down at her. "It's okay, Claire. I'm totally fine." He gave her a little peck on the forehead.

"I'm glad. When I saw him, I was worried it would ruin our evening."

"No chance of that, gorgeous. Now, let's eat."

As the clock neared midnight, Claire noticed that Cole seemed a bit distracted and was checking his watch a lot.

"Are you feeling okay, honey? You seem quiet. Do you want to go?"

"I'm great, really. I could use some fresh air, though. Would you mind coming out onto the balcony with me for a bit?"

"Not at all," Claire responded, grateful at the thought of getting out of the now stuffy nightclub.

As they walked through the door, a rush of cool

air hit their faces. The sound of the music became surprisingly quiet as the door closed behind them. Cole held Claire's hand as they walked to the far end of the balcony. The club was an excellent vantage point for London's South Bank, which provided a romantic backdrop.

"That's better," Cole said, taking in the fresh air and the silence. He shrugged off his jacket and wrapped it around Claire's shoulders. "Here," he said. "I don't want you to get chilled."

"You always take such good care of me," Claire said, turning to face him.

Cole leaned down and kissed her softly. "It's one of the few things I want to do, Claire. I want to take care of you and protect you and love you."

"Good, because I want to let you," she said, teasing him.

Cole smiled at her joke and then his smile faded. He swallowed hard, his heart pounding as he stared at her. "Claire, I had a good enough life before you came along. I had my family and the ranch, and I thought I was happy. But when I met you, I realized how much was missing. You are the sexiest, most beautiful and fun woman on the planet. You're so smart and you have the most generous nature of anyone I've ever met. When you left, it was the worst moment of my life because I knew without a doubt that you were the only woman I would ever want to be with, and you were gone."

Cole knelt down on one knee, holding her hands in his. "You're it for me, Claire. You're the only woman I'll ever want, and you're everything I need. I want to spend my life taking care of you."

He slipped one hand into his pocket, took out a little black velvet box and opened it, then lifted a ring and held it up to her. "Claire Hatley, will you marry me?"

Claire's eyes were filled with tears as she listened to him. She nodded and smiled. "Yes, Cole! Yes, I will marry you."

He slipped the ring onto her finger and then stood to frame her face with his hands, giving her a kiss full of passion and love. They would remember this moment for the rest of their lives. They held each other tight, smiling and laughing with excitement as they kissed for a long time. Inside, the crowd was counting down to midnight, champagne corks were popping and "Auld Lang Syne" was ringing out.

Finally, Cole pulled back a little. "You haven't looked at the ring yet. I want to know if you like it."

"Oh, right," she said, looking down at her left hand. "I love it! It's absolutely perfect, Cole." She stared down at the large round-cut diamond surrounded by bead-set diamonds and a diamond-encrusted platinum band. "It's the most perfect ring I've ever seen, given to me by the most perfect man I've ever known."

Cole pressed his forehead gently to hers, kissing her again. "I am so relieved. I was really nervous."

"Really? Did you think I'd say no?"

"Part of me thought you might after everything we've been through. I wasn't sure if it was too soon after us getting back together."

"Well, you can be a hundred per cent sure about me. I'm all yours."

Cole wrapped his arms around her. "Best start to a new year ever," Cole said with a wide grin.

"Definitely. What do you say we get out of here and really go celebrate?"

"I'd say I wish I had a limo waiting outside for us so we wouldn't have to wait till we get back to the hotel."

They found Janet and Ted over by the table with their friends, all looking expectantly at Claire's left hand. She held it up, and she and Janet screamed and hugged each other. Ted shook Cole's hand and then Janet hugged Cole.

"Welcome to the family, Cole!" Janet exclaimed, grabbing Claire's hand to look at the ring. "Wow! That is gorgeous! Well done, Cole!"

Ted gave Claire a kiss on the cheek. "Congratulations, Claire. I'm so happy for you both."

"Thank you, Ted! I'm so happy for me too!" She turned to Janet. "Do you mind if we sneak out of here?"

"Go! Go! We'll see you both tomorrow sometime when you come up for air," Janet laughed.

Claire and Cole blushed and said their good nights.

* * *

They made love until the sun was almost up. As they were drifting off to sleep, Cole pulled Claire to him, feeling her naked body against his. "I'm going to love you forever, Claire."

"Me too, Cowboy," Claire said sleepily. "Hey— thank you for asking me to marry you, and thank you for the beautiful ring. I'm the luckiest girl in the world because I get to wear it forever, and I get to marry you."

"I'm the lucky one. You said yes."

"You know you didn't have to spend all that money on a ring, right? I agreed to marry you on the mountainside if you lent me your hat. We already had a deal."

"Shit, I totally forgot about that. Is it too late to take the ring back?"

"Um, yes. Sorry. I could have lived without the ring before I saw it, but now I don't think I can."

Cole grinned at her. "Glad you like it, Ms. Hatley." He gave her a kiss on the lips. "Happy new year."

"Happy new year, Cole." She nuzzled into his neck and promptly fell asleep in his arms.

EPILOGUE

Colorado Springs—
Four and a Half Years Later

The sun was low in the sky, signalling the end of another hot summer's day as Claire looked out toward the meadow. She was sitting on the front porch of their cabin with three-year-old Vivian on her lap. She had been reading books with her to pass the time as the pair waited impatiently for Cole to return. The little girl's hair was still damp from her bath, and she was dressed in a cool nightgown, all ready for bed.

Vivian spotted the horses first and climbed off her mom's lap with excitement. "Dad! Daddy!" she shouted in her tiny voice.

Claire put the books down on the chair next to her and looked up to see Cole riding back with the latest group of tourists behind him. Otis, who had been dozing in the sun, perked up his ears and stood, wagging his tail.

"Let's go meet them, sweetie." Taking Vivian's little hand in hers, she started toward the meadow.

Claire's heart skipped a beat when she saw Cole riding toward her, as it always did when he came home. He had been gone for four days, and both Claire and their little girl missed him terribly when he was away.

Cole could make out the outline of his two favourite girls as he rode in. He could see that Vivian was already in her PJs, and that Claire wore one of the pretty summer dresses he loved. He spurred Dudley on to pick up the pace, not able to wait any longer to hold them in his arms.

Vivian broke into a run, hurrying as fast as her little legs would carry her until she reached the gate that led to the meadow. She grabbed onto the bottom rung with her little hands, yelling with overwhelmed excitement in her voice, "Daddy! Come home now!"

Cole laughed as he broke away from the pack and galloped toward them. When he got close to the fence, he started to dismount Dudley before the horse had even come to a full stop. Claire opened the gate and let Vivian run to her dad.

Cole swooped her up in his arms and spun around, holding her tightly. "How's my best girl?" he asked.

"Happy! I be'd a good girl," she answered, hugging him tightly around his neck.

"I knew you would. I missed you so much!" he said to Vivian, kissing her repeatedly on the cheek.

"Ouch, Daddy. Shave your face," she complained, wriggling out of his arms and chasing Otis back toward the stables.

"Bossy little thing, isn't she?" Claire asked.

Cole turned to Claire, grinning. "I just cannot, for the life of me, figure out where she gets that."

"Strange, isn't it? Me neither. No idea, really."

"She's beautiful like you, but that's really where the similarity ends."

Claire laughed. "That's right. Just so we're clear, no one thinks I'm bossy."

Cole pulled Claire to him and lowered his voice, giving her a sexy grin. "So, gorgeous, you miss me?"

Claire smiled back at him. "So much, Cowboy. You have no idea."

"Oh, I think I do. From the moment I ride off, I'm counting down the seconds until I ride back home," he answered, wrapping his arms around her and kissing her gently on the lips.

Claire returned his embrace, feeling his warm, strong body against hers. She sighed happily as she looked up at him. "Really? Well, I've been counting the seconds until I can ride you."

Cole picked her up and put her over his shoulder, making her scream with laughter. "What are you doing? Put me down!"

"No way," he responded, striding back to Dudley to grab his reins and lead him to the stables. "You're going to need to save up your strength for later." He held one hand under her skirt, letting his hand slip between her thighs as he walked to the stables.

Cole tossed the reins to Ben, who was waiting for the guests to ride in. "Can you take Dudley? I need to get little Vivian off to dreamland so I can make love to my beautiful wife."

"Oh my God, Cole! Put me down. This is so embarrassing!" Claire hissed at him as he walked away from Ben, who was shaking his head and grinning at the pair.

Cole slid her down off his shoulder. "You're embarrassed that people might know we're in love, Claire? Because I'm sure as hell not." He spun her to him and wrapped his arms around her, kissing her neck.

"*In* love is fine. *About to make love* is not meant to be public knowledge," Claire retorted, her words softening at the touch of his lips on her skin.

"Ben doesn't look offended to me. Us Mitchell boys aren't prudes like you Hatley girls."

"Prudes? Prudes? I'll have you know—"

"What does *prudes* mean, Auntie Claire?" Jake Jr. had walked up beside them, and Vivian toddled after him.

"It means your uncle and I have to remember to choose our words more carefully," Claire responded.

Jake Jr. gave her a confused look and then ran over to his dad.

Cole smiled down at his little girl and picked

her up, placing her on top of his shoulders for a ride. "Here, baby girl! How far can you see from up there?"

Vivian giggled and held tight to Cole's hands. "To the moon!"

As they sauntered up toward their cabin, the sky grew darker, allowing the first few stars to become visible. When they reached the front steps, Cole lifted his little girl off his shoulders and opened the door. He walked over to the kitchen and grabbed a bottle of Strongbow from the fridge. Taking the cap off, he handed the drink to his wife. "You go relax on the porch. I'll get this little monkey off to bed."

"I see you're not giving up the whole perfect thing," Claire said, grinning at him.

"I have to make sure you don't take off with the mailman when I'm gone."

"Most likely I won't, but only because she's a fifty-five-year-old grandmother," she replied. "Hey, how was it with the Girls' Getaway group?"

Cole shook his head. "Honestly, Claire, people think men are dogs, but women are *so* much worse. They forget we're there and they get talking, and I am shocked by how dirty they are."

Claire laughed. "Oh, I know. You poor man. Whose stupid idea was that whole Girls' Getaway thing anyway?"

"It was this beautiful chef I know who came up with it. I only agreed to it because I wanted to get into her pants. Now, go relax, so I can get this little peanut off to sleep."

* * *

A little while later, Cole joined Claire on the porch. He was dressed only in jeans, and his hair was still wet from the shower. He had clearly been in a hurry; drops of water slid down his neck and chest as he lowered himself onto the loveseat next to her. She put down her tablet and gazed lustfully at him. Suddenly, she remembered he hadn't eaten yet.

"You must be starving. I'll go heat up some supper for you," Claire said, starting to get up.

"Food can wait," he replied, gently pulling her onto his lap. "In the last four days, I've had twelve meals, but I haven't had you even once," he murmured as he leaned in to kiss her. "I've got some catching up to do."

Claire melted as their mouths met; the smell of him and the touch of his freshly shaved face on hers had her moaning with desire. He moved his hand up her leg and under her skirt as they kissed. Claire let one hand glide lazily down his delicious chest and then to the front of his jeans. The feel of his hard body still thrilled her every bit as much as it had the first time.

Cole's hand slid up to Claire's panties. He traced the outline of them with his finger and then moved the lacy fabric aside, giving himself full access to her. Claire gave another little moan as he pressed his fingers to her warm skin.

"We better take this inside," he murmured. "Someone might see us."

"Oh, I thought we'd go for it right here on the porch. You know, show the world how *in love* we are?" Claire taunted him as she turned to straddle his lap.

Cole rolled his eyes and picked her up by her bottom, kissing her hard on the mouth and starting for the front door.

Claire wrapped her legs around his waist and her arms around his neck. She pulled back from his kiss. "Prude."

Cole's lips curled up in a half smile. "I'm going to have to keep that sexy mouth of yours busy to stop you from making all those smartassed remarks, aren't I?"

"Pretty much, for the rest of your life, yes."

"Okay. I can manage that," he answered as he opened the front door and carried her up the stairs.

They made love late into the night. As she drifted off to sleep safe in his arms, Claire smiled to herself, knowing that Cole would always want her every bit as much as she wanted him. He had shown her what love was meant to be. Together they were building their dreams, they were a family and she knew her heart had found home.

Don't miss the other captivating *Full Hearts* novels by M J Summers

BREAKING LOVE
Single mom Megan Sullivan lives a quiet life
and likes it that way, until she meets Luc Chevalier,
a successful entrepreneur who has everything
he could ask for, except love.

BREAKING CLEAR
Fashion editor Harper Young reluctantly returns
home to Boulder, Colorado, to care for her ailing
father and falls head over heels for her unrequited
teenage crush, Evan Donovan.

BREAKING HEARTS
When tragedy strikes, Trey Johnson must fly to his
young son in Brazil, where he meets Alessandra
Santos, a young woman who shows him the
true power of love.

DON'T LET GO
In this *Break in Two* prequel novella, young
Ben Mitchell and Alicia Williams must decide if
they will follow their dreams or their hearts.